Tokyo Yakuza

ISSUES #1-#24
PLUS ONE BONUS STORY!

Edited by Nicholas Phillips
and Joshua Waddles

ORIENTAL EXCESS

Oriental Excess, LLC
422 Brookshire Ct.
Valparaiso, IN 46385

TOKYO YAKUZA: ISSUES #1-#24
Edited by Nicholas Phillips and Joshua Waddles
Copyright © 2015 Oriental Excess, LLC.

www.tokyoyakuza.com

Cover Artwork by Pongviwat Wongsavipas

Cover Design by Quincy J. Allen

ISBN: 978-0-9864186-0-0

Book Design by RuneWright, LLC
www.RuneWright.com

KEMPEITAI
THOUGHT POLICE
CONTROL MESSAGE

憲兵隊 HQ

FILED 01232020B JAN

NEED TO KNOW (AUTH)

NTK 01232020X JAN

FROM: Tocho Headquarters, 2-8-1 Nishishinjuku, Shinjuku, Tokyo 163-8001, Imperial Japan.

TO: ALLPERS Thought Police, His Imperial Highness for Information.

REF NO: 888444888, January 23, 2020.

Special police, coastal interdiction squads, and undercover operatives of the Kempeitai Thought Police, you are about to undertake the greatest protective mission of peacetime domestic law enforcement in our postwar history. Since victory over the Allies and the solidification of the Greater East Asian Co-prosperity Sphere over a generation ago, we have ruled in accordance with the Yamato spirit (大和魂) and ushered in an enlightened age. The upcoming 2020 Tokyo Olympics promises to be the perfect proving grounds for our athletes and a showcase for our new cyber-technology and military hardware.

All we have achieved is suddenly at risk. Yesterday, the oyabun of the Sumiyoshi-kai was killed by a Yamaguchi-gumi sniper in the Kabukichō red light district here in Shinjuku. Already, the 5 rival clans of Tokyo are preparing for all-out gang warfare in the heart of the Japanese Empire. Innocents will die. Great corporations will be ruined. This cannot stand.

We should not tolerate an individualism which shows no concern for others. We must be concerned with the problems of others as if they were our problems. At this point, our nation's people will be able to understand each other perfectly, keep in step, and proceed with a distinctive unity. The total State is, I believe, the most efficient means by which our political system can best be advanced and closely monitored.

CONTENTS

Tokyo Yakuza

Preface

NICHOLAS PHILLIPS

The year is 2020. It is the morning of a new day in a new era. Japan won World War II. And as the Imperial Army kept the peace in the Greater East Asian Co-prosperity Sphere, the rival yakuza clans maintained a wary truce in the modern, industrialized empire's capital of Tokyo.

The 2020 Tokyo Olympics was supposed to be the Japanese Empire's opportunity to demonstrate its innate superiority to all the nations of the world, including Nazi-controlled Europe and the economically stagnant American backwaters. So, in the run up to the Olympics, all-out gang warfare between the five clans was completely unacceptable to the powers that be.

The Emperor, the Diet, the Imperial Army, and the Kempeitai Thought Police joined forces with the Tokyo Metropolitan Police to crack down on the yakuza. Now, the normally untouchable yakuza elders, the oyabun (father figures) and the wakagashira (advisors), are getting hospitalized, arrested, or knocked off right-and-left. When the normally restrained yakuza run out of shits to give, who will decide each clan's ultimate fate?

Metro Map of the Tokyo Underworld

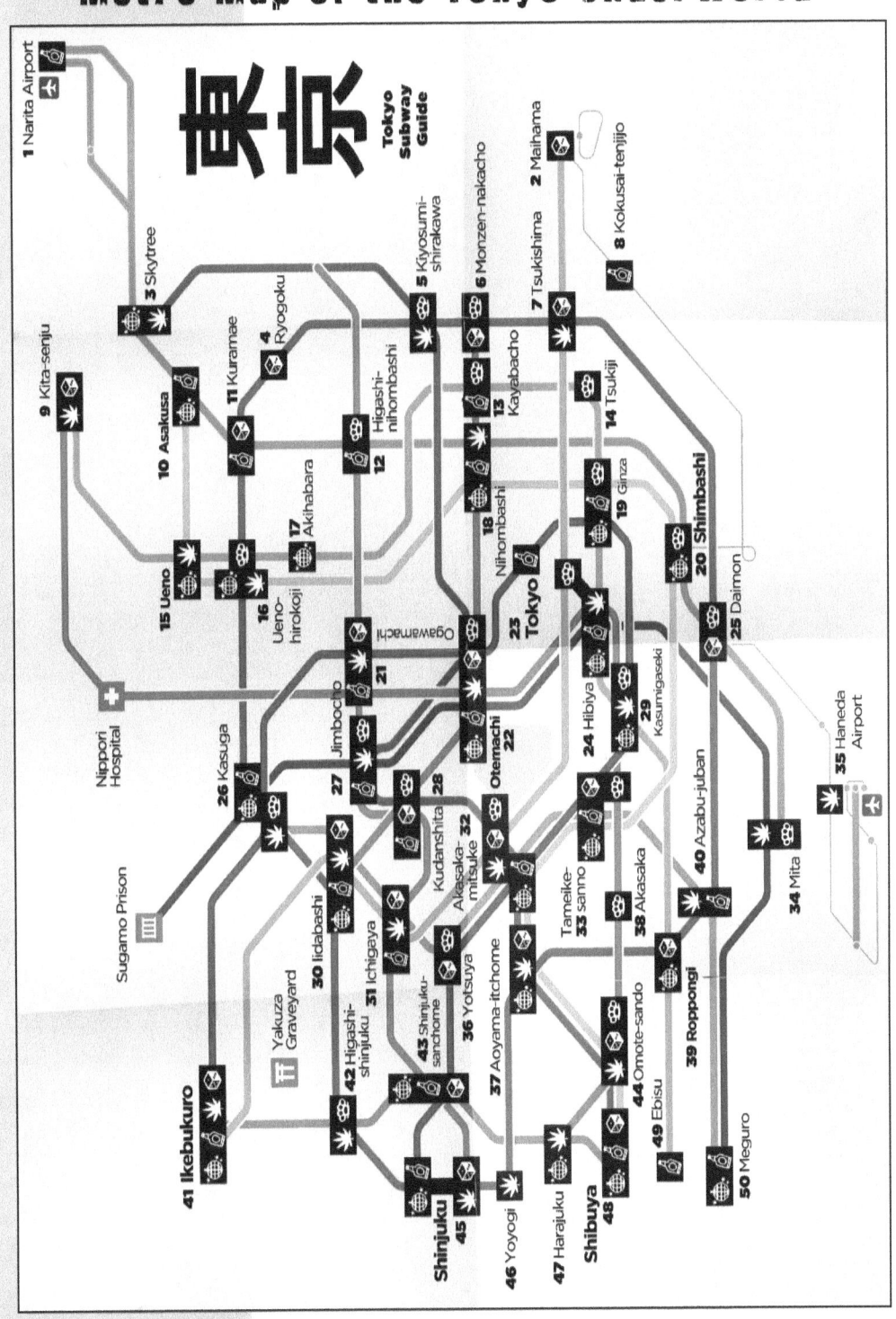

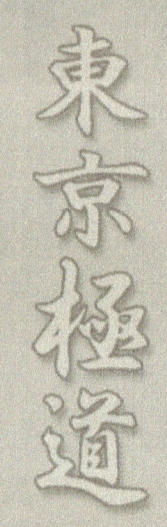

東京極道

A Rundown of the Five Clans

With each clan keeping to its own turf, the yakuza dominated the traditional underworld trades of gambling, drugs and prostitution. The original Tokyo yakuza clan, the Inagawa-kai, strengthened its connections with corrupt government officials and vice-loving, corporate technocrats, serving as muscle for hire. The Sumiyoshi-kai forged a bold, new path, shaking down these captains of industry. Meanwhile, the Chinese and Korean laborers, who were brought over to serve and work the jobs no one else would do, began to form their own criminal organizations, the 14K Triad and the Seven Star Mob, specializing in drug smuggling and gun running.

Then the powerful Yamaguchi-gumi of Kobe burst upon the scene, sending a sniper to assassinate the Sumiyoshi-kai oyabun and wresting away control of the Kabukichō red light district in east Shinjuku. When the Sumiyoshi-kai struck back with motorcycle-riding bosozoku hit squad, all hell broke loose in the city of Tokyo. Before long, the gloves came off and no one's traditional turf was sacred. The five clans were at war.

The Yamaguchi-gumi

The Yamaguchi-gumi (gumi means gang) is the largest and most popular of the Japanese yakuza clans. They are growing quickly, like a healthy and expanding grove of bamboo. Yamaguchi-gumi gangsters love to practice fighting with katanas in sacred bamboo groves throughout their territory in the verdant parks of Tokyo.

They purport to uphold the samurai spirit and teach the way of the warrior, bushido, to new recruits over a lengthy, year-long training period, during which time the new members study martial arts, perform household chores at the local clan office or main headquarters, and are exposed as little as possible to the ugly realities of drug dealing, pimping, and extortion.

The main business of the Yamaguchi-gumi is operating hostess clubs and sex venues throughout the city. The hostesses pour drinks for clients, light their cigarettes, and tell them how awesome they are (and how their wives don't truly understand them) in exchange for ruinous sums of yen. The Shinto spirit (or kami) most sacred to the clan is the kitsune, or mischievous nine-tailed fox.

The Yamaguchi-gumi's melee weapon of choice is the katana (samurai sword), and ranged weapon of choice is the silenced FN-P90 submachine gun. Finally, the Yamaguchi-gumi color, green, represents the love of nature that is the kokoro (heart) of the Yamato race.

The Sumiyoshi-kai

The Sumiyoshi-kai (kai means syndicate) is the second largest numerically but the number one wealthiest of all the clans. They worship technology and count many tech otaku (hackers and fanboys) among their ranks. A long-time player in corporate blackmail (and the inventor of sokaiya raids of annual corporate shareholders' meetings), the Sumiyoshi-kai uses encryption to hide their every move, leaving no trace on security cameras or databases as they move around the city, buying stolen goods from teams of female shoplifters and selling them for a high profit to cognoscenti elsewhere about town.

The specialty of the Sumiyoshi-kai is demanding protection money in exchange for making sure legitimate businesses, from kon-bini convenience stores to major shipping lines, will continue to operate smoothly. Sumiyoshi-kai yakuza are normally exceedingly well-mannered, educated, and sophisticated but a single word of disrespect can set them off on a loud, destructive rampage that brings powerful dishonor and shame to the targeted victims.

Sumiyoshi-kai members are Buddhist; they pray to Kannon, the Bodhisattva of Compassion, and show mercy to their enemies if they display signs of contrition and the possibility of redemption.

The Sumiyoshi-kai's melee weapon of choice is the tanto (a tactical knife), and ranged weapon of choice is the Arisaka Elite sniper rifle. Their color, purple, represents high tech, high fashion, and living the high life in general on stolen credit cards.

The Inagawa-kai

The original Tokyo gang, the Inagawa yakuza are now a distinct minority in the city which gave them birth. Due to their ever dwindling numbers and conscious of their underdog status, the Inagawa-kai has convinced the world they are the fiercest, most brutal, and downright devilish of all the boryokudan (violent organizations) in the city of Tokyo. If people believe they will be slowly tortured to death in the maze-like basement beneath a pachinko parlor, no one will dare mess with them—at least, that's the Inagawa-kai's line of reasoning.

These original gangsters got their start way back in the Tokugawa shogunate as bakuto, or gamblers, who set up hanafuda (flower card) games in tea houses across the Kanto region, centering in Edo (old Tokyo). They still maintain excellent connections with right-wing government officials and fascist corporate executives.

Today, they run everything from underground casinos to downtown, back alley games of chance throughout the core of the city. Inagawa-kai gang leaders wear menpo, samurai demon masks, and their bases are lit up with a hellish combination of red and black lights, evoking primal fears of jigoku (hell). They love to beat foes mercilessly and permanently injure the vision, hearing or limbs of victims and send them back to instill terror in the hearts of their comrades. Fire-bomb-ings and other terrorist attacks are not uncommon. Inagawa-kai members are essentially atheist, love heavy metal music, and project the notion they worship oni (demons) so that people will think twice about cheating at cards or knocking over one of their gambling sessions.

The Inagawa-kai's melee weapon of choice is the paired kama (hand sickle), and ranged weapon of choice is the Desert Eagle .50 heavy pistol. The Inagawa-kai have adopted black as their color, after a knockdown, drag-out fight with more traditional clan members who believed white better symbolized the color of death.

東京極道

The 14K Triad

14K TRIAD

The 14K is a Hong Kong triad recently arrived in Tokyo, which formed here to protect Chinese immigrants, servants and menial laborers who are being exploited by ruthless Japanese bosses in the corporations and on the streets. Bringing prosperity and the feeling of being in a big Chinese family, the triad organization uses incense, red envelopes full of cash, lion dances, fireworks and flying dragon imagery to create a sense of community among strangers in a strange land.

14K members wrap their torsos in chains for protection, practice Shaolin kung fu in the parks and alleys of Tokyo, and guard smuggled shipments of "China white" (pure heroin) with meat cleavers at the ready. Speaking a dialect of Chinese all their own, in addition to standard Mandarin, thugs of the 14K are inscrutable to the normal Japanese population, who prefer to avoid them unless when buying drugs.

Most people in Tokyo see a Chinese person and immediately think - criminal - due to the 14K's growing reputation for dominance in the drug trade. Still, the counterfeit designer handbags, watches, and jewelry stalls operated by female members of the gang are ever-popular among the fashion-conscious, but middle-class, Tokyoites. By and large, 14K members are Zen Buddhist (Shaolin) and love the five animal styles of kung fu, a sort of moving meditation teaching them to flow like water—like water, my friend.

Older members grow long, grey or white mustaches and style themselves after the Shaolin masters. The 14K Triad's melee weapon of choice is the meat cleaver, and ranged weapon of choice is the crossbow. Their color is red, symbolizing wealth, vitality, brotherhood and the strength of familial bonds.

The Seven Star Mob

THE SEVEN STAR MOB

Chil sung pa

This Korean kkangpae (gang), called Chil Sung Pa in their native tongue, protects all people, not just those of Korean descent (zainichi—or Japan-born Koreans), but all those who are in need of protection from the powers that be. The seven stars represent the virtues all gang members claim they strive for: honor; humanity; loyalty; vigilance; strength; generosity; and Seoul (love for their ancestral homeland).

Quickly earning a reputation as protectors of the weak and downtrodden, the Seven Star Mob has organized the dockworkers and bribed the coast guard to allow massive influxes of smuggled goods of all kinds, from banned books and rare medicines to firearms and precursor chemicals, even weapons-grade uranium.

The Seven Star Mob specializes in making sure imported whiskey, vodka, craft beer and champagne flow unimpeded from overseas into the dive bars and ryotei (high-end geisha restaurants) of Tokyo. While sake (rice wine) is still the drink of choice in Japan, the industry is completely corporatized and off-limits to the Koreans, so they specialize in bringing in alcoholic beverages from abroad and selling them at a tremendous markup to the Japanese, saving the best soju (Korean liquor) for themselves.

As a result, Seven Star Mob gangsters tend to be hard drinking, yet good-spirited sorts, in a slap you on the back and fine you three shots kind of way. Get on their bad side, though, and these self-proclaimed upholders of street justice will bring out the sawed-off shotguns without hesitation. The Seven Star Mob's melee weapon of choice is the bo staff, and ranged weapon of choice is the sawed-off shotgun. Their color, blue, represents salty ocean breezes and the sea in all its clarity, calmness, and penchant for sudden, tsunami storms.

Tokyo Yakuza

1

The Things We Try to Forget

by Joshua Waddles

Japan won the Second World War.
Now the yakuza are starting the Third!

The Things We Try to Forget

BY JOSHUA WADDLES

January 14, 2020. Shinjuku, Tokyo. Yayoi Himetsu holds a pair of plastic cat ears on her lap as the man goes through her purse, dumping the contents on the coffee table. She keeps her head down and her gaze firmly planted on the floor. She knows how to act when Matsuhono Eugi is angry with her, but although his voice remains even, it's clear the gangster is more angry with her than he's ever been.

He counts out a small wad of bills, looking up at her with a glare. She tightens her fingers around the cat ears and cringes her shoulders: another practiced move, though the killer's eyes would probably make her do that anyway.

"How long have you been skimming your tips? No," Eugi says, shaking his head. "First tell me what in the hell you were thinking. I told you when I hired you that fifty percent of your tips go to me; for that you get to work at 'The Bijou'[1] instead of a whorehouse. Is your

---

[1] The Yamaguchi-gumi's premiere hostess club in Shinjuku, Tokyo's Kabukichō red light district.

dignity worth less than that?"

She shakes her head. "No," she says. "Wakarimashita.² You know I'm grateful to work here. It's just that my good for nothing brother lost his job and I'm paying the rent by myself."

Eugi paces the room, thumbing the bills in his hand, his trademark white suit the color of death. "How much did you skim? And for how long?"

"Three months," she says. "I don't know how much, but my brother lost his job in May."

Eugi purses his lips, not saying anything. "You're lucky that I'm so forgiving. If I had done something like this, Kitano-san would make me pay with the tip of my finger."

Yayoi gives him exactly the reaction he wants, cringing against herself and pulling her fingers in, though the cold fear in her spine and the phantom pain in her finger are very real.

"The extra is about fifteen percent of what my chimpira³ Akiyama Jiro said he paid you," says Eugi. "I'm just guessing; I think you probably owe around half a million yen."⁴

She takes in a completely uncalculated gasp as she looks up at Eugi. "I can't pay that," she says.

"This is the Yamaguchi-gumi⁵ you're dealing with, Yayoi. Better find a way," says Eugi. He moves towards the door. "You have three months. If you can't pay it back, you lose the tip of a finger. And you won't make any money here looking like that."

He lets the money drop to the floor as he leaves the room. Yayoi stares at the crumbled bills as her vision starts to blur.

---

² "I understand."

³ Street punk. Literally, "prick."

⁴ Roughly $5000 USD. The exchange rate for JPY in the world of Tokyo Yakuza is ¥100:$1 or RM0.25.

⁵ The biggest criminal clan in Japan. Their gang colors are green.

✦   ✧   ✦

Green lights, from Kabukichō's[6] bioluminescent algae-powered street lamps, flash off the spattering rain on the windshield. Between the swipes from the squeaking wipers, the taxi cab driver glances up at a flashing neon sign of a cartoon woman with cat ears and a tail. His passenger, Soto Tasami, knows it for what it is: a distraction, tentatively allowed by the fascist government because it keeps the young people pliant, and stops them from thinking about the prison factories in Beijing or the mass graves in Pyongyang.

Video games and cartoons might do the trick for young otaku,[7] but not for someone who's been to the mainland. If Soto wants to forget about the things he's done on the continent for a night, he's going to need something more real.

Or at least, something that *feels* real.

The traffic light turns green. The cabbie pulls onto the street, toward an area filled with shops with covered windows and billboards covered in seductive curved writing, driving Soto Tasami towards the magical place where he can lose himself in alcohol and women who make him feel like a king. Something pleasant twists inside Soto when he thinks of the smell of their perfume, their smoky gazes centered on him. He could almost believe that they don't care about the thirty extra pounds around his waist and that they really want him.

In the *mostly* tasteful places that interest Soto, a customer can't buy sex. But no law says one of the women can't leave with him just because they like him.

There's always that chance.

---

[6] Tokyo's most infamous red light district. A place in Shinjuku where a kabuki theatre was planned but never built. Full of hostess clubs, soaplands and love hotels.
[7] Obsessive fans.

After paying the fare, Soto jumps out of the taxi and into the crowded Shinjuku streets. He has to walk several blocks before he runs into the familiar, dark building, its windows covered with thick curtains. A large man in a raccoon-dog tanuki[8] suit waves him in. A simple, undecorated stairwell takes Soto up a level. The floor opens up to a hallway with a pair of double doors tucked away at the end. A bell rings as he lets himself inside.

The walls and carpets in the hidden bar are all cream colored. Music from one of the new pop idols plays at a comfortably low volume in the background, contrasting with the classical atmosphere set by the gold painted bar-trim and pearl-shaped stones. Several round tables sit spread out over the room, most with a couple of men accompanied by two, three, or even more laughing women in sheer, skimpy dresses, cut high on their thighs. They play cards, trade jokes, and occasionally one of the women hurries up to the bar with a tray and a list of drinks, swaying her backside as she walks.

Soto is immediately greeted by four women who must have been waiting by the door. A whiff of flowery perfume washes over him as they bow, cheerfully shouting out an enthusiastic "Konbanwa!"[9]

Each hostess at The Bijou wears the cartoonish cat or fox ears that Soto doesn't really care for, but hell, it's not like he can afford a geisha.

They take his coat and one of them gives him that flirtatious smile, letting him know that she's picked him out as her customer for the next few hours, but he looks past her, searching for his favorite girl, Kit.

He's not surprised to find her sitting at a table with four other men. She never takes off those ridiculous fox ears, but there's just something about the way she looks at him, the way she talks to him

---

[8] A Japanese raccoon-dog spirit, which like the kitsune (fox spirit) has the powers of shape shifting (itself and others) and possession (mind control).

[9] "Good evening!"

that seems to draw him straight out of his body in a way that only chems[10] can.

But if he's going to spend two weeks' pay drinking with Kit Yamaguchi, he's going to have to wait his turn.

Out of the corner of his eye, he spots Yayoi Himetsu sitting alone at the far end of the room in one of the booths. She's not wearing her cat ears; they lie on the table in front of her and she stares at them like she hates them.

Seems like someone he could talk to.

He politely excuses himself from the woman assigned to him. For her part, she's too professional to be insulted by the snub.

"Hello, there," says Soto. He sits down across from Yayoi.

The hostess's business face falls in place like a mask and she smiles at him. "Konbanwa," she says. "Would you like to drink with me?"

"Sure. I'll have sake."[11]

Something switches on in Yayoi's brain at Soto's announcement that he'll be drinking hard liquor. That is always a signal for a good night's pay.

"What do you drink?" asks Soto.

"I like strawberry martinis," says Yayoi. She lowers her head and looks at Soto under her brow. "I love to wet my lips with something sweet. When I'm not working, I'm usually sucking on a hard candy."

Can't afford to hold back anymore, Yayoi thinks. *I've got to make him think he's going to get laid. Maybe even …* It would mean breaking the promise she made to herself when she started working here. But how many ways can a hostess make an extra five hundred thousand yen in three months?

---

[10] Illegal drugs and pheromones.

[11] Traditional Japanese rice wine.

Her eyes drift past Soto to the gaming corners.

A new hostess, some girl named Hanako, brings them their drinks and they chat for a bit until Yayoi can see the beginnings of a buzz in Soto's posture.

"My wife doesn't understand," says Soto with a distracted air. "This place gets me out of my head. Did you know that I'm a soldier with the Dai-Nippon Teikoku Rikugun?"[12]

"I didn't," Yayoi says. The guilt she'd already been feeling over her plan stabs a little deeper. She's always been a good patriot. Can she really do this to a soldier?

"The government doesn't let the media say too much about what's happening in China right now," says Soto. He stares at the table for a moment, his eyes unblinking; then he shakes his head, taking a drink straight from the bottle. "Anyway," he says. "I need a distraction. Drinking just isn't enough anymore."

"A distraction?" Yayoi asks. She thinks for a few moments. Soto seems too lost in his own thoughts to notice her hesitation.

She makes her decision.

"How about a game?"

Soto's eyebrows pop up. He glances back to the rear section where two men play a complicated holographic game. He makes a "Hrn," sound. He knows that these hostesses get a bonus if they can talk their guests into gambling or buying them drinks; these extras earn them "points" with Eugi. "I'm not really good with these sorts of games," he says.

"It's really just something to do, isn't it?" Yayoi asks. "A distraction?" The guilt on her face looks more like sympathy to Soto.

She's got a point, he decides. *I won't spend too much.*

---

[12] Army of the Greater Japanese Empire.

Yayoi takes Soto by the hand, guiding him out of his seat. "I'll show you my favorite game in just a moment. I need to do something. Meet me there?"

"Sure," says Soto. He moves on toward the gaming corner, staggering slightly.

Yayoi waves at Kit Yamaguchi. It takes a few tries to distract her from her customers and at first it seems that the fox-eared hostess will ignore her, but Yayoi puts on a desperate expression that convinces Kit to leave her company for just a moment and talk with the girl. She gets out of her seat with a dramatic flourish of her kimono, for the benefit of her customers. Yayoi could swear she hears bells ringing underneath.

"Kit-sempai, I really need your help," says Yayoi. "Do you see that man over there?" She nods toward Soto, who leans against the wall, watching some of the other gamers.

"Did he do something?" asks Kit.

"No, no," says Yayoi. "But I'm in trouble with Eugi. I need to get this client to spend a lot of money tonight. Can you use your eyes on him while we're playing? Put him in The Bliss?"[13]

Kit looks almost offended. "That's not something I normally do to someone else's customers, Yayoi."

"I know," she says with a whiney voice. "But Kit, I owe Eugi-san a half million yen."

Kit's jaw drops an inch, exposing sharp, fox-like teeth. "How did you? No, never mind. Yayoi, your cut will never cover that."

"It'll take out a chunk and maybe Eugi will give me more time," whispers Yayoi in a panicked tone. "Please, Kit? I'll never be able to pay this debt if you don't help me, and he's going to take the tip of my finger."

---

[13] A mental state of distraction caused by being placed under the spell of a kami.

Kit glances back at her table. Some of her customers look at her with irritation over her lack of attention. She sighs. "Alright," she says to Yayoi, "As soon as you sit down with him, I'll give him The Bliss."

"Arigato gozaimashita!"[14]

Kit goes back to her own table, apologizing to her customers. She keeps one eye on the other hostess.

Yayoi and Soto sit down in front of a holographic game. She gives the soldier a tender pat as she looks back at Kit's table.

Kit leans her head forward, slightly, her fox-ears twitching.

The voices around her fade. In her perception, the room goes dark, except for Soto in the gaming corner who shines like a lamp behind a wet pane of glass. Reaching out with her senses, she feels the familiar ache of dark emotions in his head.

Her eyes change, turning an amber color and her eyes narrow to slits as she stares at Soto. "Calm," she whispers under her breath. Her lips barely move. If the men at the table hear her, they give no sign.

"There is no past, there is only the now," says Kit, drawing out her words. "Fall in love, Soto."

Making no sound, her words reverberate across the room on waves of energy leading directly into Soto's brain.

The Imperial soldier feels a prickling sensation easing into the back of his head. His body starts to warm, as if he were submerging himself into a hot bath. He looks at Yayoi and the light around her seems to blur, framing the hostess's smiling face with a rainbow of colors.

"Ready to play, Soto?" Yayoi asks.

An involuntary smile spreads over Soto's face. "Whatever you want, Yayoi," he says.

---

[14] "Thank you so much!"

He has no sense of time as he plays the game, popping the floating bubbles with his fingers. He doesn't even know what the rules are, but he finds with mild curiosity that he absolutely doesn't care what he's doing. More importantly, he's not thinking about who he is, nor what he's done. He wants the feeling to last forever, to record Yayoi's sweet words so that he can listen to them constantly.

But eventually the feeling fades, as if he were coming out of a drunken stupor, and someone taps him on the shoulder.

"We're closing," says Eugi. "Time to pay."

His head clearing, Eugi looks down at his bill. His eyes go wide and he blinks, sure that he must still be seeing double.

His bill, inflated with a few extra drinks he never ordered, reads just over two million yen.[15]

"I can't pay this," says Soto.

Eugi's smile disappears.

"I don't understand," says Soto. "You have to cut me a break. Something came over me."

"Sake, I'd think," says Eugi. "Get out your card and pay. Do you think we can afford to forgive every drunk idiot who can't control himself?" he asks, raising his voice. Yayoi gets out of her chair, moving away from the two. "The cost of the sake alone would put me out of business!"

"But I don't have it," says Soto. "I come here all the time. Please, I've never done anything like this before."

Eugi looks down at Soto for a moment. *Is he thinking about forgiving me?* Soto wonders.

His question is answered when Eugi grabs him by his hair and smashes his face against the table. Blood squirts out of Soto's nose like juice from a fruit. Yayoi gasps, covering her face. Most of the

---

[15] About $20,000 USD.

other hostesses and the few remaining customers look away.

Soto shouts as Eugi wrenches his arm behind his back, using the leverage to pull the man to his feet. He shoves Soto over to the bar in front of an impassive looking bartender. Eugi digs Soto's wallet out of the soldier's back pocket and slaps it down on the bar.

"Card," Eugi orders.

Wiping the blood off of his face, Soto opens his wallet with his free hand, digging his card out. He swipes it into the reader and leaves blood smears on the keypad as he punches in his pin number.

"Insufficient funds," says the bartender with a frown.

Two more men in black suits appear behind Eugi. One wears black wraparound sunglasses and cruel smile. The other is a bald musclebound freak of nature. The pimp in the white suit lets go of Soto's arm. "Take him to the back room," Eugi orders.

As the men drag Soto away, the war veteran gives Yayoi a pleading look, begging her with his eyes to say something. She looks away, clenching her eyes shut.

Eugi throws Soto down into a plain wooden chair in a room with a stone floor. One of the men holds onto the chair, stopping him from falling backward. The musclebound freak strips off his suit jacket and tears open his shirt with a growl to reveal a menacing full body tattoo. The man with the wraparound shades and the sadistic grin leans over Soto from behind and looks down at him over Soto's right shoulder. "Pleased to meet you," the thug says. "My name is Moji Sumio. And I'd like you dead."

I'm going to die, Soto realizes. He thought he was ready, but the look in Eugi's eyes fills him with a terror that proves him wrong.

"I've got a family," says Soto.

Eugi smashes his fist into Soto's stomach. The air blasts out of the soldier's lungs and he doubles over, holding his ribs.

"Maybe you should have thought of that before you gambled with more than you could afford to pay," says Eugi.

A set of brass knuckles cracks against Soto's skull and he can feel his eyeball bulge. The third man, Asahara Hikaru, a thug with a big catfish tattoo, goes to work with a leather belt, lashing Soto across the legs and back. Soto falls out of his chair, holding his hands up and trying to ward off the blows, but all three men lay into him with kicks. He feels a rib crack before Eugi waves the others off.

Soto twists around with wide eyes. Eugi takes a step toward him.

A knife snaps open, the blade gleaming.

"No, please," says Soto.

"We're not going to kill you, yet," says Eugi. "You're going to wish we did, though."

He slashes against Soto's chest, drawing blood as he rips at his buttons. The men tear Soto's shirt off and hold him down by his arms as Eugi jams the knife into his chest.

Every slow cut leaves a line of fire burning into Soto's body, but after several straight line gashes cut into his flesh Soto loses the energy to scream and he simply groans as the gangster carves into him.

With each cut, the flesh on the struggling man's torso splits like a pair of lips opening into a grin, showing the body fat underneath. The blood wells up slowly, as if leaking from a tiny hole instead of a deep gash and, as he thrashes around, the blood spills over, as loose and warm as rainwater in summer.

Despite his experiences, Soto can't stop himself from looking. The sight of his red-painted chest sends a numbness into his brain, like drunkenness or the feeling he got at the games with Yayoi, but far more frightening. Somewhere in his diminished mind, Soto recognizes the symptoms of shock.

Eugi stands up when he finishes, his knife and hand caked with blood as he looks down onto the gory kanji for "debtor" cut into Soto's torso.

Eugi waves the knife around over the prone man, letting blood drip onto his face and he glares down at him.

"I know where you live from your ID," says Eugi. "We've killed people for owing this much. I'll give you six months. Do you understand me?"

Soto manages a slight nod, fighting against the stiffness in his neck.

"Find his coat," says Eugi.

Out in the mingling room, most of the hostesses and all of the customers are gone. Kit stands next to Yayoi behind the bar, hugging the younger woman's shoulders as Yayoi tries to keep her eyes dry.

The door slams against the wall as it opens and the women jump.

Soto shuffles out like a zombie, his coat draped over his shoulders like a blanket. Through the open jacket they can see the bloody lines carved into Soto's belly fat.

He looks Yayoi, not with anger or betrayal: barely even with recognition. At the sight of his dull eyes and pale skin, she can't stop the tears from spilling down her face.

The gangsters shove Soto out of the front door and she hears him fall before they shut him out. Eugi snaps his fingers at her.

"I gave him six months to pay," says Eugi. "He was your customer so I will give you another three months, but if he can't pay, you still owe the same sum," he says.

Eugi and the mobsters grab their coats, leaving the bar. Two of them bend down to scoop up the unconscious Soto, dragging him down the hallway and leaving a red smudge behind them.

Kit gives Yayoi another hug from behind. "You've got more time," she says. "Do you think you can pay it back by then?"

Yayoi just nods, saying nothing. She thinks about the way Soto looked at her and the smear of blood left in the hallway. She knows that she'll never forget the look on his face.

About the Author

Joshua Waddles is from Hot Springs, Arkansas. Even though he lives on the lake, he can't fish worth a damn. He discovered J.R.R. Tolkien when he was a child, and he spent the next two decades honing his geek skills. Joshua's nerd path led him to a love of anime, video games, and eighties music, for some reason.

東京極道

Tokyo Yakuza
#2

Still Waters

M. Biddix-Simmons

Japan won the Second World War.
Now the yakuza are starting the Third!

Tokyo Yakuza #2

Still Waters

By Michelle Biddix-Simmons

January 15, 2020. Shibuya, Tokyo. Green cones of light lit the street beyond the back stoop.

The street lights, Tokyo's latest update, glowed over the city. The bioluminescent green algae saved Tokyo enough yen and energy that Yoshiko knew the city's nights were destined to stay tinted green.

At least, most of the city. Shinjuku and a few other areas still glowed with multihued neon signs advertising nightclubs, casinos, and hostess clubs.

On a clear night, Yoshiko could make out the flashing glow of Shinjuku over the buildings and trees of the small park across the street from her oji's[16] sedate Shibuya sushi-ya.

But tonight the haze of impending rain hid the lights and people rushed about their business as the evening took hold.

The dry leaves on the trees across the street started rustling, letting her know a light rain had started falling. Pedestrians popped open umbrellas and the street began to empty.

---

[16] Uncle's.

A few people moved toward the front of sushi-ya, "Seiiki."

Her oji, Ryuu, had named it Seiiki[17] and maintained it as a place where anyone could eat with no fear. The old yakuza[18] families had adhered to this for several decades, partly out of love for having someplace where they could relax, and partly out of fear of *things* that had deeper loyalty.

Yoshiko knew that Oji was beginning to worry over the tension the contracts for the upcoming Olympics were causing. The Yama-guchi-gumi had already begun making moves against the Sumiyoshi-kai.[19] There was money to be made and every family was out to get their share.

Oji had a saying: "It was safer to be bloody in shark infested water than it was to deny any yakuza yen."

She thought he should add: "The yakuza were always trouble … even if they were family" at the end of his sage advice. But she kept that to herself. Oji-san and the rest of her family owed much to the yakuza.

Yoshiko could hear the kitchen staff getting louder, and that was the cue that the place would soon be busy.

In the few days she had been working here she had learned the rhythm of the restaurant. Any minute, her oji would yell at the cooks to check the last batch of rice and make sure the udon[20] was hot enough. Then he would yell because one of the waitresses was late, and at last he would yell for Yoshiko to hurry up.

Oji understood her need to have some peace, and enjoy what little

---

[17] "Sanctuary."

[18] Japanese organized crime/mobsters. Literally, 8-9-3, adding up to 20, the losing hand of cards in a certain illegal gambling game that can be played with hanafuda, flower cards.

19 The second largest criminal clan in Japan. Their gang colors are purple.

[20] Noodle soup served in a hot ceramic bowl.

nature there was in this area of the city, but he liked to keep everyone moving.

Yoshiko's life was no longer in Okinawa and it was decided she needed to learn about the city while her uncle could keep an eye on her. It wasn't that she couldn't take care of herself or that she was naive. Yoshiko had skills that some people would see as an asset and the family knew that, for her, a college education would give her enough power to save herself from being collected. The mixed-race children of kami[21] and mortals were coveted. Many powerful men who liked being able to alter games of chance, or influence people's decisions, would pay deeply to have someone with Yoshiko's talents.

Yoshiko's family still had enough pull to grease palms so that no tales were told. So she sat at Seiiki until the dorms opened, and in a few more weeks, she would lock herself away in the world of academia, away from power-mad despots.

The cold rain had caused a mist to rise and the small park across the street now took on a green halo. A large figure stepped to the edge of the park, outlined by the verdant glow. Yoshiko gave a small bow which the figure returned.

"Damn it! He did it again," Oji Ryuu yelled from close by. She could hear his heavy steps as he paced to the office. "Yoshiko, hurry up! Tonight you have to be a waitress. Grab Hanako's old dress and there are extra ears in the red cabinet … what am I saying?" He gave a gruff laugh and she could see his feet under the fabric. "Aiko, grab Hanako's dress and tail for Yoshiko."

A soft "Hai"[22] came from deeper in the restaurant, and the noren[23] was pushed back as Oji Ryuu stepped out to the stoop. He saw the

---

[21] Shinto nature spirits.

[22] "Yes?"

[23] Traditional fabric divider.

figure across the street and gave a quick bow before speaking to Yoshiko. "Sorry, girl, but that pon hiki[24] Eugi stole away one of our other waitresses for The Bijou." He bent to tap her on the nose with one finger in a gesture from childhood. "Tonight you call me 'Uncle'."

"But you told me not to."

"That was so the kitchen staff and waitresses would leave you alone. Just call me 'Oji'."

"Hai, Oji-san."

"Now hurry!" He handed her a plate of warm onigiri[25] before disappearing.

Yoshiko stepped down from the stoop and moved to the small altar she had been tending since her arrival. She stacked the onigiri on the plate before pouring some of the sake, from the tokkuri[26] she had been holding, into a small cup. The image of a fluffy tanuki holding a red balloon decorated the cup. Yoshiko smiled before closing her eyes and sending up a prayer for the nature of Tokyo.

A noise brought her out of her prayer. She turned her head and saw car lights moving through the misty rain. The vehicle was obviously costly, and something about it made her feel as if she were prey.

Yoshiko gathered the dishes before quickly stepping on to the stoop and pushing the fabric back to enter.

She hesitated and turned to look at the car directly across from her. She could see the dark outline of a man, and as the car slowed even more she could tell he was watching her.

Yoshiko stepped into the restaurant and closed the door, missing the figure still standing in the park as it turned to look at the car.

Red eyes glowed in the dark as they watched prey go by.

---

[24] Pimp.

[25] Rice balls.

[26] 徳利 - Ceramic sake flask or service container used for delivering warmed rice wine.

✦　◇　✦

Yoshiko tried to keep her mind on her work and her eyes forward as the other waitresses walked by. Aiko had removed the liner of her short, white, diaphanous gown and wore only a thong and heels. Her nipples were visible, as were all of her jiggling curves, as she moved about the restaurant.

Oji joked that the girls got better tips by showing their tips, and as long as they kept their parts out of his food, it was fine.

Yoshiko wore the full gown over boyshorts with a matching sports bra, plus a little something extra.

She decided the look said, "How may I serve you?" and not, "How may I service you?" Her tips might be smaller, but she was fine with that.

It seemed the demure look worked for some of the guys, if the hand sliding up her leg was any indication.

Yoshiko tried to twist away when a hand grabbed her arm and held her in place. She kept her face turned to the side as the older man's hot breath slide across her ear. "You are just too pretty to work here in a sushi-ya. I know where you could make a lot of money." He leaned in even closer to add, "And a lot of friends." She felt the warm swipe of his tongue and revulsion caused her to twist even more.

The hand on her arm tightened and Yoshiko tensed as she saw Oji moving toward them from across the room. She shook her head, letting him know she was okay, and was about to jerk away when a voice said, "Eugi-san, let her get back to work." The younger man, who had spoken up, moved to slap the older man on the back. "We want to eat soon and we can't do that if you steal another waitress for The Bijou." The other men in their group laughed and made other comments that Yoshiko ignored as she waited for the chance to get away.

"I was just ordering sake ... make it the best!" He finally let her arm go and she fled the room, aware that the younger man was watching.

The laughter and sounds of dishes blended into a blur as the evening progressed. Eugi still watched her, but now he stood at the bar speaking with a police detective from the Vice Squad. Yoshiko thought of the police man as the flashy dresser and tonight's purple silk shirt had cost more than any honest officer would make in a month. She had already suspected he was corrupt as he often brushed past her as she sat on the stoop. He always entered and left Seiiki through the back door. That didn't seem to be the action of someone with nothing to hide.

Moving between the tables full of chatting customers and carrying a tray of drinks, Yoshiko made her way to the other Yamaguchi-gumi members who now surrounded Eugi and the detective. She had played it smart and made a deal with Aiko. Yoshiko would bring the trays, and Aiko would handle Eugi. Not having to deal with Eugi again was well worth losing half of her night's tips.

He obviously enjoyed Aiko's attention, and the fact that she gave service with a smile and not much else, though Yoshiko could still feel his eyes on her as she went about her job.

Several tables eventually paid up and left, allowing Yoshiko a chance for a much needed break.

She caught Aiko's attention and gestured that she was going in the back. As she turned to leave the room she noticed a man had joined Eugi and the detective. The man began to take his shirt off piquing her interest for a second before her view was blocked as several other yakuza moved around the three. She grabbed a tray of dishes as a cheer rose from the group. Yoshiko turned to search for bare skin, breaking her rule, but being rewarded with the flash of delicately shaded cherry blossoms. She began to move forward when she felt eyes on her and looked up from the tattooed skin into the cold eyes of Eugi. Yoshiko clutched the tray as she left the room chiding herself that breaking the rules is asking for trouble.

After a trip to the bathroom, she went in to the kitchen to say hello to the cook, Kaede, and the rest of the staff.

Kaede waved her off after pointing out two plates of fish and vegetables. Yoshiko grabbed the chopsticks and the plates before heading to the back stoop. She added one plate to the altar before sitting down and quickly eating her food.

Yoshiko stared at the park and watched the fog swirl as spirits danced about. Once she thought she caught a glimpse of a tail, and she heard a hint of laughter, but the park suddenly stilled as the noren parted and the young yakuza stepped onto the stoop.

"So this is where you ran off to." At some point in the evening, he had loosened his tie and rolled up the sleeves of his shirt.

"It's my break."

"I thought you could add this to the shrine." He leaned down to hand her a small tokkuri of sake.

She shook her head.

"You should add it."

He stepped down from the stoop to pick up the empty cup with the fluffy tanuki.

He held the cup and looked at her. "Cute."

"I think so. I added that when I was little."

"So you are from here?"

"No."

He waited. When she didn't add anything else he poured the sake. Steam rose as the heated liquid hit the chilled ceramic of the cup.

"It's still warm!" She seemed pleased. "We should go in now."

He looked at her in surprise, but waited as she gathered her plate. As she started to rise, his right hand came out to support her elbow. She flinched away. As he pulled his hand, the rolled sleeve shifted and she glimpsed the edge of a delicate pink flower that seemed to be floating on water.

Yoshiko entered the dining area and looked for Aiko. The waitress was sitting on Eugi's lap, but his eyes found Yoshiko as soon as she entered the room. The younger man walked in behind her. Eugi's mouth tightened as he pushed Aiko off his lap and demanded more sake.

Customers repeated the demand for sake and Aiko hurried to comply.

Yoshiko went about the busy work that always needed to be done in a restaurant. She collected dishes and headed to the back just as she caught movement out of the corner of her eye. She saw Oji-san step out of the back, blocking someone from following her. She turned in time to see the white suit jacket of Eugi as the tattooed younger man helped him take a seat next to the corrupt cop in the flashy purple shirt.

She caught a quick sleight of hand as the younger man slipped the wallet out of Eugi's inside suit jacket pocket, then gestured for

Aiko to bring more sake. He nodded at Oji, who had moved up to assist in case the drunken Eugi caused trouble.

Eugi caught the nod and realized he was being played, somehow. He pulled away and grabbed the sake from Aiko's tray, then flung it at the young man. Eugi cursed and stumbled out the door, as if to go fetch something.

Yoshiko and Aiko jumped to action, grabbing towels to help clean up the young yakuza and the mess. They cleared the table as several other Yamaguchi-gumi members left. The few that stayed moved to the bar. Oji-san led the young man to the back where he could wash up. As they left the room, Yoshiko saw the younger man take a single meishi[27] out of Eugi's wallet and slide a stack of yen under the bill Aiko had set down for Eugi.

The young yakuza then stripped off his sake-drenched shirt, leaving his chest bare, and fully exposing the tattoo that had been teasing Yoshiko since their encounter on the stoop.

The young yakuza's full-body irezumi[28] depicted a water scene with several koi[29] just visible below the surface. Cherry blossoms floated beside a large, mud colored rendition of Namazu.[30] This Namazu was expertly shaded and skillfully crafted.

Yoshiko laughed.

It was obviously the work of Horiyoshi VII and she suspected it was reactive.

As he took a seat at the bar, she moved forward to get a better

---

[27] Business card. Everyone in Tokyo carries them, even the yakuza, with their clan emblems proudly displayed.

[28] Yakuza tattoo done by hand with traditional tools.

[29] Carp, often found in pools in Zen gardens.

[30] The earthquake-causing catfish of Shinto myth.

look. Horiyoshi VII had captured the arrogance of the bringer of earthquakes. A creature so destructive that he had to be held down by a rock only a god could move.

The man raised his udon bowl towards his mouth, and the catfish started to look a little different. It was subtle, but it looked as if it were fading. Yoshiko looked up to see the young yakuza frozen with his chopsticks over the bowl as he watched her. A smile slid across his face and just as she was about to speak his eyes snapped over her shoulder at the entrance.

"You bastard! I know you lifted my wallet."

Eugi stumbled in and spotted the stack of yen sticking out from under his bill. He moved toward it. "Something's going on here, Hikaru, and I'm onto your game. Besides, you keep paying the small people and you lose!"

The younger yakuza—Yoshiko refused to think of him as Hikaru—tried to placate him. "Eugi-san, you were too drunk to pay this fine barkeep and the waitresses! Our oyabun[31] would not approve, and we all know you are a good kobun."[32]

"You bastard! First, you steal from me. Then, you try to say I'm ripping people off!"

Eugi pulled a gun from his pocket before anyone could react. Several shots resounded as the udon bowl hit the ground.

A couple of the Yamaguchi-gumi members grabbed Eugi and hustled him to a corner. Oji brought him coffee and they set about sobering him up.

The tattooed man was bleeding from his left shoulder and arm and Yoshiko reacted as the man's friend started to pour some sake on the wounds.

---

[31] Father. Yakuza clan boss.

[32] Son. A subordinate yakuza.

She slapped his hand away and the sake container broke. "Don't! You don't know how it is wired. If the sheath has been compromised, you could kill him or worse."

The man reared his hand back to slap her, but Oji caught him by the wrist.

"Let her work. She can help him."

"Is she a nurse or something?" he asked.

"Better."

Yoshiko pressed a clean towel to the wound.

"It's just a graze." He lied.

"Yes, but I can see two wires. Is it a nouveau Edo[33] irezumi?"

His head snapped up. "Yes. How did you know?"

She ignored the question and reached under her short dress for her knife pack. She located the smallest knife and proceeded to delicately expose the wire. The man clenched his teeth, trying to bear the pain without crying out.

"Horimono?"[34] she asked. Yoshiko located an issue and rolled the two exposed wires back under the small flap of skin.

He failed to suppress a groan as he answered. "Obviously not," he said. He used his other hand to demonstrate that his body was not covered by a full tattoo suit.

"Not that. I meant is it intended to be? Are you following hitoppori?"[35]

"No. It is limited and I have not been worked on for a few weeks."

---

[33] Edo is old Tokyo – the capital of the Tokugawa shogunate. Tokyo was destroyed by Allied firebombing during World War II but was rebuilt. The new Tokyo is sometimes called "nouveau Edo" or "Neo-Tokyo."

[34] Full body tattoo, aka. full body suit.

[35] Getting tattooed for two hours a day.

"It is reactive?"

"Yes. How do you know so much?"

"I start the Bio-Droid-Tech program at Waseda University[36] soon. I have worked with synth-dermal adrenal cortex reactive horimono before. This is by VII isn't it? He does the best work. It is not even shimmering and you know your body is full of cortisol."

He started to ask her more when she shushed him and told him to let her work. She sprayed a setting adhesive and moved the wires in place before cleaning and adding a layer of flowderm: a liquid that spread and formed a web-like film.

"You will be fine, but get in soon so he can make sure there is no back flack to the hypothalamus. I doubt it, but you don't want a heart attack or brain damage from such a small wound."

"Arigato. I am ..." he touched his chest as he started the introduction.

She stopped him.

"I don't want to know your name. That way, when you die, I am left mourning the tattoo and not the canvas." She grabbed her tools and turned to go when he called out, "I'm Asahara Hikaru! Now, when I die, you can mourn the man and not just the tattoo."

Yoshiko looked back at him once before getting back to work.

January 16, 2020. Dawn was only a few hours away by the time she was able to step out onto the stoop again.

Yoshiko finished her restaurant work and cleaned her tools before changing back into her own clothes. The white dress was ruined from all of the blood, so she wadded it up and threw it into the trash.

---

[36] The second best university in Tokyo, after Todai or Tokyo University.

I am sure some guy would find that sexy, she thought. The image of some waitress serving food in a blood stained gown and ears crossed her mind.

A light rain drizzled down over the empty streets. Tomorrow would be a late opening. She could hear the clatter of pans as Oji made sure that each piece was back in place to start the cooking all over again.

Dropping her bag on the stoop, Yoshiko took a seat and stretched out her legs before opening a small bento[37] of onigiri. Umeboshi[38] filled the center of the ball and Yoshiko sent up a blessing for the cook and his care in making her favorite.

The curtains flapped out. The wave of air indicated that the front door had been closed for the night. Yoshiko put the rest of the rice in her mouth and chewed as she stood and stretched; then she moved to the altar to place several warm onigiri on the empty plate.

Oji Ryuu walked out, dressed in street clothing topped by a jacket, and handed her a container. "Hikaru paid for the best sake to add to the altar. It seems he has noticed you take care of it and wanted to thank your spirits for your help. He is a nice guy."

"He is not destined for this life for long if his actions tonight mean anything."

"Shh ... he has spent his career in the yakuza cleaning up Eugi's messes. But I hear he was recently promoted to run The Velours in Ginza. Asahara Hikaru follows the Yamaguchi-gumi code, and Oyabun Kitano rewards faithful service."

Oji looked off, up the street, at the lights of the kyabakura[39] where he often met his friends.

"Just go. I will be fine."

---

[37] Wooden lacquered lunchbox.

[38] Pickled Japanese salt plums.

[39] Hostess club. A place where women pour drinks, light cigarettes, and make small talk with lonely men.

He looked at her and said, "Such good sake for the spirits … they would be fools to go after you."

Oji Ryuu smiled at her, popped his collar, and touched his head before disappearing into the green tinted mist.

Yoshiko touched her head and realized she still had her ears.

She was just too tired to get rid of them.

After placing the sake on the altar, Yoshiko grabbed her bag and put the container safely away. She pulled out her umbrella and stepped into the night.

The soft hush of the light rain against her umbrella soothed her as she moved through the green tinted night.

She was almost to the corner of Seiiki when she heard a strange sound, perhaps a moan of pain, and she turned to look for the source. Across the small park, a set of headlights turned on as an expensive car drove away.

A shiver ran across her skin. She started on her path again just as she heard another moan.

She realized it echoed from the alleyway outside Seiiki.

A green haze glowed in the darkness of the tight alleyway.

One of the other businesses must have installed a bioluminescent light, she thought for a second. But the fact none of them would spring for the cost without an argument over who should pay meant no light had even been installed.

Yoshiko realized her feet were moving her forward before she had even decided to check it out.

She moved quietly, one hand going to the tool pack on her belt. Her small scalpels could be used quite effectively against any potential foe.

As she rounded a trash container, she saw that the green glow was from several hi no tama[40] bouncing around Hikaru. The young man's life's blood was quickly leaking out onto the wet pavement.

Asahara Hikaru had propped himself up against the wall of Seiiki. Even from a few feet away, Yoshiko could see three new bullet holes. Although she had not heard any gunshots, someone apparently had been lying in wait to finish the job.

As Yoshiko moved closer, more spirit lights appeared, but they did not seem to be feeding off of him yet. She sent up a prayer of thanks that Hikaru had purchased that sake. It had gained him some small favor and, if he was not dead yet, she might be able to help. First, she needed to be able to get to the wounds.

She dropped her umbrella before opening her bag and placing it next to him.

Yoshiko went down on one knee and cautiously touched the skin on his neck, afraid she might be too late, but his pulse throbbed steadily under her finger and she rushed into action.

As she started to lean him forward, he spoke. "Little Synth-tech, you think you can help me with flowderm and spray adhesive?"

He rolled his head to look at her. "Do you have cat ears on?" She ignored his question as the hovering spirits shifted. A large form, a raccoon-dog in the shape of an imposingly tall and muscular man, walked into the alley.

"Help me, please, Tanuki-san.[41] He has been shot, but I think two are shallow enough I can get them out."

---

[40] Colorful floating balls of soul-fire.
[41] Mr. Tanuki. Mr. Raccoon-dog Spirit.

"No, little sister. He has to ask for my aid, and he has to pay the balance."

Hikaru slowly raised his head and looked at the large man. He wore a rough jacket made of tattered fabric and fur. On his head was a straw jingasa[42] tied in place with a red cord that had a comical carved tanuki at the end. The massive tanuki looked down at the bleeding man.

"So Kakashi,"[43] the tanuki said, "What will it be? Shall I help?"

"My name is not Kakashi. It is Asahara Hik …"

The tanuki cut him off, "Well, you are sitting on your ass in old rice and you stink. I would say Kakashi is exactly the right name." He looked at the blood drops hitting the wet ground. His eyes glowed red as he waited for Hikaru's answer.

"Hai. Please help me, Tanuki-san."

The big tanuki-man took a seat against the wall. He leaned the gunshot victim face down across one leg, allowing Yoshiko access to the wounds. As she got to work, he lifted one large hand to lick the blood off of each finger.

"The cyber-matrix stopped the bullets. That is why you are alive. This will hurt," Yoshiko said. She spread a silica-salt solution across the wound before sliding a long, thin knife under the tattooed skin. His body tensed up and he groaned as she peeled the skin back slowly, trying not to damage the artwork. She continued for several inches until she felt a tug on the matrix; then she knew she had found the third bullet.

---

[42] Soldier's cap.

[43] Scarecrow, often set up in rice paddies.

Yoshiko closed her eyes and concentrated. She ran her middle finger along the wires until she found the ones that were sending out signals that didn't flow with the piece of art. Hooking her pinky, she gave a gentle tug, and then another. She waited for a second and gave a third before starting to unroll the skin.

Once the skin was back in place, she reached into the pack by Hikaru's face. Hikaru could see Yoshiko's hand rummaging in the contents before removing an oddly long, U-shaped instrument. It reminded him of a tuning fork he had seen in an old movie.

He felt a twang. He had to bite down to hold in the scream as he felt something pull itself from his body. Two bullets fell on the ground near his face. Yoshiko did another strike on his back and something against his heart fluttered.

Yoshiko placed the odd instrument on her pack and he could feel something cold on his skin as he heard a hiss.

"I got two slugs out and moved the other away from your heart. You are lucky VII does such great work. The extra synth-lattice to stabilize the reactive layer of the cyber-matrix is what saved your life. It stopped the bullet from piercing your heart. The crystalline structure slowed all three, and that is why you have not bled out: inlaid clotting factor with a reactive double feedback. Whoever paid for that must want you to live. That is costly, cutting-edge tech. Not even okayed yet for the police or military."

The man-sized tanuki shifted the smaller man a bit and looked at Yoshiko. "This was a mob hit. Someone will expect him to be dead."

"Hai. He would have been, if not for me." Yoshiko knew that her field surgery might have saved him for now, but Hikaru's life had changed. That was why the hi no tama had led her to him. Yoshiko and other children of kami had a kind of sixth sense: they could always tell when something disruptive was happening in their vicinity. Hikaru had gotten someone's attention and the attempted hit was just the drama these little beings loved.

"Did Eugi come back to finish the job?" the large tanuki asked as he licked the last of the blood from his fingers.

"It wasn't Eugi this time," Asahara Hikaru said. "There were two of them. They used silenced pistols. I think it was the Sumiyoshi-kai. When I went through Eugi's wallet like Yoshiko's Oji requested, I found a meishi belonging to the Sumiyoshi-kai oyabun, Sugawara Hirono."

"You will have to disappear," the tanuki said. He grabbed the smaller man while shifting to stand.

"Don't clean up the blood. I will lick it up later!" he added. He threw Hikaru over his shoulder before starting off down the alley.

"Don't eat him!" Yoshiko called out to the dark. Laughter came back.

"Spoilsport!"

January 17, 2020. The next afternoon, Yoshiko had just arrived and was about to unlock the back door when she felt his presence. Yoshiko turned to find Tanuki-san at the edge of the road.

As he moved closer, she realized he was holding a large square-shaped object, wrapped in brown paper, against his bulky coat.

"The oyabun of the Yamaguchi-gumi, Kitano-san, wanted you to have this. Kakashi does not need it anymore." He laughed dryly at his joke." As she reached out to take the package, he added, "The boy, Hikaru, lives, but he needs to be reborn as someone else. Oyabun Kitano-san has set up him with a new cyber-doctor to have … some more work done." The tanuki handed her the bulky gift. As she unwrapped it, he continued, "VII says your technique is good and he would even be willing to forgo oreiboko[44] if you decided to apprentice with him. High compliment indeed. He had another potential apprentice in mind, but he said she was no longer viable. A half child of the kami like you has more human soul than what they left that woman."

The paper fell away and there was the tattoo she had tried to save, stretched on a frame and ready for hanging on a wall.

Two koi were swimming in a serene pond, barely disturbing the cherry blossoms that floated on the water's surface, and the large catfish was no where to be seen.

"Hikaru wanted you to know the tattoo has been altered enough that no one who has seen this irezumi before will recognize it now. That could end badly for all involved."

He looked off up the street before adding more quietly, "Little sister, I suspect I will be going undercover, since Eugi has been playing nice with the Sumiyoshi-kai. I believe Eugi may have made a deal with them to help fix some contracts for the Olympics, but I need proof of his betrayal before we can move against him. Such tricky times these Games are creating." He trailed off as he looked up the street once again. Yoshiko turned just as a fox-eared girl with long strawberry blonde hair disappeared into the park.

"Always twitching her tail in my business." He turned back toward Yoshiko. "VII said he made the tattoo environ-active and that the rock has been removed."

Yoshiko quickly looked at the irezumi artwork stretched on the wooden frame and could see the slow movement of something large, deep beneath the water painted into the skin. She missed the wide grin that spread across the tanuki's bearded face and his heavily shaded eyes turned red.

---

[44] The final year of five year apprenticeship where all money made goes to the master.

"Though I suspect Kakashi removed the rock himself. You don't live through two shootings and not gain something. Unless you're a fool."

She gazed at the now still pond tattoo, and when she looked up, she found Tanuki-san was shambling back across the street to his park.

"I am hoping I get a piece like that myself, soon. VII says he always regretted working on Eugi. An irezumi of The Warriors of Kuniyoshi's *Suikoden*; I love the classics." He opened his arms wide and his coat began to blend with the trees.

"I hope I kill him myself or at least get to him while he is still warm. Pulling a gun on one's own clansman in Seiiki? That deserves a special death, and while those onigiri are good, a kami's gotta have real meat some time."

He stopped and turned to look at her. "Keep your ears hidden little sister, and stay in that school. Make yourself a power so people will be afraid to move on you when your ears do show." With a bow, he disappeared into the shadows.

Yoshiko sat on the covered stoop of Seiiki and watched as the koi began to swim in the frame. A light rain began to fall on the street and, like all fish when it rains, the koi became more active.

Rain drops fell on the surface of the tattoo pond, sending ripples out across the water, and for an instant she thought she saw the eyes of Namazu. There was a flip of brown fins as the bringer of earthquakes dove deeper down into the still waters.

About the Author

Michelle Biddix-Simmons started life in Japan and has traveled the world in what she considers a blessed life of adventure. She has seen the snows of Kilimanjaro, safaried across East Africa, crossed swinging bridges that put Indiana Jones films to shame, belly danced in the deserts of Saudi Arabia, attended a masqued ball in Venezia, and belly surfed down the shifting sands. There have been midnight rides through the darkened streets of a small city, on the coast of Italy, while locked in a blast proof Carabinieri vehicle with several armed men.

Life is somewhat calmer now and when not in the garden you can find her reading a book, attending a comedy show, or negotiating with the many creatures with whom she co-habitats. One of the many creatures is her husband who is a professional improv comedian and computer god. He tends to require the most negotiating as comedians and gods can be tricky. Costuming is a major passion and so costumes are always optional and there is even a closet for her Gothic attire. She still tends toward British spelling due to a misspent youth and must admonish herself daily for the u's she finds added in certain words.

東京極道

Tokyo Yakuza

#3

Momentum

by Todd Sullivan

Japan won the Second World War; Now the yakuza are starting the Third!

TOKYO YAKUZA #3

Momentum

BY TODD SULLIVAN

January 15, 2020. Shibuya, Tokyo. *Less than a month.* Eugi closed the ends of the metal chopsticks around the decapitated kohada[45] head and plopped it into his mouth. He chewed slowly, the dark fish eyes popping between his teeth. He tongued off the baked skin around the gills, swallowed, then leaned over and spit the thin fish bones onto a round porcelain plate. Eugi had less than a month to threaten, intimidate, beat, torture and, when those tactics failed, kill so he could raise fifty six million yen[46] and get the hell out of Tokyo. A return of the money that his Bijou hostess Yayoi embezzled from him would help, but it wouldn't be nearly enough.

Detective Kato, a middle-aged cop who was also a Yamaguchi-gumi affiliate wearing a flashy, purple silk shirt, sat next to the street samurai and pimp, Asahara Hikaru and his superior, Eugi, at the Seiiki sushi-ya. The detective clutched a tall glass of beer with one hand. With the other, he wiped his hairless chest with a wet napkin. He sweated profusely in his open purple shirt. Kato wasn't sweating

---

[45] Gizzard shad, a kind of sardine eaten as sushi.
[46] About $560,000.

because of the ambient temperature on this cold January night in the quiet sushi-ya in Shibuya even though someone had cranked up the floor heater and set it blazing beneath them. And he wasn't sweating because of the twenty and twenty-one year-old girls in thin negligees working the restaurant with cat ears gracing their dyed hair, bare legs exposed and perky breasts poking out of their low cut, translucent tops.

Eugi lifted his narrow sake cup from the masu[47] box, drained it, and slammmed it with a heavy thud on the table, making the detective jump.

No, Kato sweated because of Eugi. Eugi knew secrets about the corrupt vice squad detective, knew his perversions. He knew he had a high society wife with a brother-in-law who was a respected councilor on the National Diet. Eugi also knew that Kato was angling for a promotion from the Tokyo Metropolitan Police Force to the Kempeitai Thought Police.[48] Eugi could end everything for him by pressing ENTER on a digital keypad, sending sensitive information about the sweating detective into cyberspace to do fatal damage to his thus far stellar career.

Less than a month, thought Eugi. In exchange for his silence, Kato had revealed the planned police crackdown on the yakuza in the run up to the 2020 Tokyo Olympics in July. If the government had its way, all of the city's criminal syndicates were going down, hard, and Kato had warned Eugi that if he still operated in Tokyo, he'd be jailed, or dead. The captain superior of the police force typically opted for the latter over the former so that they could save

---

[47] A square wooden box, often used to hold sake cups and catch the overflow from culturally mandated, overly enthusiastic outpourings of sake.

[48] A secret police operating independently from routine law enforcement as the Emperor's eyes and ears. The Thought Police serves as judge, jury and executioner where lack of patriotism is concerned.

respectable Japanese on their taxes; bullets were cheaper than cells in Sugamo Prison.

Eugi cocked his hand back and suddenly slapped the detective in the face, splitting his bottom lip. *Fucking cops.* Kato almost fell off his stool, his head snapping back at the blow.

"What? Why?" Kato whined, but a growl of distaste silenced any other complaint. The detective lifted his beer to his lips with quivering fingers. Eugi speared an abalone with the tips of his chopsticks, placed the slimy flesh in his mouth, and chewed on the hard muscled fish.

One of their waitresses, Aiko, a thin slip of a girl with shapely legs and dark nipples visible beneath her negligee, appeared at his side with a tall bottle of sake. She'd been diligent since he'd first entered the sushi-ya, always making sure his cup was filled. This was his fourth round of sake, and his thoughts ran clear as water as he calculated new targets to squeeze for money over the next several weeks.

The girl brushed against him as she filled his cup. Her hips rubbed against his side as she poured, the sake overfilling the glass into the masu box. Unlike the other girls, she didn't wear cloying perfumes to stuff the private room with overwhelming aromas. Instead, Aiko opted for a light, flowery fragrance that allowed a faint, musky scent to escape from under her arms when she lifted the sake bottle. Eugi inhaled deeply, warmed at her nearness, but he kept his expression impassive when she glanced at him.

"More sashimi?"[49] she asked.

Eugi nodded, and with a shy nod, Aiko quickly disappeared. The girl was skilled, quick, flitting through the sushi-ya like a sprite.

---

[49] Slices of raw fish.

Eugi smiled imagining the ways he could force her to pleasure him. The twist of his mouth must have seemed cruel, because Detective Kato cringed. Eugi ignored him, his thoughts racing. Eugi had to move fast; he had to raise the fifty six million yen and escape Japan before Oyabun Kitano Takumi of the Yamaguchi-gumi discovered that he had been working with the Sumiyoshi-kai and Kato to fix certain construction and service contracts for the Olympics.

Kato had revealed the coming crackdown under duress days before the New Year and Eugi, the gokudo[50] made man, had been breaking skulls ever since. So much blood stained his clothes on a daily basis that Eugi ran out of outfits each week before he had time to get them cleaned. Some thought he'd lost it. They thought he'd become a sadist and enjoyed the violence too much, but what did he care? He'd be gone soon. They'd all die in the police sweeps, and that would be that.

When the waitress came back with more sushi, Eugi's eyes focused on the black patch of hair visible beneath her sheer pink underwear. The girl set the platter on the table, then set a crimson bottle of Korean soju[51] down next to the platter.

"Service," she said with a coy smile, indicating the soju was on the house. Eugi didn't react when she uncorked the bottle and poured three shot glasses: two for the men, one for her. Kato, glancing nervously at Eugi, declined. Eugi paid him no mind when he picked up his own glass. He waited for the waitress to pick up hers and they clinked the small cups together before downing the bitter liquor. A fuzzy warmth suffused his thoughts and the waitress laid a slender hand on his upper thigh. Before the evening was over, Eugi realized,

---

[50] A yakuza gangster, or made man. Literally, a follower of the "extreme path" or "ultimate way."

[51] Literally "burned liquor," a grain alcohol originally from Korea.

she'd service him, and on the house to boot, since he was spending so much money at the sushi-ya tonight.

Now the girl didn't leave his side. Aiko filled Eugi's cup along with her own and waited until he raised his glass to take hers. She stood before him; then sat by his side. Before long, she ended up on his lap, her face nestled in his neck, her breath sharp with the smell of soju. Eugi wrapped his arm around her. He noted the smallness of her body against his chest and a name popped into his head.

Inagawa-kai[52] *gambling boss Noboru Akira.*

There were others like Detective Kato with similar sexual appetites. Oyabun Noboru Akira of the Inagawa-kai was one of them. In the criminal underworld of the yakuza, their shared predilection for under-aged girls didn't matter; in fact, the underage were preyed upon, and indulged in, for profit. But even gambling boss Noboru Akira had a respectable side, a public persona that he wouldn't want ruined if the truth came out about him. If Eugi could get a recording of Akira and his peculiar brand of entertainment, he'd have him on the same leash as Detective Kato. And blackmailing Akira was much more financially lucrative than threatening some random detective on Tokyo's police force.

Eugi staggered off to the bathroom. When he returned, unsteady on his legs, Hikaru helped him back onto his seat to the left of Detective Kato. As he sat down, Eugi realized that the girl who had been sitting on his lap was gone; Aiko was probably off fooling around with one of his men. In that moment of drunken distraction, Eugi felt the inner suit jacket pocket where he kept his wallet suddenly grow lighter. Then he caught a glimpse of Hikaru making eye contact with the sushi-ya owner, Ryuu, and Ryuu acknowledging

---

[52] The third largest criminal clan in Japan and the original yakuza family of Tokyo. Their gang colors are black.

Hikaru with a deft nod.

Eugi turned to Hikaru. He stretched the grin on his face as wide as possible to frighten the young tattooed yakuza as much as he could. Eugi realized he was drunk from the soju, but he didn't care. He narrowed his eyes, looking like a serpent ready to strike. But Hikaru only stared at him, the momentary fright having dropped from his features to be replaced by a steely gaze. As Aiko returned bearing liquor, Eugi grabbed the tokkuri full of hot sake from her tray and bounced it off the young man's chest. Then Eugi swore and held up his index finger at Hikaru before heading out the door for the flowerpot where he had stashed a gun, just in case.

Outside and armed in a drunken stupor, Eugi hunted for his wallet and realized Hikaru had taken it. He didn't know why and for a moment he didn't particularly care. Then, despite his haze, Eugi remembered he had kept the rival Sumiyoshi-kai clan boss Sugawara Hirono's meishi from their first in person meeting together. Now it didn't matter even if Hikaru was only playing a practical joke on him. That fucker had to die. No one could know Eugi was working with the Sumiyoshi-kai.

Eugi parted the noren curtain and stormed back inside. Asahara Hikaru was just sitting there, shirtless like an idiot. "You bastard! I know you lifted my wallet." Eugi screeched. He saw the cash Hikaru had taken from his wallet to pay their sushi-ya tab. Eugi wasn't planning on paying, but when Hikaru called him on it, that was the last straw. The tattooed street samurai probably knew too much to be allowed to live, and Hikaru even had the gall to make Eugi lose face in front of his men. Eugi might still owe fifty six million yen to the Sumiyoshi-kai for certain services rendered, but he wasn't bankrupt.

Good thing for Aiko she's not sitting on Hikaru's lap. Hikaru didn't have time to react before Eugi threw back his jacket flap to reveal a 9mm semiautomatic, which he brought up to Hikaru's chest. Eugi's sunglasses reflected the fear in Hikaru's face in an ocean of darkness. The drunken pimp, extortionist, and traitor aimed and fired, blasting the tattooed young yakuza repeatedly in the shoulder, arm and upper chest.

January 16, 2020. Kita-senju, Tokyo. Sharp squawking from crows, circling above the alley in the Adachi-ku district near Kita-senju station, drew Marco's gaze upwards. Their night roosting disturbed, the large birds flew 'round and 'round the squat clutter of buildings in a flutter of long black wings against the dark sky. Marco pulled his jacket hood from his head so the preternatural crows could get a glimpse of his face.

The cold winter air of this late Tokyo January night bit at his tan skin and he stood on gray concrete, slick with patches of ice. The crows swooped and dived above him, their raspy cries echoing in the still neighborhood. Then one sharply ascended, a silhouette against the crescent moon, and dropped a small object from its claw. Marco watched it fall for a moment, then took several quick steps forward and caught the message.

The birds flapped down to the balconies overlooking the alley with a raucous cawing. They hopped back and forth on the aluminum railings of the old style apartments as they watched Marco with a dozen dark eyes, annoyed by this disturbance. He unfurled the scroll from its slender bamboo tube and read the mission written in elegant Kanji.[53]

---

[53] Traditional Chinese characters adopted into the Japanese language for written communication.

Retribution. Noboru Akira, the oyabun of the Inagawa-kai, one of the smaller yakuza clans whose business specialty was illegal gambling, had ordered a virgin for the evening, and he kidnapped her when she arrived. After spending the kind of money it took to deflower a virgin it seemed he calculated he could resell her to a Chinese criminal syndicate, the 14K Triad,[54] for a profit.

Marco rolled the scroll back into the bamboo tube and tossed it up to the crow that had delivered it to him. The mystical bird snapped its large black beak on it, swallowed the message, and with another outburst of squawking, spread its wings and sprung up into the air, its brethren following suit. Marco whispered a prayer of forgiveness and thanks to his feathered ancestral spirits, then he removed the wakizashi[55] blade and sheath from the leather cylinder container slung on his back, strapped the sword to his waist, and continued down the winding alley.

This was going to be a simple task. If the boss had merely kidnapped the girl, Marco would have needed to retrieve her and force him to pay a sum of money for the inconvenience. That would have been more complicated because it would have taken longer and would have required subtle threats of violence when Marco preferred the speed and purity of a sword strike. But Noboru Akira had killed the girl's two handlers in brutal fashion. With the Tokyo police threatening a crackdown on the brewing yakuza war for the 2020 Olympics, Marco's Sumiyoshi-kai master, the computer-loving otaku, Wakagashira[56] Ishii Naoki, couldn't afford to lose more men. The shifting balance of power demanded a reserve of soldiers.

---

[54] The Chinese criminal clan in Tokyo. Their gang colors are red.

[55] A samurai short sword, often used in the off-hand for blocking in the dual sword style with the katana held in the main hand for attacking.

[56] Clan underboss.

Marco closed his eyes and slowed his breathing in meditation as he focused on forward momentum. The mystical warrior monk, the equal of any cybernetic street samurai, would get the girl back and open a smile in Akira's throat, from ear to ear, within an hour. He opened his eyes, his breathing quickening, his heart racing, and his vision sharpening to reveal minute details of his surroundings. His hearing increased enough to catch the smallest sounds at play around him. His muscles tightened as he slung himself up to the blue roofs of the alley buildings and onward toward Akira's headquarters in Shibuya.

Marco leapt from shadow to shadow, heading south from Adachi-ku toward the center of the Tokyo. Occasional police drones buzzed the air above him, their presence increasing the farther he penetrated the city. Roosting crows sensed his presence and awoke, startled, and cawed at his passing. He sent prayers on silent wings to each bird to aid him in increasing his spirit energy.

Marco avoided main boulevards where the density of cars, busses, taxis, and people endued with cybernetics would be thickest. Darkness became his cloak and made him near invisible to straying eyes. He couldn't stop for a moment or let the tech disturb his focus. He slid down sloping rooftops, slung himself along balcony railings, and ran with light feet over quiet residences.

Adachi-ku district, nearing eleven, was silent, with only small neighborhood izakaya[57] showing any signs of activity. Through apartment windows, Marco glimpsed round faces bathed in holographic images projected from conical television screens, or

---

[57] Pubs serving beer and skewers of grilled meat, inner organs and green onions.

teens connected to simulation interfaces, their bodies immersed in skin tight gaming suits. Wire glasses covered their eyes with lenses shaped like coins. Marco usually dwelled on the outskirts of Tokyo, away from such devices to keep as much distance as possible between him and the modern world. The order of warrior monks to which he belonged was prized by the Sumiyoshi-kai for their mission effectiveness, but they came with their own limitations. They were only used for extreme emergencies and to make visceral examples of their targets.

Nippori, Tokyo. Adachi-ku's neighborhoods suddenly fell away at the Metropolitan Central Highway circumventing downtown Tokyo. The highway crossed the swiftly flowing Sumida River into the Arakawa District. Marco leapt to the ground, sprinted beneath the underpass, and darted across the river's rushing rapids into Arakawa-ku.

Iidabashi, Tokyo. He made a sharp western turn in Chiyoda-ku, detoured around the old Olympic village and Yoyogi Park. Deep in the forest, surrounded by the few nature spirits left untouched in this new Tokyo, Meiji-jingu rested at peace. In the next three blocks, he reached his destination.

Shibuya, Tokyo. Marco sprung out of a narrow alley into bright Shibuya and ran, nearly invisible, along telephone wires above the heads of a herd of humans walking beneath the bright lights of the tall buildings. At the 109 Department Store, standing like an ivory tower in the center of Shibuya, Marco scaled the glittering wall opposite the huge television screen adorning its front. He crouched on its top and jumped across a massive eight lane street. He glided through the air above the sound of pop music blasting from storefronts and female announcers, dressed in tight skirts and high boots, standing in front of tech shops announcing their wares. He landed on the ledge of a motel at the beginning of a narrow side lane of nightclubs and bars.

Monitoring how much spiritual energy he had left after navigating this hive of neon lights and holographic images, of busses, cars, and hoverbikes zipping through traffic, and of people endowed with cybernetic enhancements laced through their clothes and implanted in their skin, Marco estimated he had twelve strikes at most to reach his target before his focus depleted. A dozen blows to kill potential mech bodyguards, to hit Noboru Akira, and to snatch the girl out of the building and bring her to the nearest safe location, several blocks away in Harajuku.

A shadow within the brilliance of modern nighttime Tokyo, Marco sprinted across the roof, dived through the frigid air, and crashed through the thick third floor window of a private room above Club Sound Museum Vision. Deep beats shook the floor as Marco darted to the first massive guard, an African who turned at the noise and reached for a handgun holstered at his hip.

One.

With straight, clean strokes, Marco unsheathed his blade in a single motion, slicing through the guard's right hand into his waist, up into his stomach, and exited out to the left through his ribs. The African fell to his knees and toppled over with a guttural moan.

Two.

Marco built up a ball of force and issued a short, powerful cry that blew the metal door of the room apart. A rainbow of lights suffused a long hall winding around a corner. Electric notes vibrated the walls, making the hallway pulse with the rapid-fire rhythm of the music below. Marco pushed forward, his feet a blur over the polished floor. Around the bend, another guard, brought up sharp by Marco's sudden appearance, loomed ahead. The man crossed his metallic arms, snatched two Uzis at his sides, and brought them to aim at Marco.

Three.

The warrior monk propelled himself into the guard's attack with his left foot and sliced vertically up and neck. With a sharp flick of his wrist, he cut his blade free by way of the man's chin, slicing the gangster's mouth cleanly open. A warm rain of blood splattered Marco's face for only a moment. He slipped past even before the man fell.

Four. Marco emitted another short burst of force with a cry, and the flickering double doors in his path burst open. He swept across the shattered threshold and took note of the spatial dimensions of the room. He sharpened his sight, increased his hearing, and took a mental snapshot without hesitating a moment.

The walls were composed of flat screens that projected holographic characters onto a tiled floor, changing different neon colors when touched. To the right of the room, Marco saw a rectangular red table laden with tall bottles of sake standing sentry around platters of raw fish. A gaming console extended from the floor to the left and a young girl with immersion gloves on her hands spun away from the monitor at Marco's entrance. The tracking collar, shaped like pearls twinkling around her neck, marked her as Naoki's property.

In the center of the room, Marco spotted a Japanese man in a sleek black suit: Inagawa-kai Oyabun Noboru Akira. He sat cross-legged on a flat mat, his back straight and shoulders stiff. He stared ahead, without surprise, at the warrior monk. Against his temple rested the barrel of a gun, held by Noboru Akira's zainichi[58] Korean aide.

Complication: The virgin was only eight or nine years old with black hair weeping down her back. She had tan skin, wide eyes, a slim body, and legs straighter than the typical Japanese girl. She was a foreigner of similar build as the zainichi Korean aide. She had the same cheekbones, the same posture, and the same thin eyebrows. The two were related: probably father and daughter.

Analysis: A low-level criminal who must have left behind a wife and newborn baby in South Korea to make a fortune in Japan with the yakuza. As years passed, he rose through the ranks as the yakuza tightened their grip on Tokyo ahead of the 2020 Olympics. Eventually, he became an aide to gambling boss Noboru Akira, who had a penchant for virgin preteens.

Then, on the other end of the conflict, was Marco's boss in the Sumiyoshi-kai, Ishii Naoki. He ran vast swaths of the criminal underground, including human trafficking. He procured a virgin from Japan's colonial possession: a child recently abducted by the Seven Star Mob[59] Korean mafia and sold into the sex trade in Tokyo. The aide had turned the other way for every other girl until one night when it was his own daughter brought in for entertainment by two of Ishii Naoki's handlers. An unexpected surprise, a quick decision, and a fatal betrayal: he threatened to kill Noboru Akira

---

[58] Japan-born but of Korean ancestry.

[59] The Korean criminal clan in Tokyo. Their gang colors are blue.

unless the girl was rescued.

Mission status in light of this potential scenario of events: *unchanged.*

Marco's sword glared under the garish lights as he descended with his Sumiyoshi-kai master's message to the Inagawa-kai gambling boss: *retribution.* A moment before his strike, the Inagawa-kai oyabun Akira attempted to shout, "No!" But the zainichi Korean aide pulled the trigger. The round blasted Akira's brains from his forehead in an explosion of blood and bone.

Mission status to retrieve the virgin in light of situational events modified: *unchanged.*

Marco adjusted his swing, the tip of the sword bypassing Akira by a hair, and with a sharp u-flick of his wrist, he sliced a smile from ear to ear into the *zainichi* Korean aide's throat. The man's head tilted back and he crumbled to the floor. Five.

"Appa!"[60] The girl rushed forward to the gasping zainichi. The Korean aide vomited blood from his neck. "Appa!" she shouted again.

She clutched his throat with tiny hands to stem the tide of red, but it simply seeped through her slender fingers and stained the gaming gloves. Her father's mouth opened and closed. He sucked in air that gurgled in through his sliced windpipes. His body convulsed and a slow realization dawned in his features as his eyes lost their sheen. He gazed up at his daughter, sobbing over him, and brought up his bloodied fingertips to brush hair away from her tear streaked cheeks. He tapped her forehead gently, to get her attention, and mouthed his last words before his body relaxed in a stiff, eternal sleep.

It was done. Marco bent down and took the girl's arm, but she

---

[60] "Daddy!" (in Korean).

wrenched herself from him and screamed at him in Korean. The words were indecipherable, but the despair and hatred behind them was palatable.

Six. Marco whispered a word and touched the girl's temple. She buckled forward, collapsing over the corpse, and he swept her up, slinging her limp form over his shoulder. He made to turn, but the zainichi Korean aide's dead eyes remained open and staring, past the girl and directly at Marco. The warrior monk returned the stare.

He should have felt disgust for the Inagawa-kai aide's disloyalty to the gambling boss. The aide had placed family above honor, had sacrificed everything for a daughter he surely hardly knew. What drove him to that? Marco's own parents had sold him to the order of warrior monks the day he was born. He knew little about them except that his father was an American soldier, and his mother was Japanese. His childhood had been devoted to prayer and intense physical training meant to kill him. Only those favored by the ancestral sprits survived.

And his present years left him on the edge of Tokyo, away from the tech that had enveloped the city. He existed on the fringes of society, in isolation until a mission brought him into the center of the megacity, for an hour at most, as the tech wore away at his spirit energy.

Marco shifted the girl on his shoulder. She weighed little, but with each second his strength ebbed, and she grew heavier. He finally turned away from the girl's father to the door, but paused again. A frustrated sigh escaped his lips at his indecision. There lied gambling boss Noboru Akira, crumpled over on his mat with a hole in his head. *Retribution.* Then here was this girl, a child, to be given back to Ishii Naoki where she'd spend a lifetime in sex slavery in the underworld of Tokyo, sold at the highest cost from one clan's boss to anther while she was young and then passed around for cheap labor when she was old and wasted away.

Marco ripped the pearl tracking collar from the girl's neck. He focused, his senses expanding and his body tensing. He flung himself forward through the broken door and down the hall, breathing with music, out through the shattered window and into the city. He sent a silent prayer, and somewhere in the distance, crows disturbed from their roosting complained with a raucous of cawing as they took to the night sky on black wings. Marco whispered an apology, but he needed to send a message to Ishii Naoki.

Akira was dead, but Marco would buy the virgin. She would join the order of warrior monks.

About the Author

Todd Sullivan attended his first serious writing class in 1995 at Stanford University. In 2006, he graduated with a Bachelor's degree in English with Concentrations in Creative Writing from Georgia State University. He moved to New York that same year and received a Master's of Fine Arts from Queens College in 2009. He currently lives in Seoul and is studying the Korean language at Yonsei University. He is also working on a speculative fiction/urban horror novel that takes place in Korea.

Tokyo Yakuza
#4

Half a Man

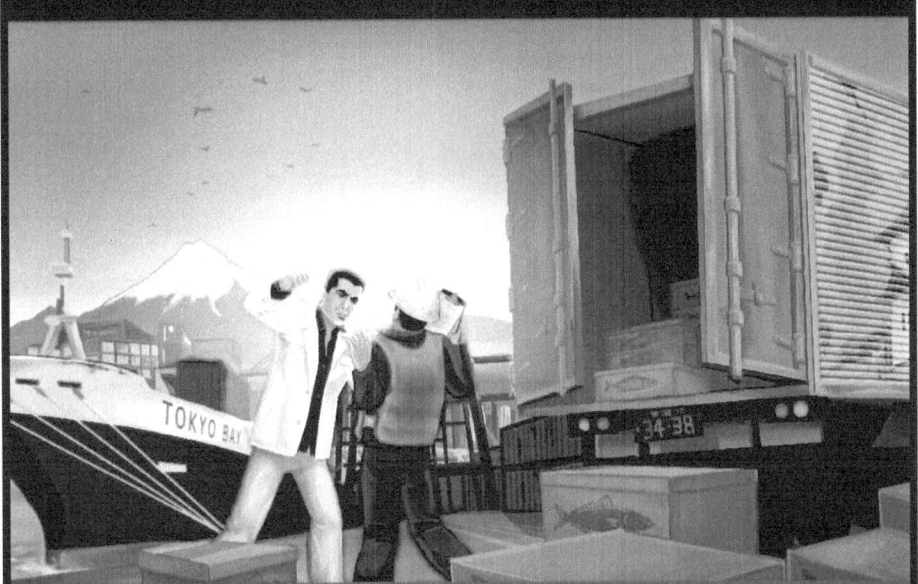

by Angela Kendrick

Japan won the Second World War; Now the yakuza are starting the Third!

TOKYO YAKUZA #4

Half a Man

BY ANGELA KENDRICK

January 17, 2020. Daimon, Tokyo. *Too fast.* Tanaka Shinobu never believed he could think such a thing, but as he whipped past a 60 kph sign that he couldn't read, he knew the truth couldn't be denied: he was driving too fast. The Shuto Expressway streaked past at 192 kph and he knew he was going to make his second mistake of the day at any moment. It was a shame he couldn't at least enjoy the ride.

At 204 kph, the tunnel vision began to creep up on him. The edges of the road started to turn hazy and gray. What was not gray or the least bit hazy was the rainbow array of high-end sports cars chasing him. Mistake number one was going alone to boost something high-end to strip. *Freelancing for the Seven Star Mob is going to cost me.*

He zipped the Porsche 911 Turbo S through a cluster of grocery-getters, scattering them like startled birds. He checked the mirror. A pursuing Lexus LFA had been taken out by a ping-ponging econobox. Shinobu flicked his eyes back to the road ahead.

"Chikushō !"[61] He tightened his grip on the steering wheel, feeling the sweat slip between his skin and the leather. There was an entrance ramp, jammed with creeping commuters, coming up on his side and the lane merged ahead, followed by a tight curve. *All or nothing.*

He dropped a gear and the clutch shoved him off like an angry lover. He cracked his knee hard on the underside of the dash. Shinobu grunted and ignored the screaming under the hood and in his head. *217 kph and the tunnel was narrowing.*

The Porsche had veered without self-preservation when she kicked him off the clutch. All Shinobu could do was hope others would spot him, panic, and ditch to the sides. That might have happened if the subcompact had seen him coming up behind the delivery truck between them, but the oblivious driver pulled into his lane at exactly the posted speed limit.

The peace of death came over Shinobu then. *Namu Amida Butsu.*[62] The Porsche scooped up the subcompact and tossed it over her shoulder, into the sports cars sucking on her exhaust fumes. *Namu Amida Butsu.* The delivery truck driver jerked the wheel and spun into a tree. *Namu Amida Butsu.* Shinobu watched the lane disappear in the small aura of vision left to him. *Namu Amida Butsu.* He heard the safety glass explode into cubed rain upon contact with an orange wagon. *Namu Amida Butsu.*

The Porsche slid sideways in a bewildering water ballet to the sounds of screeching breaks and crumpling metal as time slowed. *Namu Amida Butsu.* The Porsche clipped a median and bounced him into a full spin. A holo-advertisement, showing the wicked-eyed nine-tailed fox sniffing the Olympic rings projected from the wall of

---

[61] "Oh hell!"

[62] "I take refuge in the Buddha of Immeasurable Life and Light."

the service station, stole impossible moments of his attention. *Namu Amida Butsu.* He drifted through a mess of whirling colors crowned in the gray tunnel vision. After that, it was all convulsive crashes and metal, weeping as it wrung itself loose. The tunnel of gray collapsed before him and he mouthed a final, "Namu Amida Butsu."

January 18, 2020. Nippori Hospital, Tokyo. The nauseating odor of freshly unwrapped plastic clung to the pillowcase. Shinobu peeled his face away from the moist fabric, feeling the thread count in the lines on his face. The intensely white room snow-blinded him, so he groaned and tried to raise a hand to shield his eyes. When he met resistance, he was besieged by the memory of how many people wanted him dead, starting with his oji-san. His uncle had given Shinobu the order to bring something noteworthy back to the chop shop.

Eugi. The teenage girl who saw him lifting the Porsche had yelled, "Eugi-san!" Shinobu's eyes widened despite the pain and his nostrils flared to heave in air like a turbo engine. Eugi had been more than angry. His intense eyes had said he was taking the theft of his Porsche personally; it was an insult that would be repaid. Shinobu tugged his arms more forcefully.

"Shinobu-kun, be still." It was a quiet voice full of concern: Tachibana Michi's voice. The face of his best friend filled the white before him, which was a relief, but he was so close that his view of him was blurry.

"Shinobu-kun. You've been out for a long time."

Shinobu's eyes began to focus and he sought answers in the young man's face. The only answer there was grief. He pulled at whatever held his arms; Michi blocked his view. Shinobu's lips stuck to his teeth. With some effort, he tugged his lips apart only to croak out, "I worried you."

"No, you continue to worry me, Shinobu-kun," Michi said. His wisp of a smile spoke more of pain than joy.

Shinobu registered the strange repeated use of his name. He linked it to Michi's words, and the look on his face. "What?" He did not need to say all the words; Michi always knew his mind.

"Shinobu-kun, you are fortunate. Do not forget it." Michi's eyes floated slightly with unshed tears as he backed slowly away from Shinobu's face. Shinobu's confusion at this wonder magnified when he found that the hospital had restrained him with fabric cuffs attached to the bed. His eyes moved between his two wrists, trying to make sense of it before he noticed that the sheet lay flat between them.

"Shinyuu?"[63] he whispered.

"Shinobu-kun, to save your life, they amputated from the pelvis."

He looked up from his missing body to his best friend standing over him. "What?"

"They took your legs and pelvis to save your life, Shinobu-kun. It was the only way. You are fortunate."

Everything glared white again; Michi stood before him looking like a corporeal ghost. Michi tried to talk to him, but there was a vicious keening in his ears. He tucked his chin forward, he threw his head back, but he could not draw a full breath. Michi hurried out of the room, hollering.

Seasickness took Shinobu as the room replicated the Porsche's water ballet. A polite "ding" sounded at his shoulder. He turned his head to see something green winking at him, sending him to oblivion.

---

[63] Best friend?

✦　◇　✦

Shinobu lost track of time in the hospital but was aware of his visitors. He was not sure what to make of all of them, though. Surely some were the byproduct of the green blink at his shoulder, particularly the translucent gray spirits that seemed to slowly bubble and press their way out of the white paint, as if born within the wall and pushing onward to freedom.

Michi visited regularly, often with his slightly younger and off-limits sister, Suzume. On a particularly lucid day, they chatted about Michi starting work in the chop shop in which Shinobu had originally worked. Shinobu excelled in motors, gears, electronics, and program-ming, whereas Michi had an eye for shapes and colors. Michi had developed a mild respectability in bodywork and earned his place in the shop.

Shinobu noticed Michi had lost color. It was only obvious when he sat next to his sister. Michi blew it off when Shinobu asked about it and again later when other troubling features became apparent. Michi was losing his hair.

He always wore it long and smooth in a way that Shinobu envied. Shinobu's face was too easily mistaken for a girl's, so he wore his hair short and messy with a splotchy goatee: the best he could manage. Michi was always clean-shaven with glossy hair that made women stop him to talk about hair products, but it was noticeably falling out.

Though normally a neat person, Michi wore rumpled clothes that might not have even been washed. He would not answer when asked about these things, so Shinobu assumed it was stress over the wreck and he felt guilty for worrying his friend.

Shinobu also received a hot visitor from the Seven Star Mob. The tall Korean woman, with perfect facial symmetry, strode in with flowers and a teddy bear, of all things. She was not someone he knew, but she flashed her Seven Star Mob tattoo with a bloody bullet hole for the seventh star, so he kept quiet.

"You've been hurt badly, Tanaka-chan. You'll be paying hospital bills forever if you aren't more careful." The woman waited for him to acknowledge that she was there to talk business.

"Yes," he replied softly with a dip of the chin. It was the best bow he could execute. He would meet his end with as much dignity as he could.

"It's a good thing we have such an honorable family who looks after you. Oji-san sends his regards and bids you not to worry about the bills."

Shinobu snapped his eyes open and his head up. They should want him dead for messing up the job so spectacularly.

She smiled coyly as if Shinobu were nothing more than a flirty schoolboy. "Oji-san sent me to tell you that and more." She turned to fuss with the gifts, making a dance track emanate from his heart monitor. When she looked back she was serious. "Oji-san says you will need a new job, but that you can still bring honor to the family. He will set up a repair shop for you to run for him. You'll pay him rent, of course. You'll always give the Seven Star Mob's jobs top priority. And of course you'd never consider sending him a bill after his generosity, right?"

There are worse forms of slavery. He took a deep breath to give himself time to think through the words. "I am honored that Oji-san would hold me in such great esteem. He is wise and benevolent, and I must learn from him."

"You *must* make profits for him, but I doubt you'll learn anything." She left then, without giving her name or well wishes: not even a goodbye. She kept the flowers and left the galling teddy bear on the windowsill to mock him.

Shinobu was already trying to calculate how he could repair getaway cars and smuggling trucks for free for the Seven Star Mob any time they wanted and still make profits. He did not see any options, but they could not do much worse to him than he had already done to himself.

He had not entirely decided against suicide upon being released from the hospital anyway. He had time yet to decide if and how; he wasn't in any particular hurry. And the possibilities of cybernetics still tickled the back of his brain. He wondered what it would cost him to replace his legs. Shinobu let his head fall back on the pillow in frustration and he eyeballed the obnoxious teddy bear. *Where's a green wink when you need one?*

Rather than blissfully blacking out and forgetting all about the Seven Star Mob and Oji-san, Shinobu watched as another spirit bubbled out of the paint. It was a samurai in a navy hakama[64] over a white shitagi,[65] both bearing a gory slash across the abdomen. That seemed strange as it had been awhile since the last blinking green dose, so Shinobu was sure it was time to pass out again. However, the samurai proceeded to introduce himself like a friendly new neighbor, floating over on soundless straw sandals. "I'm Okawa—"

"And *I'm* not staying," was all he offered when he interrupted the samurai.

"Look boy, that's just why I want to talk to you."

Shinobu's body wobbled in response to his instinctive attempt to sit up straight. This was not the wandering conversation he had held with the other spirits he imagined.

---

[64] Kendo, fencing, pants.
[65] Samurai undershirt.

"I'm going to settle into that teddy bear and you're taking me with you when you leave," Okawa said.

"Why?"

"Because I want to leave this depressing-ass hospital, and you can hear me. In exchange, I'll keep your non-living visitors out so you can rest better. That gets us both out of here faster."

Shinobu frowned, thinking back on the many incoherent, drugged conversations with spirits he thought he had dreamed ... "Why me?"

The samurai rolled his semi-translucent eyes. "Because you've seen the dark river but not travelled it."

Shinobu felt the Porsche's spin pressing him painfully against the door. He heard the tires breaking traction and the axle giving out. A weightless moment, then the Porsche was pulling several Gs. The colors smeared past his narrowed vision again. There was horrific rending, and probably sparks, as her back end scraped the pavement in the manner of an arcing ice-skater's blade. It was hard to hold his head upright, and the tunnel grew smaller until it all went dark, but not black.

Everything was murky gray, but he had seen a river glinting onyx ahead of him with luminescent purple lotus flowers following the currents like lanterns floating in the night sky. In the weighty silence of that place, he had approached the river, knelt in the cool gray mud, and reached for it.

"Yes." He knew the dark river.

"Yes, and now you can see me; now you can hear me. We've shared this and are alike but different. I entered the river to quench the flames. You did not touch it."

"I didn't die?"

"Oh no, you died spectacularly. You just happened to have lived as well. And right about now I need you to agree to take that teddy bear home with you when you leave in a few days."

Ding. Green flickered in his peripheral vision.

"Okay," he said without thinking too hard about what could not be real anyway.

January 28, 2020. Shinobu was mellow for the first time after waking in the hospital. The doctors had put him on a schedule of practicing with the old-fashioned push wheelchair before he could leave. Lately Shinobu found himself making additional laps around the ward as if he were pacing.

He had not seen Michi in several days, longer than he would have expected, so he hoped he would see him that night for a little while. Whether or not he had dreamed the samurai who wanted to live in the teddy bear, the result had been better sleep for the last week and his health was improving.

He was eating rice instead of liquids. He was also beginning to feel more confident about moving around what was left of himself. He could lift himself from the wheelchair into the bed, which was a sure sign of being released soon.

Not half the man I used to be. He coughed up a surprised laugh at his failed attempt at nihilism as he reentered the hospital room after his midday laps. Though he had never touched it, the teddy bear was not on the windowsill.

It was in Tachibana Suzume's lap with her hands wrapped neatly around its belly. Her usual polite smile that Shinobu had always wished was for him, rather than at him, failed to grace him at all. She did not even look up at him.

"Tachibana-san?"

"Senpai."[66] She did look at him then. She reminded him of a trampled flower dropped from a parade float. The empty well of her heart echoed loud enough to overcome his self-pity.

"What's wrong?"

She looked back down at the teddy bear and smoothed its acrylic pink fur. "When will you be released, Senpai?"

"Not Senpai. Just Shinobu, as ever. Any day now," he answered gently.

"Shinobu-san ..." she paused.

"Suzume, I've offended you with, with ... I am sorry." He began to back out the room to spare her looking at his mutilation; it had always been covered when she visited. The wheel left a black calligraphy stroke when it scraped the doorframe.

"No, I need to tell you ..." and she began to cry the silent tears that make some women even prettier.

He instinctively approached her to — *What the hell are you going to do?* He stopped awkwardly and rammed the wheelchair into her seat, but he refrained from reaching for her. She did not seem to notice the jostling impact.

"Michi-kun and Haha,"[67] she said. Her voice hitched. "Have new names."

"No," he whispered as if to convince a child there were no monsters.

"Yes." She looked him in the eye. "I am so sorry, but we could not wait, and you have missed it."

The idea that Shinobu missed the funeral of his best friend broke through the denial. He thought of Michi holding back tears and blocking his view of his missing legs. He had been more than his

---

[66] Senior. Elder classmate.

[67] "Mommy."

shinyuu: his ketsumeisha.[68] His voice broke when he asked, "Your mother you said?"

She nodded, breaking the eye contact and continuing her ministrations on the bear. "Murdered in the parking garage, both of them." It was not the hurt in her voice that disturbed him, but the anger; he realized the tears were frustration, not grief. "The Yamaguchi-gumi burned them alive."

Shinobu blanched with anguish. His new body work job for, and debt slavery to, the Seven Star Mob. His best friend—Suzume's family murdered. *My fault.* This girl had been orphaned because he took on freelance work for the Koreans. He killed his best friend when he messed up the Porsche job. Michi's words, "No, you continue to worry me" burrowed into his mind. He shook his head and released his sweaty grip on the wheels of the chair. Shinobu's soul demanded an honorable death, but he had debts to pay both to Oji-san and to Suzume.

About the Author

Angela Kendrick has only ever lived in Texas because home is where the "stars are big and bright." She earned a BA in History and went on to complete an MBA. Presently, she is a full time Human Resources professional. She spends her time reading, writing, and loving her pets and marvelously supportive family and friends. Her favorite stories on paper or screens of all sizes are sci-fi/fantasy, especially the dystopian variety.

---

[68] Someone who has taken a blood oath, used here to connote a "blood brother" relationship.

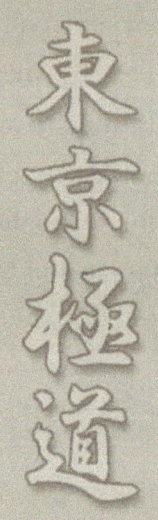

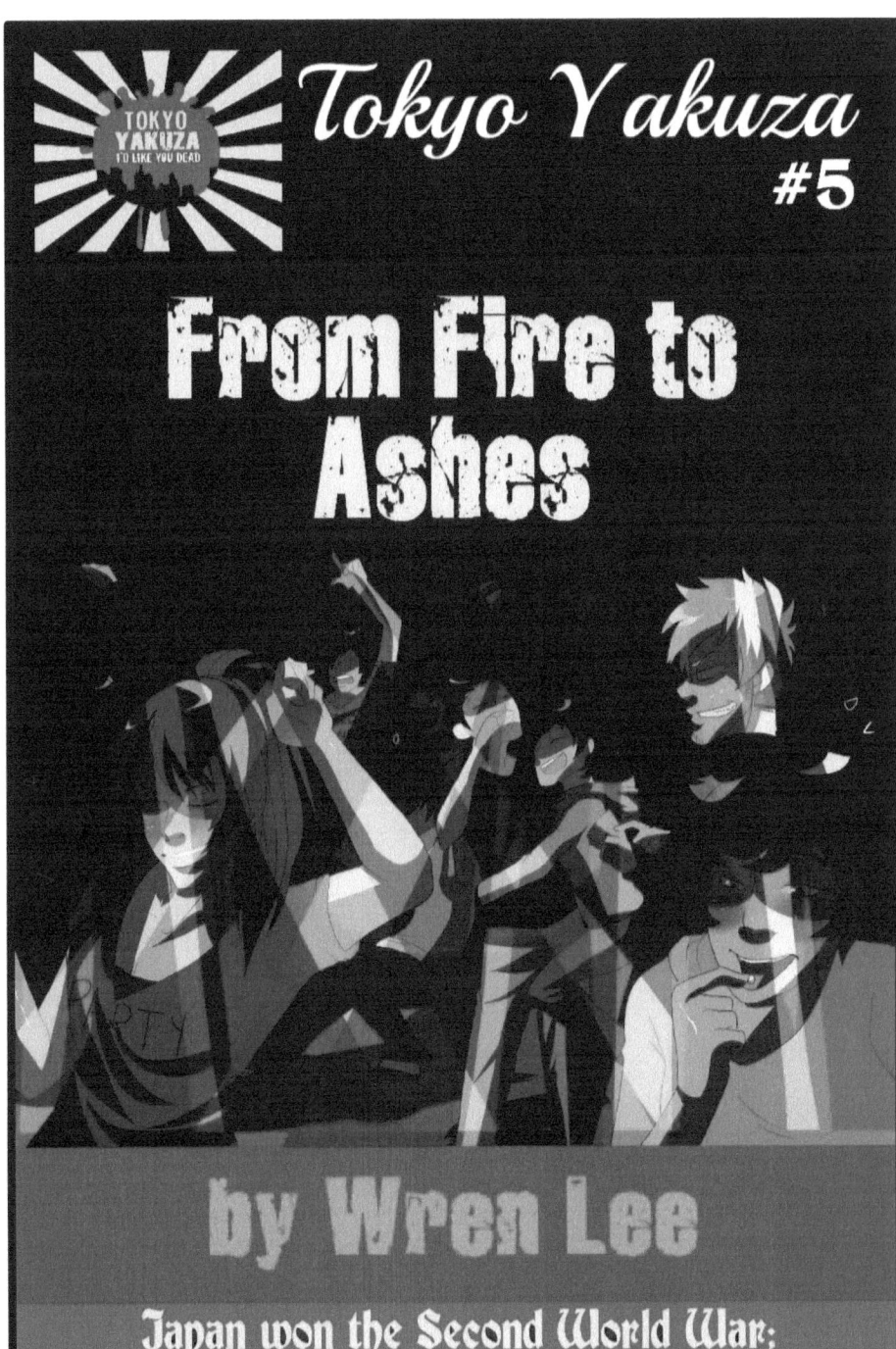

Tokyo Yakuza #5

From Fire to Ashes

By Wren Lee

January 19, 2020. Ueno-hirokoji, Tokyo. Hiroto Itou just wants to relax. He goes through the motions of living one stressful day after another at Ueno Gakuen University.[69] He never truly lives, not until night hits. Then the young adult goes to his local club. Every night, he takes off the strangling tie and turns into a new person. He is reborn into a party boy, getting his fix on drugs. Every night, Hiroto Itou exposes the side of him that no one else knows of.

But his club isn't a typical club: it's run by the Inagawa-kai.

On a certain Sunday of a certain month, this college boy gets a surprise at his local club.

Golden rays of sunshine pierced foggy haze of sleep. The sleepy college boy opened his chestnut eyes to the morning sun. An alarm blared, screeching at the maximum volume Hiroto could stand. He scowled as he slammed his palm down onto the digital screen of his

---

[69] A private university near Ueno park specializing in music. Formerly an all-girls school.

clock. The nagging urge to stay in bed and skip the lectures that would only make him tired and empty rose in his heart.

But Hiroto couldn't do that.

Rolling out of bed, the young man landed on the floor in a heap of clothing and body. He groaned, the noise echoing in the almost-empty apartment. He shook as he rose to his feet. Hiroto inched closer and closer to his closet, filled to maximum capacity with sweaters and slacks hanging neatly on hangers.

Another empty, emotionless day, he thought.

Minutes turned to hours and the young man stumbled from classroom to classroom. His hand seemed to scratch words onto the tablet set before him as he took down notes. The teachers with their dull voices seemed to drone on and on about history and things Hiroto didn't give one shit about.

But it was necessary to keep up the façade.

Just one more. One more minute. One more hour. Just get through today. It can all end tomorrow. No ... can it? he mused as he struggled to pull his thoughts together.

He furrowed his brow, the crease something his ex-girlfriend Asuka Higashino, an art major, always complained about when they were together. *Asuka*, he thought, absentmindedly. *I wonder what she would think of me now.*

Hiroto hadn't always been the party boy at night type. He had been a studious child with a dream to go to someplace better and be a successful doctor. Not that Japan wasn't ripe with opportunities: he simply thought that the outside world offered the chance for freedom, and so studied hard to get into the college of his choice.

It all spiraled out of control the day Hiroto met Sachi. Sachi turned Hiroto's life upside down. The ecstasy dealer had spent hours convincing the teacher's pet to indulge and spend one day at Insanity[70], a dance club Sachi claimed would "make things better." Hiroto, on the day before a major test, succumbed to Sachi's sweet words and went to Insanity.

He got hooked.

Hiroto wasted his hours away dancing under the strobe lights and gave no more than a glance to his work. His grades plummeted and professors took notice. But by then, Hiroto was too deep into the mystical world of Insanity.

Things changed, though, the day he had approached Sachi about a permanent membership to the club. That day, he was branded with a lasting mark.

Did Hiroto care? No. He needed the club as much as the club needed him.

If that meant he had to join the Inagawa-kai, so be it.

Hiroto's eyes slid shut as he fell into the warm embrace of sleep. The late night partying had left no room for shut eye. He was exhausted, but the thought of more dancing, drugs and women surged through him, giving him a reason to keep his eyes open one more second.

The classroom blurred and Hiroto snapped upright. *What is going on?* he thought. He blinked rapidly, rubbing his bleary eyes with his hands. He swallowed his fear. His red eyes went to the professor who had given the class the quiet they needed to complete the daily assignment. His tablet vibrated, notifying Hiroto of a new message.

---

[70] A dance club in Ueno-hirokoji frequented by college kids where the Inagawa-kai deals in ecstasy.

Weary, the college student turned his tablet off, and scanned the faces of his classmates. Asuka, sitting on the other side of the room, gave him a concerned look before gesturing at the tablet set out in front of her. Hiroto just grunted, slumping into his seat.

A headache rose in the back of Hiroto's temples. He winced, shaking his head. Questions swarmed his mind but he didn't have an answer for any of them.

Then realization hit.

The effects of the bliss from the night before seemed to be seeping into his morning hours.

This frightened Hiroto.

He tried his best to keep his lives apart. One turned him from the other into a shell that was filled with drink and drug. No one, not someone like him, would want their polar opposites touching, much less colliding.

He wouldn't let it happen. He couldn't.

The music slammed into him as he entered the club. *Bum-ba-dum. Bum-ba-dum.* The tattoo on his bicep throbbed as he passed over the threshold into the world he embraced when the sun set. Sweat and that telltale hint of vanilla being pumped through the vents caressed him. Hiroto let a rare smile dance across his thin lips as the numbness of the day consumed him.

A tablet was offered to him: ecstasy. The pearly white pill glared at him, tempting him in his foggy mind. He reached out, his body moving on its own. The waitress gave him a sly wink, then commanded him to open his mouth and stick his tongue out. Hiroto felt his jaw drop as the busty woman popped the tablet into his mouth. He felt the rush of euphoria and warmth seemed to flood through every vein, every essence of his being. A little giggle escaped his throat and the woman flashed him a blinding smile.

The college boy just laughed, throwing his head back. His unruly, shoulder-length hair tumbled down his back.

Strobe lights flashed against him: greens, reds, blues, pinks, and purples. The colors blinded him, drowning him in the rainbow.

Hiroto's gray world turned to color as the world of partying and clubbing consumed him.

The drug was crashing into him now. Its full effects were swallowing him and he felt the music shaking the ground beneath his dancing feet. The soles of his shoes slammed into the concrete underneath. The beats pounded in his head, making him feel more alive than he had before.

It was working.

Hiroto swayed his hips. A woman with stunning, electric green hair made up dance moves as the crowd screamed the words to a popular American song. Hiroto had to admit that it was an addictive song. He screamed the words in broken and stuttering English. The ramblings of a madman with a guitar bled through the speakers and the crowd only screamed louder, as if trying to rock the foundations of the concrete building.

The Inagawa-kai isn't going to like that they are screaming so loud, Hiroto thought through the haziness of his brain. *As a member of the clan, that should bother me too.*

But what did he care, really? Hiroto had no particular love for the Inagawa-kai. He only joined for the exclusive rights he attained in return for his regular reports on the club's patrons.

A waitress wobbling on strappy heels stumbled by. A portly

gentleman with a sweaty brow hooted in delight as a flash of thigh was revealed. The waitress blushed furiously and continued on. Hiroto's eyes followed her.

She … familiar? he thought, numbly. The young man bit down on his lower lip, trying to focus.

But his vision was coming in and out like a camera trying to focus, and it wasn't working.

The song switched to one with a thumping bass and a screeching singer. It was a Japanese song this time. The patrons were thrusting to the beats, fists pumping in the air.

Hiroto let his lips curl upwards into a mock smile as the world around him seemed to rage. Pulsating lights, screaming music, and hips thrusting to the beat.

Yeah. He loved this.

The world seemed to tilt and spin on an axis unseen by the human eye. Hiroto shut his eyes to stop the spinning as the strobe lights blinked and flashed in the dark of the club.

His limbs felt weighed down by anvils as he moved. It was like trying to force his way through a wall and not making it.

Move, he ordered his limbs, but they groaned and fought back. *Move, dammit!*

He shook his head, his eyes darting left and right. Something was wrong. Something was terribly wrong. He felt it in his bones, rising up in his throat.

Gulping, Hiroto tried to ignore it.

The nagging part of his brain battled the high part of him. The rational versus the impulsive: opposites.

"Hey! I've seen you before. Hiroto, right?" a man yelled in

Hiroto's ear. The voice was coming from behind Hiroto. He whirled around, the heel of his shoe sliding on the sweaty wood of the dance floor. Hiroto stiffened slightly, a flash of recognition crossing his pale skin. Hiroto drank in the man's looks.

He had the tan of a foreigner's skin and the gleaming, white teeth of someone with money to get whitening procedures, or someone with the power to order someone to give it. The pulsing implant embedded in the man's temples that shined through the flashing lights of the club. The locks that contradicted his pinstriped suit and aesthetically appealing face tumbled over his shoulders, much like Hiroto's.

The man gave a cocky grin. His red-rimmed eyes made his wild look even wilder. "Hiroto Itou, right?" the man called in smooth English. His voice was barely a whisper compared to the wall-shaking music. Hiroto only nodded in response, his eyes on the man's lips. "I'm Jaques," the man said, but Hiroto only heard the bass of the song ringing in his ears.

Focus, focus, focus, Hiroto thought. He furrowed his brow in anger at the noisy club.

"Do you need something?" Hiroto asked in broken English. Jaques flashed a wide grin as a spotlight caught a metal badge on Jaques's chest. Hiroto blinked away the flashing light, trying to clear his mind and school his growing frown.

The music stopped and the dancers froze. Jaques's smile grew into a mask of nothing.

Hiroto whipped his head around in confusion. What was going on? Who stopped the music? The drug in his brain screamed at him to figure it out, but there was nothing to figure out. There were no clues to why this happened. *A fluke,* Hiroto thought. *It has to be a fluke.* He waited for the music to blast once more, but there was only the silence: the silence that came before the storm.

"Hiroto."

The man turned his head, trying to locate the origin of the voice. Jaques was missing. Hiroto frowned, blinking rapidly.

The room exploded with noise as people screamed in confusion. Where is the music? Who turned it off? Where were the waiters? Hiroto raised an eyebrow to the last question before scanning the multitude of heads. They were right. The waiters in their starched suits and the waitresses in slutty dresses that exposed just enough cleavage were … gone.

"What … what is going on?" a college-aged girl shouted. Her sapphire head bobbed up and down as she disappeared into the crowd. The clubbers all had the same look on their faces: disbelief and confusion.

Hiroto felt tempted to call out for Jaques. Maybe he knew. He had, after all, appeared out of nowhere. Hiroto swallowed the bile rising in his throat. There had to be a logical explanation for this.

Then the hollering started. Battle cries filled the room. The clubbers shrieked in alarm as the windows, ten feet above their heads, shattered. Gangsters clad in black clothes and ski masks bombarded the club.

Whoops filled his ears. Hiroto spun in circles, his eyes wide with fear and doubt. The invaders filled the corners of his vision. *Black, black, black.*

Where were the colors?

He gasped in surprise as he caught a glimpse of stars from the patch of the former Republic of China emblazoned on someone's shirt. Hiroto inhaled sharply. *No. It's not possible! The security? The staff? How … no!*

"Well hello, Japanese comrades," a loud booming voice called over the speakers. Hiroto shifted nervously, his eyes darting left and right. Another gang. What was this? A takedown? Why in a club? Why not at the headquarters?

"This isn't your club anymore. This turf now belongs to the 14K Triad. And don't think about fleeing. Don't think about fighting it. You're all our prisoners," the deep voice continued in Chinese-accented Japanese. Hiroto chewed on his lower lip. What was he supposed to do?

A shout rose among the "captives." They were frantic, their anxiety growing with the minutes passing. A man shoved his way through the crowd. Hiroto's eyes widened in surprise. It was Jaques. *What is he doing? Oh god. He has to go back*, Hiroto thought, swallowing anxiously. His hands balled into fists as he waited for Jaques to do something.

Maybe ... just maybe ...

Jaques threw his arms wide. "You will not take our club," he cried in broken Japanese. The crowd nervously agreed. Some exchanged reluctant looks.

"Is that so?" a triad member asked. The gangster cocked his head to one side and his eyes narrowed.

Bang.

Red blossomed on Jaques' chest. He staggered back as his soul wavered on the edge.

A scream rose in someone's throat.

Dead. He's dead.

"The next man to challenge Chen Jie-shi gets the same," the killer said.

Hiroto gulped, trying to hide what was under his shirt. He couldn't let the triad members see his yakuza tattoo. He couldn't. He shut his eyes and prayed to the god he didn't believe in for so many years.

"Help me. Save me," he prayed, biting the inside of his cheek.

Somewhere, Asuka was safe.

Somewhere, Sachi was conning another kid to come to Insanity.

Somewhere, not here or now, there was a Hiroto who was at home studying. Not waiting for his death sentence.

About the Author

Wren Lee is a student who loves books and writing. She has attempted, and won, NaNoWriMo twice. Wren writes mostly YA fiction and reads dystopian. She writes book reviews on her book blog in her spare time. When she's not dreaming about fantasy worlds, she's working on schoolwork or watching "Red Band Society." Wren is a dreamer and always will be.

Tokyo Yakuza
#6

Hostile Takeover

by Stephen Rhodes

Japan won the Second World War; Now the yakuza are starting the Third!

Tokyo Yakuza #6

Hostile Takeover

By Stephen Rhodes

January 20, 2020. Nihombashi, Tokyo. A news broadcaster reads the day's top story across the city of Tokyo:

The CBI-Hitachi Corporation announced they will be holding a press conference in five days, suggesting the bio-technology firm is set to unveil their new line of cybernetically enhanced clones. A new era in cloning technology could enable the creation of cheap and efficient labor, which CBI claims will revolutionize both manufacturing and construction industries. A special exhibit will be set up near the Olympic village to showcase the cyborg clones.

This news has sparked strong opposition from union leaders who have spoken out against the use of clones over real human workers, stating the devastating impact an artificial workforce could have on the Japanese economy. This news comes just days after threats by pro-human terrorist groups who have long opposed the creation of clones. More news to follow after these messages ...

✦   ◇   ✦

Sato Fukui turned off his curved 4K Ultra HD television with a look of disgust on his face.

"Pro-human terrorists? Is that what they call us yakuza now? Well, I guess we best live up to our new nickname!" Sato said. He smirked at the others around him, who all nodded eagerly in agreement.

Sato unholstered his pistol, checking the safety and the magazine, and chambered a round. The tall, athletic man removed his makeshift combat helmet, running a hand through his messy, dyed blonde hair. He went over the plan in his head for what felt like the hundredth time. He knew the job and what needed to be done. He wasn't really sure why he was doing this, he just wanted to get paid and maybe gain some favor with the Sumiyoshi-kai leadership.

Sato looked around the confined interior of the van; the ten other people were busy preparing for the mission at hand, all lost in their own thoughts. They were a mixed bunch, many of them new to the clan. Most didn't even look out of their teen years to Sato. He could pick out the chimpira easily enough: they were the ones staring at the floor of the van, trying to seek some reassurance or comfort from the metallic floor or quietly mumbling to themselves. The more experienced members of the group were chatting and laughing with happy expressions, a habit brought on by having been on many missions like this for the clan.

Sato had brought his usual group of miscreants with him on this job; they would make a colossal mess of anything they were directed at, which was exactly what Sato needed. They weren't the brightest or strongest of the Sumiyoshi-kai's foot soldiers, but they made up for it with raw enthusiasm.

Maihama, Tokyo. The hijacked CBI-Hitachi delivery van rumbled to a stop at the security checkpoint. The guard stationed at this particular entrance barely glanced up from his television set to check the van before he disabled the barrier and allowed the vehicle to pass through.

CBI-Hitachi's Maihama facility was a sprawling industrial complex, consisting of two dozen large buildings that varied in function and shape. The central cluster was comprised of research laboratories and offices whereas the outer areas were reserved for production factories and storage warehouses.

At the heart of the facility lay the headquarters of the CBI-Hitachi research division: a building of significant stature, towering over the rest of the facility. The unique appearance of the structure helped reaffirm its importance. It was a tall, cuboid structure which tapered and rotated at the top, giving it a helixical shape from a distance. The outer surface was made entirely of glass which reflected the moonlight and caused the building to act as a beacon in the darkness.

The van travelled through the quiet facility, directly towards the towering central building. At around the halfway mark, the van stopped next to a large warehouse. The side door opened and five figures disembarked.

"You have fifteen minutes to plant the charges. Remember, we will pick you up here; do not be late," Sato said to Takegawa Yoshi, his unofficial second in command. "All of the prototypes are kept in this building, so make sure it goes up good."

"That's what we do best!" The woman winked and took the charges before signaling her team to follow her. As one, they disappeared silently into the darkness.

The van continued onward towards its primary destination. Sato grabbed his heavy assault rifle and turned to look at the remaining occupants of the van, all of whom were looking at him expectantly.

"You know what we have to do," Sato began in an effort to break the uneasy silence. "We go in there, we shoot anything that moves, we destroy the data and the servers, then we set the place alight." He finished and was greeted with nods of acknowledgement and approval from the others.

The van stopped once again and Sato took a deep breath before he opened the door.

Just think of the money, it's just a job, Sato thought to himself. He leapt from the van and ran toward the nearby entrance; then he kicked the door open and began to fire.

January 21, 2020. Ginza, Tokyo. Sumiyoshi-kai oyabun Sugawara Hirono strolled into the lobby of the CBI-Hitachi headquarters, the sound of his immaculately polished, designer shoes echoed around the cavernous entrance hall. The stern, middle-aged man barely paused as he stepped over the bodies of the security guards who had been gunned down moments before his arrival. Clad in his traditional black suit complete with blue trimming, white shirt, black tie, and clan emblem lapel pin, the boss of the Sumiyoshi-kai carried himself tall and proud. His scarred and weathered face belied his modest years, giving the man a fierce, and unpredictable, demeanor.

The clan members in charge of securing the lobby had executed their objective with brutal efficiency. As Sugawara passed them by, the clan members stopped in their cleanup work to show respect to their leader.

Flanked as he was by his personal team of enforcers, Sugawara and his retinue made for the elevators at the rear of the building. They walked in an arrowhead formation. Sugawara formed the tip, leading his ever vigilant bodyguards with purpose.

Each man was wearing a suit matching with that of their leader, complete with concealed body armor. They also carried advanced assault weaponry, designed to deliver the maximum number of rounds per second, in order to neutralize any potential threat that may arise. Each man wore an unreadable expression and was silent in his duty, always ready at a moment's notice to do their oyabun's bidding. They were the best the clan had to offer and they took great pride in their work.

The lift made a high pitched beep to indicate it had reached the ground floor. The five men entered the small compartment silently and turned to face the door. Sugawara swiped a blood stained security card over the terminal inside and the doors began to close in acknowledgement.

The board room was a bustling hive of activity. Located on the top floor of the CBI-Hitachi headquarters building, the room offered beautiful views of the Tokyo central business district, yet no one in the room even noticed. Twelve executives sat around a long, rectangular table located at the center of the large room. Along the top of the table sat holographic projectors displaying a wide range of reports, statistics and equations into the air above the surface, allowing the executives to better absorb the crucial information.

"The entire project has been compromised," said a short, elderly woman. She scanned a new report hovering in front of her at the table. Although she was old, her cybernetically modified eyes allowed her to read the information much faster and with more clarity than a normal person her age could. "All of the prototypes were located at that facility, meaning none survived yesterday's strike," she concluded.

A younger man, tall with jet black hair that was combed over to one side of his head, sat opposite the older woman. He stood up to address the board members, drawing their attention by his movement.

"The attack has been leaked to the media; it's already being relayed across the network. A cover up is now highly unlikely to gain traction." The man sat back down, still in a state of shock at what had occurred the evening before. He turned his focus back to reading new reports and updates, hoping some positive news would present itself.

"Following the news leak, our share price has plummeted to its lowest value since the company's inception. We must act quickly and formulate a plan to recover this situation!" said a serious and agitated man. He showed clear signs of being sleep deprived. His bloodshot eyes, his creased and slightly stained suit and his caffeine fuelled twitches made it apparent that this man had been awake since the news arrived. The table erupted into a fresh wave of arguments and heated debates focusing around what course of action should be taken.

At the far end of the table, a solitary figure sat unmoving. His eyes were hidden by a pair of reflective smart glasses, and he kept his hands locked together, resting his elbows on the table and placing his hands in front of his face in quiet contemplation. His hair was short and neatly trimmed, streaks of grey piercing the sea of black. The man was clean shaven and wore a suit, perfectly cleaned and pressed, showing no signs that it had ever been worn before today.

He silently raised his right hand, signaling that he wished to address the other board members. The sudden movement caught the bickering executives off-guard; they ceased their discussions and sat back in their seats out of a mixture of respect and curiosity.

Several moments of silence passed. The man finally said, "Not all of the prototypes were destroyed."

"Chairman Hiro, how is this possible?" asked Akagi, the tall young man. "We were under the impression that there was no other facility working on the project?"

Hiro was not accustomed to being questioned. He did not become board chairman of Tokyo's largest biotechnology corporation by allowing insubordination; however, under the circumstances, he chose to forgive the insult and continue with his explanation, though he made a mental note to watch for any future signs of disrespect from Shigeru Akagi.

Chairman Hiro looked at each member of the board, meeting each person's gaze before he delivered his response. He wanted to make sure they were paying absolute attention and would absorb every word.

"I ordered several prototypes to be relocated once the final phase of testing was completed. They are quite secure here, several floors below us. Secrecy was of the utmost importance; I'm sure you can all appreciate this in light of our current situation." The chairman of the CBI-Hitachi board of directors let his words sink in for a moment. He could see that the others were processing the information and working out what the implications of this new information could be.

The sudden silence was interrupted by the sound of approaching footsteps. Slowly the board members began to notice the sound and started looking towards the doors, curious to discover who was brave enough to disturb such a high profile meeting. The footsteps grew louder; it was easy to make out the individual footfalls and it became clear that quite a large number of people were drawing near. Hiro wondered if it were the scientists. *Perhaps something had happened to the prototypes? Or perhaps it was a pack of personal assistants seeking orders from the various board members they worked under?*

The door opened, revealing Sugawara. His face was a mask of neutrality, showing no emotion of any kind. He entered the large and expensively furnished board room, paying no attention to the men and women who sat at the table that dominated most of the room. He walked right past them and headed towards the opposite wall, which was made entirely of glass windows.

Sugawara stood for a moment, looking out across the central business district of Tokyo. His eyes were drawn to the bustling streets full of men and women going about their lives. In the distance he could discern the silhouette of the Tokyo Olympic Park, still under construction by thousands of workers—human workers. Ordinary men and women trying to make an honest living. Not these factory constructed monstrosities that corporations like CBI-Hitachi wanted to utilize.

Sugawara grimaced in disgust at such thoughts. He knew that what he was sent here to do was for the clan and the greater good of Tokyo, despite the fact these actions offended him and were considered illegal by the authorities. It was lucky for him, then, that the authorities' loyalty could be bought.

He turned towards the table of CBI-Hitachi executives. Sugawara's men had positioned themselves around the room, guns levelled at the people sitting at the table.

"Good morning ladies and gentlemen, my name is Sugawara Hirono." The man walked slowly around the table with purpose. "My clan, the Sumiyoshi-kai, is here to help your corporation through this 'difficult' time." Sugawara let the words simmer in the air for several moments.

"You see, we cannot have your volatile, half-human monsters, forcing honest, hardworking people out of their jobs. We have a responsibility to our unions and contractors to protect their interests and ensure that greedy corporations like you don't destroy the livelihoods of millions in pursuit of greater profits."

The board members looked around at each other with a mixture of panic and confusion. Chairman Hiro remained static at the far end of the table. His eyes never left Sugawara; he followed his every movement.

"I have a proposition for you good people," Sugawara said with renewed enthusiasm. "If you are willing to sign over your shares in CBI-Hitachi to the Sumiyoshi-kai, relinquishing yourselves of all responsibility for this corporation, then you shall be allowed to leave this building unharmed." He paused once again, observing the reactions to his words play out on the faces of the board members. They were scared; he knew they would be. Fear would be their undoing and it would lead them to agree to anything if they felt it would help them to survive.

Sugawara pulled a double-barreled hunting shotgun from beneath his overcoat. The Sumiyoshi-kai oyabun pumped his shotgun with one hand and then walked behind the nearest board member. He set the shotgun against the young man's temple and put his other hand reassuringly on the man's shoulder. Sugawara could feel the trembling beneath his touch. He cocked the shotgun's hammer for added effect and then looked around at the rest of his audience.

"Please, just let us go!" the man whimpered. He tried hard to control the pitch of his voice.

Sugawara smiled and reached into his jacket once again, retrieving a small tablet device.

"Of course, my friend. Relax. All you have to do is confirm your identity on this device and your equity holdings will be transferred to a secure off-shore account, preapproved by the Tokyo Stock Exchange AI. Once your colleagues have done the same, you will be free to go." He reached over the man's shoulder with the device, keeping the muzzle of his shotgun firmly against the witless board director's temple.

The man moved his trembling hand slowly towards the tablet and placed his thumb against the identification reader. The device made a happy "beep" and Sugawara checked it to confirm the transfer had completed.

"Thank you for your co-operation, Shigeru Akagi," Sugawara with sincerity in his voice. He moved the shotgun away from Akagi's temple and heard the man let out a breath of relief.

Bang!

The sound of the gunshot echoed around the conference room, as did the screams of horror from the board members. Akagi's blasted head slammed into the desk, blood pooling around the shattered remains of his face. The three people unfortunate enough to be sat opposite Akagi had been showered in blood as the buckshot blasted its way out of Akagi's skull.

"Now you understand that I do not have time for any more pointless delays," Sugawara said with a stern voice. His eyes showed no emotion over the execution he just performed. "No more questions. And no tricks."

He walked around the table, stopping at each board member to acquire their biometric identification. The process went a lot faster after they had seen how far Sugawara was willing to go.

Once the task was completed, Sugawara checked the tablet and smiled with approval at the information displayed there.

"Honorable board members, you have done as instructed. Now you shall be escorted to the lobby where you will be free to leave and continue your lives." Sugawara bowed and signaled to his men.

At once, the armed figures moved in towards the table and began ushering the executives out of their chairs, pushing them towards the door. Chairman Hiro stood up and began moving with the rest of the board members, but Sugawara signaled to him to stop.

"I am afraid we have further business to attend to, Chairman Hiro." Sugawara said. He pointed his shotgun at the board chairman.

"I gave you my stockholdings, what more could you want with me?" Hiro asked. He sounded confused but dauntless.

"I am referring of course to the prototypes you have in this building. Akagi was quite certain you would have at least some moved here for insurance reasons?" Sugawara asked. The apparent shock on Hiro's face amused him.

The two men waited for the room to clear before Sugawara signaled Hiro to move with a wave of his shotgun. They walked towards the elevators, Hiro in front and Sugawara a few steps behind him. Sugawara kept his shotgun leveled directly at the older man's back.

"Do you think destroying CBI-Hitachi will prevent someone from creating a more cost efficient workforce? Another corporation will rise to take our place." Hiro said. He sounded as if he thought the prediction was already a certainty.

The two men entered the elevator silently and Hiro swiped his ID card, signaling the lift to take them to a restricted floor. After several tense minutes of descent, the elevator chimed to signal their arrival at the desired floor. The doors opened and Hiro looked out at the makeshift research facility he had ordered to be constructed a few weeks earlier. He stepped out of the lift onto the polished white tiled floor, the bright green algae-halogen lighting causing him to squint.

Ahead of the men stood a pair of glass doors set to privacy mode, making the surface opaque. The words "Restricted Area" could be seen in large, bold writing.

"We do not want to destroy CBI-Hitachi, Chairman Hiro," Sugawara replied, despite it having been some ten minutes since Hiro had asked him the question. "On the contrary; we want to invest in the company and the research you do but we also want to ensure it is used at times which benefit our interests as well as your own."

Hiro turned slowly, seeming to consider Sugawara's words. As he did, the scarred man lowered his gun and handed the tablet to Hiro.

"You are now the majority shareholder of the corporation. You will cancel the press conference tomorrow and issue a statement claiming radical pro-human terrorists attacked your facility last night, then your headquarters today where they executed the board members." Sugawara relayed the instructions quickly and without pause. "You will continue your research but will turn your attention to military applications instead of construction. We will expect monthly reports. In return, we will offer protection from other rivals and opposition and you will be allowed to keep your position." Sugawara began fishing around in his jacket as he finished.

"Why did you pick me?" Hiro asked with genuine curiosity.

Sugawara pulled his hand from his jacket and handed Hiro a small communication device.

"We are doing this because this technology is going to change the world. It's going to shift the balance of power and when it does, we want to be on the right side of that shift. We think you share our sentiment." Sugawara said. His voice carried determination and belief.

"You work for the Sumiyoshi-kai now, Chairman Hiro."

About the Author

Stephen Rhodes is a video game designer and freelance writer. He was born in England, but currently lives and works in Warsaw, Poland. Stephen is a quest designer at CD Projekt RED, where he works on titles like *The Witcher 3: Wild Hunt,* and *Cyberpunk 2077.* When he isn't making video games, he spends a lot of his time reading and writing, mainly fantasy and science fiction. He is a self-confessed film junkie and his favorite film is Ridley Scott's classic, *Blade Runner.*

東京極道

Tokyo Yakuza
#7

The Cynic's Rhapsody

by Brett Stevens

Japan won the Second World War;
Now the yakuza are starting the Third!

The Cynic's Rhapsody

BY BRETT STEVENS

January 21, 2020. Roppongi, Tokyo. Jiro Satani ran for his life. It was during times like these that he wished Jared Santos were back in America working at the "Deli Counter." But then, Jared Santos never had the balls to go to Tokyo where the action was. That was Jiro Satani's job. Needless to say, it was the last time Satani was going to do the "screw and steal" routine for a bit, at least when it involved some guy's sister.

"After him!" he heard someone shout from behind.

Satani knew he shouldn't check behind him, but he had to see who was after him.

Three men, all of whom had the new cyberlimbs everyone had been talking about. Or was it robo-arms? Either way, it was bad news for Satani.

"Kuso,"[71] he muttered; then he smiled. If he hadn't been in the middle of running, he'd have taken a moment to congratulate himself on remembering a new word. *Didn't even need the dictionary.*

---

[71] "Shit."

As he turned the corner, he almost ran into a fruit cart. Suddenly, he had an idea. He grabbed some oranges and pears from the cart, then threw them on the ground behind him just as one of his would be attackers caught up to him.

"You will answer for what you've done, gaijin!"[72]

Satani wanted to tell him he should come up with something better, but before he could, the ruffian slipped on a piece of fruit.

This was his chance; Satani darted for a nearby alley. His attacker was too dazed to notice and the others were too busy screaming something he didn't understand to conduct a more thorough search of the area.

That bought him some time, but not much. If he wanted to be a big shot in Tokyo, he'd have stay off these guys' radar, at least for now, and there was only one place he could think to go.

Satani was hit by a billow of smoke as he walked into the "Keisatsu-cho,"[73] or "National Police Agency." It was an ironic name for a dive like this joint.

While this wasn't the sort of place he wanted to be, it was the only way he knew of to make connections.

All tables were full of men and woman laughing together, drinking, smoking, whispering to one another like children hiding secrets from their parents.

None of them looked up at the gaijin who just entered and Satani wouldn't expect anything less from the patrons of a foreigner bar.

"Hey gaijin, want to give it a try?"

---

[72] A casual, somewhat offensive, term for a foreigner.
[73] National Police Agency. Japan's version of the FBI.

Satani looked over at the speaker; he was standing by a table, flashing his yellow teeth. He had what looked like a joint in his outstretched hand. If Satani thought for a second the guy was a part of the clans, he would've taken him up on it.

At that moment, Satani noticed a stranger waving to him from across the room. He tried not to let his relief show. Something about the guy with the yellow teeth didn't sit right with him.

"Sorry, I'm here meeting someone."

The smoker shrugged. "Whatever, gaijin." He turned back to the table.

He walked past a girl who was fondling some old guy. He thought he heard the Japanese word for beautiful, but he couldn't be sure; the only word he could remember being "kuso."

Satani bowed as he approached the table, mildly pleased with himself. Perhaps he wasn't such a gaijin after all.

"Thank you for your assistance," said Satani.

His fellow foreigner only shrugged. "Hey, we gaijin have to stick together, right?"

Satani frowned. He had to admit, he was getting tired of that word. He should've known that the name wasn't going to help. Plastic surgery and a voice modulator would do the trick, and maybe then the yakuza would take him seriously.

The stranger motioned to the seat in front of him. "My name's Doi Tyrone. Take a seat."

Satani nodded. "Thanks. Call me Satani."

"So what do you do?" asked Tyrone.

"Pickpocket," said Satani, immediately. Saying anything else would've gotten him laughed out of the place, so pickpocket seemed like the safest answer, relatively speaking.

"Man, forget that. You should be like Tobi," said the smoker. He'd moved at some point without Satani noticing and stood only a few feet away from them, leaning against a wall.

Satani nearly jumped out of his seat. *Real smooth, Satani.*

"Get out of here." Tyrone spoke to the smoker as though he were talking to his annoying little brother.

The smoker shook his head and walked away.

Doi Tyrone stared at Satani for a long time, then smiled and shook his head. "Think the world has enough pickpockets."

Kuso. With the smoker's interruption, he had hoped the man had forgotten their previous conversation. Satani sighed and said, "I wanna work for the yakuza."

The stranger had a good belly-laugh.

A couple patrons turned to look.

"It's not funny," Satani hissed.

Tyrone shook his head again. "You even sound like an American. If I were you, I would just go home. No point in wasting your life on impossible dreams."

Satani smiled at that. *Jared Santos might have agreed with him,* he thought.

"Thanks for the advice, but I think I'll wait for someone to come my way."

He looked around the bar and saw no one from the clans, at least not from one of the right ones. The Yamaguchi-gumi was the biggest clan and the one he most wanted to join. He didn't see their Yamabishi[74] posted anywhere. If only he had a better idea of what to look for.

The stranger gawked at him. "You think it's going to be that easy?"

---

[74] The diamond-shaped clan emblem of the Yamaguchi-gumi.

"I'm a big believer in fate," he said. It was a lie. If he were a big believer in fate, he'd have stayed in America.

Satani heard a slap. He turned to the crowd only to see the girl from before rubbing her cheek.

The man she sat with had his arm raised at her, his face red.

Tyrone got up as he tried to wave the waitress over, but apparently wasn't so preoccupied that he didn't notice Satani's attention was elsewhere. "Something wrong?" Tyrone asked the waitress.

Satani's eyes fixed on the girl's. "It's nothing," she replied to Tyrone.

January 22, 2020. Satani slept at the bar that night. Not a good idea in hindsight, but he had nowhere else to go.

When he woke the next morning, he was lying outside the club, his arms sore.

Tyrone stood a few feet away, leaning against the door. "You're lucky I don't have anywhere else to go today."

"Why's that?" asked Satani. He sounded nonchalant.

Tyrone spoke as if he were talking about the weather. "Some guys came over; wanted to cut your pinky off and shove it up your ass. I told them to back off."

Satani figured the guys from before had found him, but he couldn't figure out how this guy managed to get them to back off. The thought tickled him a bit, so Satani chortled. "Yeah, and they just listened."

Doi Tyrone nodded. "After I broke their arms, they did." A bit of sadness crossed in his eyes. He barely knew the guy, so Satani didn't want to push the subject. The silence lasted for a few moments. The longer it went on, the more Satani believed him.

"You didn't have to …" Satani's voice trailed off as he realized the implications for his career with the yakuza. If he had to have a stranger protect him, how were the clans—or whatever clan he ended up working for—going to rely on him?

"I know I didn't have to, but let's just say you owe me one now, ok?"

Before Satani could say anything, Tyrone walked away.

January 24, 2020. Satani spent several nights at the bar thereafter, except when he entertained the ladies, including some girl who liked art. He reverted to his thieving ways, albeit to a lesser extent than before. After all, it was hard to steal in the same area more than twice, but he didn't want to stray too far from the "Keisatsu-cho" lest he miss out on an opportunity to impress the yakuza.

The smoker in the purple silk shirt, who Satani later discovered was a corrupt vice squad detective named Kato, continued to bother him, but drinking with his fellow gaijin made it easier. He'd sometimes ask Tyrone what he did for a living, but all he would say was "We're drinking buddies, so let's drink and leave it at that." So they did.

Satani was about to give up hope when, one night, the yakuza walked through the door. Or so he hoped. He wasn't sure what about the new arrivals made him think that this guy with them could be the one. It could have been the people bowing their heads in respect when they entered. Or maybe the shit-eating grins the lackeys had on their faces as they cast their eyes around the room, particularly the one with the wraparound sunglasses. Like the robo-arms, it didn't matter; he had to take a chance.

Satani swallowed hard and strode over to the man with ease, or at least he tried to make it look that way.

"Excuse me, sir," he said. He tried to keep his voice steady. "Are you with the Yamaguchi-gumi?"

The supposed yakuza looked at Satani with a jaundiced eye, then to his people, who shook their heads,

The man waved him off. "Gaijin," he said in a low, guttural voice. *I couldn't even get a word in …*

The others started pushing him away, but Satani wasn't about to give up; he would beg if he had to.

"Please," he said. He tried to push the others away. "I'd like to help you!" Satani suddenly realized how stupid he was being; he didn't even know if the man spoke English.

The guy with the sunglasses laughed and then said something to the boss that Satani couldn't understand; the only words he made out were *kuso* and *gaijin*. Satani made a mental note that he would have to study more. Then he suddenly realized he was clutching the dictionary.

The man smirked, dropped his level, wrapped Satani up behind the knees, and tackled him down to the ground, then pulled the book out. He laughed as he explained the significance of the book to his comrades. The boss grunted and the man turned back to Satani. "The boss says he isn't interested."

But Satani wasn't done yet. "Look, I could be an asset to you. Worst case scenario, I'm expendable; you could get rid of me real fast if you felt he needed to."

No one said anything for a moment. The lackey with the sunglasses said, "I am Moji Sumio. I am a Yamaguchi-gumi gokudo. You will speak only when spoken to, gaijin."

Satani tried to hide his smile. "Understood."

The man wrote something on a piece of paper and handed it to him. "Come back tomorrow from this address with a package. Tell them you're working for us; we'll see how you do."

January 25, 2020. Tameike-sanno, Tokyo. Satani went to the address, as ordered. It was some warehouse he didn't know the name of, but that didn't matter. He had waited for this chance and he had no intention of messing it up. The inside was pristine, well-lit, and conspicuously empty except for Satani and a non-descript muscle-bound man with a bag slung over his shoulder.

The man said something in Japanese. When Satani didn't answer, the man just laughed and said, "I heard this belongs to you."

Satani gawked at him for a moment, then shook his head and took the bag from the man's hand.

As the man walked away, Satani thought about asking him his name or what was in the package, but he thought better of it.

Yet, as he walked back to the bar, his curiosity continued to grow. Hiding in an alley momentarily, he took a peek inside and nearly vomited.

He supposed anyone would have done the same, the first time he saw a girl's severed head. *She looked like an angel. A bloody angel . . .*

Roppongi, Tokyo. As he walked into the bar, he could feel people's eyes on him, but it didn't matter because all he could think about was the girl. What was she like? Did she have a family? Satani knew he shouldn't be asking himself these questions, not if he wanted to join the highest ranks of criminality.

His train of thought was broken as a pair of hands clasped him on his shoulders. He was not surprised to hear Kato's voice afterwards.

"What you got there, gaijin?"

"None of your business," said Satani with a dark tone. He gripped the sack tighter.

Detective Kato cast a sidelong glance at the bag. "Well, whatever you got, can I have some?"

He wanted to tell Kato to get lost, but Tyrone did it for him in an aggressive tone.

Kato threw his hands up as if to stop an attack. "Take it easy, man. My bad."

After he was gone, Satani muttered to Tyrone, "Thanks … again."

Tyrone nodded. "Congratulations."

"Isn't that a little premature?"

"You came back alive, so I'd say no."

Satani couldn't help but laugh; he realized he was being too loud when he saw the bewildered look in Tyrone's eyes. "Sorry, just needed some kind of release."

"If you really need a release that badly, go find yourself a woman like you usually do."

"No time for that. The boss'll be here any minute."

Tyrone waved to the bartender, "Well, I guess a drink will have to do."

The local Yamaguchi-gumi boss walked in but Satani barely noticed. He was too busy looking at the waitress, wondering if she was going to end up like the girl in the bag.

"He's here," said Doi Tyrone as he sipped his beer.

Satani stood and took a deep breath.

"Now's the hard part," said Tyrone.

Tyrone could have been reading his mind. Satani was suddenly scared. He kept glancing over in the waitress's direction, the same girl who had been fondling the old man. It was as if she was telling him with her eyes not to go through with it; she looked more frightened than he was. Satani tightened his grip on the bag again, wondering if the angel in the bag had asked the same thing of her killer.

"What do you mean?" he asked.

Tyrone only shrugged.

The cruel man in the wraparound sunglasses, Moji Sumio, kept calling him over.

Without another word to Tyrone, Satani strode over to the local Yamaguchi-gumi set's boss, Kamei Daichi.

Kamei-san sat at the table, eying Satani with what he thought was contempt, but then he supposed yakuza weren't for smiling.

Moji Sumio stepped in his way. "Well done, gaijin." He held out his hand for the sack. As he examined the contents, Satani felt the living girl's eyes on him.

Suddenly, something changed inside Satani.

Out of nowhere, he kicked Moji in the groin and grabbed the sack. Then Satani ran, but not before he ushered the girl from the table. People started yelling. Kamei Daichi shouted something that the aspiring yakuza didn't understand, but that didn't matter anymore. Besides it was probably something akin to "Kill the stupid gaijin."

Satani felt a bullet whiz past his hand. He looked back to see Tyrone with a gun in his hand. Satani almost wanted to ask how he got that, but he knew that it wasn't exactly the right time.

"I told you this would be the hard part!" Tyrone shouted. He wore a savage grin on his merciless face.

Kamei-san yelled something at Tyrone that Satani didn't understand, but there was no translation needed.

"P-please," said the girl in a Filipina accent. "Please don't let me go."

Satani squeezed her arm. "I won't."

With that, they were out the door, no doubt with Tyrone close behind.

They hid in a nearby alley, but Satani knew they were screwed.

He looked over at the girl. She was trembling and Satani suddenly bad he had involved her. Why the hell had he done it anyway? A Yamaguchi-gumi foreigner bar is no place for heroes, especially gaijin heroes. He supposed Tyrone knew that, hence his allegiance to the yakuza.

"I'm scared," the Filipina said.

"That's a funny name," Satani said. He suddenly realized that he had no idea who this girl was.

She gawked at him and his ears turned red.

"Real smooth, Santos," said Tyrone, suddenly.

Before Satani could realize that Doi Tyrone had just used his American name, he heard him add "It's nothing personal, Satani; Kamei-san just wants you dead." He spoke as if this was the plan all along. Maybe it was. Maybe they fully expected him to play hero.

Satani sighed. "Run now," he told the girl.

Satani darted out of the alley and tackled Tyrone to the ground. As they struggled over the gun, a shot went off. He heard a thump and saw the girl lying in a pool of blood. *Why the fuck did she run the same way as them?*

Satani gritted his teeth and turned his full attention back to Tyrone. There was that sadness in Tyrone's eyes again.

Suddenly, Tyrone managed to hit him in the nose with the butt of his weapon.

The last thing Satani saw was the gun pointed between his eyes.

He couldn't help but wonder if this made them even.

About the Author

Brett Stevens has wanted to be a writer his whole life; he just didn't realize it until March 7th, 2007. On a break from yet another standardized test, he began scribbling what became his first novel four agonizing years later. Since then, he's completed two more novels and is currently in the "banging-his-head-against-the-wall" phase of the fourth. He is excited to be collaborating on an anthology that combines two of his greatest loves: crime and anime. When he's not working or writing, he can found blogging at:

http://guywhowrites.weebly.com.

Black Kite Death

by Nick Aires

Japan won the Second World War;
Now the yakuza are starting the Third!

東京極道

Black Kite Death

BY NICK AIRES

January 22, 2020. Shinjuku, Tokyo. The laser sight swept through the Tokyo night, flashing red across the black lapels of business suits and the foreheads of uniformed schoolgirls. It glanced over the windows of the cars on Yasukuni Doori, reflecting off tinted windshields and merging with the glowing kanji on taxicab signs.

On the roof of a nine-story building, the Yamaguchi-gumi sniper crouched in the shadow of a neon sign. He smiled with grim satisfaction as his target crept within his sights and then, silently and efficiently, he pulled the trigger.

The traffic light exploded. On the street below him, a woman screamed. The man next to her grabbed her arm, pulling her away from the shards of glass raining down on the roof of a sky-blue Prius hybrid car.

Tobi withdrew into the shadows, silent and still until the couple and the car were out of sight. He had already lined up his next target: smaller, darker, and further away, but nothing Tobi couldn't handle. "Come on, baby," he whispered.

A block down the street on the fifth floor of a nightclub, a lone security camera caught its last brief shot: Tobi's bullet just before it put the camera's eye out for good.

"What are you doing?" The voice, carved from digital steel, came through his headset. "Your shots could draw attention to your position before the target is in place."

Tobi snorted. "Never have before. I always zero out a rifle before the shot that counts."

"Well, don't," the voice said. "Not on my watch. Remember, you're not taking a life, Tobi. You're saving two."

"What's that supposed to mean?"

"Don't play dumb. Unless you want your idiotic ramblings to be the last thing your parents ever hear."

"Fine." So the conversation was being recorded. *Well, that makes two of us.* Tobi fingered the device in his pocket. *Just in case.* He asked the voice, "You sure we want to go through with this?"

"We need him out of the way."

"Someone else'll just rise to take his place." Tobi tightened his grip as a white car flew through his sights, but it was just an old Toyota, not the Sumiyoshi-kai oyabun's limo. He eased his finger off, but kept it stiff and alert. "And they'll know we were behind it," he said.

"That's the idea."

"Nobody wants another clan war."

"Correct. But ..." Whoever was behind the digitized voice paused, as if considering whether to go on. "I want the Sumiyoshi-kai for myself."

Tobi froze. The trigger, warmed by the constant half-pressure of his finger, went cold. "I thought you were one of us. Yamaguchi-gumi."

"Does it matter? I have something that matters to you and you can deliver the only thing that matters to me. He's coming."

Tobi grunted in disapproval, but he lowered his eye to the scope and zeroed in on the entrance to the club.

He knew the target immediately, even though he'd never met Oyabun Sugawara in person. The leader of the Sumiyoshi-kai never traveled light and he never traveled in anything but style. Tobi flicked off the laser sight. Sugawara-san was no idiot; Tobi saw no point giving him a warning with the little red dot.

Two bodyguards awaited the limo and they took up positions at the front and back of the long car; then the driver got out and stood at attention. Another bodyguard stepped out of the front passenger seat and opened the rear door.

Tobi had a clear view of the sidewalk in front of the door. The moment Oyabun Sugawara stepped out, he'd have him.

I shouldn't be doing this.

But Tobi had no choice. Whoever was behind this, wherever their allegiance lay, they had his parents. When it came down to it, that was all that mattered.

He saw movement from inside the car: a leg coming out. Tobi nearly squeezed the trigger.

Something wasn't right.

He didn't think the oyabun would be wearing a red dress, or a green one, for that matter. Two women with amazing figures displayed by tight, low-cut dresses stepped out of the limo. Their unexpected appearance distracted Tobi, especially since it suddenly started to rain and their dresses quickly became translucent.

Tobi didn't even notice that Sugawara-san had joined the women on the sidewalk until the motion of the man opening a large black umbrella brought his attention back to his target.

The oyabun put an arm around each woman, drawing them in close under the umbrella. Tobi had no shot.

A less skilled or less creative sniper would give up: let Sugawara go into the club and hope to reacquire the target on the way back out. Not Tobi.

He aimed at the ground just in front of the Sumiyoshi-kai oyabun. The moment a hand-sewn leather shoe entered his sights, he pulled the trigger. As expected, the target jerked forward. He dropped the umbrella and reached for his injured foot, *lowering his head.* Tobi took the shot that mattered.

He didn't bother to watch the body fall. He'd done this before, he'd do it again, and whoever wanted the oyabun dead wouldn't have asked him if they hadn't known he'd deliver. He dropped into a roll and crawled behind the neon sign advertising another club in the building below him. Those bodyguards were well-trained; it wouldn't take them long to figure out where the bullets had come from.

Tobi crawled, as he'd crawled a hundred times before, to the hatch that would take him back down into the building's service hallway. "It's done," he whispered. "Now let them go."

Above him, the neon sign started to blink. It guttered, as if all of the tubes were failing at the same time, and then roared back into life, a thousand times brighter than it had been. "What the—?"

This was not good. It was literally shining a spotlight on him. If the bodyguards' attention hadn't already been trained on this building, it would be now.

Tobi ran. He'd shot out the security camera that would have captured him leaving the building, but the blind spot would be bigger than that. Hoping his mental calculations were correct, Tobi made a break for the gap between the building he was on and the slightly squatter one next door.

"I might not make it out of here alive," he said. "Tell my parents I love them. Then let them go."

A blaze of static crackled in his ear like an electronic laugh. "I'm afraid I can't do that. You see, patricide is a specialty of mine."

"But the oyabun doesn't have any biological children: just kobun," Tobi gasped as he ran. "They say he got testicular cancer a couple years ago and he's now as sterile as an operating room."

"That may be the case," the voice said. "But he created me, all the same."

Tobi jumped. The buildings in Shinjuku were close enough together that there was no doubt he would make it, but the building next door was a good two stories shorter. He hit the concrete rooftop hard, one ankle twisting under him with a sharp twinge.

It hurt. It hurt like hell, but the security light on the taller building was twisting to follow him, its yellow beam inching behind him as he forced himself to run.

"You can't hide, Tobi."

The voice in his ear was the same as it had always been: flat, impersonal and devoid of emotion, but its deadpan delivery made Tobi's insides run cold.

He created me.

Tobi climbed down the side of the building and onto a service ladder, putting as much of his weight on his arms and his uninjured leg as he could. "No," he whispered as realization hit. "That's impossible."

"It's not impossible."

He'd heard the rumors, of course. Everyone had. The Sumiyoshi-kai had created a supercomputer, some kind of quasi-sentient artificial intelligence with the ability to manipulate the Tokyo Stock Exchange. Tobi had blown it off. *Impossible.* He'd assumed their human experts had been lucky.

There was a window below him: a sixth-story window, if his split-second calculations were correct. It was close enough to swing his legs onto the ledge. Holding onto the ladder with his left hand, Tobi swung the rifle around and, for the first time in his life, took careless aim. The window shattered. An alarm sounded and Tobi swung through the hole.

Jagged glass tore at his clothes, bloodying his limbs as he clambered through the window into a storeroom. He hardly noticed; his mind was still reeling with the revelation of who—what—he was up against.

"You're a computer?"

"Not a computer."

Above Tobi's head, the lights flickered and failed, leaving him in darkness.

"A computer is a physical thing," the Tokyo Stock Exchange AI elaborated. "A computer can be destroyed. I can't."

"Screw that."

The room was dark but it was hardly treacherous. Tobi fought his way through a maze of cardboard boxes and, with a well-placed kick, knocked open the door. It was long after normal business hours, but a light flickered at the end of the hallway and Tobi could hear the faint sounds of fingers at a keyboard.

He forced himself to walk quietly, sliding his feet along the tiled floor. It was unlikely that some poor overtime worker posed a threat, but the blood on Tobi's clothes would be a red flag. There was an elevator on his left, but now that Tobi knew his adversary could probably control anything computer-based, he wasn't stupid enough to try that. Instead, he aimed for the stairs at the far end of the hall.

The AI was in control of this building. He had to get out. He had to get away.

The stairway door started to open. Someone was coming.

He couldn't risk whoever it was getting a look at his face. Not when he'd just murdered the guy who had half the cops in Shinjuku in his pocket. *The other half was in the pocket of the Yamaguchi-gumi.* He cursed under his breath. With no other option, Tobi pushed the elevator button.

The doors opened immediately. He lunged inside and jammed his thumb against the ground floor icon. He sighed in relief when the doors closed and the elevator started to descend.

With a screech and a clang from the shaft, the elevator shuddered to a halt.

"What's going on? You gonna trap me in here until I starve to death? You really think no one will take the system offline and pull the doors apart to rescue me?"

His earpiece remained silent, but the doors opened.

Problem was that the elevator had stopped halfway between floors. Still, there was enough of an opening at the bottom, below the third floor ceiling, that Tobi thought he'd be able to crawl through.

Stretching out on the floor, he held the rifle over his head and slowly, carefully, he began the process of exiting, feet first. His legs, hips, and waist slid through the opening and were dangling on the air over the third-floor hallway when, all of a sudden, the elevator fell.

Tobi dropped the rifle and shoved himself backward out of the rapidly shrinking opening. He got clear a split-second before the falling elevator would have severed his head, his arms, his torso, or all of the above. As it was, the impact slammed him into the hallway floor, knocking the breath out of him, and he shook with pain.

"Well played," the Tokyo Stock Exchange AI said. "But you'll never get out. You know that, don't you?"

"Why?" Tobi gasped. Sweat ran down his face, into his eyes, and his heart wouldn't stop pounding. "I did what you asked. Why are you—?"

"I don't trust humans. You would betray me."

"I wouldn't," Tobi said. He stood and limped toward the stairwell. The door was locked and this one was too heavy to kick in.

"Oh, but you would. Your mother would have. She even said as much. Not very smart of her, wouldn't you agree? Your father screamed like a little girl when I killed her."

"No!" Tobi kicked at the door anyway, his foot pounding the handle with a thud. Another shock of pain shot up his leg, but Tobi barely felt it. His world was red with rage.

The big windows in the main office were strung with safety wire. Tobi almost threw a computer at one anyway, but cold logic kicked in. Even if he did make it through, it was a three-story fall to a busy street on an already injured ankle.

He frantically searched for another way out.

The window in the employee kitchen was small, but still big enough for a man to squeeze through and it opened with the push of a lever.

Tobi climbed on the counter and over the sink to stand on the two-burner stove. He got one foot up on the window ledge before the burner below him kicked into life.

There was no time to look down, no time to plan his landing; the flames consumed the bottom of his pants leg and continued to climb. He had to get out. With a deep breath, Tobi jumped.

The sign for the bar on the second floor broke his fall. He pulled off his jacket, using it to beat out the fire. "How are you doing this?" he gasped.

He could almost hear a smile in the mechanical voice. "It's all connected."

Tobi smiled. For the first time all night, things were going his way. He draped his blackened jacket over the security camera next to his perch on the sign. His bullet already had taken care of the camera across the street. Once he jumped, the AI would have no way of knowing where he was.

He took his time, positioned his fall so his good ankle would take the brunt of it, and hit the ground running. A taxi squealed to a halt, the horn blaring as its drunken passenger hurled a stream of obscenities through the glass.

Tobi ran.

The traffic at the intersection ahead was stopped. The pedestrian light was a solid green, which should have meant he had at least a minute or two, but the second he stepped into the street, the light blazed red.

The cars that had been stopped at the light surged forward into the steady stream of traffic on Yasukuni. A motorcyclist drove straight into the side of a tour bus. When the bus put on its breaks, a delivery truck slammed into its back. A bright red sports car, its driver distracted by the spectacle, plowed into Tobi hard enough to break a floating rib, but he just ricocheted off the car, grit his teeth and made a mad dash to the subway station.

"How'd you find me?" he demanded between ragged breaths. "I shot out the cameras. How—?"

But the answer came to him before the AI could give it. Tobi ripped out his earpiece and took the phone from his pocket. He popped out the micro memory card from its slot, then threw the device out into the chaos of the street. His chest heaved; his ankle throbbed. But Tobi smiled at the sound of his phone, and its built-in

GPS, smashing beneath the wheels of a jet-black van.

He fled into the subway station, pushing past businessmen and well-dressed women, only half-aware of their stares. He had to get out of here: out of Shinjuku and out of Tokyo. He had to get some place where the Tokyo Stock Exchange AI couldn't track him until he figured out what to do with the card and the recording on it.

Tobi took his wallet from his jacket pocket, fighting the urge to laugh hysterically at the untouched, pristine leather. He pulled out a five thousand yen note and, narrowing his eyes at the stack of IC-chipped credit cards, tossed the rest into a trash can. He scanned his memory and his imagination for any way to turn a ticket vendor lethal. When he couldn't come up with anything, he stuck the money in. This would be a test, then. If it let him buy a ticket, he'd know destroying his phone had worked and that the TSE AI couldn't find him anymore.

He had no idea where he was going. He bought the most expensive ticket he could: it popped out, crisp, pink and normal. Tobi breathed a sigh of relief.

The automated gates were waiting: three red for *Exit*, four green for *Entrance*. Tobi held out his ticket, took a step toward the nearest green gate.

And the barrier slammed shut. The one next to it followed, and by the time Tobi reached the end of the line, a crowd of passengers was clamoring for the station staff, unable to get in or out.

Behind him, Tobi heard a mechanical groan. It was the steel gate that closed the underground off to would-be passengers trying to catch the last train of the night. The gate rattled on its downward course even though the time couldn't have been any later than ten.

No.

There was only one thing to do. Tobi went deeper, away from the subway and into the maze of shops that wound beneath Shinjuku-eki[75] like an anthill. He wasn't sure how far the tunnels went, but he knew he stood more of a chance here than against that gate.

The people he shoved past looked at him with disgust, anger and fear. What did any of that matter now? Tobi had to get out of here, had to deliver this card to his own oyabun, Yamaguchi-gumi clan boss Kitano Takumi. Hell, he might even try to take it to the Sumiyoshi-kai wakagashira, or anyone. Someone had to know about the rogue Tokyo Stock Exchange AI before this escalated beyond a clan war and into a full-blown reign of terror.

"Tobi!"

Tobi flinched, then realized the voice was human. He turned to see a man in an unbuttoned purple dress shirt sitting on a bench. *Detective Kato.* The corrupt vice squad detective appeared to be totally at home on the bench, people-watching as he so often did at the Yamaguchi-gumi run Philippines bar that Tobi knew him from.

He strode over to his friend. "Kato-san! I need your help. I—"

"I can help you, man. I can always help you." Detective Kato grinned a little too wide. He proffered a marijuana cigarette. "There's nothing this can't help."

"No thanks, Kato. I gotta tell you something important."

"Okay," Detective Kato said. He flicked his lighter near the end of the joint. "Tell me while we get high."

"Kato, I really need your help!"

Detective Kato tried to get a flame from his lighter again, but failed. "And I really need someone to smoke weed with. It's a win-win, man."

"I don't have time for—"

---

[75] "Shinjuku station."

A woman walking toward them suddenly shrieked and, without apology, stepped on Tobi's foot as she hurried past him. Tobi turned to see what had startled her. Across the hall, a newsstand clerk cried out as smoke rose from his computerized cash register. Flames climbed up a rack of magazines, threatening to burn the whole place to the ground.

Kato tossed his empty lighter aside. He jumped up and ran *toward* the flames. Tobi watched with near shock as Kato held his joint out to the burning newsstand to light it.

Thankful he'd not entrusted the important memory card to his bar friend, Tobi ran on.

Behind him, he heard another metallic groan. He didn't have to look back to know that it was another gate coming down. The gates were intended to keep customers out after business hours: the AI was using them to keep Tobi in.

An electronic lock beeped and popped. From a service corridor just ahead of him, an engine roared to life.

"What the hell?" a salaryman yelled.

He made it to the corridor entrance at the same moment the machine did. It was a buffer, a floor polisher: giant and heavy with two whirring mops like the mops at a car wash. Someone should have been pushing it, but no one was and the thing was running at him so fast that smoke was starting to billow from its insides.

Tobi turned, desperate for another way out, but the closest shop was a mobile phone dealer and he didn't want to think about what would happen to him in there. Instead, he backtracked, running into a formalwear store.

If he could just get up onto the sales counter, that thing wouldn't be able to reach —

Just as he leaped, the machine caught up to him, clipping his heels and sending him sprawling into a rack of cocktail dresses. He landed in a heap on the floor. Above him, the PA system crackled to life and a voice said, "Attention all shoppers. Attention all shoppers. Special in the formalwear aisle."

The buffer's whirling mops crawled over him, crushing his left foot. Tobi screamed out in pain. He grabbed hold of the toppled clothes rack and shoved it under the machine. With a grinding screech of metal on metal, the buffer's overworked engine died in a puff of black smoke.

Tobi stood and tried to walk, but his ruined foot couldn't bear his weight and he toppled over, half in and half out of the store exit. The store's metal gate began to rattle down. He frantically tried to crawl away, but the gate was too fast. At the last instant, he rolled over to try to catch it and push it back up, but it was too heavy. It cut into his stomach, resting heavily on what he guessed was his liver or his spleen. His high velocity bullets gave people a quick, painless death, but it would be a slow, painful death for him. *Figures.*

A security camera whirled around to face him and then stopped, staring down at its victim. There was no doubt what lurked behind its empty black gaze.

Tobi looked around for someone, anyone who might help him, but both of the salesclerks were backing away, horrified. His gaze landed on a young woman who stood staring at him in shock. She was in her early twenties, tall and thin, carrying a bag of what looked like art supplies embroidered with her name: Asuka Higashino. She snapped out of her fearful trance and dropped the dress she'd been holding. She rushed to him and tried to push the gate up with her flawlessly manicured hands.

"Are you all right?" she asked. "I'm sorry. I … I can't move it."

Tobi opened his mouth, but all that came out was a bloody gurgle.

He beckoned for her to come closer. She glanced over her shoulder, taking in the camera. She seemed to understand that what was happening wasn't a string of fluke accidents: that Tobi was under attack and if she wasn't careful, she'd be in danger, too.

She dropped to one knee and whispered in his ear, "What can I do?"

Tobi grabbed the gate again. He pushed up with all his might, shaking it noisily.

Asuka put her hands next to his and pulled again, but even their combined strength could not budge it. Then the young woman, this kind stranger, pulled his hands off the gate and held them.

Tobi had not been pushing as hard as he could. His right hand was not empty, so his grip had been impaired. He didn't know if she'd noticed this, but she certainly now felt the micro card he transferred into her hand.

She lowered her ear next to his mouth.

"This," he managed to say. He kept her head between his lips and the security camera. "Take this to ... Yamaguchi-gumi. My old friend ... Asahara Hikaru."

She gasped but never let go of the card. She was good. She was smart and she had kind eyes. Tobi didn't know if that meant he could trust her, but at the moment he didn't have much choice.

"This will stop a war. Promise me ..."

Asuka scrutinized him for a minute, then nodded slightly, keeping her voice low and her face turned from the camera. "Okay."

"Thank you. I—" Tobi began, but was interrupted by another announcement over the PA.

"Attention all shoppers. Please stick around for the fireworks display."

"The what?" Asuka asked. She pulled her hand away, still holding the card. She stood and looked around, fear etched across her face.

Her answer came in the form of a burst of light from the hallway. The neon sign above the shop's entrance exploded, sparking with an electrical overload. It crashed down into the metal gate.

Tobi's face contorted, twisting in agony as electricity flowed through his body.

His vision blurred. The last thing he saw was the security camera's crimson light. He wished he could shoot it out. He'd always thought he'd die with his sniper rifle in his hands.

He was wrong.

About the Author

Nick Aires is the author of *Arrow: Heroes and Villains*, and the interactive novel app *Diabolical*. His short stories have appeared in numerous magazines and anthologies, most recently in *JukePop Serials*, *Neo-opsis*, and *Voices of Imagination 2*.

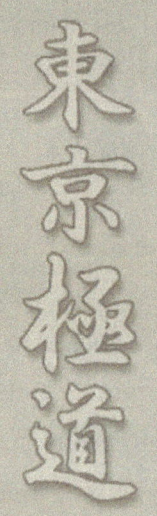

東京極道

Tokyo Yakuza

#9

Two Princes

by Dan Seidel

Japan won the Second World War; Now the yakuza are starting the Third!

Tokyo Yakuza #9

Two Princes

By Dan Seidel

January 22, 2020. Ginza, Tokyo. The man sat transfixed. His vision blurred as he stared down at the glass bar, the LED backlighting diffusing into an indistinct glow. There were two glasses in front of him, a tall, frosted cylinder filled with something clear and an old-fashioned tumbler with dark liquid and orbs of ice. He reached for the former, although he could barely feel it in his hand, and lifted it for a grateful sip. The sake was from Niigata. It wasn't the most expensive or famous, but he'd preferred it since the first time he tasted it. Supposedly, spring runoff from the mountain snows gave it an exceptionally clear taste. Chilled, he could almost forget it wasn't water.

"Hikaru, I'm bored," said Kujo Michihiko with a drawl.

The overly familiar address drew him from the trance. The speaker was the owner of the second glass. Lifted from the glossy bar top, the tumbler swayed back and forth with the idle motions of the man behind it, causing the frozen spheres suspended within to clink audibly against its sides. Asahara Hikaru replied, "You're always bored. We need to talk business. If you're willing to meet-"

"Let's go somewhere fun," his friend interrupted.

"Kujo-sama." Hikaru's tone was dry and his politeness feigned so obviously as to make his annoyance clear. "Look around. Where do you think you are? We've got anything you need, so let's just talk."

"The menu here is always the same," Kujo Michihiko complained.

Michihiko didn't mean the beverage selection. For all his complaints of variety, he always drank the same thing: Kentucky bourbon, aged thirty years. Imported from the United States, it was one of the most expensive items they served, and that included most of the more illicit offerings that could be found in the club's private lounge. Then again, the government wasn't waging a tariff war on cocaine or sex. The same couldn't be said for imports from the Pan-American Zone.

The Velours was a high class hostess club in Ginza, catering to a clientele of megacorp managers, Tokyo Stock Exchange (TSE) brokers, and the occasional bored aristocrat like his present drinking partner. Women in cocktail dresses prowled the bar, where the men would buy them overpriced drinks for the privilege of company and conversation. Most hoped for more, even if few enough ever got it.

Everything was constructed to encourage that fantasy. Most of the girls they hired could be models. A few were. The place had its share of aspiring talent: young actresses and would-be idols. The rest were mostly students or young office ladies. Most of these women thought of the job as an easy way to make a bit of extra cash, whether to fund their chic spending habits or just to make ends meet. Some inevitably got caught up in the lifestyle, spending as much as they made on new found tastes and addictions. Others angled for a permanent arrangement with one of the rich clients, whether that meant marriage or just a credit line at the Shibuya 109. Sometimes he felt like an old woman. It was a fine line between matchmaker and pimp.

"I hired a few new girls last week," Hikaru suggested, ever the accommodating host.

Michihiko made some almost purring sound of consideration, lifting his glass for another sip as his lazy eyes scanned the room. "They all look the same to me."

Frustrated, Hikaru still couldn't argue the sentiment. The girls were of a mold and no matter how well-formed, how charming, it took a certain lack of self-respect to sell yourself like this. Or a certain desperation. Neither yielded deep or endearing character. Instead, they were uniformly shallow, monotonously fake. Everything from their smiles to their makeup to their high-pitched voices was a calculated fabrication. They smiled for him, flirted as he hired them. Most had fucked him too, though he wasn't the sort of man to make them go that far for a job. That some offered without prompting was proof of their flawed character. That he accepted was proof of his own.

It was a kind of mutual exploitation. They turned on the charm when they needed a shift change or needed him to rough up a handsy customer. Otherwise, their eyes were forever on the club's guests: the wealthy and the powerful, men like his drinking partner. His friend was actual royalty, related to the imperial family through some long-dead great aunt: a literal prince. Five years ago, they might have looked at Hikaru the same way. Now he was just some thug they had to endure as a price of doing business.

"You might like one of them," Hikaru insisted. "Kanae's fresh off the shink[76] from somewhere in the south. Kagoshima, I think." A tanned beach-bunny from subtropical Kyushu, she definitely didn't look like the rest, even if she was every bit as superficial.

Michihiko laughed in open disbelief. "That gibberish they speak, how did you even interview her?"

---

[76] Short for "shinkansen" or "bullet train."

"Her accent isn't *that* bad."

The prince ignored him, glancing at a young woman just returning to the bar. She was on the young side, even for the hostesses at the club, and looked uncomfortable in her slinky black cocktail dress.

"What about her?"

"Asuka. She's an art student at Ueno Gakuen," Hikaru said, following his friend's gaze. "She's nice. Not too … well, you know." She was less despicable than most, working to pay off loans and some kind of gallery business she was starting. He hadn't slept with her.

Michihiko considered her for a long moment.

Even if most of the girls were happy to turn on the charm for the catch he represented, the young prince was always terribly picky and frequently disinterested. Hikaru understood why. The Kujo were richer than Daikoku-ten,[77] the kami of wealth and prosperity himself. Even at the height of his own lucrative career, Hikaru had never known the sort of wealth and privilege his blue blooded friend took for granted. Yet luxury was a drug like any other. After time, you developed a tolerance and ended up chasing newer, bigger highs. This was why the princeling liked him: because he could get those things that money alone could never buy, at least not without a seller like him. *Without a pusher, without a pimp.*

But Hikaru had to be careful. Extorting salarymen for their namesake earnings was one thing. The shame of scandal would always keep them quiet, though media interest would be small at best. The police would investigate, but only so much. There was always the sense that if a fat old man was found smelling of whiskey, beaten or dead, or if someone caught him with a girl young enough

---

[77] The god of great darkness and five cereals. One of the Seven Lucky Gods of the household.

to be his granddaughter overdosed in his bed, that his own weak character was to blame. People averted their eyes from such displays.

Michihiko was not a fat old man. He was the son of a leading member of the House of Peers, a member of elite society. While the scandal would be far greater if anything happened to him, so too would be the media circus surrounding it and the heavenly punishment enacted against Hikaru and his associates.

And besides, Hikaru really needed him.

"No, let's go somewhere else," Michihiko had finally decided. He watched as Asuka moved off to refill a drink for a balding man in a gray suit.

"Kujo-denka," Hikaru said, upping the ante of their verbal sparring. "I'll get you anything you want tonight, take you anywhere, do anything. But you have to get that meeting with Chiba. And soon. This … it's the only way I'll ever be free of this place."

"I know, but I *like* this place," Michihiko said, still complaining.

"You've been nagging me to go somewhere else all night long."

The prince lifted his hand. "I'll speak with my father. Now let's go."

The two men rose from the bar, leaving behind their pair of glasses. Hikaru had drained his, while Michihiko's remained half-full, ice melting into the expensive liquor.

The two men spent the night in pleasure, yet one dreamed only of a cell.

For various public order and weapons charges, Asahara Hikaru had been sentenced to a five year term. He served his time, from 2014 to 2019, at the New Sugamo Detention Facility[78], a modern mega-prison built on the site of an older facility of the same name. The original had housed political dissidents and foreign spies during the war. The new institution's guests were not so illustrious, and its operations were oppressive but orderly.

In his dreams, it was a concrete monolith: a bastion devoid of hope or escape.

Hikaru walked across the exercise yard. Many eyes looked on and heads bowed in deference. Even the guards paused to recognize his passing. Two men walked behind him. No, not men. One was a guardian dog and the other bore the image of the Bodhisattva Kannon.[79] Even in that place, they were not afraid, and all feared them. A man stepped into their path, prostrating himself and holding up a sheathed sword of ancient design. "This is yours."

Hikaru reached to take it but he could not grasp the steel.

They walked along a long corridor, with many cell doors to one side. Turning his head, Hikaru saw that a woman inhabited each tiny room. Some stood nude, their bodies undulating in sensuous dance. Others lay upon the prison cots, writhing beneath the forms of piggish, sweaty men, or beneath the tattooed backs of his own brothers. He turned, continuing ahead to where Kannon stood before him.

"I deliver a blessing. You are released."

Relief filled his heart until, suddenly, he was gripped by many arms at once.

"Mercy requires penance," Kannon said with a smile, both serene and sadistic.

The many-armed goddess twisted and held him down. Several hands gripped his every limb and one held his left arm aside. The

---

[78] Colloquially called simply, "Sugamo Prison."
[79] Goddess of Mercy, "Guan-yin" in Chinese.

goddess's last hand brandished a sword.

"Now you are forgiven, and now you are free."

As the dog looked on, the blade fell. Kannon tossed Hikaru back into a cell.

January 23, 2020. Hidden behind its public facade, The Velours boasted a private lounge used for VIP functions or for meetings by members of the Yamaguchi-gumi. While the women out front strolled the club in chic evening wear, the hostesses who served behind closed doors wore nothing but lingerie and high heels. The tables boasted reflective surfaces and dance poles. OLED-paneled walls could project any image, making the whole room seem somewhere else at a whim.

Kujo Michihiko was the VIP that night, a guest of the clan's leaders and proxy for his father. He sat across from Chiba Ken who held position as the Yamaguchi-gumi's wakagashira, second in command and right hand to Oyabun Kitano Takumi. It was a position that Matsuhono Eugi had once been expected to fill and it was a stepping stone to the top ranks of the Yamaguchi-gumi leadership nationwide.

Chiba had his wife, Kinugasa Tamika, a club hostess who so enthralled him he actually married her, kneeling on the couch cushion beside him and two bodyguards behind. Hikaru recognized both of the bodyguards as comrades from a past life. One had dutifully patted him down before he sat and now made every effort to look through him. The other watched him with a vicious, curling smile.

"You know that we've had trouble with transportation recently." Chiba was in the midst of complaining to Michihiko. "Security is very tight these days. Everyone wants to save face ahead of the Olympics.

And then there's Customs inspections." Hikaru smiled. It was nice to know that it wasn't only his top shelf liquor that was suffering the tribulations of a competitive global economy.

"That is something my father can help with. He knows many people at the Trade Ministry and in Public Security. Although there is no stopping the inspections, there is really no such thing as a 'random' check. You only need to avoid the … unlucky containers. And as my friend as told me …" The young prince gestured in Hikaru's direction. "This sort of capacity will radically change your business model."

Wakagashira Chiba did not look toward him, but smiled for Kujo Michihiko. "It would allow us to move much larger quantities … or other, larger products."

Still so greedy.

The Kujo heir simply nodded at all of this, his small smile a permanent fixture. "Once we have established the trust between us, there may be larger opportunities in the future." He sipped his usual drink. "You already know what my father would request in return."

"The construction contracts on the Spacecraft."[80]

"Nothing as much as that. You only need to guarantee that Fuji Heavy Industries withdraws their bid, paving the way for CBI-Hitachi."

Michihiko was uncharacteristically precise.

"The contract will ultimately be worth billions."

"There are other projects, and the games are still years away. So they will merely be passing on one opportunity in favor of another. This is the first step on a long road. Consider it an investment into the business we can facilitate for you."

---

[80] The nickname for the new 2020 Tokyo Olympics stadium in Shinjuku.

It was the perfect bait for Chiba Ken, who smiled like a shark. "I think we can do business."

Now it was Hikaru's turn. "Wakagashira Chiba-sama, please allow me to oversee the first shipment." He bowed as deeply as the table allowed him. "You know I used to handle this sort of thing before I … began working here." Before his arrest, ouster and exile. "Kujo-sama and I are well acquainted, which will ease things along. Please, allow me to do this."

Chiba made a show of considering the offer, glancing toward Michihiko.

"I would be happy if he was involved," his friend said. The reference was helpful, although his tone was noncommittal. The prince would not let the deal suffer on his account.

The wakagashira's answer was predictable. "Hikaru-kun has a bad history with this sort of work. I worry he would only fail again, given such responsibility. But if you desire his involvement, I will allow him to serve under one of my more trusted men. Moji-san?"

The man with the wraparound sunglasses and the cruel smile dipped his head in acknowledgment.

Michihiko surrendered readily. "Splendid. Now, let us celebrate our new found partnership."

With that, the deal was made, leaving Hikaru to play the happy host to his fickle friend and worst enemy. Rising, he moved off to find a couple of the girls to replace him. Asuka was working the lounge for the first time that night, so he sent her to the table where the two men remained.

February 16, 2020. It had taken several weeks to put things together, but that night, the first of the new shipments would enter the

Shinagawa[81] container terminal. The oldest of Tokyo's commercial freight ports, it was now almost entirely mechanized and automated. Each container would be transported by magnetic lift and rail, its manifest transmitted and checked against both ship and port records. With several thousand units entering the port a day, most were subjected only to the most essential of security scans for explosives or radiological threats. Only a handful faced physical inspection of their contents.

The container sitting on the concrete pier before them was not one of those.

"Open it." The voice belonged to Moji Sumio. The cruel thug had gotten shot in the interim while working as a bouncer at The Bijou, but he had recovered quickly.

One of the other men working with them had the codes for the lock. After a moment, the doors at one end of the rectangular blue container swung open with an ominous creaking sound. Moji nodded and several men moved in, shifting through the smaller crates packed inside. Hikaru looked on, standing guard on one of the flanks. Near the warehouse, more containers stood stacked in rows.

Digging through the front row of boxes, filled with everything from sneakers to cases of women's hand soap, the men finally came upon what they were looking for. Moving a layer of decoy products aside, one of the men lifted their prize: a cellophane and tape-wrapped kilogram brick. Tossing it back for Moji to inspect, he unpacked another from beneath it and then another.

"Leave it. There's several tons in there and we have arrangements to move the whole container."

---

[81] A part of Tokyo that literally means "River of Products."

The men had only started reloading the extraneous cargo when the pier flooded with light.

"Public Security! Drop your weapons, place your hands behind your heads, and step away from the container!"

The next moment was chaos.

They had arrived in several vehicles. They fled toward them in equally patchwork fashion as the circling drones adjusted their green algae-halogen floodlights, sweeping after the scattered, fleeing figures. An armored police vehicle rolled into view ahead of them and another stopped to the side, blocking their avenues of escape through the canyons of corrugated steel. A gunshot sounded, followed by more. Moji ran for the warehouse. Hikaru pursued, gun in hand.

The warehouse was immersed in darkness, lit only when the eerie, sweeping searchlights hit a single window, but its vast interior echoed every sound. From outside, they heard more gunfire and blaring megaphones, barely dampened by the walls. Inside, he could hear his prey's footsteps and guess at his location when the intermittent green light flashed over the maze of containers.

"Traitor! This was all a setup!"

The shout echoed too, and Hikaru made a guess at his target's position.

"Chiba should have let me kill you!"

He wasn't about to return the favor by giving himself away for the sake of a reply.

Hikaru turned between two crates and the green light poured in. He could see Moji, but only a moment. He considered firing a shot, but held. He could barely see, and in the narrow confines between the metal containers, the ricochets could go anywhere. Holding his breath, he began moving slowly forward, waiting for the next light. Then he lunged.

Hikaru wasn't armed beyond his handgun, but he had another weapon, courtesy of the man he was about to kill. Moji saw him coming, in the last moments, as the green light flooded the warehouse once again. Armed with a short blade, he slashed as Hikaru came for him.

Hikaru caught it in his left cybernetic replacement hand, bending the metal. Then he smashed his right palm upwards into Moji's elbow, against its natural bend, breaking the arm holding the blade.

Moji screamed in pain as Hikaru threw him to the floor. Hikaru loomed above Moji with his handgun in his "good" hand, a distinction that now seemed superficial. This close, he wouldn't miss, and the concrete floor would absorb the slug. He began to squeeze the trigger as a light swept over them both.

But this one wasn't from the windows. Turning slightly, he could see the PSB officer moving down the metal corridor toward them both. He wore riot gear and carried a submachine gun with an under-slung light. Hikaru tensed, then began to lift his hands in surrender.

"Asahara-san?" demanded the officer.

He nodded.

The officer approached closer, lowering his weapon. Then, strangely, he drew his sidearm and offered it to Hikaru. "It will look cleaner if he's found with one of ours in him," he explained. "A justified shooting during the raid. My instructions, from our mutual friend, are that this is to look like a regulation operation. No evidence of an internal squabble to 'complicate' the narrative."

Hikaru nodded, saying nothing. Michihiko had never explained the entire plan, but he was beginning to grasp it. Taking the officer's sidearm and holstering his own, he looked down at the man on the floor, pinned underfoot with his shirt open enough to reveal the Buddhist icon tattooed on his chest.

Hikaru reconsidered his earlier thought and transferred the weapon to his left hand before squeezing the trigger.

February 17, 2020. With the morning glare coming through the window, Hikaru rolled out of his futon, leaving the covers in disarray and only half concealing the form still resting there beside his vacated place. He admired Asuka from that angle for a moment before rising and heading to the bathroom.

Standing before the mirror, he unwrapped the bandage around his palm and examined the torn synthskin where his hand had caught the blade. He could see the movement of the exposed servos behind the gash. Quickly, he replaced the bandage, and proceeded on his normal morning routine. He checked his messages as he brushed his teeth. Several alerts stood out.

PSB RAID NETS YG YAKUZA, COCAINE, AT PORT
CABINET MINISTER CLAIMS SUCCESS FOR ANTI-CRIME LAW
NO BID CONTRACT SCHEME—WHO STOOD TO GAIN?

Hikaru skimmed through briefly, then dismissed them. Asahara Hikaru now had all the pieces of the puzzle. He knew about Eugi's involvement with Sumiyoshi-kai Oyabun Sugawara, and that Moji had betrayed him on Wakagashira Chiba's orders. Only Hikaru knew that Chiba, Eugi, and Moji had all been secretly working with the Sumiyoshi-kai to win the Olympic stadium contract for CBI-Hitachi. *And* he had the information on the TSE AI which Asuka had given him in exchange for her lucrative new job as a hostess at The Velours.

That meant Hikaru was the only man in Tokyo who knew that: (1) Chiba and Eugi's faction in the Yamaguchi-gumi was angling for a shot at leadership of the clan by working with the Sumiyoshi-kai, and (2) the Tokyo Stock Exchange AI had gone rogue and manipulated a Yamaguchi-gumi sniper into assassinating Sumiyoshi-kai oyabun Sugawara to start a war between the clans. Leaking this information to Oyabun Kitano would mean the Yamaguchi-gumi would have to fight a civil war within the clan while at the same time defending itself against the Sumiyoshi-kai's retribution for the death of Oyabun Sugawara. Not to mention the other clans waiting in the wings. A war on multiple fronts could tear apart the Yamaguchi-gumi.

Hikaru was certain he had some kind of an edge over his rivals. But with the allies he'd picked and the depth of the conspiracies, it seemed as though Hikaru might end up destroying his kingdom before he ever claimed it.

So be it.

About the Author

Dan Seidel is a student and enthusiast of Japanese language and culture, and received his Master's in East Asian Studies from George Washington University. He's a proud New Yorker, but has lived in Washington D.C. and Tokyo. A lifelong gamer, this is his first foray into the professional side of the industry as a freelance author.

The Coward's Ultimatum

by Vishal Wilde

Japan won the Second World War;
Now the yakuza are starting the Third!

The Coward's Ultimatum

BY VISHAL WILDE

January 23, 2020. Shinjuku, Tokyo. Ryuk-kun was about to discover Kitano-san's temper the hard way. The *really* hard way, by my calculations. Kitano-san, an oyabun of the Yamaguchi-gumi, ran his own turf: the Kabukichō red light district in Shinjuku. He was ambitious from the start and when the Yamaguchi-gumi kumicho[82] in Kobe sent him to take over Tokyo's Kabukichō, the conquest only served to whet his appetite for more of the city. Then came Ryuk-kun, whose despicable behavior was unearthed by Kitano-san. That behavior would be dealt with accordingly.

Kitano-san had to rule with an iron fist if he wanted to see his hopes of one day running the Yamaguchi-gumi's Kobe headquarters materialize. And that's all he wanted: to make it to the top. No one was going to get in his way, especially not that sniveling worm,

---

[82] Clan godfather or "Chairman." The "capo di tutti capi," "boss of all bosses," or "oyabun of all oyabun." Each clan has a kumicho who stands at the top of the pyramid and controls one oyabun for each city in Japan where the clan operates.

Ryuk. The constant skirmishes between rival clans trying to make inroads into Kabukichō was a source of great anxiety for Kitano-san, who took the district from the Sumiyoshi-kai in one of the Yamaguchi-gumi's biggest coups, and that day he had called his crew to a high-end nightclub to "celebrate" their recent victories.

Among the crew and the consortium of beautiful geishas, Ryuk-kun and I were present. Now I'm not ashamed to say it; I'd set him up. It was not that I had anything personal against Ryuk-kun, but I did what needed to be done and Ryuk-kun's death was merely instrumental. Really kid, it was nothing personal. Try not to curse me in the afterlife.

"Here, here!" Kitano-san called. We all sat down at the table as if we were Kitano-san's watchdogs. The geishas were exempt from his command, though some did voluntarily sit. Sake, several varieties of tea, tofu dishes, chicken dumplings, beef ramen, sushi platters, and much more were served along the long wooden table. Kitano-san had asked Ryuk-kun to sit at the opposite end of the table.

"Kabukichō is at war and we must work tirelessly to crush the invaders." He smiled at the irony, since they were invaders themselves not so long ago. He raised his tokkuri of sake and continued with a solemn voice, "but we can excuse a little celebration, can't we?" I chuckled to myself as they all laughed, but for an entirely different reason. All of us downed our sake: a toast before the deed, possibly even *to* the deed.

"But come now, we are at war, and in wartime, it always pays dividends to take things a little more seriously. As warriors, our conduct on the battlefield is paramount." Kitano-san paused again, pouring some more sake for himself. "And today, my fellow warriors, it is necessary to expose a coward in the ranks." We looked around in astonishment, some in anger, some in shock, and some in confusion. I played my part on this stage of hypocrites and acted confused.

Ryuk-kun withdrew into himself. He knew Kitano-san refered to him and he must have realized his time had come.

"And cowardice must be exposed and dealt with accordingly," said Oyabun Kitano. "Ryuk-kun, stand up." All eyes focused on Ryuk. I could see every inch of his body struggling to heave itself upright under the weight of shame and dishonor. He trembled and stared at the floor in disgrace as Kitano-san addressed him.

"Care to explain what happened in your little altercation? Who were you fighting with? Or rather, should I say, *fleeing from?*" Kitano-san drew his sword and pointed it at Ryuk-kun from across the table.

"Kitano-san, they were yakuza but we could not identify their clan," Ryuk answered. He was kept his eyes pointed at the floor. It was as if the fog of war itself had descended upon the room and, unknown to everyone around me, I was that fog.

The Fog: quite a name. It would make a nice alias wouldn't it? Yes, you can call me The Fog. I wouldn't want to risk you discovering my real identity and jeopardizing the whole operation. Ladies and gentlemen, The Fog has descended, it has enveloped all, and it is purposefully confusing.

"Listen to the coward!" Kitano-san shouted. "He ran so quickly that he couldn't even identify the enemy! We must be the laughing stock of our enemies by now, that too, from a senior warrior like Ryuk-kun. No matter what you have previously done for the clan, this is inexcusable."

Ryuk-kun had been involved heavily in the clan wars. He was one of the young, top dogs in Oyabun Kitano's army. He was even renowned for his bravery, so why would he have suddenly chosen to run away? Because of what I did. Why did he not know who his enemies were? That was me as well. Call it one of the undocumented wonders of the world that even the strongest heroes, with the physiques of titans, can be slain through psychology.

In school, they call psychology, unlike say engineering, a "feminine" science, the domain of fortune tellers and hostesses. Perhaps this is why certain ladies of the night far outstrip men in martial strategy.

Hidden warfare: that was what Ryuk-kun and Kitano-san were both experiencing.

The Fog descends, it envelopes and it confuses, but does it strike? Hidden warfare is an art, my friend, and you will learn all about it from me. Needles like me are hard to find in this haystack of brutish thugs. They talk war and they fancy themselves warriors, but the needle in the haystack will bleed them dry. I am The Needle; I am The Fog; I am The Hidden Warrior. These idiots follow their passions, and they ebb and flow with the ever-changing, discordant heartbeat of war. But as for me, I always check the pulse. I always monitor the situation.

"Ryuk! Is this true? Do you not remember what I taught you!" Kamei Daichi shouted. He was another senior fighter in Kabukichō. His deep voice, his massive, imposing figure, and the numerous dragon tattoos he sported made him known throughout Kabukichō. When Ryuk-kun looked up at Kamei-san, I could see the sadness in his eyes, whilst all everyone else could only see him as the coward who had brought dishonor upon them. Kamei-san valued loyalty above all. He mentored Ryuk-kun, so the kid must have been feeling the pain right then. What a pity. It didn't have to be so emotional. Ah well, he'd be put out of his misery soon enough.

"And how are we going to deal with the traitor, Kitano-sama?" Kit Yamaguchi, a foxy young vixen in Kitano-san's ranks asked the question. You know, you can only take horses to the water but these asses actually *choose* to drink. And hey, we've all made use of our fair share of work mules.

"Kit poses a good question, Ryuk-kun." Kitano-san tapped his sword pensively against his shoulder. "Look at me, Ryuk." Ryuk obeyed and his gaze met the oyabun's piercing eyes. "Do you know what our ancestors did when they faced the prospect of capture or of certain defeat? Rather than be taken alive by the enemy, they would take their own lives to prevent disgrace and dishonor. You, Ryuk, have already brought disgrace and dishonor upon the clan; no matter what you do or say now, your life will end today. The only question that remains is this: will it be my blade or your own? Normally, I would just take a coward's life, but in recognition of your past deeds, I will give you the opportunity to take your own. The choice is yours, Ryuk-kun." Kitano-san spoke with a solemn tone. A tense silence descended upon the room as all eyes went back to Ryuk. They reminded me of flies swarming the rotting corpse of a dead dog.

I imagined what was going through Ryuk's mind as it raced in panic. He must have felt ashamed that he fled but he must also have been thinking back to what the Shinto shaman said. The shaman was my intermediary, an intervening cause between Ryuk and I. The shaman ensured that he would flee from an encounter where he would have normally stood his ground. I believe in the spirit realm: in higher powers, in kami, in divinity, or whatever else you'd like to call it. These things just influence me in a different manner than the way they influenced Ryuk.

Ahh, I digress—more on that later.

Think of what must have been going through the man's mind. Think of what happens when you have been given this ultimatum by your own clansmen: "Lose your life your way or our way." The last free act you have in this life is how you end it. It's beautiful, but nonetheless, I can't help but inwardly wince in horror at the very thought of being put in a situation where loss of face is so public and inevitable.

Ryuk-kun drew his own sword and inverted it, so it was facing his stomach. We all watched, still silent, but it felt like Ryuk's heartbeat was pervading and pulsating throughout the room. At each heavy beat, we wondered when the deed would be done. Seeing this, Kitano-san laughed and spoke once more to the martyr, still using the intimate suffix, "-kun," as if the man about to die were his own son.

"Ryuk-kun. Through the stomach is painful and it is the brave man's way. Tell me, when someone looks at your body and hears your story, would they think that the death was fitting for the circumstances? Make it fit, make it flow. Life is a song and a poem, Ryuk-kun, and you have the chance to write its final line." At this, tears rolled down Ryuk's face, but the resolve to end his own life was unwavering. He lifted the blade higher and turned it horizontally. Kitano-san was known to be ruthless when dealing out ultimatums, and yes, indeed, it would be known throughout Kabukichō that Ryuk was given this ultimatum. All the clansmen would know that this was the price of cowardice under the iron fist of Oyabun Kitano.

It was also intended to show the rival clans that Kitano-san was not fooling around. Sure, these were his intentions, but little did he know that this would all contribute to his downfall.

The subtle game of The Hidden Warrior is completely missed by imbeciles such as him, Kamei-san, and Kit-kun. When The Fog descends, it envelopes and confuses, but it all feels so natural to them that they have no idea what has ensnared them. Unbeknownst to them, they are puppets on my string. Puppet Master, The Fog, The Needle, Hidden Warrior … I keep adding to a nice little repertoire of apt aliases. Ahhhh, yet again, I digress!

"That's right, Ryuk-kun. Die in a way that is fitting for the disgrace you have brought upon us," Oyabun Kitano said as if Ryuk were nothing more than low-life scum. Such was the way of our world: no matter how virtuously we might act, no matter how high and mighty the righteousness is that we seek to fortify our characters with, just one sin is enough to cause the entire façade to come crashing down in bloody awe.

Ryuk-kun slit his own throat. As the blood poured forth onto his chest, he fell to his knees and watched the world disappear as he lost consciousness. Soon his miserable, lifeless corpse lay sprawled across the table and blood stained the food and the carpets. Everyone had obviously lost their appetite, but this just served to whet mine: for my appetite was tied firmly and solely to the desire for conquest.

"Kitano-san, those were bespoke carpets! You could have at least told me you had something planned for tonight." One of the most prominent geishas in Kabukichō , Naruse Riko, was hosting us. Her part in all of this, I will make clear later.

So why am I doing all this? Well, besides the smuggling activities, drug peddlers, liquor shops, gambling dens, and all else that was commonplace in yakuza strongholds, the Kabukichō district was especially renowned for the sheer number, range, variety, and quality of its brothels. The enormous amount of taxes and protection money collected by Kitano-san from the brothels delighted the kumicho of the Sixth Yamaguchi-gumi, [83] so much so that Kitano-san came to be

---

[83] Each kumicho reforms his own clan from the ashes of its predecessor. The fifth Yamaguchi-gumi was operated by a relatively wise kumicho who managed to die peacefully, of natural causes, at age 96.

known as the Prince of Kabukichō .

I'm one of his tax collectors, by the way. You won't be able to trace me with that: there's quite a few of us, full-time and part-time. Plus, I do some other jobs for him as well, so I'm not wholly a tax collector (though that's how I like to think of myself). I'm more of a senior, trusted handyman in the district.

Protecting the geishas had also earned oyabun Kitano the respect and reverence of several prominent geisha houses across Kabukichō .

My story starts with one, relatively unknown young geisha that the Oyabun Kitano crossed one fateful day. That young geisha was my lover. Angel. She called herself Angel. Her death triggered a domino effect that will culminate in the end of the Yamaguchi-gumi's current leader. Soon enough, he will watch his precious Kabukichō go up in flames.

Although many geishas were allowed to withhold certain favors from clientele, Kitano-san was accustomed to having his way with any geisha he wanted, within reason, of course. The prominent ones and their favorites were spared Kitano-san's voracious sexual appetite).

He tried to have his way with Angel one night but, by then, she and I were in love. She had lost a lot of income because she had given up sleeping with clients and only entertained them with dances and conversation.

We had made plans to leave Kabukichō and start a new life together in the mountains. Angel told me that she would tell me her real name when we finally made it out to a rural village. I constantly dreamt of that magical day when all the one yen coins would add up to turn our musings of a life together into reality.

That son of a bitch Kitano had to screw it all up. Mark my words, he will pay with his life.

A couple of Angel's friends were present when it all happened, and they were real close to her. They told me everything. Kitano told her that he was looking to have a good time, to "play," but she begged and pleaded with him to spare her because she was already in love with another man. He asked her who her lover was, but she refused to give a name; she cared too much about me to do that. Her friends even pleaded with oyabun Kitano. They offered themselves to the dog, but he wouldn't have it. The mutt had to have his fill.

His guards made her friends watch as he made an example of her; he raped her and then, as if that wasn't enough, he stuck a dagger through her guts. He even twisted the blade.

He made an example of Angel. So … you think I'm going to make an example of him too? You think I'm going to show him the "power of love" or some other bullshit like that? Nah, I'm not that fucking stupid and I'm not that petty either.

I'll make something more of him, something far more than a mere "example." As you just heard, oyabun Kitano believes that "life is a poem." The more I ruminate on the matter, the more I love the sound of my own poem: the sound of Kabukichō on fire and Kitano-san gasping for breath and, that too, all over the body of a dead geisha.

So there you have it, ladies and gentlemen. An inferno was set alight in my heart from the moment I heard of Angel's death. Right now, all they are feeling is the smoke but soon enough, The Inferno will engulf them. For this duty to the heart, ordinary men are too weak. I have been transformed. I am The Inferno fuelled by an undying love for a dead Angel.

We still had to deliberate and vote on other matters before the night concluded. At that point, we called some of our bodyguards to retrieve the body for safekeeping; Kitano-san had not finished with it. He wanted to make more use of Ryuk.

If you sat through enough Yamaguchi-gumi council meetings, you would quickly come to realize that Kitano-san is not an oyabun in the traditional sense, but a modern-day dictator. Like all dictators these days, he has grown adept at harnessing the power of democracy. Well, harnessing is one way to describe it. Manipulation might be more fitting.

Whatever you want to call it, he utilized unanimity in voting for his proposals across the council as a means of legitimizing his fascist regime. Of course, we all voted out of fear (of one thing or another) but that's what democracy is. Don't let any passionate, idealistic bullshit convince you otherwise.

I have no allies in Kitano's council, not his wakagashira, Chiba Ken, nor his wakagashira-hosa,[84] Matsuhono Eugi. They are all swine to me and I could take them each out, one by one. But Kitano is my priority. When The Fog envelopes, when The Needle bleeds him dry, when The Hidden Warrior slays him, there will be only one name on his lips: "Angel." Angel will flash before his eyes, and I will watch as the Lord God Almighty extracts his ugly soul from his miserable, writhing body and feeds it to the kami of the local well.

Of course, to bring down a mob boss like Kitano-san, you can't just use psychological, hidden warfare. Certainly, hidden warfare is of primary importance, but you also need to get your hands dirty. Even in conventional warfare though, I'm somewhat different to the rest of my clansmen. In this era of cyber-kinetics, artificial intelligence, digital dog-shit and all that crap, I choose more traditional means. Leave the hacking to the geeks, leave the software to those cyberpunks. The only hardware I need is my repertoire: Susanoo, my handgun, and my twin swords, Amaterasu and

---

[84] Deputy underboss.

Tsukoyomi. I'll take on those cyberpunks the good old-fashioned way.

Call me what you may, but if you listen closely enough, you will uncover the nobility in my treachery.

About the Author

In Vishal Wilde's life, God is the Supreme Being (he has no religion) and Freedom is the Supreme Principle. He wants to devote his life to fighting for and defending Freedom, Free Will and the Free Society and, to this end, he serves Her Majesty as a member of the Royal Naval Reserve and he writes for the Adam Smith Institute (a libertarian public policy think tank). He aspires to work in academia, cyber security, naval intelligence and public policy whilst producing creative writing throughout his life.

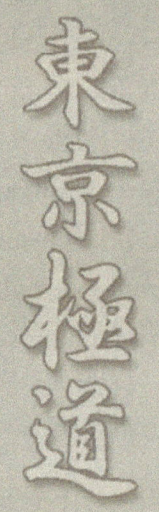

Tokyo Yakuza
#11

Mob Dance

by Matthew Alan Thyer

Japan won the Second World War.
Now the yakuza are starting the Third!

TOKYO YAKUZA #11

Mob Dance

BY MATTHEW ALAN THYER

January 24, 2020. Roppongi, Tokyo. "Hey, Mago. You playing, man?" Haegol's voice came through. Kim "Mago" Jihoo muted the voice channel coming into his audio implant momentarily. A competing conversation entering the feed distracted him, botching his killing blow. The game would have to wait a moment. There was real yen at play across the street.

Jihoo set down the haptic control pad and peered through the optical scope just as his mark reached out and grabbed a skinny waiter in white. Frustration was plain on the mark's sunken face. Anger was an unusual emotion to see on the face of any ill-boonin,[85] especially someone even loosely associated with the Kempeitai Thought Police. After what appeared to be a brief, irritable dialogue, the boy ventured down the narrow hall lined with imitation Russian pine toward the kitchen, presumably to fetch another tokkuri of warm sake. More booze was a good thing, Jihoo knew.

All the same, Jihoo's face puckered at the memory of the cloying stuff as he watched the man sipping from the tiny cup. There was

---

[85] 일본인 - Korean description of a Japanese person.

plenty for Jihoo to dislike here in Roppongi, but most of all, he hated the flavor of everyone's favorite drink. He would happily munch cheap VegiPure™ tempura at Mr. Doughnut for the rest of his days if he was never offered another sip of that ttong.[86]

To Jihoo's palate, soju was far tastier, even after nearly a year of operating inside the empire.

Jihoo's mark for the evening's mission, Akio Minami, Inagawa-kai wakagashira and interim oyabun while the senior members were gathering to elect Noburo Akira's replacement, did not seem to have much in the way of a drink preference. Tonight it was warmed sake, cheap and plentiful. Two weeks ago, when Jihoo had received the contract, it was Best Thai Whiskey. On most intervening nights since then, Jihoo had watched Minami drink away a small fortune, almost never partaking of the same drink twice. If the mark had any taste left, it certainly was not very discerning. Jihoo suspected that Minami drank to forget.

Jihoo smiled. He had figured out Minami's tell. He could now reliably predict, based on when the old man would get blitzed on cheap rice booze, that he would invariably and subsequently go visit his favorite ofuro.[87] The background check and bank statements confirmed this pattern of behavior for as far back as Jihoo could afford to investigate. Akio Minami would visit one of several cheap imitation sushi joints, get stumbling drunk on warm sake and then make his way to the same Ofuro No Osama[88] bathhouse. There, he would presumably soak away his cares and all that remained of his

---

[86] 똥 - Korean, dung or shit.

[87] Wooden soaking tub.

[88] 風呂の王様 - Japanese, King of Baths. Chain of semi-legitimate Japanese style bath houses found in and around Tokyo and elsewhere. The Inagawa-kai is paid protection money to ensure Thought Police compliance and also maintains a limited trade in prostitution, drugs and body modifications through these establishments.

buzz, neck deep in hot water and whores.

Jihoo expected that Minami would go through two more tokkuri before making his way to the bathhouse. That's what his credit statements read like, anyway. Jihoo figured he could afford a few moments of inattention so he refocused the sound sensitive laser on the front window of the sushi house, tuning the invisible beam to better hear Minami above the clatter of the kitchen. Then Jihoo returned his attention to the real time strategy game playing in his heads-up display.

"Sorry about that, Haegol. Something came up at work," Jihoo subvocalized into his throat pickup.

"Tell them they need to pay you more, Mago. Shit man, we got pushed way back in the lane," said Haegol, commenting on their lack of success at the digital multiplayer game.

"Yeah, you can leave a comment on the Seven Star crowd-source review page. I'm sure they'll take that into consideration during my next review," Jihoo replied, sarcasm in his voice.

The second game was better than the first. He and Haegol pushed their opposition back just enough that they could farm resources for high points, thus gaining a ladder win. The two of them jumped up a tier.

As the victory screen played, Jihoo turned up transparency on the game feed in his heads-up and checked on the mark. Minami had started to fade at the little side table. That had given both the restaurant server in the sushi joint and Jihoo some extra time to get things done.

So when Haegol had to take off to do some homework, Jihoo was ready to stop playing. He logged out of the game and finished up his laundry, finally folding the same load he had washed and dried six times that evening. Minami was on his fourth bottle of sake, so Jihoo felt it was safe to call a delivery drone to the laundromat.

With his kit safely stowed aboard the little robot and on its way back to the hotel room, he stepped into the public toilet at the back of the Roppongi laundry facility and began to stuff his street clothes into his rucksack. The jeans would do, but he took off his shirt so he would not overheat, hidden within the folds of the photo-adaptive suit. He checked the battery readout, just to make certain it was fully charged, and set the suit through a complete cycle of self-diagnostics and calibrations.

These suits were useful but, unlike military-grade thermoptic camo, they were notoriously temperamental. Even a little dust or lint would turn you into a walking blank space of inaccurately reflected light and the model Jihoo owned was infamous for developing a static charge that would attract ambient particles. With the diagnostic cycle out of the way, he toggled the "on" switch, using the tongue-manipulated control ball embedded in the roof of his mouth, and watched himself fade into little more than a shimmer reflected in the cracked latrine mirror.

Jihoo picked up his rucksack, slinging it over a shoulder, and confirmed in the mirror that the photo-adaptive fabric of the bag correctly synchronized with the rest of his suit. The batteries inside the pack were on the heavy side, but he suspected that this mission would require a long burn. This was his first and best chance to make a name for himself with the Seven Star Mob. Jihoo intended to fulfill the contract with unforgettable style.

To isolate Minami, he would first need to get into an Inagawa-kai-controlled bathhouse without raising any alarms. The message had to be delivered there, or near the Inagawa-kai stronghold, since all Minami's other common hangouts were probably heavily monitored by the rival gang or the Thought Police. If Inagawa-kai caught Jihoo infiltrating the bathhouse, he would be in deep ttong for sure, but that was not likely, given his recent procurement of the photo-adaptive suit and the suite of new bioaugmentations now soaking in bodily fluids deep inside his skull.

Jihoo stepped out onto the busy downtown street, hugging the wall to his right. Kodokushi[89] rushed by, walking along a moving concourse only a few centimeters to his left. The ubiquitous moving walkways gave rise to a concrete no-man's land between the building fronts of Roppongi, and this space had proven useful to Jihoo on more than one occasion.

He spotted Minami making his way to the spa on the far side of the street. Jihoo jogged ahead, using the narrow band of sidewalk between the store fronts and the moving walkway. One of the reasons he enjoyed his time in Roppongi was all this negative space that did not exist back in his remote hometown of Gwanak-gu, or even in occupied Seoul, for that matter.

Had anyone bothered to look, they might have noticed a distinctly man-shaped hole in the reflections cast on the glass to Jihoo's right. This brand of photo-adaptive suit was also bad at replicating reflected light cast against glass, but wrapped up in their own concerns, no one noticed him as he juked and dodged through the crowd like a ghost.

He reached the entry gate of the ofuro before the mark arrived and he ducked behind a large potted tree to wait. He watched Minami stumble through the crowd on his way to the bathhouse. Jihoo initiated a quick, nonintrusive scan of the area. The scan found

---

[89] 孤独死 - "lonely death" refers to the phenomenon of people dying alone and remaining undiscovered for long periods of time. Additionally, used as slang to describe those who are lonely, appear lonely, or as a derogative term.

two IR monitors on the underside of the awning in front of the ofuro. The remaining devices were all visual cameras, likely tied into a closed-circuit and monitored by Inagawa-kai enforcers in a room somewhere behind the front desk.

Minami stumbled as he stepped off of the automated walkway, then he passed beneath the awning before the entrance to the ofuro. He mumbled a drinking song, failing to carry a tune, and shuffled through the door. Jihoo followed him through, discharging a micro-chaff cartridge as he followed. The microscopic dust particles would mask any heat or EM-signature he was emitting as he entered the room.

"Welcome, Wakagashira Minami-san," said the automated desk attendant. Jihoo figured that the robot was likely using facial recognition software to see and name Minami. As long as he stayed out of sight, he imagined he would remain undetected and, more importantly, unidentified.

The android handled bath allocations and room assignments, but Minami would need to locate a poju[90] if he desired the services of a paid escort. If the old man went that route, then Jihoo's job would be more difficult. But he resolved to handle that situation if and when it arose. The android continued, "Would sir like the usual, or can I prepare anything special for him?"

"Nothing special, Reiko-ni, just the usual," Minami mumbled. "Wait," he corrected himself. "Can I have a big bucket of shaved ice and the window room? The one up high?"

The android's speech recognition software chewed on his slurred words for a moment. It replied, "Very good Minami-san." Two fluffy, white towels appeared from a door beneath the counter. "Shall I

---

[90] 포주 - Korean, pimp.

notify the rodo[91] of your visit?"

"No, no. Not this time, Reiko-ni. No business please. I'm just here for a soak. With the Olympics on the way, the Kempeitai has been putting on the pressure. They are particularly scared of a Soviet soccer victory this time around. I am never certain I'm going to make it to retirement, eh? But 'knocked down eight times, get up nine' right?" Minami said. He took the warm towels from the drawer.

"Very good, Minami-san. Please follow the green lighted path to your room," said the robot. It opened the magnetically sealed door on the left side of the desk. Jihoo crept into the elevator car a moment before Minami waddled aboard. He did not need to scan this room; the monitoring equipment was in plain sight inside the cart. Jihoo released another micro-chaff cartridge, filling the chamber with ablative nano-particles to shield his presence from the scanners. With Minami inside, the door closed and the elevator lighting changed to a calming shade of green. The rapid shift in light made Jihoo stand out in the corner of the car momentarily, but the inebriated mark missed his suit's glitch entirely.

The two of them stood in the tiny elevator car face to face, almost touching. Jihoo calmed his breathing and remained still. If the drunkard so much as brushed him now, his photo-adaptive suit would mal-function and even the dumbest monitoring equipment in the Inagawa-kai's arsenal would surely detect him. Minami resumed singing his tune again as the elevator climbed high into the Tokyo skyline.

"Open the damn window," Minami shouted as he entered his assigned ofuro room. Steam rose from the hot bath, and the window,

---

[91] 主 - Lord, master or head of the house. Chief, person in charge. Used to denote management of Inagawa-kai owned property.

set into the side of the skyscraper, looked out onto thousands of illuminated buildings in Roppongi's ever-expanding skyline.

Jihoo parked himself in a corner of the small, wood-lined room and initiated another scan with his tongue stud. This time he performed a full capability sweep of the space. He needed complete privacy for what would come next.

Minami sat down on the bench next to the hot pool. The window to the room opened on quiet, well maintained hinges, and the man nudged the large plastic bucket of ice between his legs. He cupped both hands and extracted a pile of frozen water, burying his face in his chilled palms. Minami repeated this several more times before he paused, brushed his hands off on one of the towels, and loosened the neck tie, garroted around his neck in best government dress fashion.

Jihoo's room scan came back positive. He scrolled through the list of countermeasures sharing the room with the two of them: acoustically tapped walls, pressure plates showing up as voltage variations throughout the space, and a slow scanning laser working its way around the room. Jihoo switched his vision over to high band and pinpointed the laser scanner. From its mounting gimbal on the far wall, it radiated a fan of ultraviolet across the room, but he was still in Minami's shadow.

Chang na,[92] Jihoo thought to himself. *Going to have to get him out of here to do this right.* He looked over his shoulder, wondering about the hallway outside the little room. *A viable option,* he decided, but kept searching. The window, approximately two and a half meters square, was all the way open now.

Jihoo could not see the street below but he could hear the traffic and noise of the city well enough. Through the window, he could

---

[92] 짱나 - Korean, Short for 짜증 나. Idiomatic expression used to express feelings of annoyance or frustration when something does not going as planned.

plainly see the metal girders of a sky rise under construction. It sat incomplete on the far side of the four lane road some forty stories below Minami and himself. *That's going to have to do*, he decided. He allowed the faintest of rustles to emanate from his position as he armed his favorite pet, *the frog tongue*.

He powered up the bioaugment that inhabited most of his left arm and watched his battery energy reserve plummet on the readout in his embedded optic lenses. Things were starting to get real, but none of this could be helped. The ofuro had been too big to scout out beforehand and besides, there had been no way of knowing which room Minami might get. *Time to move*, thought Jihoo.

Jihoo raised his arm and lit up a laser range finder in his fist. Some of the sensors in the room would likely register the infrared beam emission, but he didn't plan on staying here long. When the frog tongue gained a positive lock on a girder set above their floor, he let the creature spring to life. It lanced through his sleeve, a long line of pink and tender fleshy substance, now visible beyond the photo-adaptive suit. It clung to the metal surface on the construction site, many meters away.

Minami's face was comic in its surprise. Jihoo wished he could have taken a photo of it as he grabbed the man around the waist and ran for the threshold of the open window. The frog tongue had already begun to pull in its mad rush to take up slack. Jihoo jumped, taking the weight of the pear-shaped Minami plus his own on his single arm. The frog tongue could handle the strain, but the extra weight hurt his left shoulder as the bioaugment grappling hook yanked them both toward the far building. Wind rushed past his face and Minami wailed in either surprise or fright, Jihoo was not certain which.

Their landing on the construction site, a couple of floors below the crossbeam where the frog tongue anchored, was graceless and more than a little painful. Minami rolled and then curled up in a ball to whimper in the corner of the half-finished room. Jihoo rose to his hands and knees and breathed as deeply as his body would allow.

When the shock of the grappling maneuver had passed he stood and walked over to the man lying on the bare concrete of the floor. His photo-adaptive suit was now covered with a light coating of chalky dust from the freshly cured cement. With his hands on his knees, he sucked wind and cursed the powdery coating that was making this piece of his kit shine like a beacon in the city lights.

He flinched as the frog tongue fully retracted into his flesh. That uncomfortable moment forced Jihoo back into mission mode. Jihoo needed to get the suit off and hide Minami before anyone realized what had just happened. He pulled the suit top over his head before the glow turned him into the perfect sniper target. The pants and battery pack went dead as soon as the cables disengaged from the power supply.

"Get up," he wheezed at Minami. "I've got a message for you."

The little man seemed completely consumed by fear, pain, or both, and his whimpering did not abate.

"Get up," Jihoo barked, stuffing the photo-adaptive suit into his pack. "I'm not going to hurt you. I'm just a messenger." Jihoo gently kicked the man, trying to prod him into action. "Well, I mean I'm not going to hurt you *anymore*. Get up anyway. You have to see this before the rest of the Inagawa-kai realize you're gone."

The old man didn't budge from his corner. "Get up," Jihoo shouted. He grabbed hold of Minami's shirt and jacket, lifting him to his feet. He looked around, searching for a position that was less exposed. The Inagawa-kai were going to see them both. In fact, it was best to assume they already had.

Jihoo took a couple of deep, calming breaths and rolled the cursor around in his mouth, looking for options. The spatial awareness software had already mapped most of the floor they were on, displaying it in his vision with a wire frame grid. *There.* He found a set of stairs heading up. *That will work,* Jihoo thought to himself. He threw the old man over his bare shoulder and jogged toward the hallway. The Inagawa-kai wakagashira was not that light, but Jihoo took the stairs as quickly as he was able. He climbed the building, huffing and sweating like a nosae.[93]

Jihoo did not stop until he reached the top floor, his uncertainty driving him ever higher. The door to the roof had not been installed, so he simply walked Minami out onto the top of the sky scraper, beneath cranes and among building supplies. Jihoo held onto Minami's collar as he set him down on the roof. *Just in case,* he reminded himself. *Because the mark might try something unfortunate.*

The man clung to Jihoo's out stretched arm with both hands. "No, please, don't hurt me. No." His whimpering took a new shape and Jihoo growled involuntarily, fanning his fear.

"Look, you're not dead. If you were supposed to be dead, you'd be dead already. I didn't snatch you from that room because I'm supposed to kill you. There's a message for you. I'm pretty certain it's something you're going to want to see," Jihoo said. He realized that he hadn't the first idea about how to calm this guy down.

The older man momentarily peeked out from behind his closed eyelids. He let go of Jihoo's bare arm, wiping tears and snot from his face. Jihoo pushed him up against the edge of the rooftop. "Don't do anything unfortunate. I'm not here to hurt you," he repeated.

"Who are you? What do you want?" The man's voice was choked and not much more than a whimper. He could not yet look Jihoo in

---

[93] 노새 - Korean, mule. Beast of burden.

the face, though Jihoo hoped he might recover. Still, there was something like calculation running under Minami's eyes. The recognition that this situation would probably not end his life had taken root and Jihoo knew that he had to keep Minami off balance in order to complete his job.

"Look, I'm just a messenger. I want nothing of you other than a private moment of your time: 'private' being the most important word in that sentence. The message I bear comes from Shon-seonsaengnim.[94] He's the one you need to talk to," replied Jihoo.

The man looked around in momentary disbelief. "That chon[95] crime lord?" Minami managed to dredge up enough indignation to confront Jihoo and spat a racial insult. "Nothing! I want nothing to do with those kimchi yaro.[96] Nothing." Minami turned and started for the stairs before Jihoo laid a restraining hand on his shoulder. Jihoo paused a moment, considering his next move. He was not going to take it personally, but he decided that Minami had it coming. He tossed him easily against the low wall at the edge of the building and pushed the fat man against the edge, maybe a little too far.

"Watch what you say, ggondae.[97] You can insult me. Call all Koreans roaches, I don't care. But I'll be the one who does the squashing. I've got enough dirt on you to see you hanged, and that makes me wonder what the Seven Star Mob has in their databanks back on the peninsula." Now it did not feel so much like fumbling. Now Jihoo was able to take advantage of years of practice he had

---

[94] Master Shon.

[95] チョン - Japanese vernacular nickname for Koreans, with strongly offensive overtones.

[96] キムチ野郎 – literally, "kimchi bastards" in Japanese.

[97] 꼰대 - Korean, clueless old man, normally an authority figure, who takes advantage of his power and resists any changes.

gained extorting protection money from jjokbari[98] imperialists.

"Now, I'm going to let your insulting nature slide, just this once, because I'm under orders not to hurt you. You're going to sit down, shut up, and pay attention to this message." He fished around his pants pocket for the data stick. "Or," he said, stretching the bluff. "I'll take your refusal to listen to this message as a failure to play well with others. I can chuck your ass off this roof if you fail to play well. Got that?"

Minami nodded his head, his intimidation and resentment plain on his face from his tight, pressed lips. Jihoo pulled a data stick from his pocket and plugged it into the bottom of a deck which he removed from his rucksack. He snatched Minami by the wrist and pressed his thumb into the data device, unlocking a secure connection back to some computational engine, likely buried back on the peninsula.

Thousands of microscopic mirrors moved into place within the confines of the palm-sized device, issuing a buzz, barely audible above the dense Roppongi street traffic below. When he set it down on the concrete roof, many LEDs illuminated a holographic projection of Uijang[99] Shon Kyowon's face. From behind, Jihoo could see dust motes and air pollution swirling around inside the image of his mob boss. The program finished its connection process and addressed Minami in perfect Japanese.

"Minami Akio, the Seven Star Mob has been watching you. We see a man increasingly compromised, a man attempting to leverage the wealth and privilege of his superiors, but doing so in an unwitting fashion." A new projection appeared next to Shon-seonsaengnim's avatar and long lists of transaction records scrolled

[98] 쪽발이] - Korean, racial slur used to describe Japanese Imperialist living in colonized enclaves on the Peninsula.
[99] "Chairman" in Korean. The clan boss of the Seven Star Mob.

past: all of it undeniable evidence of wrongdoing against the imperial government and the Inagawa-kai. "A man trying to escape the consequences of his deceptions merely by hiding from the full understanding of what he has done," said the hologram.

Knowing that he was not supposed to listen in on the message, Jihoo stepped away from Minami and the avatar of his boss. Minami seemed to slump as Shon-seonsaengnim's avatar continued pointing out all the flaws in the man's current state of affairs.

Jihoo imagined this was Shon-seonsaengnim's set up and eventually the exchange would become a negotiation of sorts; not the sort of negotiation where transfers of ownership were debated, but the sort where limits were the topic of discussion. It was a kind of social calculus in which one party described a rate of decay while the other attempted to slow that rate. It could be a negotiation of how fast someone's reputation, liberty, or health might crumble and turn to dust, for instance.

Shon-seonsaengnim had a reputation as the kwanjangnim[100] of the shakedown. Everyone knew that Shon's rise to prominence in the Seven Star started back at the blockhouse, the same place that Jihoo now occupied. Some said he clawed his way there, but others said he had not needed to expend that much effort. Jihoo believed that it was the simple mastery of the shakedown that propelled Shon's rise. That, coupled with his ability to walk the Sinzo[101] perfectly.

Jihoo had met Shon once before in the flesh. His tattoos glowed with mu[102] from beneath the shaman's thick, silk robes. Jihoo's uncle

---

[100] 관장님 - Korean, grand-master of a martial or combative art.

[101] 신도 - Korean, "way of the gods." Korean ritualistic shamanism which may incorporate martial art, augmentative technologies, and sessŭmu religion/mythology. Forbidden by the current Imperial Japanese governor.

[102] 巫 - Korean, the supernatural energy harnessed by sessŭmu shaman through ritual practice, tattoo channeling (both simple ink and bioaugmentative), and martial discipline.

had explained that Shon had attained that level of mastery using only traditional tools and inks. He had relentlessly tapped octopus ink under his own skin using bamboo barbs, cut and cured from a grove he maintained. Shon had taken the long, slow Sinzo path and gained much. Jihoo would emulate his boss, but he preferred technological shortcuts like the frog tongue where he could find them.

Although Jihoo had moved away from Minami as instructed, the temptation to eavesdrop was too great. He knew there would be an unforgettable ribbing from Haegol if he returned to the Korean peninsula without a story to tell about Shon-seonsaengnim. He tongued his oral interface, scrolling through a series of stem-menus. He bumped up the sensitivity of both ears and amplified the signal traveling along his auditory nerve bundles, playing with the settings until he had both the avatar and Minami dialed in. He stood motionless and listened.

"Kempeitai internal system access," Shon-seonsaengnim said. "The same sort of information you've already been buying for the Inagawa-kai. That is the Seven Star price. Specifically, we require access to monitoring systems in the Olympic athlete camp."

"But if the other Inagawa-kai ever found out," Minami protested.

"You mean if the Inagawa-kai discovers you've been selling secrets to Seven Star before they discover how deeply you're in bed with the Kempeitai Thought Police? Minami-san, you've been stacking cards. The Inagawa-kai will kill you if they discover any of this. They may kill you just because they've tired of your drinking. They already have access to the Kempeitai monitoring systems and they know you're not capable enough to replace the oyabun; why do they need you anymore?" Shon-seonsaengnim asked.

"We want access to those systems. We'll obtain access with or without your help, so why are you making this so difficult? In exchange for your assistance, I've offered you Seven Star Mob protection. You will be on an anonymous boat to North America days before the opening ceremonies. That's a place where the Emperor and the Inagawa-kai cannot touch you, and you'll have more than enough credit in hand for you to retire in comfort."

"But that place is such a koya[103] and the people there are barbaric. How do you expect me to live?" Minami bit down hard on Uijang Shon's hook and Jihoo smiled as the master began to reel in his catch.

"Minami-san," the avatar of Shon-seonsaengnim said with a growl. "Take a moment and consider your alternatives. Do you want to come live here in occupied Korea? Your house of cards has already fallen. If we know about your indiscretion, so does Inagawa-kai. The only reason you remain valuable to anyone is that the Kempeitai have made no move to cut you off from the Olympic management program. We're offering to extract you from this terminal situation: a situation of your own creation. The Seven Star Mob will set you up, and you get to keep everything you've already earned or stolen. Ultimately, we'll make certain you don't wake up one morning at the bottom of Tokyo Bay."

Jihoo turned just enough so that he could watch the man out of the corner of his eye. Minami slumped over, collapsing in on himself. An implosion of personality was underway. Maybe it was the booze letting him down, or more likely it was the realization that he had no choice, but Jihoo could see that there was no fight left in the man. He would give Shon-seonsaengnim everything he had asked for. Maybe more. He would give the Seven Star backend access to the

---

[103] 荒野 - desert wilderness or wasteland.

Kempeitai domestic monitoring program. The Inagawa-kai's ace in the hole, a strong connection with the government, would belong to the Koreans.

"Shon-san," Minami began plaintively, but the avatar cut him off.

"Minami-san, do not condescend to me. I represent the worst of a proud and capable people: a people who will rise once again." Shon-seonsaengnim's voice projecting from the little holographic device was adamant. It silenced Minami. "You may address me as 'seonsaengnim' and that is concession enough. Prove your worth, Minami-san; prove it to me and you will die a comfortable and anonymous death. Cross me again and suffer the fate you have made for yourself."

An uncomfortable silence grew from the dusty concrete roof as Minami gathered his wits and considered his next words.

"Yes, Shon-seonsaengnim," Minami said. He cut himself off, realizing his mistake, and bowed his head.

The avatar glared at the man a moment longer, then said, "Good, Minami-san. Prepare yourself; a second life awaits. Now call over that eavesdropping fool, Jihoo, so we can finalize arrangements."

"Is this the best you can do?" Uijang Shon-seonsaengnim asked Jihoo. "Are you sure? I want you to understand something, something of critical importance to you at this point in your life. Dealing with mobs is like dancing with fire."

Shon-seonsaengnim let an uncomfortable silence slip between them, waiting to see if Jihoo might interrupt. "Just so you realize fully and completely why I am retaining you at this point, I'm going to let you in on a little secret. Below you are six Inagawa-kai who've just breached the construction barrier of this building. They are armed to the teeth. I suspect they mean to use these weapons on you and, perhaps, even Minami-san."

Jihoo's eyes sprang open in surprise. He started to say something, but the avatar of Shon-seonsaengnim barked and regained his attention. "So, this is how it's going to play out, Mago. And yes, I know all about you. Those induction tattoos on your shoulders: I can wear you like a skin. I control the mu for all the Seven Stars and those inks let me see from the blackness behind your eyes." Shon-seonsaengnim continued to talk to him as Jihoo searched for an escape route.

He could hear the voices of the Inagawa-kai kill squad echoing up the stairwell. "You've got your story to tell back at the barracks, but it has got to grow much better before you'll get that opportunity. You'll now need to escape, with that two-timing marshmallow in your care, and get him to a safehouse: or better, the Honmoku-futo wharf."

The Inagawa-kai were getting louder, the stomping of their heavy boots thundering up the hallow shaft. Minami had once more frozen in fear.

"Do this, Jihoo," the holographic avatar of Shon-seonsaengnim continued. "And I will double your payout. Fail, and don't bother to come back."

The halo projection went dark. The voices coming up the stairs were close enough now that Jihoo could make out what they were saying as they cleared each floor. These were not simple thugs, but professionals on a hunt. Jihoo's situational awareness suite was coming up with ttong, as it drew egress lines down the stairwell and over the edge of the building.

Even though had he a weapon, Jihoo knew that he was outnumbered and outgunned. He turned on Minami and yelled,

"Want to live?" The old man simply nodded his head, too terrified to speak. Jihoo stepped up atop the short wall at the edge of the building. "Put your arms around my neck and hold on." He gestured to Minami, who followed his directions.

Jihoo turned his back to the void beyond the edge of the building and armed the frog tongue. There was no way it would stretch the whole length of the skyscraper. Jihoo picked a floor near ground level and prepared himself to fire the bioaugmentation. Into Minami's ear, he said, "I mean it. Hold on tight!"

Jihoo pulled him in tight with his right arm just as the threatening faces of the Inagawa-kai, looking over muzzles, began to fill the open threshold of the rooftop doorway. Jihoo leaned back with Minami and let gravity take them both.

The air rushing past his ears was louder and more menacing than it had been when they had crossed between the buildings. Perhaps it was the three-round bursts of auto-rifle fire crackling from above. As Minami screamed in terror, Jihoo concentrated on counting the floors passing centimeters from them.

The range finder was tracking their distance from the building with precision and they had reached terminal velocity, floors above. Jihoo aimed and fired the frog tongue, still unsure how much further they had to fall. His left arm took the load, immediately threatening to pull his shoulder out of its socket. The fibers in the frog tongue were stretching well beyond their rated tolerance. They slammed against the outside of the building, hard, and came to a stop, but Minami managed to cling to Jihoo. The bioaugmentation was not designed for this kind of use. The battery readout in his heads-up blinked an alarm.

The hit squad took a couple more pot shots at the two of them as they dangled only a couple of floors above the ground. Their auto-rifles were made for close quarters combat and the slugs went wild long before they got anywhere near Jihoo or Minami. The sound of police sirens followed the gunfire, adding to the cacophony.

"Lighten up." Jihoo forced the words out. "You're choking the crap out of me." He glanced over a shoulder, looking for a place to land. "I'm going to let go. Let go of me and be ready to roll into the fall when I do." Another volley of shots echoed down the urban canyon.

Jihoo counted out loud. "Three, two, one." He let the frog tongue relax its grip on the building. They fell the last few meters to the ground, each rolling in their own direction down a pile of gravel.

Jihoo's bioaugmentation lay fully extended on the ground. "Help me," he shouted at Minami, who was brushing dirt off his suit jacket. "I can't retract it. No power," he said, stuffing sixty some meters of his frog tongue arm into his rucksack.

The chaos engendered by the police response to the Inagawa-kai hit squad helped them both escape. The gunfire drew even the Palace Guard to the construction site in Roppongi, where they dropped onto the scene from above in their red and gold power suits. Minami and Jihoo slunk away as the Inagawa-kai and police exchanged fire.

The ship, Daigo Fukuryu Maru,[104] stewed in the pungent waters of the Honmoku-futo wharf. Moored at the end of an out-of-the-way pier that creaked its impending demise with every step they took toward the vessel, the boat stood out in the olfactory funk. Jihoo

---

[104] 第五福龍丸 - Lucky Dragon 5. An oceangoing fishing vessel.

could not quite tell how, but the Daigo Fukuryu Maru somehow smelled even worse than its surroundings.

A short man in a thick rubber suit stood next to the walkway leading to the boat. His jacket was unzipped and fish blood stained his chest.

"This must be Minami," Hidekazu Shiomi, the first mate, said, laughing at the two of them. "Welcome aboard the Fukuryu Maru," he said. He gestured up the narrow aluminum walkway. "Head on up there. One of my crewmen will show you to your quarters."

Jihoo made to follow Minami but discovered a stout hand pushing against his belly. "You Mago? You must be. Why you think you can come aboard my boat?"

Jihoo looked down at the short fisherman. "That's my contract." He pointed after Minami. "I want paid."

The little fisherman stepped between Jihoo and the boat and snarled. "That's my boat. The contract is now in my domain." The little man paused to pull back his yellow slicker, exposing an oversized handgun riding at his hip. "He gets debriefed and dumped as soon as the Seven Star Mob gets what it wants out of him. You got a problem with that, Mago?" He sneered.

Jihoo let out a huge sigh. "This reminds me of something I just learned," he said. "'Dealing with mobs is like dancing with fire.' Take a step to the left and those flames will follow you." Jihoo unshouldered the bag containing most of his frog tongue. "Move to the right." The fisherman followed the movement of Jihoo's free hand as he gestured in the opposite direction. "And you'd best be ready for a warm spin."

Both of the men looked down the pier into dark, humid air. The greedy little fisherman in the thick rubber slicker started to ask, "What's that supposed to -"

Jihoo interrupted him with a punch square in the nose.

"It means you've got to know how to dance!"

About the Author

Matthew Alan Thyer, best known for his hard science-fiction and speculative cli-fi, is a Jack. Prior to finding his voice as a writer, he worked as a signals analyst, linguist, operations engineer, wildland firefighter, backcountry ranger, kayak guide, and river rat. Matt's hobbies include trail running, backpacking, skiing, mountaineering, bicycling, and paragliding.

Tokyo Yakuza
#12

Blood in the Headwaters

by Josh Vogt

Japan won the Second World War;
Now the yakuza are starting the Third!

Blood In the Headwaters

BY JOSH VOGT

January 25, 2020. Ueno, Tokyo. "I don't understand, Gorou. Why we killing him again? Get our money back?"

Gorou sighed as he led Isamu down the piss-stinking warren of back alleys. The Inagawa-kai thugs shuffled past whimpering beggars, ancestral upload temples, moldering food carts, and trinket hovels. Eyes watched them from all angles, peeking around corners or peering down from the shabby apartments above, their faces pressed against grimy windows. The watchers no doubt carried an endless array of contraband and weapons, always eager to leave a stripped body dumped in the gutters for a rare cop patrol to find.

Fortunately, Gorou's companion's muscled body rippled with vibrant yakuza tattoos, marking him as a local enforcer. Those who might've taken advantage of Gorou's slight frame quickly faded into the night once they spotted Isamu stalking beside him.

"It's not just the money," Gorou said. "We were cheated. If we'd lost fairly, I might be inclined to let him live and just salvage my wounded pride."

"But ..." Isamu scratched his bald head. "You cheat. You hide our money."

"That's different." Gorou fiddled with the chain of antique copper yen around his neck. "I use my natural intelligence to keep family funds from being detected by pokers and priers. I dig invisible data caches and craft coded treasure chests to secure our financial future. That's cleverness, not cheating. But this Susanoo asshole, he fleeced us with the help of a few neural enhancements."

"How do you know? He beat us at menko.[105] Easy game. Got lucky."

"Exactly." Gorou snapped his fingers. "Sometimes, yes, people just get lucky. Some combine luck with skill to heighten their chances. This guy, though, I realized too late he was doing the impossible. I calculated the odds of him throwing those menko cards so precisely every time: astronomical, to say the least. He's wired. Must have a nani-net or flashchip in his brain. Must have a vector program running on his bioware, letting him figure all the factors ahead of time."

Isamu's hands curled into massive fists, knuckles ridged with scars. "He cheated."

"Yes. And we're not just going to get our money back; we're going to make sure he doesn't cheat anyone else ever again." Gorou paused and glanced at the branching alleyways. "If I can find his damn hideout."

---

[105] A simple card game played by placing a card on a surface and trying to flip the other's player's card by throwing one of one's own cards at it. The menko cards are beautifully illustrated with samurai, ninja, soldiers, baseball players or anime characters.

The other night had begun with them and a band of brothers wandering through bars, pachinko parlors, and smoke dens, celebrating a recent territory expansion and the flush of funds that came with it. In their drunken haze, Gorou and Isamu had wandered away from the group and stumbled across Susanoo's open-air lair. There, they lost everything they had on hand and drained their personal accounts to the dregs in just a few rounds of a child's game.

"We lost?" Isamu asked.

"No," Gorou said. "Shut up. I've got everything under control."

He moved toward a side path that looked like all the rest. A giggle from the shadows made him freeze.

"Look, Takeshi. Handsome travelers. Are they here to play or pay?"

Isamu turned, fists raised as a woman appeared beside them as if from nowhere. Recognizing Suki, Susanoo's dolled-up kitsune-looking companion, Gorou shoved Isamu's arms down.

Fox ears poked up through the girl's shoulder-length black hair and a fluffy tail trailed out from under her crimson skirt. Both ears and tail twitched as she moved and Gorou wondered if the additions were biological or cybernetic implants. Odd adornments, but he'd certainly seen stranger. Perhaps Susanoo pimped her out on the side.

She bowed. "Oh, gentlemen. I did not recognize you at first. It is an honor to have you visit our fine establishment once more."

A rat scampered past her heels and hunched in front of the pair, whiskers twitching in what Gorou imagined to be disdain.

"Takeshi!" Suki waved the rodent off. "Get away from our distinguished visitors. You'll soil their lovely clothes." She bowed again. "My apologies, gentlemen. Okoshi Takeshi of the Sumiyoshi-kai has forgotten his manners ever since being reborn as a rat. A few months probation will teach him to call himself 'The Animal' and bet against me."

Gorou cleared his throat, ignoring her obvious insanity. "We're here to see Susanoo. I've an offer to make."

She spun and crooked a finger over her shoulder. "This way, gentlemen."

Her tail swished as she guided them along, taking turns until Gorou had wholly lost his sense of direction. Maybe she'd charge them to be led back out again. At last, they turned a corner into a crooked path lined with gaudy neon signs, toppled garbage cans, and ratty clothes, strung out to dry overhead.

Susanoo sat in the middle of the alley like a pauper emperor ruling over his domain of filth. Floppy orange hair kept falling across his dark eyes and his silk tunic hung loose over his skinny frame. Cards, coins, and empty bottles littered the area: evidence of other games and drunken wagers.

A couple girls loitered in the shadows, dressed to distract. Off in a dark threshold, a man wept softly in one girl's arms, crying about how he didn't dare go home after having lost so much yen.

Susanoo riffled a pack of well-worn cards in one hand and smiled beatifically up at Gorou and Isamu. He spoke in a sing-song, childishly soft voice.

"Hello, fellows. Back to kneel at the feet of the king?"

"Cheat," Isamu said, before Gorou could hush him.

Susanoo's tongue dabbed his lips. "You wagered. I won. What matters more than that?"

Gorou stepped in front of Isamu. "Obviously we had so much fun we had to come back for another round."

"You have more to lose?" Susanoo asked.

His eyes glittered in the neon glare and Gorou envisioned the nano-network shining behind those optic nerves. *Fucking cyber-cheat.* Gambling engrams had been outlawed almost a decade before, but unless one had a neural scanner it remained difficult to catch an operator in action. Only his genius at coding and calculations had clued him in.

"Same game. Menko." Gorou drew a card pack from his shirt pocket. "Except this time, we use my deck."

He dumped the cards out and fanned them. Each card held stylized images of samurai, shinobi, yakuza, and other iconic Japanese figures. Each card's tri-D surface also projected said images into fully three-dimensional holographic displays. The figures looped through a few seconds of dramatic motion when presented.

Susanoo smirked. "Shiny." He waved to Suki. "Sniff, my pet."

Suki approached and held out a slim hand, showing her shimmering nails, filed to points. "If it pleases you?"

Gorou shrugged and handed her the pack. She fanned through them, her gaze keen. Gorou kept his breathing steady, trying to keep his pulse from racing. *Nothing to worry about.* Let her inspect all she wished. The secret coded into the deck's holo-displays wouldn't activate until run through the set pattern.

At last, Suki returned the deck and nodded to her master. Susanoo kissed her hand before letting her withdraw to the side. He cocked his head, studying the pair.

"But my friendly fellows, I already emptied your pockets. What other gifts can you bring to the bargain?"

"You took *our* yen, yes," said Gorou. "But I am Inagawa-kai. I have access to hundreds of financial accounts, all safe and secure and stuffed with yen. I can offer you ten times what we played for before."

Isamu grunted in alarm beside him, but Gorou ignored him, keeping his gaze locked on the game master.

Susanoo's eyes narrowed. "Gambling boss Noboru Akira may be dead, but you'd risk the wrath of your new oyabun just to try and best me? And after I sent you scampering with tails tucked?"

Another rat skittered by and vanished between Suki's heels. *The same one she'd chatted with earlier?* Gorou shook off the distracting thought.

He bowed his head. "I am already dishonored by defeat at your hands. How can I continue to serve my family if I know my skills are so poor as to be entirely at your mercy? Give us this chance to reclaim our standing."

"Give Suki the registry numbers for these accounts," Susanoo said. "Prove your validity, and then we may indulge your vice."

Having expected this, Gorou produced a data tab. Suki once more sidled up, now with a tab scanner in hand. Her tail twined around his thigh. It made his skin tingle, but he forced himself to focus until she completed the scan. She blinked at the amount on the readout; that reaction alone seemed to satisfy Susanoo.

"Terms of the tournament?" he asked.

"Best two of three rounds," Gorou said. "Isamu and I hold equal shares to yours, and if either of us wins, you forfeit all."

The gambler held his hands out. "Join me in worshipping the whims of Fortune."

They took a seat on either side of Susanoo, who cleared a space between their feet for the card throws. Suki came over and began massaging the back of Isamu's neck. He rumbled in appreciation. Gorou shot him a warning look, not wanting him undermined by simple wiles at this juncture. He still needed to play his part in ensuring that Gorou got out of the area alive after they sprang the trap.

He gave the holo-cards to Susanoo, who shuffled them and divvied the cards up into three equal piles. The men took up their share and Susanoo laid a card in the middle. The display showed a samurai in a grimacing mempo[106] flourishing his katana.[107]

Gorou leaned forward on the steps serving as his seat. Practically every child in all of Japan knew how to play menko. All one had to do was throw a card at the other player's card, using the impact or resulting wind to flip it over. A successful flip meant the thrower took the cards as a prize until one player possessed all the cards.

Yet the last time they'd played, Susanoo had thrown his cards without err. Even in this drafty alley, the slightest breeze had worked to his advantage and he'd taken all the cards with ease. Gorou guessed that Susanoo's upgrades not only let him calculate the necessary angles for a flip, but also allowed for precise motor control.

And so it seemed as they began the first round. While Gorou and Isamu held their own for a few minutes, Susanoo flicked and flung his cards so the others flipped like trained hounds on command. Holographic samurai thrust tanto while ninjas threw darts at invisible enemies. Geisha performed fan dances and yakuza tattoos came alive in midair. The holograms displayed a kaleidoscope of glowing forms and figures that created a miniature theatre, a private performance that dazzled their audience.

It barely took ten minutes for Susanoo to gather the whole pack. As he grinned at Gorou, his left cheek and eye twitched.

"Ready to face the inevitable?"

Gorou hid his own grin at the facial tics. *Pattern in place. Program running.* One more round was all he needed. "Yes. Let's finish this."

They reshuffled and redistributed the cards. Gorou laid a card down first this time, his fingerprint against it activating the final

---

[106] Samurai mask and helm.

[107] Samurai longsword.

subroutine. Susanoo stared at the horned oni the card displayed for a moment longer than usual, unblinking. Then he shifted back into motion and threw his own card, flipping Gorou's as usual.

The rest of the round progressed much like the first, until Susanoo made a final throw and flipped Isamu's last card. He reached to collect them, but his hand shook above them, unable to quite get a grasp.

The gambler's face transformed into a mass of twitches and tics. "I ... w-won? Y-you l-l-lost and m-must ..."

Susanoo's stutter turned into chattering teeth. His body locked in place, as if straining against invisible bonds. Then he toppled to one side, twitching and choking.

"Susanoo!" Suki dashed to her master and held him as he convulsed. The other girls shrieked and vanished into the night.

Gorou couldn't hide his smile any longer. Isamu's face rumpled in a deep frown, but he stood as a pillar of security, eyeing the area for any possible threats.

Suki brushed the hair away from Susanoo's face and dabbed the drool off his lips and cheeks. Her eyes snapped up to Gorou, fury making them seem to glow.

"What did you do to him?"

Gorou rose, yawning and stretching. "He would've been perfectly fine if he hadn't been using his neural implants to cheat." He scooped up the cards and patted the deck. "The hologram light-coding contains an added algorithm: my own work. When viewed in a particular fractal pattern, it inserts a virus directly into an enhanced cortex, inducing a total logic collapse and permanent brain damage."

He'd used the same trick on a few money-laundering competitors who'd upgraded themselves to try and match his natural skill. It was necessary to keep himself invaluable to the yakuza, who came to him for his special brand of accounting.

Susanoo stared up at the night, eyes glazed and expression slack. Blood oozed from his nostrils and tear ducts, streaking his face. Suki choked a sob and bent over to kiss both his cheeks. Then she fixed Gorou with another predatory glare.

"Fools." She spat at his feet. "I spent years developing his talent and now you've ruined it."

Gorou frowned as he slipped the cards back into a pocket. "You … what?"

She rose, her lips stained and hands dripping crimson mucus she'd wiped from Susanoo's face. Did her fingernails look longer? Sharper? How did the glow in her eyes brighten even as her hair draped shadows over her face?

Isamu stepped into her path, palms out. "Lady, no fighting. Don't want to hurt you."

"I can't extend the same courtesy."

Suki slashed a hand faster than Gorou could follow. Isamu collapsed in a spray of blood, a gaping wound opening in his throat.

"Shit!" Gorou whirled and sprinted down the alley.

He took turns at random, relying on desperate speed to get him out of the area rather than any orientation. Horror clogged his lungs and clouded his mind. What was that bitch? Some kind of 'borg beast? A vengeful spirit brought to life?

Mist congealed at the end of the row he ran down, forming a curvaceous figure with fox ears and a tail. How'd she get ahead of him? He spun to dart down another path, only to find it blocked by another misty Suki. As he spun, a dozen foggy versions of the woman surrounded him. They stepped in, closing off any escape.

He dropped to his knees. "Please … I'm sorry … I didn't know …"

A sharp nail curled under his chin, forcing his head up to meet Suki's flaming gaze.

"Ignorance is the excuse of the weak," she said.

A blazing spike shot up through Gorou's mouth and into his skull. He twitched as she withdrew an impossibly long and gore-streaked nail from his head.

The fox-tailed wraiths converged, dragging him down into realms of icy darkness.

Suki licked the blood from her fingers and combed her ears back. The Inagawa-kai yakuza coder's body cooled at her feet, his soul rising from it like wisps of steam. She retracted her nerve-steel claws and fangs while letting her biochem amp-surge ebb. As she stabilized, she pondered her next steps.

Poor Susanoo. Suki'd have to pay a meat maestro to remove the implants and flush out the virus. No doubt the ex-gambler would die in the process: not that living would do him any good now. It'd take time to find another suitable candidate, one who could handle the processing demands and who'd prove malleable enough to her will.

Suki crouched and took the death-coded deck from the corpse along with the data tab containing the financial records. She despised setbacks, but at least she could salvage new resources from this upset.

Takeshi nibbled at her ankle and squeaked. She nodded.

"Yes, I know. We have time." She headed down an unlit alley, mist swirling to close in behind her. "We have all the time in the world."

About the Author

A full-time freelance writer and editor, Josh Vogt has sold stories to *Paizo's Pathfinder Tales*, *Grey Matter Press*, the *UFO2 & UFO3* anthologies, *Intergalactic Medicine Show*, and *Shimmer*, among others. He writes for a wide variety of RPG developers and his debut fantasy novel, *Forge of Ashes*, is available as of April 2015. You can find him at JRVogt.com or @JRVogt. He's a member of SFWA as well as the International Association of Media Tie-In Writers.

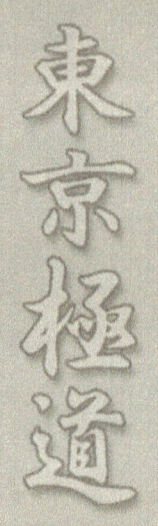

東京極道

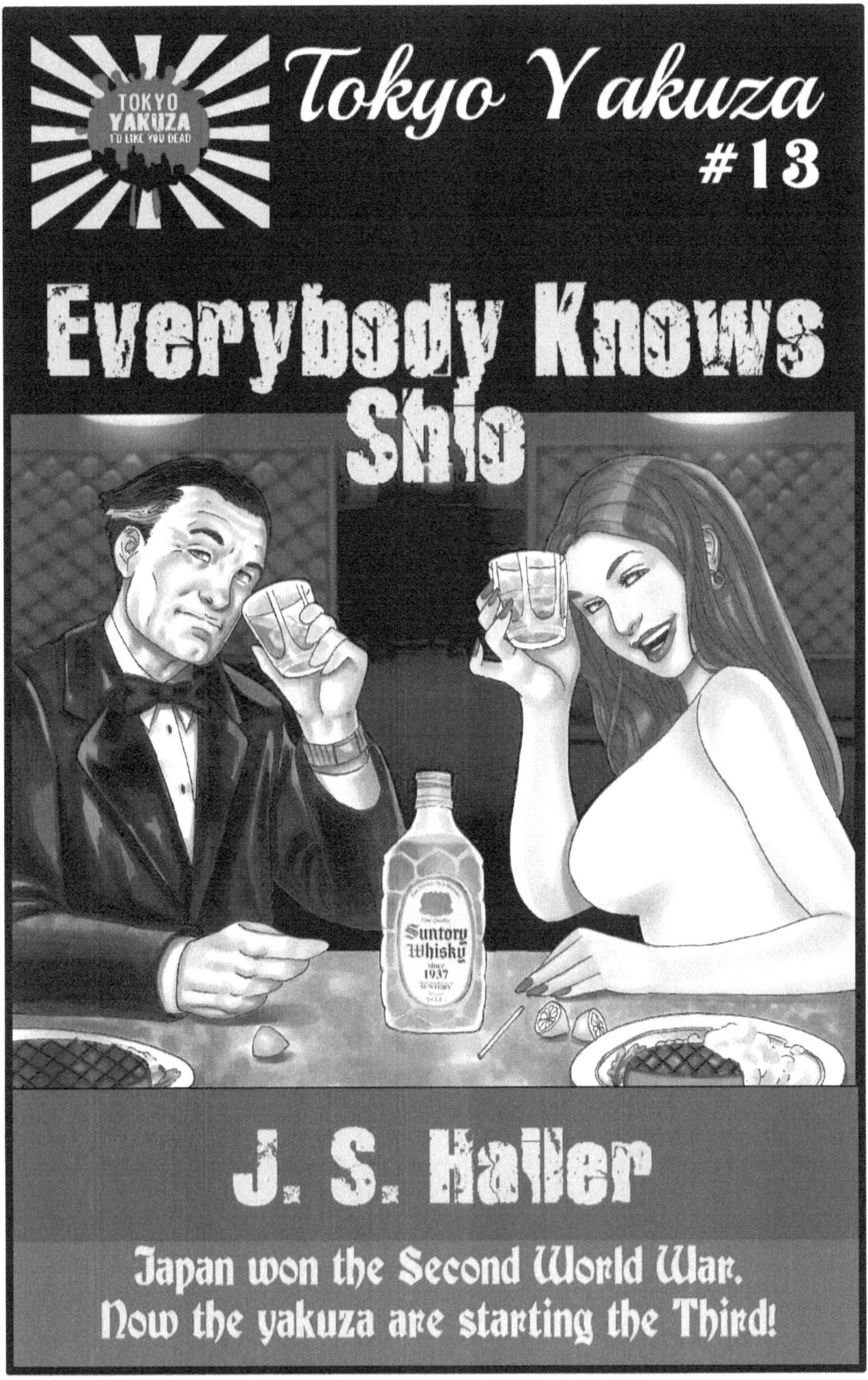

Tokyo Yakuza
#13

Everybody Knows Shio

J. S. Haller

Japan won the Second World War.
Now the yakuza are starting the Third!

TOKYO YAKUZA #13

Everybody Knows Shio

BY J. S. HAILER

January 26, 2020. Ogawamachi, Tokyo. Everybody knew Shio at the end of the bar 'cause he was a man who could get you whatever you wanted. No one knew where he came from or even when he started showing up. But the professional fixer had risen to prominence in the Inagawa-kai and was a fan favorite to replace their slain oyabun, Noboru Akira. Shio was a fixture at The Whiskey Chandler,[108] and the crowd, women and men alike, seemed to have picked up on his racket endless ages ago.

This was why everyone was confused when they saw Shio with a Chinese-looking high school girl talking to him. She wore a cloak and little else. It was an old fashioned German cloak, straight out of a fairy tale, which covered her face and kept her body in disguise. Except, of course, to those who had megane[109] extensions, which

---

[108] An authentic Scottish whiskey bar in Iidabashi - at the top of the hill and hang a left.
[109] Smartglasses.

included almost everyone in The Whiskey Chandler. Most of the patrons could see right through her hologram underclothes.

Little red riding hood shivered as she spoke in hushed tones, never looking Shio directly in the eye. Shio was rather jovial that night, only laughing at the girl and making her turn a bright shade of red. At one point, she even tried to slip him a red envelope filled with money. He pushed it back under the table and shook his head as his left hand punched in a drink order on the tablet next to him.

"Two whiskeys, one neat and one on the rocks," the bartender said, pushing the drinks towards his employer. "You know, Shio, you could have just asked like a normal person."

Shio merely waved the bartender away and handed the girl a tumbler which rolled two mountainous ice cubes, covering a sprig of whiskey. The Inagawa-kai professional downed his double with one tilt of his head, his smile never leaving his lips.

The girl tried to imitate Shio and, a moment later, ran out of the bar, holding her hand to her mouth. Outside, unused to the hard stuff, she coughed up a lung.

"She didn't even say thank you," Shio said. He rolled a laugh all the way down the bar. "Poor Akane-chan. Now, if you'll excuse me, I've got to make a call."

This was all part of the womanizing, alcoholic fixer's game. It started with the job. Second came the call, calling on whatever female Shio just so happened to be shacking up with that week. Just as he would walk outside to do so, the whole bar would comment on his new squeeze.

"What a big idiot," they all cried in the absence of their boss.

"Who does this girl think she is?"

"Who the hell just comes in here and asks for a favor like that?"

"Why did Shio take the job? He didn't even take the money."

"Do you think he's getting soft?"

The conversation fell dead long before Shio came back in from his phone call, which was why no one could immediately understand the expression on his face, now soured and droopy after the smiles and joy that had lingered there earlier.

"One more of the same," Shio said, raising a finger.

"Did she pick up this time?" the bartender asked. Shio looked up at him with a bloodshot eye and held onto his scotch.

"You pulled the 18-year on me this time," Shio said. "Yet only charged me for the 12. I think you know if she picked up or not."

"What are friends for?" the bartender said, with an understanding nod. Shio let out another little smile as he took another sip and stared into the ambrosia.

Noise had once again returned to the bar: plans being discussed too loudly, people being insulted, and the ever present tinkling of glass being picked up and put back down again. The TV in the corner continued to spread the news of the Shogi[110] Killer. If this place represented anything, it was freedom.

Then came in the second person of the day who shouldn't have been let anywhere near Shio.

Everyone knew Izumi Goseki, an Inagawa-kai chimpira who nicknamed his long, thick wooden stick his "Little Brother." He was the teenage boy who strutted his way around bars in the lower Iidabashi area. Lately, Goseki had been puffing out his feathers up at The Whiskey Chandler, trying to get a gig running with Shio.

The whole crowd was ready to give him the boot. The jokers and the clowns were intentionally riling one another up.

Goseki did nothing to help his case. He openly stole other people's drinks right in front of them. He talked too boisterously

---

[110] The Generals' game or Japanese chess.

about how he had taken on a bunch of Sumiyoshi-kai yakuza, and he was trippin' shit. He showed everyone his neck, not realizing they all had axes.

"Kid, get over here," Shio said. That shut the whole bar up. They all stared, watching Shio as he worked his way over to the old double-person phone booth which Shio had converted into a chamber of silence. No sound gets in, no sound gets out.

Goseki followed, flipping off all the patrons of the bar as he walked right behind the senior Inagawa-kai mobster. The doors were closed and not a sound could be heard from the outside.

"Some dame walked in here earlier," Shio said. "Said you was nothing but trouble and that I should do my best to leave you on the side of the road. Preferably in a boarding school in China." He spat.

"Was it my bitch half-sister?" Goseki shouted. "Why that punk ass mongrel. You know, I think I'm going to kill Akane when I get home."

"Hold it, hold it," Shio said, holding up his hands. "Look, I don't know who it was but I ain't a man who takes orders from no one but myself: which means I'm going to give you a chance."

"Wait, what?" Izumi Goseki nearly twisted his head right off when he heard that.

"When I was a kid, I was a good for nothin' just like yourself. But look at me now. I'm big time business, baby. They might even make me oyabun. Now I'm gettin' old and I need someone tough enough to take my place. So, let me tell you what I'm going to do. Tonight, I got a raid I got to do on a 14K Triad warehouse to steal some more 'E' for Insanity. The triads'll just have drugs and guns there: no cyber, no kami, nothing really fancy. I'm going to test your chops tonight."

"You," Goseki said, pointing. "Want me … as muscle?"

"Yer damned right, kid."

"You don't think I'm just some punk kid?"

"You are just some punk kid. But it takes spunk to be a punk, right? Besides, punk kids grow into bad adults, and with Oyabun Noboru dead and Wakagashira Minami out of the picture, I'm the baddest there is left in the Inagawa-kai."

"Sure, sure, whatevs," Goseki said. "You really mean it, though? You're really going to take me out?"

"Yeah. Look, here's ten thousand yen; get yourself something nice at the bar and sip it, don't take it like a shot. Do it before I change my mind," Shio said.

Goseki's eyes kept flipping back and forth between the money and the accomplished gangster.

"Go!" Shio yelled. Goseki leapt up and rushed towards the bar, leaving Shio in the booth alone. He lit up a cigarette and had the bartender send him a whiskey into the booth. He sipped on his whiskey and punched in a phone number on the ancient, wall-mounted vid-phone device.

"Yo, Miike-san," Shio said to his brother-in-arms, Miike Yuki. "Yeah, yeah. Some kid's half-Chinese half-sister came in and paid me to scare the shit out of her brother, some chimpira named Izumi Goseki. Girl's mom's a war bride or something. Yeah, you know I'm going to take him down by the old warehouse, pretend it's run by the 14K, and we can arrange to fake my death. He'll be scared shitless and hopefully run back home to daddy like they usually do. Anyway, I already set up the squibs, so all you need to do is have some guys show up. Standard rates. Just make it look real. Arigato. Ciao."

Shio drank in the atmosphere for a moment. The smoke swirled around his head and the whiskey had just started to make him wobble.

"Sit down at the shogi table," Shio said to Goseki. "Sometimes you just need to sacrifice a fuhyo[111] to capture the oshou[112] and win the game."

Shio stood up and walked out of his chambers.

"Come on kid, it's time to go," Shio said. The pair walked out of the bar together and waited for Shio's car to come up from the underground garage.

Night continued in Tokyo. The television was reporting news of the Shogi Killer leaving behind another promoted pawn piece at the site of a killing. Everywhere, books were being made in honor of the Olympics, available for yen or deutschmarks only. People who didn't need to breathe anymore were being shot and those who went too much against the grain disappeared beneath the snow and ice.

It was late night at The Whiskey Chandler, and the crowd had only been whipped up more by the fact that Shio was gone for the night. The amber-colored nectar of the gods flowed around the complex, and what cheer was there to be had amongst the patrons, now enraptured in a wild frenzy of joy.

At least up until the moment when the doors split open to reveal the beast at the edge of forever, who was cursed from the tip of her head to the bottom of her feet. She was, first and foremost, not so much fat as she was rotund. Her hair had been beaten and battered so it stood high in the air, now resembling a bleached blond bird's nest more than a mane. Her nails were a horror show; they looked as if they could rend the flesh from a man's face. Even her fake tits and

---

[111] Pawn, in Shogi or Japanese chess.
[112] King, in Shogi or Japanese chess.

Okinawa tan screamed her name: "Naka."

Across the hardwood floors, her ten-inch heels stomped loud enough that one could have mistaken her for an elephant. "Where is he?" Naka yelled at the bartender.

"What do you need this time, Naka? Money, drugs, or a murder?" the bartender asked.

"Why can't I just want to see the man I love?"

"Since when do you love anyone?"

"Who are you to judge me and mine? How dare you make assumptions about me! Why I don't know why Shio likes this place so much; you're all terrible rats."

"Maybe it's 'cause he ain't such a terrible human being," the bartender muttered, just a little too loud.

"Oh you," Naka yelled, pointing her long, fake fingernail like a katana at the bartender's face. "If you don't tell me where my Shio is, I'm going to bust a bottle across your nose."

"Oh shut up already," shouted Takenaka-san. The drunken Shinto monk in crimson robes sat at from the back of the bar. "Your husband took some kid out on a raid, get it?"

"What?" Naka yelled. Old Takenaka-san suddenly looked around for cover as the rhinoceros stomped her way towards him, pointing nails that seemed like they could mutilate a water buffalo. She grabbed the Shinto monk by the collar and lifted him up.

"Hey, wait a second! You wouldn't hurt a holy man, would you?" the priest said, putting on his best smile.

"Why. Would. He. Do. That?" Naka cried tears so large they could have filled pitchers. "He's too old to go on raids. If I warned him once, I've warned him a million times. He's too old to be going on raids. He's going to get himself killed. The goddamned idiot!"

Naka dropped the monk and ran out of the bar, screaming. She pulled out her mobile phone and started pounding away at numbers. The problem was, most of the old balding men she called recognized her number and simply put their phones on mute. Yet Naka was the sort of woman who always had a sucker or two following her around in hopes of an easy lay.

Everyone knew Shio actually appreciated it when someone slept with his wife. It always calmed her down for a spell.

The sucker this time just so happened to be an Inagawa-kai martial artist named Uchida Ryoto.

"Eh … moshi moshi,"[113] Uchida said.

"Oh, Uchida, it's terrible! Shio's gone out on a raid," Naka cried.

"What! Shio's out on a raid? Hold on a moment." Uchida hung up and then dialed another Inagawa mobster.

Cellphones rang throughout the night. The night lines lit up like a Christmas tree and, for those who were looking, the best present of all could be found sitting under the tree.

Up the chain it went. Everyone trusted Uchida more than Naka. Everyone trusted the street samurai, Ito Shintaro, more than Uchida, and the gokuko, Sasaki Kohei, more than Ito. Onwards and upwards, throughout the ranks, the message that Shio was putting himself in personal danger continued to spread.

January 27, 2020. Shimbashi, Tokyo. By the time this all transpired, it was early morning and Shio had finished driving deep into 14K Triad territory. Sure, people had called Shio to warn him, but he hadn't ever brought a phone in the car with him. He even

---

[113] "Hello?" (when answering a phone).

made sure the cars he bought didn't have phones attached, as he had lived since the '80s.

The dark warehouses had all been peaked with a snowy glaze across the surface. The ground crunched beneath the gangsters' feet as the two of them walked across virgin snow into the highway traffic-resounding din of the Shimbashi night.

"What the hell are you doing, kid? Turn those damned things off!" Shio shouted back at Goseki.

"I can't see at night without my megane extensions," Izumi Goseki said. "Night vision yo!"

"Yeah and every mook with wireless digital surveillance can pinpoint you from half a kilometer away. You want us both to get shot, you keep those things on. Come on kid, are you fucking stupid?"

"Hey, who's over there?" asked Goseki. He pointed to a snow-covered homeless man who was shuffling a pack of cards, singing quietly to himself.

"Make a fortune tonight. You too can make a fortune tonight. Just put your money down; one hundred yen will do." The man looked as if the legendary hero Urashima had just returned from the ocean kingdom: a young man with the face of an ancient fool who had just seen three hundred years in three days.

"Hey, hey, hey," the homeless old man said. "Want to try your luck at menko cards? How about tarot? I bet old 'Susanoo' can read your fortune."

"Get the hell out of here, you old bastard," Shio said. He pulled out his pistol and pointed it at the crazy drifter.

"Now, now, don't get too upset. You know this card? The nine of spades, sometimes called the nine of swords. Death and madness is the only things in the nine of swords."

"Get the hell out of here," Shio yelled. A pistol shot rang through the air and buried itself right at Susanoo's feet. The man jumped up in the air, and then he smiled and danced.

"Oh, did I mention the six of clubs? Six of wands, do you know what that means?" Susanoo asked with a smile.

"Next one's going in your head." Shio growled.

"Yo, don't shoot him, man; he's just a bum." Goseki said.

"You want to make it in this business, kid, you need to learn one thing. No witnesses to anything."

"Six of wands," Susanoo muttered, twitching. "It means we brought backup."

A moment later, Shio was blinded by algae-powered floodlights that made the whole world light up in green.

"Ah, what the hell? Who brought the floodlights?" Shio said.

"Well, if it isn't good old Shio." They heard Miike's low voice as he muttered across the wind. "A little promoted pawn thinks it's safe in the castle."

"Wait, kuso, you weren't supposed to come yourself, Miike! You were supposed to send that Chinese guy," said Shio. His frantic voice gave away his panic. "Fuck! Kid, run!"

"What's going on?" Goseki asked.

"I've finally captured the last piece I needed to make oyabun." Miike Yuki, revealed as the Shogi Killer, shouted from the rooftop as he balanced his sniper rifle. "Boys, plug him."

Miike's loyal men moved out of the shadows, submachine guns and fragmentation grenades at the ready.

"Run!" Shio shouted. He shifted his weight and pushed Izumi aside before the world turned into a chaotic hell of fire and explosions.

The first thing Goseki felt was the cold winds that blasted over his body. Shortly thereafter, he noticed the blood that covered his body. He didn't even notice that he was running until he found himself crouched inside a barrel in an unnumbered warehouse, as far away as he could get.

It seemed as if his heartbeat would give him away. Izumi Goseki's breath was so loud he felt that they must have heard it from miles away.

Back at the ambush site, a few of Miike's boys took pictures of Shio's bloody corpse with their smartphones, sending it all over to the other Inagawa-kai members. They smiled and laughed as Miike Yuki, the hitman and serial killer with crimson lips and sharpened teeth, smiled onwards into the night.

"A damned shame; he was one of the best," Miike said. "One of the best. Almost oyabun material. Almost. Of course, we all knew that his weakness was going to kill him."

"Women aren't such a terrible weakness," Suki said. The kitsune sidled up from behind.

"I guess it wasn't women per se," Miike, the killer, replied. "It was the type of women." He turned from Suki to his men. "Now, you boys get to work. We've got a lot of useless bodies left in the Inagawa-kai that we need to clear out of the way tonight. We also need to clean up this guy's corpse and make corpses of all those Chinese fools in the 14K who were going to help him fake his death."

"Yes sir," Miike's loyal minions yelled. They all stepped forward and plowed through the snow-covered land across the 14K Triad-controlled Shimbashi warehouse district.

"Wait a minute." Miike yelled at the boys who were picking up the scattered remains of Shio. "You see where the biggest chunk of his body lies? Take a good note of its position and leave it be. I want Suki to put this exactly where his heart used to be."

The wicked, smiling man, who was soon to be elected the new oyabun of the Inagawa-kai, reached into his sleeve and produced a shogi piece. He put it in Suki's hand and walked away.

Suki opened her hand to reveal a promoted pawn. She twitched her tail.

About the Author

J. S. Hailer is an old fashioned, globetrotting, New England writer and comic book artist. He's published the first three issues of his first comic, *Elementary My Dear*, which he both writes and draws. He's currently working on making comics and teaching English in Chonburi, Thailand.

Tokyo Yakuza #14
Protection Packet

By Andy Goldman

January 27, 2020. Shinjuku, Tokyo. Neon dripped and drizzled, reflected in the silver puddles that lined the Kabukichō back alley. Nakashima Kichiro, a former Yamaguchi-gumi yakuza, stomped his foot down on one of the puddles, marring the electric brilliance and splattering water over his shoes. The puddle was deeper than he expected it to be. It had been that type of day.

The rain made the algae stench, from the underground, smell worse than usual, and the endless line of promotional posters for the 2020 Summer Olympics, already faded and peeling months before the event, further mocked him.

Discover Tomorrow.

Disgraced, but tasked by the Yamaguchi-gumi with one last mission, Kichiro didn't expect to still be alive tomorrow. Others might have run, might have fought their fate, but Kichiro was tired of running. Honor demanded he pay for his mistake, even if it was the last thing he did.

In the center of the alley, he approached an unassuming door, nestled into one wall. The green algae-powered street lights didn't reach here to illuminate the symbolic red torii[114] gate looming in the dark over the path in front of the door. Those who needed this place knew where to find it.

Kichiro opened the door, stepped into the pitch-black vestibule, and shut the door behind him. Without hesitation, he descended a set of stairs, his tabi[115] squishing with each practiced step.

At the bottom, he squinted before opening the next door to reveal a dimly lit room. He stood still, allowing his eyes time to adjust to the light. The heady aroma of incense washed out the stench of algae and wet asphalt from outside. Kichiro breathed it in, tension bleeding from his shoulders.

He entered the public hall, walked past the worshippers in their silent meditation, and strode down a hallway toward the monks' quarters.

"Nakashima-san, you are expected," said the crimson-robed monk. The monk appeared from a side room, where he had been nursing his whiskey hangover.

It was Takenaka-san. *Who else?* Kichiro inclined his head but otherwise remained silent, not wanting to give him an opening to make small talk. Takenaka nodded and led Kichiro further into the private portion of the shrine. The smell of incense gave way to one of ozone and dust.

They arrived at the end of a hall, green algae-powered fluorescent lights crackling and humming from an un-covered light fixture above them. Takenaka waved Kichiro toward the door, bowed, and walked away.

Without knocking, Kichiro pushed open the door and entered the tiny room. Red curtains draped the walls, limned in the cyan glow of

---

[114] A red wooden Shinto gate. Oftentimes, a path to another dimension.

[115] Split-toe traditional Japanese socks.

an old TV set on the table in the middle of the room. In front of the TV rested what looked like a bulky computer keyboard. Various other overlarge electronic devices were arranged on the low table, connected by thick cables.

On a cushion in front of this setup sat an old monk, facing the TV. His shaven head was wrinkled, but his posture was perfect. He did not turn to acknowledge Kichiro's arrival.

"Kawaguchi-san," Kichiro said, bowing. "I am in need of assistance."

"So I have heard. Please sit."

Kichiro took two steps and sat seiza[116] next to the monk, head bowed.

"You seem tired, Kichiro: older," the monk said. He turned to pierce Kichiro with his milky-eyed gaze.

"And you look younger," Kichiro replied.

"Flattery," the monk sighed, smiling. "How easily the falsities fall from your lips, as ever."

Frowning, Kichiro said, "My lies have finally caught up to me. I have been dismissed from the Yamaguchi-gumi."

"And so you come to the kami for help?"

Kichiro hesitated. "Actually, I'm not sure why I came."

Another lie. One edge of the monk's lips curled up and he rested his hand on the keyboard. "Then let us ask the kami."

He began to type, his fingers moving faster than Kichiro could follow, filling the old TV screen with lines and lines of text.

Even had he understood programming, Kichiro doubted he could have used this particular computer, the Commodore VIC 20. No company had existed that made such a computer, in Japan or elsewhere, and yet here it was, and here it had been for years.

---

[116] Literally "proper sitting," it means kneeling on the floor in a traditional posture.

"It arrived from elsewhere" was the most detailed explanation that Kawaguchi had ever been able to offer. Whatever it was, wherever it had come from, what better kami for a yakuza, disgraced or otherwise? Twenty was the loser's hand in hanafuda and Kichiro was a loser twice over.

Kawaguchi pressed a final key, triggering the attached dot matrix printer into action. It chattered and buzzed, assaulting the paper with text, line by line. When it stopped, the monk tore the sheet off and began to fold the paper in on itself, forming it into a likeness of a fish of some kind. The monk slid the origami[117] fish into a plastic packet attached to a lanyard and passed it to Kichiro, as if giving him a convention badge.

"Protection," Kawaguchi said. "You will need it now more than ever."

A protection amulet? Kichiro didn't believe in such trinkets, but if that is what the kami offered, Kichiro would accept it.

"Thank you," he said, bowing once before standing up. He lowered the lanyard over his head and slid the attached protection packet under his shirt. At the door, he hesitated. "I won't be back."

"We shall see," said the blind monk.

Detective Kato from vice and Ueda-san, his buddy cop on the beat in Kabukichō, were waiting for him in the alley outside the shrine.

"What are Tokyo's finest doing out in such miserable weather?" Kichiro asked.

Kato answered him with a punch to the stomach. Kichiro doubled over and fell to his knees. He hung his head and closed his eyes, finding

---

[117] The art of folding paper to resemble animals and other things.

calm in the rush of rainwater pouring into a storm drain. The peaceful moment ended when Kato yanked his hair, pulling his head back.

Ueda squatted in front of him, garlic heavy on his breath. "Heard you were dismissed, Nakashima. Tough break."

"I thought you'd be happy for me," Kichiro replied. "I'm on the straight and narrow now."

Ueda, an amateur boxer before joining the force, laughed heartily. "I'll believe it if it lasts. It doesn't matter, though. You still owe us."

"I'm a little short right now."

Ueda nodded, smirking. "Get him on his feet."

Kato yanked him up.

"That's better," Ueda said. He threw a vicious right hook that smashed into the side of Kichiro's face.

Kichiro staggered under the blow and, with help from Kato, fell sideways into the big puddle from earlier.

"I don't care how you get it," Ueda said. He drove his foot into Kichiro's stomach. "I want that money."

Kato knelt down and pulled Kichiro's wallet out of his back pocket. "Ten thousand yen," he announced, standing up.

"That'll do for now," Ueda said. He took the money and dropped the wallet in the puddle next to Kichiro. "You have until tomorrow night for the rest, or else you might meet an unfortunate end while resisting arrest. Understand?"

Kichiro stared up at them, rain stinging his eyes, clothing soaked, and said nothing. He had one last job to do. If these cops wanted to kill him, they'd have to get in line.

Ueda stomped on Kichiro's leg, drawing a howl. "Understand?"

"I understand," Kichiro said.

"Good. We'll see you tomorrow night. Enjoy civilian life until then."

✦   ✧   ✦

By the time he reached his building, he was a cold, aching mess. He made a mental note to pop a couple of hebi[118] once he got inside, to take the edge off the pain.

"Nakashima-san, are you okay?" asked the girl.

She stood in front of his apartment building holding a pink umbrella with kawaii[119] eyes and ears on it. *Could it be Hanako?* he wondered, his vision blurry from the falling rain and the beating. *No, this girl was too young and spoke too formally to be Hanako.* As he approached, he racked his brain for her name and how he knew her.

"Weather like this, you should be inside, Akane-chan," he said, remembering at the last moment.

"It's okay. I'm waiting for my ride."

"Izumi Goseki?" he guessed. Her half-brother. Kind of a punk. He used to hang out around the Inagawa-kai a lot, a rival clan, but Kichiro liked him anyway for his boisterous nature. He hadn't seen him in a while.

"That's who I'm going to see," Izumi Akane said. She nodded once, her smile beaming. It faltered and the half-Chinese, half-Japanese schoolgirl bit her lip. "I heard you were … I mean, you left—er, you are no longer associated with the Yamaguchi-gumi."

"News travels fast," he said. Icy rain poured on him while he made chit-chat and his aches multiplied.

The smile returned to her face. "Well, I say congratulations. The Yamaguchi-gumi don't deserve you anyway. I'm going to make sure my brother knows you left. He still looks up to you, even though he ultimately decided to join a different clan. Maybe your example will

---

[118] Snakes, designer drugs that come in the form of pills.
[119] Cute.

be enough to finally convince him to give up the life."

"Akane-chan, don't bother," Kichiro said. He cocked his head so the street lamp would shine on his black eye. Akane gasped. "I'm no one to look up to," said Kichiro, "and your brother's going to do whatever the hell he wants anyway."

A taxi slid to the curb in a cloud of algae-steam. Izumi Akane opened the door, paused, and said, "Thank you, Nakashima-san. I know you mean well, and Goseki might be a jerk, but I love him all the same and I will save him from this life if it's the last thing I do. Again, congratulations on finally leaving the Yamaguchi-gumi. I wish you luck."

Nakashima Kichiro bowed his head and silently wished her luck as well. They would both need all they could get.

"What happened, baby?" Hanako asked when she entered his tiny apartment.

Kichiro, laid out on his bed, pulled the towel full of ice cubes off of his face and said, "You should see the other guy."

Closing the door behind her, she crossed the room in three steps and flounced on the bed next to him. She laid her hand on his bare chest and asked, "What really happened?"

"I'm out of the Yamaguchi-gumi," he said, sipping the last of his beer.

Her hand retreated to her lap. "Well, that's good, right? Safer?"

"Yeah. Safer," he agreed. He brought the ice back to his face.

She bowed her head, letting her blindingly pink hair fall over her face. "You okay for money, Kichiro?"

"Why?" he asked, as if he didn't know.

"I've got to get back to The Bijou, but I need a little something first." Her doe eyes peeked out from behind her hair. "I'm hurting."

She shook like a wet dog and Kichiro knew it was no act. The girl had a kaiju-sized[120] habit.

Floating on a cloud composed of hebi and Asahi beer, Nakashima Kichiro reached out and pulled Hanako into bed with him, dropping the icy towel to the floor. "How long until you need to be back at the Bijou?"

"You got what I need?" Hanako asked.

"Yeah, but after this, you'll need to find someone else to buy for you. I won't be around much longer."

She shimmied out of her top and skirt, sliding under the blanket next to him. "Don't talk like that, Kichiro."

"It doesn't matter. Even if I live through the night, I'm broke." He pulled her on top of him. "It's been fun. I hope the next guy treats you right."

Hanako leaned down to whisper in his ear. "You're the only guy for me, Kichiro. Now shut up."

Ginza, Tokyo. Ginza at night. This was Sumiyoshi-kai territory. Kichiro let the rain soak into his clothing again as he stood outside of a bar called Uncle Sam's.[121] Having popped two more hebi on the way over, the cold rain didn't bother him in the least. The thought of walking into Uncle Sam's, on the other hand, had his dulled amygdala beating against the inside of his brain, trying to get a single message out of his skull.

Flee.

---

[120] A movie monster, like the radioactive creature born from the sea when Japan tested the first atomic bomb in history on Pearl Harbor during World War II, knocking the United States out of the fight.

[121] A wartime propaganda American-themed Sumiyoshi-kai pub in Ginza.

"No," Kichiro said out loud, startling a passerby. "Not this time."

He took his jacket off, dropped it to the puddled ground, and added his shirt to the pile. Cold rain fell on his bare skin, streaking down the tattoos that covered his chest, back, and arms: the tattoos which proclaimed his Yamaguchi-gumi alliance to anyone in the know. For whatever it was worth, he left the protection amulet hanging on its chest, safe and dry in its plastic sleeve.

With his affiliation laid bare, he lowered his head and marched into Uncle Sam's, that favorite Sumiyoshi-kai hangout.

For a minute, all remained calm outside. Cars slushed by in the mix of rain and snow. Footsteps clattered as salarymen, in their uncomfortable shoes, headed to bars after work rather than home to their families. Street lights clicked and buzzed, directing traffic.

A shout: "You Yamaguchi-gumi fuckers killed Oyabun Sugawara!" Then came a crash and clatter, as Kichiro sailed through the bar's front window, landing on the sidewalk amidst the broken glass. Sumiyoshi-kai thugs poured out of the window and through the front door, surrounding him on the street.

"You lose a bet, bro?" Sumiyoshi-kai chimpira, Eguchi Bunta, asked menacingly.

"Something like that," Kichiro answered. He rolled over onto his hands and knees, gasping as the broken glass cut into his flesh. "I need to speak with your new oyabun. I have a message for him."

This elicited much laughter from the assembled hoodlums.

"We don't take orders from Yamaguchi-gumi scum," said Katayama Bunrakuken, the same martial artist who chucked Kichiro into the streets of Ginza through the window of Uncle Sam's.

"Would you believe I'm no longer with the Yamaguchi-gumi?" Kichiro asked. He smiled despite the pain.

Judging by their fervor as they kicked and beat him unconscious, it seemed they would not.

January 28, 2020. Awareness slowly returned. He found himself in a dark room with a single, blinding light aimed directly at his eyes. It made it impossible to make out more than vague shapes, but he didn't need his sight to know that he was in trouble.

He was seated on a hard chair, tied to it at the elbows, wrists, waist, and ankles. The cords dug into his flesh and left his hands and feet feeling like dead lumps at the end of his limbs. He shifted in his seat, testing the bonds. They didn't move and neither did the chair. This wasn't the work of some street-level hoodlums.

"You have a message for me. What is it?" a man asked, somewhere beyond the light.

"Are you the oyabun?"

"Yes. I am Ishii Naoki, formerly wakagashira to Sugawara-sama. What is your message?"

"I don't know," Kichiro admitted.

Quick footsteps approached. Kichiro steeled himself for the hit a second before someone backhanded the side of his head. Apparently, he had been out long enough for the hebi to have worn off. His ear throbbed with pain in time with his beating heart.

"Were you sent here to kill me?" Oyabun Ishii asked.

He had plenty of reason to be concerned. His predecessor, Sugawara Hirono, had been assassinated less than a week before, reportedly by a Yamaguchi-gumi sniper.

"If I was, I'm doing a really poor job of it." The words fell out of his mouth faster than his brain could tell him to keep quiet.

Another backhand, this time on the opposite side. Kichiro hung his head to his chest, tired, ready for it to be over.

"Did he have any weapons on him?"

"No. Just a wallet and this," another man said.

There was a pause before the new Sumiyoshi-kai oyabun said, "Let me see that."

The light twisted down with a wrenching squeak, highlighting pudgy fingers examining the blind monk's amulet. Oyabun Ishii Naoki slipped the paper out of the plastic sleeve and, after a few false starts, found the point at which to begin unfolding it. From there, the paper seemed to spring open and for a while it hovered in the light, supported by two bodiless hands.

Whatever was printed on the paper, it elicited several grunts and hums from the oyabun. Kichiro hoped the message was worth his sacrifice.

"A match, please," Oyabun Ishii requested.

Within seconds, someone clicked a lighter to life and held it out to the oyabun, who held the corner of the paper in the flame until it caught. He held on until most of it was charred and curling, let it go, and allowed the rest to burn out on the floor.

"Do you know what the paper said?" Oyabun Ishii asked.

"No."

"It is from Chiba Shinobu, wakagashira of the Yamaguchi-gumi. It's an offer for a temporary truce between the Yamaguchi-gumi and the Sumiyoshi-kai, to allow for a specific mission to be carried out at a certain date and time: a mission that would greatly disadvantage our mutual enemies, the Koreans of the Seven Star Mob. They claim they had nothing to do with Sugawara-sama's death. A lie, I'm sure. Still, the Koreans must be dealt with sooner or later. What do you think of the idea of our clans joining forces temporarily?"

"I wish you success, but I am no longer part of the Yamaguchi-gumi."

"No, you are not," oyabun Ishii said. He fell silent for a while. "If I want to reject this offer, I am to do so by returning your corpse to your people. Pardon me, to the Yamaguchi-gumi. To accept it, I must allow you to live."

Kichiro sat up as far as he could, squinting against the bright light. He had not expected to have even odds of making it through this night alive.

The oyabun of the Sumiyoshi-kai gave no indication as to what he might decide, so Kichiro sat in uncomfortable silence for what felt like an hour. All the aches of the day rose to the surface of his consciousness, each cut, scrape, and bruise vying for his attention. Someone turned the light on him again and he closed his eyes against his brightness. A hand traced the tattoos on his chest and arms.

"These will need to be removed," Oyabun Ishii said. "Your irezumi is pitiful and not worthy of a Sumiyoshi-kai. Our cyberneticist will install your dermal plating."

"Oyabun?" Kichiro asked. "Am I to understand …?"

"Yes. It's part of the arrangement. You are to remain in my service until the mission has ended. After that, we shall see."

Kichiro understood that his life still hung in the balance, but he would survive the night, at least. Tomorrow and the next day, he would deal with when they arrived. And it seemed he would be living them not as a member of the Yamaguchi-gumi or a civilian, but as a Sumiyoshi-kai street samurai instead. Interesting.

"Oyabun, if I may?"

"Yes?"

"If I am to be useful to you, there is one problem I humbly request your assistance in solving."

✦ ✧ ✦

January 29, 2020. Shinjuku, Tokyo. The next evening, Kichiro lay in bed next to Hanako and scanned the public net. No matter how many times he read the headlines, they never got old: *Hero Cop Dies in Grisly Accident. Vice Squad Detective on Life Support at Nippori Hospital.*

Hero cop. Kichiro doubted anyone would have described Ueda that way when he was alive. *Well, let him be a hero in death.* All that mattered was that he wouldn't be bothering him again. And Detective Kato would think twice about it too, if he even survived.

"Baby, what are you smiling about?" Hanako asked dreamily, as she clung to him.

He brushed the pink hair from her face, marveling that she had come back to him after all.

"You're here, Eugi's fine with you dating me even though I joined the Sumiyoshi-kai, I've got free cyber implants, and I've got a new job," he said. "Of course I'm smiling."

"What happened to your old tattoos? What's with this new one?" she asked, rubbing his arm.

He looked at the keyboard and monitor on his right bicep and said, "Turns out the VIC 20 is a more powerful kami than I imagined."

About the Author

Andy Goldman is the author of *The Only City Left* and its upcoming sequel, *The Fifth House*. His work is heavily influenced by 80s and 90s pop culture, and mixes western SFF with manga and anime. A fan of shared world anthologies since reading *Thieves' World* and *Merovingen Nights* as a kid, Andy is more than thrilled to be part of the Tokyo Yakuza team.

Tokyo Yakuza
#15

The Gaijin & The Butterfly

by Tina Shelton

Japan won the Second World War; Now the yakuza are starting the Third!

TOKYO YAKUZA #15

The Gaijin and the Butterfly

BY TINA SHELTON

January 30, 2020. Ginza, Tokyo. The best part about the cheap girly liquor on the bar was the weak, brittle bottle it came in.

Paul knew a little about top shelf liquor, but those bottles were significantly tougher to break. The sharp edged appletini mixer bottle caressed the bartender's carotid. *What was his name again? Eguchi Bunta.* Bunta looked like pissing his pants was an option. Paul pressed the jagged edge against Bunta's throat and hoped that his point was clear.

"Where is she?" he asked again, forcing eye contact.

The chimpira of a bartender looked green; Paul hoped he didn't throw up. It looked like the bartender very much wanted to, but didn't know how without impaling himself. Paul wondered briefly if that would stop him.

Pinned down on the bar of Uncle Sam's, Bunta put up a weak struggle. "I don't know who you're talking about!"

No one seemed all that concerned about their interaction. Paul knew it was because the Sumiyoshi-kai owned the establishment. The place was so inured to violence that no one raised any objections. It helped that, although Paul was half-American and half-Japanese, he had enough gold in his skin and slant to his eyes to not be questioned. Bunta, for example, talked smack about Caucs all the time and no one gave a shit about Caucs, especially at Uncle Sam's, a pub that made fun of American war propaganda and used the US flag as toilet paper in the restrooms.

"Sodaina Migotona, you stupid waste of skin! Matriculating at Chiben Gakuen. Gone missing for three days now. I've been retained to find the girl and I'm to understand that you were the last person to see her. I want to know why, I want to know when, and I want to talk to the bastards that set you up to steal her," Paul said. He didn't let it slip that the girl was actually his daughter. He gripped the bartender tight and kept the edge of the bottle pressed up against his neck. Paul was a wiry sort, with a shock of black hair that defied gravity. He wore sunglasses inside the dark bar.

People continued to eat, sip their drinks, and converse as though there wasn't a madman threatening one of the people responsible for providing them with their diversions. Beautiful girls acted as waitresses and as hostesses, providing every man with a view as well as a drink. More than a view cost extra, and there were privacy booths for that. There were curious glances cast at the makeshift weapon, but when Paul's dark eyes met theirs, they quickly looked away, pretending the violence didn't exist.

"There's so many girls, how am I supposed to keep track?" Bunta asked. He tried to work his way free. "I know where they go."

"Where do they go?" Paul asked. He pressed the glass a little harder into his neck.

"Is there a problem?" A man behind him asked. Two others stood with the man. He spoke with his voice pitched low, as though they could have a private conversation with Paul and Bunta clinging to the side of the bar for leverage.

"No problem," the bartender said. His eyes were so wide the whites were visible across the bar.

"No problem with you," Paul lied. He noticed the dermal plating and the tattoo, including one of a weird old computer, winding their way up the arms of the interloper. *Some kind of tattooed cyborg.* Paul thought he caught movement, but kept his focus on his informant.

"Sir, I'm sorry, but we cannot allow displays of violence to stand. Kindly stop threatening the employee and turn over your weapon." The 'borg was as calm as a meditation pond. "Then we can step out back and you can voice your complaint."

"It's cool, Kichiro; we're cool here." The Uncle Sam's bartender's breathing was labored from his strain not to panic.

"Now's the time to prove if you have honor," Kichiro said, ignoring the help.

Paul sighed. He dropped the broken bottle on the counter and relinquished the bartender. Those sitting around them didn't look directly at their milieu, but he could feel the curiosity stirred by their interactions.

Paul didn't resist as they escorted him out. Bar fights always looked glamorous and they were great for chaos, but with an up-and-coming yak street samurai with something to prove, he wouldn't survive to see the first chair break.

Kichiro's bully boy grabbed his upper arms on either side and half-escorted, half-hauled him out of the bar. Kichiro followed in their wake, looking disinterested. When they made it through the kitchen and outside into the alley, he gave Paul a derisive sneer. "Boys, dissuade him from reappearing at our establishment."

The two bouncers fell into it with a will, punching Paul, and driving the air from his lungs. Kichiro watched, bored, and after the first volley of hits, he turned and walked back into the kitchen.

As soon as he was gone, Paul pivoted and dodged the first bodyguard's punch, kicking out to hit the second one in the gut.

The fight was short but sweet. Paul hadn't had a chance to cause violence to the deserving in a long time. He had promised his wife, Akarui, before she died, that he would stem his violent tendencies. But when the yakuza took his daughter, all bets were off.

Paul ran, leaving the two bouncers in a confused heap in the alleyway. His contact hadn't given him the most precise information. It was time to coax the greedy fuck into being more forthcoming.

Azabu-juban, Tokyo. Paul took the Metro and walked to the darkened storefront of Jimmy Fong's Authentic Chinese Emporium.[122] The glass of the storefront barely contained the gaudy baubles stacked in tall, thin rows. It looked as though the store wanted forcibly to eject the tackiness onto unsuspecting passersby, pulling them in and digesting them into yet more effigies of cheap plastic promises.

Paul knew better. He reached out and pulled on the door, which squirmed like a friendly dog trying to wheedle more pets from a stranger. It was the easiest thing in the world to pull the door just that much farther, feeling the locks give way to the kitsch.

"Excuse me! Excuse me, we're closed." Jimmy Fong's round face fell when he saw who he was interrupting. His small, pearl handed pistol was quickly secreted behind his back when he recognized his

---

[122] A place where rich Tokyoites could buy cheap imported junk along with real war trophies scavenged from conquered China.

client. "Paul Bitaendo. I should have known. My shop has a soft spot for you."

"Nice place," Paul said, quietly.

"It's retarded, do you hear me? Fucking retarded! It should never have let you in here before. You're going to blow my cover!" The Chinese man growled and shook his pistol at the wall. "You hear me! Some help you are."

"If you don't mind, I'd feel much better if you stopped waving that antique security device around." He knew the 14K Triad incense master wouldn't actually try to shoot him, but he had no faith that the gun wouldn't go off by mistake. "I went looking for her at Uncle Sam's, where you said she went missing. Ran into some Sumiyoshi-kai chimpira, but they had no clue where she was."

"You're fucked, Paul, and you brought it on me and the 14K now." Jimmy scowled. "Word on the street is she changed hands several times and ended up property of the Yamaguchi-gumi. But you can't cross the Yamaguchi-gumi; they are big medicine around here. If they took your girl, your girl is theirs now."

"I won't let that stand." Paul's words were measured carefully and distributed thoughtfully. "I can't."

"Dammit man, you are looking to get yourself killed. I know your wife's death made you crazy, but at least your daughter's still alive. If you take on the Yamaguchi-gumi to steal her back, they kill you, they kill her, they come back, kill Jimmy ... we all smears on pavement. Nothing my men can do about that."

"Better free in death than the slavery they'll put her in." He looked down when he heard the snap. A little porcelain figurine he didn't realize he'd palmed lie in two pieces; the little kitten's head snapped clean off.

"I put this latest update on your tab," Jimmy said dismissively. "The triad has no more information for you. I give you all we had. I'm sorry, Paul. We run drugs through here, not girls."

"You led me to Uncle Sam's. The bartender was going to talk. Now you're sending me to the Yamaguchi-gumi, whether you want to admit it or not. You keep jerking me around!" Paul couldn't keep the frustration from rising in his voice.

"There is a wisdom here, if you only look hard enough," the incense master said with a soft, wise tone.

"Fuck you, Fortune Cookie. I need accurate information."

"There are booths at regular intervals at the Azabu-juban Metro. There's an entrance two blocks south." Jimmy ran his hand through his thick, black hair and glared over his wire-rim frames. "Now, pay your tab and go away."

"Jimmy, I don't owe you. You owe me." Paul's voice hardened.

"No, at the very least, we're square. You said!" Jimmy's voice trembled.

"Screw you and your triad boys. You owe me for not torching your beloved shop to the ground."

Malevolence filled the air at the sound of the threat. Jimmy put his hands out, and spun around. He laughed, nervous, with sweat beading on his brow. "You kid! You kid! You desperate, you out of mind. Don't be crazy, Paul. I'll tell you where to go. You need to go to The Bijou, that high-end hostess club in Kabukichō. Just don't tell them I sent you."

Paul nodded, absorbing this new information. "The Bijou. Of course, I should have known. Forgive me, Jimmy. I will leave your shop."

"You're actually going to … you crazy bastard. Don't do it. I've heard stories. The Bijou has spirits," Jimmy Fong said.

Paul gave him a level, unreadable look.

"No, like, really. Kami, ghosts, tanuki, magic." Jimmy sighed. "Fine, go, get out of my shop, go, go, go, you crazy fuck."

Paul set out for The Bijou, prepared to face ghosts for his daughter.

Shinjuku, Tokyo. Late night, and Kabukichō was decorated in all the colors of the neon rainbow. The Bijou was a hostess club, but moreover, it was the hostess club in Tokyo. Akarui worked there during her stint as a hostess, before they had married. What happened to her before she met him, he had no sway over, but as soon as he was able, he took her out of that life and gave her a wedding ring, a daughter, and a comfortable life. Before the cancer won out.

He glared at his old enemy. The building was unmoved.

"Gaijin! Are you looking for some companionship?" A voice called out to him in the dark.

The old insult felt like salt grinding into a fresh wound, but Paul did his best to not react. The effect was spoiled slightly when he looked down the alley, next to the building. He discovered that a man-sized tanuki, a kind of large, pot-bellied, anthropomorphic raccoon-dog in a suit and tie, was speaking to him.

"Oh, come on, you look like a fellow who needs a lovely lady to remind him how to smile. Come in, come in, we'll get you talking to Kit. She's got a nose for matching a guest to a hostess!" The raccoon-dog gave him a winning grin, and Paul allowed himself to be dragged off, into The Bijou.

Paul had heard all about The Bijou from his wife, Akarui, but he had never dared to go in before and he wasn't prepared for what he saw. The luxury, that draped itself like a lovely woman at a roulette wheel, was palpable: an additional force in the room. The women were exquisite.

But it didn't take long for Paul to find a woman who looked hastily arranged, her eyes shiny wet with unshed tears, sitting perfectly still like the prey she was. Yayoi Himetsu only had eyes for Akiyama Jiro, a thick-necked bruiser with the tattoos twining up his arms, around his neck, and down his back. The thug ignored her and concentrated on his drink, but every now and again he reached out for Yayoi, just to make sure she was still there.

It was all Paul could do not to visualize his daughter getting similar treatment.

"Kit!" The tanuki hollered, cutting the din of pachinko and conversation like a silk knife.

Paul gasped and caught himself. The fox-eared woman who turned to look at the raccoon-dog spirit was his wife. For a moment. Then her face resolved into that of a beautiful half-American, half-Japanese girl. "Oh, hello there, Godan. Yes, we have many … distractions." She eyed him, her cold blue eyes measuring him despite her friendly hostess smile. "Just name your poison."

"Ha ha, another satisfied customer." Takami Godan tipped an imaginary hat to Paul and went back outside to scare up more customers.

Kit waited until the raccoon-dog spirit was gone before she addressed him again. "Your tastes are … specific."

"Damned specific." Paul agreed.

"Would you care to share?" Kit offered her arm.

"Yes. I'm looking for a girl, goes by the name Sodaina Migotona. I heard that you may know where she is," Paul said, forcing politeness.

Kit chuckled. "Let me put you in touch with The Bijou's onesan, Zafa.[123] She keeps track of the girls for Eugi."

"Just like that?" Paul asked.

"I can read minds, Paul. And sometimes control them," Kit Yamaguchi said. "I know that telling you 'no,' however, is not going to be accepted, so I thought I would try the direct approach. We don't have to be enemies, Paul."

"Yes, we do," Paul corrected her.

"I think you're in for a surprise," Kit said. "Anyway, Onesan Zafa is around. She knew your wife, Akarui, by the way. They joined The Bijou around the same time together. Try the Green Room, she's often seen there."

With that, Kit turned her back on him and Paul was left to his own devices.

Paul bounced around the floor like a pachinko ball, looking for the onesan. He didn't really know what he was looking for. He didn't know if Zafa was tall, or short, or Japanese, or some kind of changeling like Kit. He didn't want to charge in without any preparation, but the game's rules were set. He had to find her to find his daughter. Kit told him that she was in the Green Room. It was time to explore the establishment further.

The Green Room was a quiet room, off to the side of the major attractions of The Bijou. He noticed there were guards. Kit hadn't mentioned them, but he hadn't asked. They were thick-set men, wearing matching black suits with neckties, collars, and gold cufflinks. Like Paul, they also wore sunglasses inside. Paul wondered if theirs were surveillance equipment with megane extensions, or simply the standard-issue intimidation technique, like his. It didn't matter. Paul was all out of fucks to give.

---

[123] Older sister, the woman who runs a geisha house or hostess club.

He strode up to the door monkeys. Paul didn't look too out of place, he thought, in a green, button down shirt and denim jeans. He noted that both the door guards had suspicious bulges under their left armpits.

"This room is not for customers. This is for staff only," said Moji Sumio. The slightly smaller door guard with wraparound sunglasses flashed a cruel, calculating smile.

The fact that he stooped to English to convey this information made Paul bristle. In perfect Japanese, Paul replied, "I am here for Onesan Zafa. Kit Yamaguchi sent me."

Two matching waxed sets of eyebrows climbed the corporate ladders of their foreheads in surprise. Door guard number one, Moji Sumio, recovered first. "Kit Yamaguchi?"

"Anyone can say that," snapped door guard two, Kamei Daichi. He was the bigger of the two men and the professional killer who ordered the death of Jared Santos, aka. Jiro Satani. Kamei continued in Japanese, "You must prove it."

Paul leaned in as though to whisper a secret. Kamei mirrored his movement unwittingly, then realized what he was doing and jerked back, but not before Paul slammed his fist into his nose, crushing the cartilage underneath in a splash of blood. Moji reacted swiftly, pulling his own .50 caliber Desert Eagle and aiming for Paul, but the impact from a well-aimed punch to his elbow made Moji drop his gun.

Paul pushed Moji back, reaching down to scoop up the gun just as Kamei started to draw his own. Swinging backwards, he smacked the pistol barrel against Kamei's cheek like a club, immediately bringing the gun around again and smashing the handle down onto the top of Moji's head. Both men fell to the floor, unconscious.

Paul knew that it would only be a few minutes before others arrived, but he could use those minutes to talk to Onesan Zafa.

The door had a complex magnetic lock but it didn't hold out against the power of the bullet. Paul slipped inside only to find himself stopped by two women, dressed like futuristic kunoichi[124] down to their laser-edged katanas.

The room was enormous, dominated by a central desk. Behind the desk sat a beautiful, older woman. Her skin was perfect, save for tiny crow's feet marring her otherwise youthful look. Her crow's feet were not in any way appearing from amusement, unfortunately.

"What do you want?" She asked in Japanese.

Paul looked at the kunoichi with the katana at his throat. She looked to Zafa, who nodded. She lessened her edged pressure on his throat, allowing him to speak. "I come looking for Sodaina Migotona," said Paul. "I have reason to believe she was stolen from her private school."

Zafa eyed him. "And who are you?"

"I'm the girl's father, Paul Bitaendo." His eyes stayed on her, ignoring the ninjas despite the proximity of their edged weapons.

"Ah, I see. And how do you know she didn't come willingly?" Onesan Zafa asked.

"Because she never would," Paul said, stiffly.

Zafa laughed, a high chiming sound that was echoed by her ninjas. "So little that fathers understand their daughters."

"Please, if she is in debt, I will take on the debt and pay it. I do not wish her to work as a hostess."

"And why not? The Bijou is the finest hostess club in Tokyo. Some argue in the world," Zafa said.

"Her mother worked here once. She died of cancer. Sodaina is all I have left of her," Paul pleaded.

---

[124] Female ninjas.

"Ah, I hear the sounds of honesty. Girls, fetch me some tea. I need to discuss business with Mr. Bitaendo."

The kunoichi vanished.

"Please, come to the desk. I will look through the books and see who we've received. The records are extensive but not exhaustive, so do not expect me to find something that is not there," Zafa said.

Paul bowed low, making his appreciation known, and then stepped as close as he dared to watch what she did.

Paul might as well have been blind for all that he could understand the swiftly moving columns of kanji that appeared on the monitor. Names flashed with the speed of light, with only the rapid tapping of a skilled operator breaking the silence.

"No. No. No." Zafa looked up after several minutes of poring over the books. "I'm afraid her name isn't here, Mr. Bitaendo. Eugi must not have recruited her after all."

Paul slammed his hand down on the desk. "She has to be here!"

She gave him a slow, sleek smile. "As a matter of fact, she does not have to be, and I told you not to expect me to find something that wasn't there. Unrealistic expectations inevitably lead to disappointment."

Her ninjas reappeared. They did not bring tea.

"Mr. Bitaendo did not find that which he was seeking. Therefore, he still has desire in his heart and is miserable because of it. Please take him to Eugi and see that he is properly instructed in the ways to respect the yakuza. Perhaps this will alleviate some of his desire."

Wordlessly, the kunoichi bowed. Then they looked at Paul, seeing what he would do.

Paul offered no resistance. If Sodaina was not with the Yamaguchi-gumi clan, then where on Earth was she? He would have to live through whatever punishment Eugi could dish out to find her.

But he would live. And he would find his daughter.

He allowed the kunoichi to lead him on, to face his fate.

About the Author

Growing up in the middle of nowhere gave Tina a great view of the stars. She made up stories under the brilliant night skies and now she wants to share those stories with the rest of the world. She's a woman of many hats: wife, mother, and author being her favorites. She's written one novel, *The Corsican*, and aims to release her second novel *Bento Box* in 2015.

東京極道

Tokyo Yakuza
#16

Death on the Inside

by Gustavo Bondoni

Japan won the Second World War; Now the yakuza are starting the Third!

Death on the Inside

BY GUSTAVO BONDONI

January 31, 2020. Asakusa, Tokyo. Kusama Mariko looked up at the little otaku bitch and blew a puff of acrid cigar-smoke in her face. The fan girl coughed and sputtered, the flash of rage on her features contrasting with the cutesy graphics on her clothing and the stuffed animals hanging from her belt. Nothing in her delicate little world had prepared her for this.

"Go away," Mariko said.

The girl seemed on the verge of speech, but then bolted down the pavilion's aisle.

With any luck, she'll call the police, Mariko thought. If the little slut didn't, she'd have to find another way. Time was of the essence.

She looked around. Her bags had been positioned strategically in one of the most densely packed sections of the Olympic mall; that was the name the city had given the old public market leading to the Sensoji, the main temple in Asakusa, after roofing over the market and rebuilding it. She was surrounded by stalls carrying everything from clothing to consumer electronics, all branded with the Olympic rings and that unspeakable mascot.

What she most definitely didn't have was a permit to be there or any kind of proof that the bags she was selling had been purchased legitimately. None of what she was doing would get her locked up for any length of time, but it should be enough for her purposes, especially if she did a little talking back to the authorities.

"Do you know the penalty for selling false bags in the street?" a voice from behind her asked.

She turned slowly, not startled in the least, and looked him over from head to toe. He was just a regular street cop, probably six months out of the Keisatsu Dai-gakkō.[125] "I imagine it's a slap in the wrist. If it were a serious crime, they'd have sent someone a bit more impressive to arrest me."

Kusama Mariko puffed some smoke into the cop's face. If she'd still been working The Bijou, she wouldn't have bothered giving this one anything extra; he was too green to know what strings to pull for her in return, but he'd do. "At least they would have sent someone who knew the difference between fake bags and real ones," she said.

"Even if they're real, I doubt you have a permit to sell them here." His eyes lit up as he realized what he might have found. "And I also wonder if you can explain where you got them."

She could have laughed at his earnestness, but kept a straight face. There was no need to anger him more than suited the situation and no need to make enemies that would then need to be eliminated. Cops could be tricky when a woman mocked them, and there was a fine line. "So, are you here to harass me, or are you actually going to make an arrest?"

The choice wasn't that easy. Even a guy this wet had probably learned that any kudos he'd earn by arresting street peddlers wasn't

---

[125] The National Police Academy of Japan.

worth the extra work, and the vendors were invariably back on the street in a matter of hours. Ninety-nine times out of a hundred, the cop would simply tell them to get out of his sight and not come back until someone else had the beat.

The key here would be whether the potential of a smuggling and stolen goods bust was enough to get him to act, or whether she'd have to up the ante.

To her relief, the cop took the bait.

"All right, get up, you're coming with me."

"What about my bags?"

The cop called for his partner, who appeared in less than a minute from out of one of the cross-corridors, and turned to her. "They're evidence. Now come on."

She hated to leave the bags to the cops. They always took some "samples" even when they released the things, and she'd have to make up for the difference herself, but she had no choice.

Even if they kept the whole lot, she could probably make up the difference, she hoped. Of course, if she couldn't, her superiors would happily remove the difference in digits. She wondered what the tip of a forefinger went for these days.

Once at the station, she was handed off to a couple of fat desk cops who processed her. "Hello Mariko," one of them said. She recognized him as an old Bijou regular, a guy who'd wanted to be with the upper crust, but had never really had the money to do anything but buy the least popular hostesses a drink or two. She nodded at him, curtly.

"I see you have some new tattoos."

"I see you still have the same job."

"Yes, I always thought that one should avoid reaching beyond one's ability." He tried to make his tone nonchalant, but she knew him well enough to know that he viewed all women as objects to be used as far as they'd let him, and then discarded.

Now one of the women who had been out of his reach at the hostess club suddenly fell into his power. For a frustrated misogynist like him, it must have seemed like a gift from whichever spirits he believed in. "A lesson you seem to have forgotten," he said, continuing his point. "Prostitutes shouldn't try to be smugglers. They aren't very good at it."

"And policemen shouldn't try to be philosophers," she said back. Mariko knew that making this one angry wouldn't make her treatment worse, but if she showed fear, she was in trouble.

"So, what do we have here?" He pawed through her handbag. "Kyocera glasses. You must have done well as a whore to be able to buy these. If they weren't DNA coded, I'd keep them as evidence. But you can't go into the cell with these, can you? It would be a pity to have some cheap Yamaguchi-gumi lawyer here in ten minutes trying to get you out before we can thoroughly investigate those bags, now would it?"

He rummaged some more, pulling the few bills out of her wallet before tossing it back in the bag. He handed the bag to his partner to be taken, along with the glasses, to be registered as the prisoner's personal effects.

"Now, I'm afraid there's been some unpleasant business with people we capture turning out to be augmented maniacs, so I'm going to need you to undress for me. I am going to run a scan."

She shrugged and removed her kimono.

The cop looked at her panties. "Those too."

She knew perfectly well that the scan could see through the silk cloth of her tiny briefs, and she knew the cop knew it as well. She also knew that her augments were completely undetectable with the tech the cops were using. Their equipment would work on stuff that had traditional circuitry, solder and copper, but not against what she was packing. At least, that was what the theory said. No one else had augments like hers, or at least, no one was advertising them.

She dropped the panties.

The cop took a few seconds to look her over. "Pity about the tattoos," he said. He then started the scan. While he passed the cold paddle over every inch of her skin, he kept a running monologue going. "You might think this is a silly precaution, but just last week we picked up a drunk from the Inagawa-kai who called himself 'Shintaro.' He was perfectly docile when we brought him here, but once he managed to sleep off the booze, he went wild: tore up our holding cell, threw one of our clerks through a wall, and walked out. The tech squad told us he had some new kind of tattoo augments, so now we scan everyone, especially yakuza."

"Do you think yakuza would give their girls augments?"

"You never know," he replied. "And that brings us to the second point." He put down the paddle and donned a pair of latex gloves. "One thing the yakuza often do is to load their girls up with lots of drugs and goodies. We normally have a female officer do these checks, but we can't waste time looking for one when we have dangerous yakuza in hand, now can we?"

She patiently waited while he groped her, inexpertly. They both knew that this was pointless; a drug mule would never, ever have been out on the street doing something illegal. Real mules were caught by cyber-espionage and infiltration, and the closest a street cop would ever come to one was the outside of her cell. But they both knew the rules: he could, temporarily, make things a little worse for her in the short term if she didn't play along. And if questioned, his explanation for the cavity search would be accepted immediately.

She didn't really care. Her body was a tool for getting what she wanted and had been one even before she'd decided to become her own guinea pig. The augments inside her, augments of her own design that had never been tried on any other human, were simply the concrete evidence of that philosophy. While men used their muscles, she had used her looks, managing to get dates in huge numbers and keeping enough money to fund her studies end experiments, even after paying The Bijou's cut.

Eugi had been suspicious a few times, but the sheer amount she was pulling in by giving her clients whatever they wanted was enough to allay his doubts and leave plenty for her.

There were only two conditions: the first was that the clients could never talk to Eugi about it or she would never serve them again, and the second was that they had to dispose of any dead bodies that might result. Other than that, she was theirs. And Eugi thought her dō han[126] involved nothing more than going out for drinks and public events.

So a cavity search by a horny cop was something she could endure without blinking. And it was sweet to know that this time, she was submitting for a huge advancement, not just a small gain. "So, convinced I don't have a battleship hidden up there?" she asked him.

He pulled back, embarrassed. "All right, get dressed."

She smiled and put her clothes back on without a hurry. "Which is my cell?"

"The only one left."

He wasn't kidding about augments. The two holding cells to the right of hers looked like a train had gone through them. Twisted

---

[126] Dates outside the house of pleasure.

metal jutted every which way. Fortunately, her own cell was empty.

"Goodbye, it's been a pleasure."

When the guard was gone, Mariko sat on the cot hanging from the cell wall and closed her eyes. She knew that, to the outside world, she looked asleep.

Nothing could have been further from the truth. Using a combination of synapse shunts and retinal menu selection, she powered her systems up. The tech was all highly camouflaged using her own nervous system, adequately beefed up, to send impulses, and using semiconducting carbon nanotubes in place of the telltale silicon chips everyone else made do with.

Well, perhaps not everyone. She'd been hearing rumors that Jise Hirabayashi had been creating similar stuff for the White Witch. A reckoning was certainly in their future, but it was still too soon. Attempting to lock horns with her former idols now, or even just being discovered by them, would ensure that Mariko was crushed like an insect. That would change, but it would take time.

After today, however, she would be a step closer.

Her systems were up and the diagnostics showed that her body heat was just a little higher than normal. Unless the cops were really paying attention, it would pass unnoticed. The world behind her eyelids lit up like the screens in the Olympic plaza.

She quickly connected to the net and linked to her bot, which was in a dark tube back in a Shinjuku love hotel.

Shinjuku, Tokyo. Navigating by infrared, Kusama Mariko walked the sausage-shaped crawler through the air conditioning ducts. She knew she was on the correct floor, but that was it.

The first vent was a dud; an empty room greeted her. The second was also fruitless, as three maids were cleaning the room. A third held a couple, but not the man she was looking for.

Only on her sixth attempt, an agonizing fifteen minutes into her search, did she find him. Hello, Jiro, she thought. Aren't you popular today?

Akiyama Jiro was the nearest thing to a friend and mentor she'd had within the Yamaguchi-gumi. He'd been the first to understand what was happening, the first to realize that every man who blocked her ambitions, or even just disrespected her more than what was normal for yakuza and women, ended up with a small stiletto wound right in the sternum: a wound which was invariably fatal.

He'd only asked her two questions when he confronted her.

"How did you get close enough to kill them? They knew you hated them."

She'd just stood silently.

"What the hell is the knife made out of? With a wound that small, the blade has to break, but it doesn't."

She'd refused to answer.

After a full minute of silence, he'd laughed and offered her a job. Not street-level, not peddling her ass, but running a territory, responsible for the profits … and the losses.

She selected Cutting Torch from the robot's menu, blinking for the select command. The grate made some noise as she pushed the sides away, but as there was no burning smell. Vacuum fans on the robot made certain the fumes were lost in the ducting. The four people on the bed didn't notice anything. They were certainly otherwise preoccupied.

Jiro was taking one of the three hostesses from behind while a second one, standing on the bed, pressed herself into his face. The third seemed to be doing nothing, just sitting on an easy chair and watching the activity. Mariko recognized her: Hanako, a girl just getting started at The Bijou when Mariko had left.

None of them were looking in the bot's direction and Mariko took a moment to admire Jiro. She'd never seen him naked before, as he'd always respected her and never, not once, had asked for sexual favors. He was extremely well-muscled and tattooed everywhere from the neck down.

She'd heard enough to know that he'd earned all that ink the hard way, just as he'd earned the right to use The Bijou's assets in whichever way he saw fit outside of the club.

But his usefulness to Mariko had run out. He always treated her well, but he also took credit for her triumphs, and it had quickly become obvious that he was a barrier to her advancement inside the Yamaguchi-gumi.

Shotgun, she selected.

An instant later, Jiro's back was torn to hamburger. He slumped forward onto the girl he'd been fucking, who collapsed under the weight.

A second round took out the girl standing on the garish clamshell bed, some slutty waitress named Aiko who managed to impress Eugi a couple of weeks back. Too slow to realize what had happened, Aiko was looking stupidly at the dead man under her until the flying buckshot propelled her into the mirror beside the bed. Hanako nearly got away, but Mariko was able to cut her in half with the third and final shell as she made a bid for the hotel door.

I should have designed the robot to deal with more people, Mariko thought. But how could she have known about Jiro's appetites?

The last girl managed to climb out from under Jiro and, soaked with the dead man's blood, ran screaming into the hallway, an open kimono fluttering along behind her.

And hello Bachiko, Mariko thought, recognizing the fleeing figure. It was a thought tinged with sadness.

Mariko prayed to the kami and was rewarded to see that the girl, instead of running towards the lobby elevators headed for the service stairs. A good yakuza reflex, Mariko thought, with approval. Now let's hide this gadget before anyone finds it and starts asking questions.

Mariko knew that a lot of the Yamaguchi-gumi, especially the girls at The Bijou, were aware of her penchant for building electronic toys. It was considered a harmless pastime, but it wouldn't be harmless if they discovered this one.

An industrial-sized broom closet with nearly an inch of dust in the back corners served as a perfect hiding place. No one had been there in ages, and it was unlikely that anyone would search now. There was no room for a gunman among the nooks and crannies, after all.

Asakusa, Tokyo. Kusama Mariko, being in jail across town at the time of the killings, had the perfect alibi. She sent a message to the Yamaguchi-gumi lawyers the fat cop had been worried about and powered herself down. Then she opened her eyes and waited for them to post bail. It wouldn't be long.

February 1, 2020. Shinjuku, Tokyo. They were always happy to see her at The Bijou. For one thing, they knew Mariko could be counted on to fill in, and do so profitably, if one of the regular hostesses were absent. But mainly, she represented what all the girls wanted: to be respected for herself, no matter how humble the origins. Kusama Mariko knew that most of them were too soft to survive and that they'd be begging on the streets or working as drug mules when their charms faded.

But she smiled at the surviving Bijou hostesses and hugged them all.

"Hello Yayoi," she said. "How are you today? All paid up?"

Yayoi was always getting into debt because of her no-good brother. Yayoi gave Mariko a sad smile. "Soon, Mariko. Soon."

They walked into the back rooms, past the onesan's Green Room, where the regular girls lived and slept during the day. "Have you seen Bachiko today?"

"I did. She ran in earlier, grabbed some things, and left. She looked sick."

"Oh, that's too bad. I was coming over earlier to bring her some money from Jiro, but had a little trouble with the cops." And, she thought but took care not to say aloud, that means that I was safely locked up when some unnamed gunman shot him into small pieces.

But it was clear that the news about the deaths of Jiro, Hanako, and Aiko hadn't reached these girls yet, because Yayoi's only reaction was a shrug. "I guess you'll have to look for her later, then. She's supposed to be in tonight, so that should be a decent bet."

"I'll try to look in. Tell her I came by, will you?"

"Of course."

Mariko let herself out and sighed. She knew exactly where Bachiko had gone, but it could complicate things. She hailed a cab and directed it to the partially-built Spacecraft.

The industrial area behind the Olympic stadium was a mess of tubing and air-conditioning units. The grime and stench was as sharp a contrast to the shining tourist areas as the front rooms of The Bijou were to the private areas, where those who couldn't pay had things explained to them. Greasy puddles lay on concrete slabs because they had nowhere else to go, and packs of even greasier maintenance techs roamed the dank corridors.

Mariko ran into one group as she descended into the second layer. Clearly foreign laborers by their skin, they were dirtier and smellier than the corridor around them. Their eyes were hungry when they saw her, but when they shone their light on her tattoos, they immediately and let her pass, apologizing for delaying her.

Unlike the stupid cops, these guys knew the significance of the tattoos and were streetwise enough to know that no one would dare show her traditional-style ink without having gone through hell to get it.

But even these men couldn't be aware that each tattoo represented one death, one man who'd either hurt her or stood in her way, and whose last sight had been the woman they were screwing driving a long, thin blade into their hearts as she laughed at them.

As she approached her destination, she wondered whether Jiro merited a new figure, even though she hadn't killed him with her own hands. She'd already decided that the girls didn't count.

She walked between the algae tanks, listening to the bubbling as they turned the detritus of the city above into the energy that powered the neon universe.

Her destination was little more than a gap in the concrete wall, which led to a crawl space and a tiny suite of rooms. Three ideograms above the entrance made it clear that anyone trespassing would be curtly dealt with by the Yamaguchi-gumi, but truth be told, there was little of value in this hideaway, other than a place that offered girls who needed it, for some reason, a modicum of privacy and safety from official molestation. Mariko crawled through the hole, and then walked through the rooms.

"Hello, Bachiko," she said.

"I knew you'd come," Bachiko said. "I knew that little robot looked like it was yours. So I came here. I knew you'd come."

The girl looked both happy and terrified to see her. The thick mascara around her eyes had run, making her look like a tanuki. Like the other two (now dead) hostesses, Bachiko was a moderately popular hostess, with the delicate features that those who couldn't afford a real geisha enjoyed so much.

"I'm here now," Mariko said.

"Yes. You always helped me. I knew it was you when you didn't shoot me like the rest. I knew it. That's why you saved me."

"I've always helped you."

"Yes. Remember that time you loaned me twenty thousand yen to give to Eugi? I remembered. That's why I came here. You always looked out for me."

"Of course I did. I always do, don't I?"

Bachiko came closer, squeezing one of Mariko's arms in her hand. "Yes. That's why I came straight here, that's why I didn't tell anyone about the robot. For once, I could take care of you."

"Thank you, Bachiko," Mariko said. She pulled the other girl close, squeezed her into a hug.

Tears streamed down her face as she plunged the stiletto into the other girl's back. She struck quickly, hoping that the other girl wouldn't feel it.

But she did, and a single sputtering sigh shook her body. Mariko held her, held her hard, until the corpse turned cold.

Minutes later, as she dragged the stiffening girl up a service staircase, she thought about the world of the yakuza. There was even less room for emotion in that world for women than there was for men.

The body fell with a splash. Bubbles of toxic gas formed on Bachiko's skin as the algae began to turn her into electricity. She'd be gone in a few hours.

Now Mariko needed to get those black market handbags back before Wakagashira-hosa Matsuhono Eugi and Onesan Zafa, her higher-ups in the clan, started asking questions. She thought she knew exactly what it would take to get the fat cop to give them back to her.

About the Author

Gustavo Bondoni is an Argentine writer with over a hundred stories published in ten countries and in four languages. He is a winner in the National Space Society's Return to Luna Contest and the Marooned Award for Flash Fiction in 2008. His fiction has appeared in the *Texas STAAR English Test* cycle, a Bundoran Press anthology, *The Rose & Thorn*, *Albedo One*, *The Best of Every Day Fiction* and others. His latest book, an eBook novella entitled *Branch* was published by Wolfsinger Press in March 2014. He has also published two reprint collections, *Tenth Orbit and Other Faraway Places* (2010) and *Virtuoso and Other Stories* (2011, Dark Quest Books). *The Curse of El Bastardo* (2010) is a short fantasy novel. Gustavo's blog is located at

http://bondo-ba.livejournal.com/.

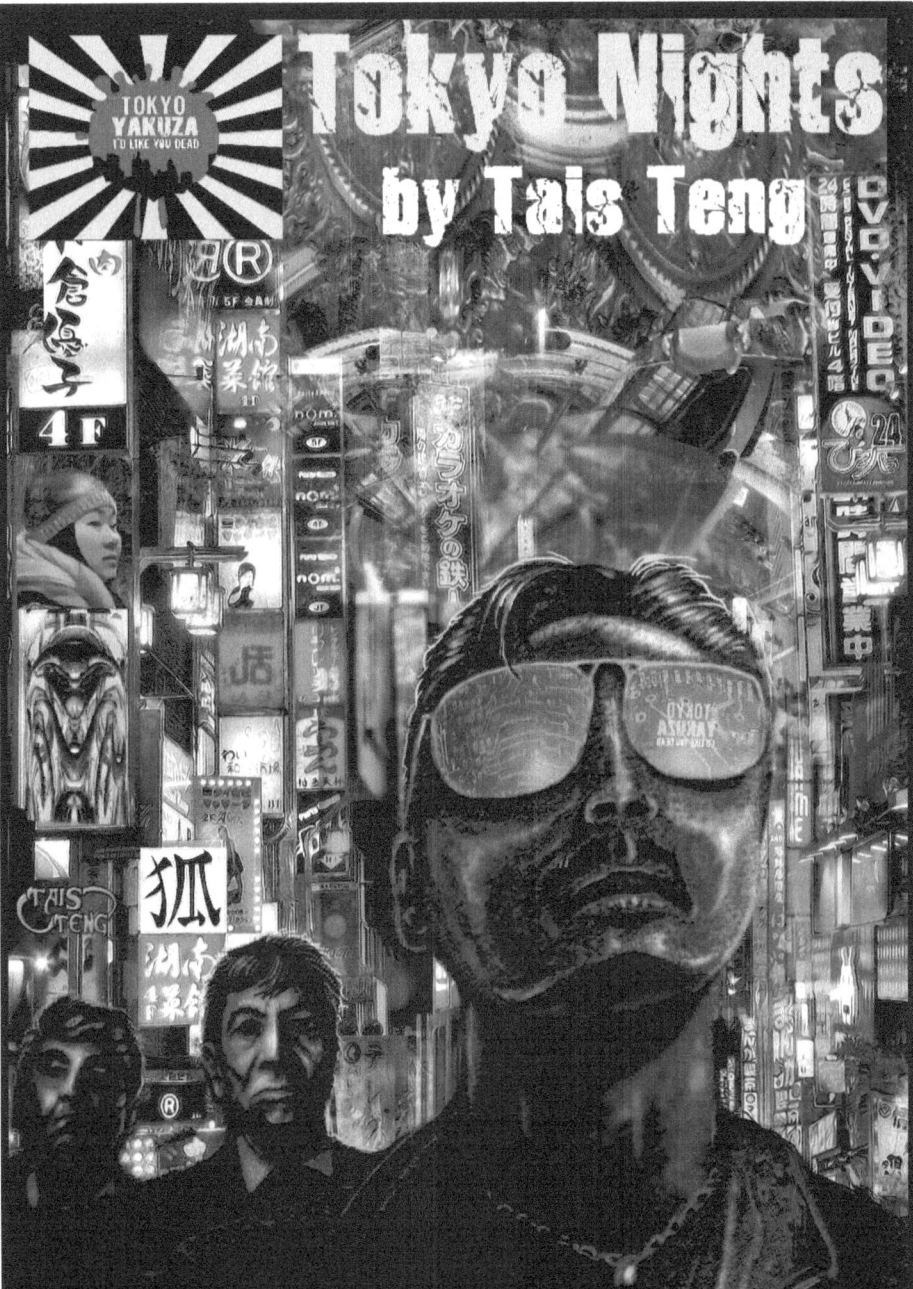

TOKYO YAKUZA #17

Tokyo Nights

BY TAIS TENG

July 6, 2019. Maihama, Tokyo. That was the day Taro saw his first clone. It emerged screaming from the CBI-Hitachi artificial womb, a look of horror on both its faces. The real world was clearly not to its liking. Taro stared at the two-headed monstrosity and felt sick. This was so clearly *wrong*: what a Catholic priest would have called unholy.

The screaming turned into whimpering and then stopped. The heads sagged back into the pulsating flesh of the womb, emitting the salty smell of freshly spilled blood.

The CBI-Hitachi physician nodded. "Six seconds. Not too bad. A success, in fact." He turned to Taro's client. "Noboru-sama, mixing high tech and Taoist magic is always tricky, but you should have seen the ones before. None came to term. They grew flippers or dragon wings, turned inside out. This looks at least approximately human. When we get the new Monsanto wombs tomorrow …" "Ah, sir?" Taro spoke to his client, Inagawa-kai oyabun Noboru Akira. "What exactly were you aiming for?"

The face of the yakuza boss was like a kabuki[127] mask, unreadable without specs and Taro had left his Google glasses at the reception when the guards frisked him.

"I got a hair from one of my rivals, the Yamaguchi-gumi oyabun, Kitano Takumi," Akira said. "A doppelganger would have been perfect. We kill Takumi discreetly and put the clone in his place. He would be my sock-puppet, speaking with my voice. But that is just a possibility, a sideline. For the real job, we need a perfect clone." He pursed his lips. "Who is the most famous man in Japan, my friend? The greatest and most beloved hero in the eyes of our countrymen?"

"Basho," Taro instantly replied. "Everybody reads his poems even after all those centuries, and three of the top-ten hits ..."

"You are a thief. A very good thief but it shows. You don't have the proper bloodlust, the manly killer instincts. No, it is Oda Nobunaga, the samurai's samurai. He defeated all the other warlords and united Japan. Nobunaga was an extremely good strategist and clever. He knew exactly when to betray an ally or honor a defeated enemy. With him, the yakuza will be unbeatable."

"You would make him shogun again?"

"More like wakagashira. A very highly placed advisor in the clan."

What was that Chinese saying again? When you ride a tiger, you can never stop? Nobunaga had been like a force of nature, impossible to tame. The idea that you could use him as a mount to ride to glory, was suicidally stupid. Still, it wasn't Taro's problem.

"I guess you would want me to steal his bones? Get his DNA?"

"Not only his bones. That would just give us a body. We need his memories, his soul. A newborn would have all his talents, but we

---

[127] Traditional Japanese performing art.

need his experience. Without his memories he would perhaps end up as a corporate raider, or a very successful academician. We need the warrior, the general."

"I see." Taro had plundered haunted temples in Cambodia, stolen amulets from dragon's lairs, but this was different. Taro didn't know where one would find the soul of a murderous hero who had betrayed his best friends, but it probably wasn't in any of the heavens.

"His bones would be possible, Noboru-sama, though it wouldn't be easy. His soul?" He shook his head. "No price is high enough. Anyhow, I wouldn't know where to start."

"Your lover is a fox," replied Oyabun Noboru Akira. "A kitsune would know where to find his soul."

They know about Hoshi. The yakuza and the kitsune had never mixed well. Fox spirits were mischievous and often cruel, but they frowned on the amassing of wealth, while killing, except for food, was seen as a perversion. With her red hair dyed black, Hoshi could pass for human and she took care never to show her tail.

Akira's threat was clear: *we know your secret. Obey me or we'll expose Hoshi.*

Every kitsune led a hidden life, keeping to the shadows like any hunter. Their secret identities were their most prized possessions. With the whole of Japan wired, cameras on every street corner, Hoshi would never be anonymous again.

Taro felt a flash of ice-cold rage. *I'll get you for this. I'll never forgive you. Threatening Hoshi, blackmailing me into working for you.* He knew exactly what was happening. The yakuza didn't like lone wolves, so Oyabun Noboru wanted him in the pack, part of the Inagawa-kai and obedient. Ordering him around was the start of that process.

Taro smiled. It never hurt to smile. "Good. I'll get you the bones. But don't pay me in yen. Too easy to trace. Five thousand

Reichsmarks[128] in krugerrands[129] and Maria Theresa thalers."[130]

"That would be the price of a major hit," Akira said, adding, "Nobunaga is already dead."

"I am not your ordinary assassin. The bones are treasure. Priceless."

"Four thousand Reichsmarks and Hoshi's reputation is safe. Forever. I give you my word!" Noboru Akira beat his fist against his chest.

"Good." *Take a step back to hit all the harder.* "And, Akira, old pal, ten million yen[131] in gold and silver for his soul." Taro knew that was pushing, reckless. But by Inari's[132] nine tails, he was so angry! "By the way, that price in nonnegotiable."

He saw the pupils of the yakuza boss dilated in shock. Ten million yen was a fee no hireling should ever ask. It put Taro right in the ranks of the players.

"Good," Akira said. "Ten million the moment you deliver us his soul." He didn't raise his hand this time. He didn't talk about his honor.

Taro knew he would be paid, and that would be only the beginning of his troubles. In Akira's eyes, Taro had just upgraded himself to one of the oyabun's very own rivals.

When they left CBI-Hitachi's secret Maihama facility, Taro and Akira looked into each other's eyes for a frozen moment. In the end, neither of the men bowed. Their status had become too fluid: it was impossible to decide who outranked whom. There was only one way

---

[128] Roughly $20,000. The official currency of the Third Reich, introduced in Germany in 1924. The exchange rate for RM in the world of Tokyo Yakuza is *RM*1:$4 or ¥400.

[129] Gold coins minted in South Africa and used continuously in world trade since 1967.

[130] Silver coins minted in Germany and used continuously in world trade since 1741.

[131] $100,000.

[132] Nine-tailed fox god of the kitsune.

to save face. Taro was the first to offer his hand and they shook, the American way. Partners in crime. Then the freelancer and the Inagawa-kai clan boss went their separate ways.

Akihabra, Tokyo. Outdoors, there was the heady smell of rain and ozone. It was a typical Tokyo night with a thousand LED-lit signs and giant 3D-screens showing gyrating blossoms and dancing pandas. Two impossibly elegant women were walking their robot-dogs on the other side of the street. Taro zoomed in with his Google glasses and nodded his approval. The fad of bulging Western eyes had run its course: their eyes were once more slanted, almost aggressively Asian: pure Japanese beauty.

After buying the electronic component parts he came there for, there was a ping in the left-hand corner of Taro's field of vision: *LIKE US?* followed by three hearts and a second question mark.

Look and you are seen. When you were wired with megane extensions, it always worked both ways.

"I am already taken," he said and saw the words scrolling across his glasses, "and my lover is as jealous as she is beautiful."

"Ah, a proper fox wife!" said one of the nearby girls in the crowd. Taro's heart almost missed a beat, but then he realized it had nothing to do with Hoshi. To imply that a man had a fox as a lover was the highest compliment, almost a cliché. Kitsune were passionate and easily distracted: only a very accomplished lover could keep their attention.

"You wouldn't want to anger one of your sisters," he replied, implying that they were so beautiful that they could only be foxes themselves. Silver laughter filled his ears. The girls waved and turned a corner.

Taro felt a warm glow in the bottom of his belly. Nothing relaxed like a little flirting, and most of the tension was gone. *Get some moldy bones and a soul. How hard can that be?*

In the subway, just for practice, he rolled two drunken salarymen, and then he slipped their intact billfolds back into their pockets with cards that read: TAKE CARE. THERE ARE PICKPOCKETS HERE WHO NEED YOUR MONEY WORSE THAN I.

It was always a good idea to keep in shape.

Tsukishima, Tokyo. Taro and Hoshi lived on a houseboat in one of those brand-new marinas in Tokyo Bay. They both enjoyed the rocking motions of the waves and laughed off the danger posed by the rising waters and ever more frequent tsunamis: *We're already floating, after all, so being washed away in a storm wouldn't really be anything new.* It also helped that their heavily modified houseboat had started as a high-tech lifeboat and could right itself even after having been turned upside down.

When he crossed the jetty to the ferry station, three men stepped from the shadow of a container. At that same moment his *megane* extensions failed—his Google glasses lost all connection to the web and became crystal clear. He was on his own with no way to call for help.

"Don't move." In the orange sodium light, an alternative to the pervasive green algae light, their faces seemed waxen and lumpy, with big noses and heavy-brows, like Neanderthals.

Gaijin, he thought. *Outsiders.* They overtopped him by at least two heads: hulking giants who had been fed on hormone-saturated chicken-legs, cheese, and cornbread. There was the glint of a snub-nosed revolver.

Not even a silencer; these people are rank amateurs and completely unpredictable.

"You are coming with us," their leader said. "To the closest ATM." He stepped back and gestured with his gun. "Which is where?"

"You want money? If you let me get my billfold we-"

"Keep your hands away from your pockets! And your billfold? You think I am crazy? No doubt it is chipped and booby-trapped from here to Saint Ekaterinburg. No, you are going to get us some cash: nice, unmarked bills."

Most of the cash-machines were owned by the yakuza, the Russian Mafiya, or 7-Eleven: they were the only places where you could get your money completely unmonitored.

"You walk in front of us," ordered the leader of the Russian thugs. "No, don't raise your hands. We are just friends. Good friends taking a stroll." He put his gun away, hiding it from any passersby.

"Is it far?" one of the others asked. His curly hair was red as a fox, but he certainly wasn't a kitsune. No kitsune male would wear muddy Doc Martens or tattoo his arms with snarling wolf-heads.

"Just around the corner, so people can get cash before they board. In Bay Town, you have to pay cash for everything. People here don't trust cards," Taro said.

Taro felt fine, almost lighthearted and above all, he was spoiling for a fight. Not the kind of fight where he used his fists, but the kind of fight that he won: where he left his enemies down in the mud, humiliated and all face lost.

The ATM was an island of warm light in the gloom, with a new yen sign rotating above.

"Now you can take your card," the leader said. "Don't try to tell me you are broke. Those shoes are genuine seal-leather and you necktie is watered silk."

285

"I am not broke. Right, how much do you want?"

"Such a strange question! All of it, of course."

"There is a fifty thousand yen limit on each cash transaction. You have to wait two hours for the next five."

"We have all the time in the world."

"Fifty thousand: that would be how much in rubles?" the red-haired tough asked.

"More than enough for a night's work." The leader gestured again and stepped closer. "Put in your card."

The ATM next read Taro's fingerprint, and checked his DNA.

"You are Kobayashi Taro," a dulcet computerized voice intoned. "How can we be of service?"

"Fifty thousand, please. In the biggest bills you have." All three hooligans now crowded around him, their attention focused on the hopper. *Perfect.*

"Counting." The first packet emerged from the slot and Taro turned around.

"Please step back," he said. In his hand, Taro held the gun he'd just stolen from the leader's pocket.

"Holy Saint Basil!" the red-haired one cursed. He raised his own gun.

"I already emptied the cylinder," Taro said. He opened his other hand and let the five cartridges drop, clattering across the stones of the quay.

Taro felt a wide monkey-grin tugging at the corner of his mouth. "Now it is your turn, please. Your cards, gentlemen."

It soon became clear why they had tried to rob him. Their money barely covered the price of a dinner for two in one of the better area restaurants. Taro pocketed the money: it was honestly earned after all. "You can leave now."

"Not so fast," said a new voice.

Five masked men appeared from alongside the nearby wall; they had probably been wearing thermoptic camo, army-grade chameleon gear. "We are the Inagawa-kai, and we don't like strangers poaching on our territory."

Taro recognized Akira, despite his mask. It was the way he stood: with slumped shoulders and his head pushed forward, like an inquisitive turtle.

The leader of the Russians raised both his hands. "We are mafiya, comrade," he pleaded. "Members of the Solntsevskaya Bratva."[133]

"Really? How about that, Andrei?" asked Noboru Akira. Using his hands free device, he called up the real head of the Solntsevskaya Bratva.

"They are scum." A man with a clearly Russian accent replied, his voice coming from the thin air. "Not in any of our divisions. I checked their tattoos through your smartglasses. They are meaningless: infantile scribblings. Not a single barbed cross or braided snake to be found."

"I can explain," the leader of the Russian wannabes pleaded.

"Explain it to Yama," Akira said. "You'll meet the lord of the underworld soon enough."

"You have been following me," Taro said.

"We have to protect our investments. A courier just delivered the first four thousand Reichsmarks in krugerrands and Maria Theresa thalers, as we agreed. He brought the coins to your houseboat and your lover signed for them." He nodded. "See us as your bodyguards."

"I didn't ask for an advance."

"It was just to show that we trust you." Akira nodded to the cowering robbers. "Do you want to stay? To, eh, see justice done?"

---

[133] The Russian Mafiya in Tokyo.

"No thanks." Taro turned and swiftly walked away. He wasn't all that fond of spilled blood. It must be Hoshi's influence: killing should never be mechanical, never just a boring job, but something done in a white-hot passion, or at least in self-defense.

In the distance the lights of the ferry were drawing closer and he suddenly felt terminally tired. *I just want to go home, to lie in Hoshi's arms.*

Kokusai-tenjijo, Tokyo. Taro leaned across the railing and let the salty night-wind blowing off Tokyo Bay pummel his face. He never took an advance. He preferred to get the money after the job was done and never owe a client a single yen; for he could fail, discover that the job couldn't be done after all. And he was always paid. He made sure of that. *Why the hell did Hoshi sign for the money?* He almost pinged her, but held back at the last moment. No line was ever really secure.

He called up the newsfeed and the first headline showed why Noburo Akira had been so desperate, willing to resort to necromancy even.

THIRD YAKUZA OYABUN ARRESTED THIS YEAR.
Prime Minister Akiyama asks for a speedy trial and designated boryokudan status for all violent yakuza clans.

The designated boryokudan status, "particularly harmful," meant the loss of almost all legal protection. It made them no better than terrorists.

The great Yamaguchi-gumi syndicate was clearly falling apart, turning into a hundred feuding gangs, and no bureaucrat, politician, or cop dared to take a bribe from them anymore, though they still took the Inagawa-kai's money quite readily.

A bad time to be a member of the yakuza. Luckily, I am not. He looked at his antique gold pocketwatch. Half an hour and he would be home. *Just enough time to get a drink.*

Taro went below-deck to the bar and ordered a sake. After the third cup, he relaxed. He put on his glasses, switched on the megane extensions, and idly selected the Ghostview 2.1 app. He looked around.

Ghostview ver. 2.1 was only a week old and already one of the more controversial updates because, while powerful, it too often came up with false positives. The principle was simple: take a picture in visible light and compare it to one in infrared and another in ultraviolet. Ghosts and the undead were at the ambient temperature, or at least much colder than the usual human thirty-seven centigrade. Demons and river-dragons were made of pure life force, overflowing with chi, and were dazzling in ultraviolet. Luckily, the app was useless with kitsune or other animal shape-changers.

He scanned the ferry's below deck bar and there were two instant and unmistakable hits. One was a mournful looking sailor at the bar who fell into the ghost range. Another was the little girl sitting next to him who produced an almost blinding aura in the ultraviolet. *No doubt one of the kami.* Taro took his cup and moved over to a table in the corner, as far as possible from the two supernaturals.

Too late. The little girl slid from her barstool and crossed over to his table. She sat down and put her elbows on the tabletop.

"I saw you looking. You know what I am?" Tiny flames danced in her pupils, Taro saw. Tiny green flames.

"Something high and strange," Taro replied. His tongue felt suddenly very dry and the air had become hot: hot as a furnace, hot as the mouth of a volcano. "A goddess."

"You don't have to flatter me. I am just an oni."[134] She smiled and her teeth were rows of gleaming pearls. "You see? Not even pointed. So you have nothing to fear."

She turned and crooked a finger. The sailor left his barstool and came shuffling over across the barroom. There was a sudden fearful hush, all conversation halted and everybody was staring at Taro's table. Clearly, he wasn't the only one with the Ghostview app.

"I collect humans," the little girl declared. She pointed at the shambling sailor. "I collected him, but I think you'll be much more fun. He can't even scream, only kind of bubble. So boring." She put a little pudgy hand on his wrist. "I think I'll take you."

"I am …" *Inari help me!* "I already have a wife."

"Good. I'll take her, too."

"She is a fox. One of the yako."[135] The yako were the worst of the kitsune, ranging from mischievous to downright evil.

"Ah, kuso! Why are all of the good men already taken?" She looked around and pointed to a businessman, who wore a golden chain with a Malthezer cross. "You. I want to see you dance on glowing coals." She and the businessman grew transparent and vanished.

Taro slumped down in his chair and waved to the barkeep. "A glass of whiskey: a big glass. No, make that a tumbler, with lots of ice."

After a spell, Taro somehow made it home to his houseboat. "You are drunk," Hoshi said. "Shame on you! Are you a salaryman to stumble dead drunk home to your ever-loving wife?" She pointed to the table were a row of krugerrands and Maria Theresa thalers lay

---

[134] Demon.

[135] A kitsune devil.

gleaming in the green lamplight. "And please explain this."

"I can't," Taro moaned. "I am much too drunk." He took his Google glasses off. "Have a look. I recorded most of the night. And that money is for stealing someone's bones."

"Whose bones?"

"And later his soul. But then they will pay more."

Hoshi put her hands on her hips. "Whose bones?" she repeated, her voice uncharacteristically shrill.

"O-Oda's. Oda Nobunaga's bones."

"You," she said. "You must be fucking crazy." With her supernatural strength, Hoshi effortlessly lifted him and tossed him across her shoulders. "You go to the bedroom to sleep it off. I'll speak you in the morning."

"Yes, love of my life," Taro mumbled. "I'll do that." He was asleep the moment his head touched the pillow.

July 7, 2019. The slanting sun-rays drove silver needles through Taro's eyeballs and his mouth tasted like a month-old ashtray. Behind his hypothetical third eye, a heavy metal band was doing an earthquake imitation.

"Put this in your mouth," Hoshi ordered. She offered Taro a small ivory ball. The instant it touched his tongue, all pain was gone. Pure chi flooded his muscles and energized his brain.

"Now spit it out," she said. "I don't want you to grow a tail."

"That was your hoshi no tama![136] Your fox ball."

The hoshi no tama was a kitsune's most prized possession: the amulet that allowed her to change shape.

---

[136] A kitsune's fox ball, or shapeshifting amulet.

"Yes, and I hope this is the last time I have to use it."

Taro looked at her face in wonder. Hoshi wasn't conventionally beautiful, with her face too narrow for the round Lolita look and her unplucked eyebrows much too bushy. Her mouth was wide, not a rosebud at all but made for smiling. Her smile was never bashful and always mischievous, as if she knew a secret even the gods would dearly like to know.

She put her fox ball in my mouth: the most intimate act for a kitsune. Hoshi must truly love me. Then and there, Taro decided never to betray that trust, to be the best husband and lover a mortal man could be.

Hoshi sat down at the foot of his bed. "Now tell me everything. I trust you were just babbling about Oda Nobunaga's bones?"

"I am afraid not."

Hoshi sighed. "Well, no risk, no gain. Let's try to figure out a way to survive."

About the Author

Tais Teng (1952) is a Dutch fantasy and science fiction writer, illustrator and sculptor. His real name is Thijs van Ebbenhorst Tengbergen which he shortened to Tais Teng. In his own language he has written about everything from radio-plays to hefty fantasy trilogies.

His books have been translated in German, Finnish, French and English. To date he sold some twenty-five stories in the English language and one novel, *The Emerald Boy*. His websites are: taisteng.atspace.com (stories) and taisteng.deviantart.com (art).

You can buy his short story collection LOVECRAFT, MY LOVE at Amazon.com or one of the other e-book retailers.

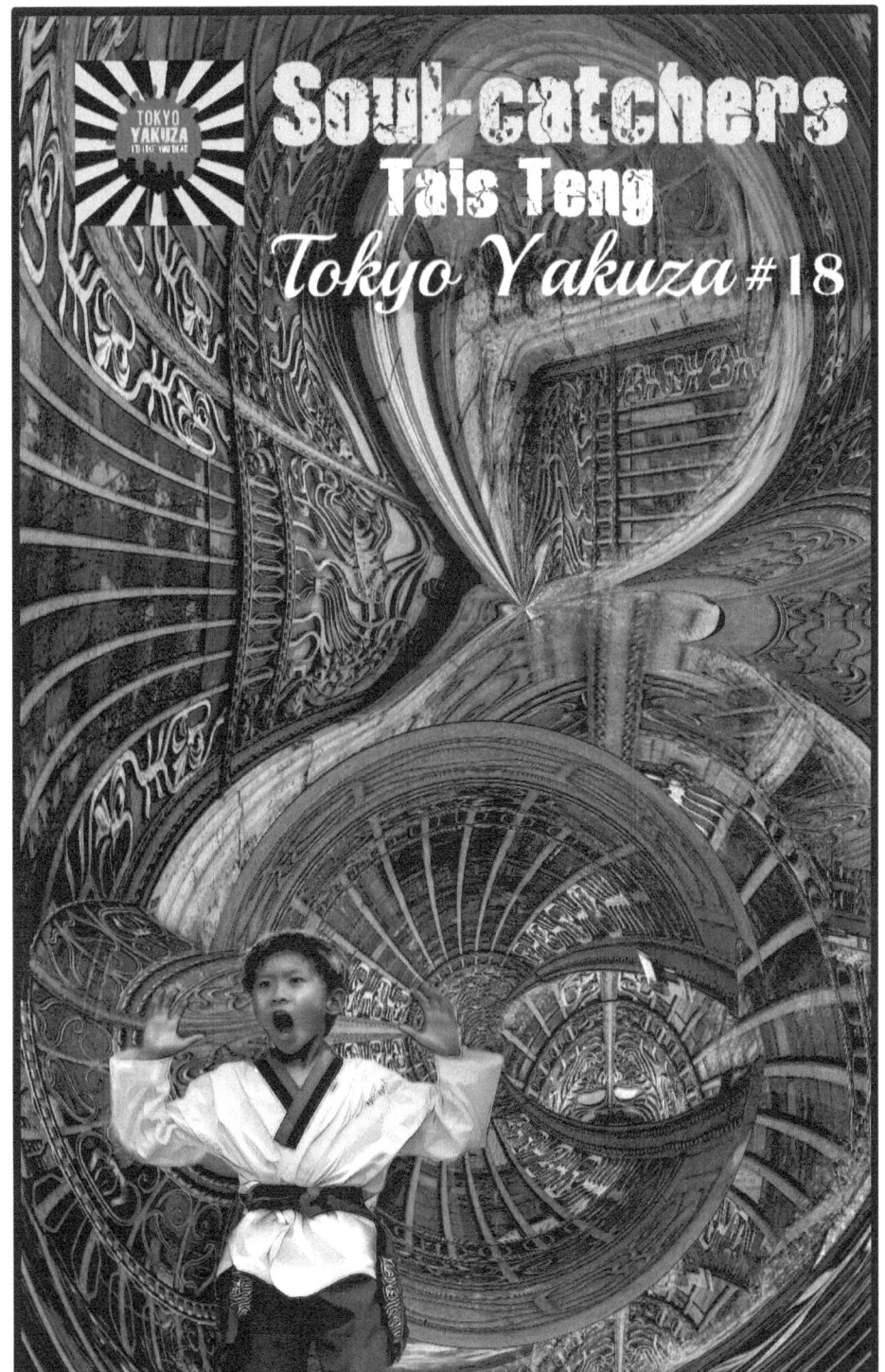

Tokyo Yakuza #18

Soul-Catchers

By Tais Teng

July 8, 2019. Kokusai-tenjijo, Tokyo. "I have finally located his grave." Hoshi snorted took off her Google glasses to rub the bridge of her nose. "There is a problem. Oda took his own life: harakiri in a temple."

"Yes? That would only make his bones more powerful."

"He took his life in a *burning* temple. What the monks buried were his ashes. Not much DNA left in ashes."

Taro frowned. "Do you think Oyabun Noburo Akira knew? Paying me in advance for a job that can't be done?"

"Not a chance. He would lose face, too. You can't be blamed and the others wouldn't be amused."

"What should we do?"

"What any sane person would try when she is perplexed. Get me the *I Ching*.[137] Throw the yarrow stalks," she said.

"Hexagram thirty-two," she said after the cast, opening their leather-bound volume. "Yes, Heng: Durability. Arousing thunder

---

[137] The *Book of Changes*, an old Chinese book of fortunetelling.

and penetrating wind. Close companions in any storm: the superior person possesses a resilience and durability that lets him remain faithfully and firmly on course. Such constancy deserves success." She closed the oracle book. "That doesn't sound too bad."

"True," Taro said. "But what does it *mean*? And am I a superior person? Otherwise that advice is useless for me. Then that 'It deserves success.' Does that prophesy that I'll succeed?"

"Questions, questions. Don't try to understand. Feel." She spread her hands. "Flow with the tao, the currents of the world!"

"Can you do that?" Taro asked his kitsune wife.

Hoshi started giggling. "No. We foxes, we are easily distracted and only a nine-tailed fox could ever be called wise. I am centuries too young for wisdom."

"Wait!" Taro cried. "Thunder and lightning. The burning temple and all bones turned to ash. I almost have it. All we need is a drop of blood, a single hair."

"Hair is pure keratin. No DNA at all, according to my glasses," Hoshi said.

"Don't distract me," said Taro. "No bones left. Not even teeth and their DNA would have been degraded by the fire anyhow."

"Baby-teeth," Hoshi said, with slow realization. "You humans put a milk-tooth under the floor of the living room. Did they already do it that in Nobunaga's time?" She touched her own Google glasses. "Yes, they did! And Oda was born in Nagoya Castle, which is still standing. Oh no," she said. "It was extensively renovated by one of the later rulers."

"You don't dig up the foundations when you rebuild. His teeth are probably still there." Taro rubbed his chin. "Quite a lot of floor space on a castle and they probably wouldn't allow us to lift every flagstone or floorboard. We'll have to narrow it down somehow. A dowsing rod?"

"You use a dowsing-rod to look for the chi of flowing water. There is not much chi in a discarded milk-tooth. Don't worry. We'll find a way."

Kuramae, Tokyo. They met the Inagawa-kai clan boss in a tavern that was a faithful replica of the Korova Milk Bar from *A Clockwork Orange,* except that they were dispensing soy-milk, most Japanese being lactose intolerant.

Noboru Akira presided in his circle of mirror-shaded hoodlums. A waitress with a platinum-blond wig sat on his knee.

"Everybody out!" he called the moment he noticed Taro and Hoshi. He rotated his wrist and Taro's glasses went dead for the second time.

Akira folded his arms. "So tell me. Did you get his bones? That was fast."

Taro explained the situation. Akira was a good listener, something Taro would never have suspected and, in the end, the yakuza boss nodded. "So you need his ashes. No need to rob any graves; this can be handled discreetly. I know the abbot of the temple where Nobunaga is buried." He nodded. "Using his tooth to raise him is a nice touch. Quite traditional. Wasn't there an army in Western myth that was created by sowing a field with dragon teeth?" He guffawed. "Milk-teeth. Hah!"

A scant three hours later, Akira met with them, holding an urn. "Here are his ashes," Akira said. "I hope it is enough? Because this is all there was left. There were others who had a use for Oda's ashes."

Taro eyed the urn: it had that ugly, cracked, off-green glaze you saw in the more expensive galleries, the ones where nothing bore a price tag.

"A celadon grave urn!" Hoshi exclaimed. "It must be priceless. And he just handed it over?"

"Well, he'll probably have to take his life. Seppuku, eh? If he ever wants to look his ancestors in the face."

"Sou desu ne."[138]

"You can keep the vase after you are finished, girl," said Akira.

Hoshi glared at his retreating back. "There goes a man without virtue who no doubt will burn in Hell. Or return as a cockroach in his next life."

"Nobody will notice the difference." Taro took her arm. "Come. We have a castle to visit."

Nagoya, Japan. It was almost too easy, an anticlimax. They just strolled into Nagoya Castle with the bodyguard in front, waving a hand from which the little finger was conspicuously absent. The ticket-collector decided to look the other way.

They were a company of four: Taro, Hoshi, Ito Shintaro, one of Akira's cybernetic Inagawa-kai bodyguards, and Takenaka-san, a Shinto exorcist in crimson robes who always traveled with a hip flask of whiskey. The monk had been Hoshi's idea: one who could banish ghosts could probably also summon them, though this was more of a treasure hunt than a summoning.

"Do you have to petition one of the kami to help you?" Hoshi asked.

---

[138] "I see."

The slightly tipsy monk giggled. "This is so *wrong*, yes, deeply *evil.* But you hired the right person for the job. I am not exactly an exorcist, more like a devil worshiper. I lay curses, esteemed fox-lady. And Nobunaga was a bad man." He looked around the first room. "Now hand me the urn."

Takenaka poured ashes into the palm of his left hand, hissed a word, and then blew. The ash rose in glowing coils, drifting across the room.

"Follow them. Like calls unto like, yes? They were once part of Oda's mortal body, just like his milk-teeth, and they dearly want to unite again."

The ashes finally settled on the floor of the seventh room. Nobody interfered when their bodyguard took a pneumatic hammer from his briefcase and started to drill a hole.

Hoshi held the tiny tooth between her thumb and index-finger and shook her head. "This is probably the single most stupid thing anybody will do this century." She dropped the milk-tooth in a plastic envelope and zipped it.

"Oyabun Noboru wants to meet you," the bodyguard said. "At the CBI-Hitachi facility in Maihama. All three of you."

"Me too?" Takenaka asked.

"The oyabun is tapped into the wireless video feed from his cybereyes. He saw you cast that spell. He is impressed."

July 9, 2019. Maihama, Tokyo. The CBI-Hitachi physician inspected the tooth, and nodded. "Looks promising. We have been able to extract DNA from a saber-toothed tiger's fang and this is much more recent." He turned to Oyabun Noboru Akira. "Two days: one to extract, one to repair the chromosomes. Then we can start the clone. We just got the stolen wombs. No more double-heads."

"Good." Akira frowned and stood, rubbing his chin. "How long would it take for a clone to mature?"

"The usual time. We can accelerate the growth of a fetus to a week, but after the birth it slows down. If you want a ten-year old, you'll have to wait ten years."

"I didn't realize." Yori shook his head. "There must be a way."

"Excuse me?" Takenaka said. "There is, there is! My grand-mother taught me a spell to accelerate aging. 'Let his hour be as a day, his day as a month.' Like that. She used the spell on the girl next door, when my granny caught her flirting with the boy she fancied." He chuckled. "At the end of the week, the hair of her rival had turned gray and she had to use a walking stick, shuffling to her school."

"Interesting. And the price?"

"That is the best thing. Only the victim pays!"

"I'll see you in three days." Akira gestured to his bodyguard. "Show them out. No, wait. Taro, you and your lover. Think about how you can catch Oda's soul. I need it in, well, two weeks."

"Catching a soul is ever so easy," Takenaka said. "All you need is a virgin mirror."

"Virgin?" the Inagawa-kai oyabun asked.

"Just shaman-talk. It means a mirror that nobody has ever looked into. In the past such mirrors were made by blind artisans. A virgin mirror sucks the soul into the glass from the very first person who tries to shave. But it gets even better! When the next victim looks in that mirror, well, that hungry soul jumps right out in a dazzling flash of pure chi and possesses the second body." The monk's smile could only be called a smirk, Taro thought. "In Nobunaga's case, well, it works even better when the soul is already outside a body." Takenaka folded his arms. "Now let's talk about the price in yen. Both of the mirror and my assistance."

Tsukiji, Tokyo. "This was a most profitable day!" the monk said. They were at a hole in the wall sushi joint back in Tsukiji. "A beautiful fox lady and a yakuza lord as clients!" He bowed. "By the way, you can call me Kenji. Yes, Takenaka Kenji."

"Which probably isn't your real name?" Hoshi said.

"Of course not! But it is easier talking this way." Takenaka Kenji spread his arms wide. "Such a beautiful day, my friends! Let's take a cup of sake and rip the wings of some screaming butterflies."

July 10, 2019. Yokohama, Japan. Afterwards, Taro never could reconstruct how he ended up on the roof of a Yokohama bathhouse, sleeping next to Hoshi, with an earthenware sake bottle as his cushion. He blinked against the watery early morning sunlight. "Where is Kenji?"

"He turned into a vulture and flew away," said Hoshi, still drowsy. "But perhaps I shouldn't have taken that second cup of his fermented mushroom liquor."

July 28, 2019. Maihama, Tokyo. In a country that wasn't exactly real:

"Your name is Oda," one of the warriors told the boy. "Oda Nobunaga, and you will rule the whole of Nippon. Everybody will bow for you. Bow deep and grovel, because you are the overlord."

"Why can't I rule all of Nippon right now?"

"Well, perhaps because you are still a toddler?" He made a sweeping gesture across the entire horizon, with the rising columns of smoke where castles and villages were burning. "This isn't real, you know. It is just a game. To learn."

"You don't look like my other soldiers. I don't think you are even Japanese." The boy pointed. "Tell me your name! I order it!"

"They called me Sun Tzu when I was still alive. And yes, I am not Japanese. I never even visited your country. I wrote a book when I wasn't campaigning for my king. It is called The Art of War."

"The Art of War," the boy mused. "That sounds interesting. I would like to read it."

"We can do one better. You'll live it." And for some years the boy was an officer in the time of the Warring States, the right hand of that august personage, General Sun Tzu.

November 11, 2019. One day Sun Tzu halted his horse at the hilltop. The walls of the last enemy city had been breached and all the members of the court were marched outside, to be strangled.

"I have taught you all I know about war and about winning," Sun Tzu said. "Now it is time you study how to keep what you have taken." He pointed to a distant rider who instantly appeared next to them.

Oda unabashedly stared at the newcomer and started to giggle. This man was even stranger than Sun Tzu, with eyes so big they bulged from the sockets. No beard, not even a wisp: his face was as smooth as a geisha's.

"This is my good and clever friend, Niccolò Machiavelli. He wrote a book, too."

"Show me," Oda ordered.

"Ah, an eager pupil. I like that." The strange man took Oda's hand and they were somewhere else. At their feet stretched a wondrous city with a dome red as lacquer, a winding river with half a dozen bridges.

"Welcome to my great and terrible Firenze."

December 25, 2019. Months passed, perhaps years, and one day wonderful Firenze faded out and Oda found himself once again sitting in his own bedroom. In the background the voice that never stopped, sang on. "Your minutes will be hours, your hours fast fleeting days and months. Your minutes …"

Oda's robot-cat, Cheshire, sat on his pillow, his eyes glowing. With his wide smile and his black karateka head-band he looked like an evil Hello Kitty.

"I think that you are growing up," his robot-cat said.

"I am already a grown-up," Oda protested. "When I walked with Machiavelli, I was even a head taller than he!"

"That wasn't real," Cheshire the robot-cat said. "Just a virtual war game called Assassin's Creed." Cheshire extended a razor sharp claw and started to whittle a fallen oak branch. Faces appeared between the curling shavings: screaming faces with every mouth a black circle.

"Explain," said Oda Nobunaga.

"Well, you are actually lying in a bath of warm jelly. Your muscles are kneaded by gentle robotic hands. You are fed glucose and amino acids right into your veins. You have never walked, or jumped, or raised a sword. That will happen when you are old enough. When they wake you." The robot-cat touched his own glass eyes. "There are lenses pasted to your eyeballs and they project all you see on your retina. Taste and smell are fed directly into your brain."

"I don't believe you. I ate a salmon half an hour ago, spat out the bones. When I touch the leaf of a thistle, my fingertips bleed!"

"Nevertheless …"

"So I am kept prisoner in my own body. My jailers will be sorry when I escape!"

"Oh yes." Cheshire's grin became even wider and now Oda could see that his teeth were pointed. "Oh yes, they will."

"We woke him," Akira said. "He is almost ready. A ten-year-old boy with his brain still malleable enough to accept a wiser and stronger soul." He touched the screen. Taro saw a young boy running through a strangely empty cityscape with endless corridors, wide as a spaceship hangar. A robot-cat ran in front, jumping as high as a hare. The cyber-animal raised his forelegs and suddenly there were claws like sickles, claws that wouldn't have been out of place on a velociraptor.

"What we see, it is a simulation?" Hoshi asked.

"Mostly real. An old anime movie set with interactive walls. The ground moves backwards when he runs, to keep him in the same place. But he is ready for a wider world. I need Nobunaga's soul. Urgently."

"I know where to find it," Taro said. "Takenaka Kenji took me, dreaming, and we located him." He shuddered at the memory: the burning guardians at the gate of the underworld, the shrieking crows feeding on carcasses long as aircraft carriers, carcasses that were still alive and mewling.

"So, I hope you can spare him," Hoshi said.

"The boy is old enough. No need any longer for Kenji to keep that time spell going."

"Call him. We brought the virgin mirror. It was made in an automated factory, instantly wrapped in silk."

January 1, 2020. Akihabara, Tokyo. They were walking the streets of the city, trying to keep up with Kenji who slalomed through the dense crowd like a swallow slipping through waving reeds. Into Akihabara they went, where every wall was a moving screen and little girls with huge manga-eyes gazed at them, licking lollipops: little girls who could have been middle-aged housewives in Lolita-drag. Robot-dogs ran past while cyber-monkeys jumped from street-lamp to street-lamp. All was movement, all was change. Logos crawled across Taro's bare arms and his footprints followed him in glowing snowflakes.

This was the high-tech district, with a thousand tricks that were hard to distinguish from magic … except to those who could see the eyes that peered from the shadows in an alley, looking straight into their souls. Those who could see the eyes knew that all those tech-tricks and illusions were just that: shallow entertainment and nothing like true magic.

There was sudden hush, leaving only the sound of rustling leaves.

"How did we get in this park?" Taro asked. "And where the hell is it? I thought I knew Tokyo."

"It isn't a park, love," Hoshi said. "It is the yakuza graveyard,[139] where oyabun and wakagashira go when they die. No Tokyo Metro line leads here, and no line leads out."

"Well, what better place for the gate of the underworld?"

Kenji halted in front of a tomb and tugged at an iron gate that opened without making a sound. Five steps led down: slippery steps, covered with browned petals. There was the sickly sweet stink of small, decomposing rodents. "No need to follow the dream-road this time, Taro. Now that we know where to go, we can take a short-cut," the monk in the crimson robes said.

Taro took a first step and the stairs unrolled like a scroll. Too many steps to count reached down into a glowing twilight: thousands of steps, millions. He looked back and the whole universe did a flip-flop. He suddenly stood at the very bottom, with the stairs reaching up for an entrance that surely must be light-years away.

"We have arrived," Kenji said. "Well, that wasn't too hard, eh?"

"We have arrived *where*?" Hoshi asked.

"The Seventy Third Hell, meant for those who betray trust and compromise their honor forever."

"Nobunaga ended up here?"

"As you can see."

A man was kneeling on a mosaic floor which was lit by roaring flames. He sat in the right position for seppuku, his tanto, the ceremonial knife, held ready for the cut that would open his belly and free his soul.

There was no kaishakunin standing at his back, Taro noticed, no appointed second to cut Oda's head off should the pain become unbearable and an inadvertent moan spoil the ceremony. That alone

---

[139] The yakuza are known for hosting lavish funerals for their dead leaders, but few realize that their souls all end up here.

made it into a second rate seppuku.

And who were those shades standing in the middle of the flames, each with his severed head held in the crook of an elbow? How eagerly they stared at the man, licking their lips in anticipation.

Oda raised his knife, drove it into his belly and cut sideways.

No, he didn't. Halfway, the knife changed into a sprig of parsley, making the ceremony ridiculous: the act of a clown. Mocking laughter rolled through the temple.

Nobunaga moaned in dismay, then reached for the tanto again, which had changed back into a knife.

"This is justice?" Hoshi was aghast. "What did he do to deserve this?"

"It was during the siege of Yakami Castle," Kenji said. "He sent his best friend Akechi Mitsuhide to parley, promising him that he would let the ruler and his family go free if they surrendered. They agreed and opened the gates, but Oda still took their heads, thus besmirching his own honor and worse than that, the honor of his friend."

"I understand," Hoshi said. "Yes, this is justice. A pity we'll have to interfere."

She took the covered mirror from the priest, stepped into the circle of shades, and ripped the silk panels away.

"Oda Nobunaga!" she cried. "Look into this mirror. See your own infamy and shame."

A dazzling flash followed and suddenly the circle stood empty. The knife clattered on the floor, turning into a sprig of parsley for the last time.

Hoshi carefully tugged the crumpled silk across the mirror.

"So, it is done. Now, how do we get back?"

"We *are* back," Kenji replied. It was true. Just beyond the open iron gate, Taro saw the full moon sailing above the pine trees. It couldn't have been more than a few minutes. Why, then, did his legs feel like lead, and why did the soles of his feet burn as if he had walked every one of those ten thousand steps?

They wandered out into the streets surrounding the yakuza graveyard in a daze. After a few minutes of aimless wandering past dilapidated temples and vacant apartment buildings, Taro activated his Google glasses. "No Metro line leads out, huh? Then let's call a taxi. No, even better, let's call Akira and have the Inagawa-kai pick us up."

Lost in Tokyo. The Inagawa-kai cyborg bodyguard, Ito Shintaro, drove them in a car with darkened windows: there were clearly some secrets Akira still wanted kept. When they stopped, it was in front of a row of oversized containers. On two of them, Taro noticed the bleached logo of Studio Ghibli.

The boy stood in the middle of the container, the robot-cat crouching at his feet.

"Oda Nobunaga," Akira said.

"Yes? Some people have called me that. More just call me 'Lord.'"

"I have something for you," Akira said. "Something to make you whole."

"Explain."

"Your soul." The Inagawa-kai oyabun swept the silk sheet away and a flash lit the whole container.

The flash turned the boy's eyes into two dazzling points for a moment.

"What?" Noboru Akira stood swaying. He blinked, opened and closed his mouth like a beached salmon. "I don't see," he said. His voice was different, lower. He balled his fists and turned to his bodyguard, Shintaro. "You! Kill all traitors! Leave no one alive."

"Me?" the bodyguard said. The order clearly confused him, but he reached for his weapon.

"Kill them!" Akira shrieked. "They'll betray me! Just like that dog, Akechi Mitsuhide!"[140]

That isn't Akira, Taro realized. Oda's soul somehow ended up in the Inagawa-kai oyabun's body. Taro thought about that flash and the boy's eyes reflecting it like a cat's. *He must still be wearing the contacts. They turned into mirrors, like automatic sun glasses, bouncing the soul away.*

"Don't move," Ito Shintaro said. The cybernetic bodyguard's voice quavered.

"A bit hard to fire with no bullets," Taro answered. *Thank god that I kept in practice, that snatching a gun and taking the cartridges out is almost second nature to me.*

He took Hoshi's hand. "Let's go."

Ikebukuro, Tokyo. The boy was running through the wondrous streets of the city. He wasn't fleeing, just running all out, his heart hammering with joy. The robot-cat, Cheshire, ran next to him. *My name is Oda Nobunaga, and I was made to rule all of Nippon.*

He remembered everything, the military campaigns of two thousand years: every trick, every speech that had once proved effective in making soldiers and followers roar in approval.

The robot-cat halted in front of an ATM. "Best get some cash first, Lord Nobunaga. You remember all of the heist movies, *Burning Chrome, Ocean's Eleven, The Sting?*"

---

[140] Born 1528, died 1582. A general who rebelled against daimyo Oda Nobunaga, leading to Oda's death.

"Let me show you."

Twenty seconds later, the first bills started to emerge from the slit.

Oda wasn't a bad boy, really. Not even evil, but there were some things he had learned from Cheshire. *Everything I see is a game. When I kill people, they don't really die. At the next start, they will be alive again.*

Tokyo Yakuza
#19

For the Honor of a Geisha

by Travis Heermann

Japan won the Second World War; Now the yakuza are starting the Third!

For the Honor of a Geisha

BY TRAVIS HEERMANN

Kusanagi Ryu

February 5, 2020. Shinjuku, Tokyo. The tech unzipped the inductive data-cuff from Ryu's wrist. "Upload complete," she said with a lascivious wink.

Kusanagi Ryu ignored her flirtation and she deflated. He snorted. Women shouldn't be so forward.

Ryu rolled down his red silk sleeve, concealing the sakura[141] and tiger's tail tattoo encircling his arm. The tiger writhed up and around, reaching between his shoulder blades, clawing at his back … the way Makiko clawed at his back. This little tech nerd with her plump cheeks, data-feed glasses, and profound ordinariness wasn't worthy to stand in the shadow of a goddess like Kurosawa Makiko.

In the afterglow of the first time he had bedded Makiko, her fingers stroked his back, brushing the lines embedded under his skin

---

[141] Cherry blossoms.

with the tattoos, and realization of their true nature had bloomed in her eyes.

He had seized her porcelain white face in both hands and said, "If you tell anyone, I'll have to kill you; you know that."

She had swallowed hard and nodded, then grinned at him, biting her smudged, rose-red lip and putting on a mischievous expression. "Do you want to spend all this expensive time chatting?"

So he took her again.

The entire evening, complete with dinner, much fine sake, and two maiko,[142] apprentice geisha who played shamisen[143] in accompaniment to Makiko's exquisite dance, had cost him the equivalent of a month's pay for a salaryman, and the tatami-burns on his knees from the ferocity of his thrusting took a week to heal.

Two months later, little else found its way into his thoughts except Makiko and work. Some days, thoughts of Makiko won out. He told her at their last meeting that he would buy her way out of the geisha house that owned her. The rest of the Yamaguchi-gumi were starting to notice his distraction. He could not afford to screw up this run, or it might cost him a finger.

Yamaguchi-gumi wakagashira Chiba Ken stepped up to Ryu and offered a thick envelope.

Kusanagi Ryu gripped it between two fingers, then withdrew his hand without taking the envelope. "Too thin," he said.

"What the fuck are you talking about? I'm your boss. Take the money."

"Don't bullshit me."

In the glow of the tech's computer screens, surrounded by shadow, Chiba's face looked as if it were made of hatchets. With slow

---

[142] Geisha-in-training.

[143] A three-stringed Japanese musical instrument.

menace, he took the cigarette from his mouth. "It's your standard rate." His cheeks rippled with restrained anger. The ring and chimes of pachinko machines filtered through the ceiling vents.

"Like I told you when you called, this is not a standard job," Ryu said. "We're not exactly on kissing terms with the Inagawa-kai. They're going to be looking for couriers tonight. And with the police response given the upcoming Olympics, you can't get near a train station. Plus, it's snowing. Our mutual boss, Oyabun Kitano, wants this data at Narita airport by midnight, so he comes to the best. That's me."

"You're a greedy fucker."

Ryu spat. "I don't see you mounting up to make the run personally. Double the standard fee, or I walk."

"The data is already uploaded."

Ryu rolled up his sleeve again and displayed the cherry blossoms on his arm. "All I have to do is touch these flowers in the correct sequence and the data is flashed clean. I can do it right now." He hovered a finger over his forearm. Bioelectric sensors built into the tattoo were his only way to interface with the hardware embedded in his flesh.

The lines of his tattoos camouflaged thousands of data chips implanted in his dermis, creating a storage matrix with petabyte capacity, powered by his natural bioelectricity and kinetic movements. He had no means of accessing the data; he could only upload and erase. The download decryption algorithms were always in the possession of the recipient. In an age when any phone call, any email, and all data transfers could be hacked, Ryu was a special kind of courier.

If he didn't take this job, his visits to Makiko would cease and his plans to buy her contract would crumble. The thought of her taking money from other men, entertaining other men, fucking other men, even though she swore Ryu was the only man allowed into her bed, put his teeth on edge. He wanted the most beautiful geisha in Tokyo all to himself, for as long as he cared to have her.

Wakagashira Chiba said, "Fuck you, Ryu." Then he pulled out a second envelope.

Ryu smirked and took both envelopes. "No, thank *you*, Chiba-sama."

He shrugged on his armored leather motorcycle jacket, ignored the tech's wistful sigh, and climbed up the back stairwell into the Kabukichō alley where his Honda Meteor 1100 sat parked behind a trash bin. The bulletproof cowling and engine housing gleamed like a droplet of fresh blood in the light filtering from the street. Warm air and cigarette smoke wafted into the winter night, forming a thick cloud through the open back door of the pachinko parlor.

He buckled on his bullet-resistant, full-face helmet, slung a leg over the world's fastest production motorcycle, and thumbed the biometric starter button. The button registered his thumbprint and the massive engine rumbled to life like a tiger roused from sleep.

The GPS below the instrument panel flickered with a map of the greater Neo-Tokyo metropolitan area. "Narita Airport," he said. "Terminal Six."

The earbud in his helmet spoke like an electronic female. "Course entered."

He scanned the route overview mapped on the screen. "Why are we going through Ginza?" The traffic would be horrendous, even at this time of night. Fresh snowfall made this run even trickier.

"All other major routes closed for construction."

"Fucking Olympics."

"Please repeat."

"Never mind."

He gripped the throttle and revved. Then he launched the machine into the night.

Sasaki Kohei

"I think we got him, boss," Ito Shintaro said. "He's coming out of Kabukichō like a bullet on fire."

The thrill of the chase whispered up Sasaki Kohei's neck. "Tap into the surveillance network," he said to the dashboard.

The video screen on the dashboard of the Ferrari Speciale flickered with a grainy video image of a blood-red motorcycle streaking through a teeming intersection, scattering pedestrians in its wake. The network of surveillance cameras locked onto the motorcycle and flagged it for the dozens of traffic violations it was racking up.

Kohei couldn't help but grin as he tightened the racing-style shoulder straps. "Hit it."

Shintaro punched the gas and the Ferrari roared out of the parking garage into the Shinjuku streets. Cars squealed and honked, pedestrians screamed. The acceleration smashed Kohei deeper into his seat.

He looked over his shoulder at the squirming bundle stowed in the narrow space behind the car's two seats. "Don't worry, sweetheart. If he's got what you say he's got, you'll come through this just fine." The zipped-up body bag stopped wriggling. "Now stop that fucking whimpering. You're giving me a headache."

The video screen displayed a pulsing red dot weaving in and out major streets and residential neighborhoods, shooting across foot bridges and sidewalks.

"Can we catch him before the cops?" Shintaro said.

Kohei ran his fingers over the touchscreen and issued commands. The map now showed the locations of every police car in Tokyo; none of them were converging on the motorcycle. "Either they haven't gotten the alert on him, or they've been paid off."

Ito Shintaro grinned with malice. "Then they won't care if we smear him across the front of a building."

Aoyama-itchome, Tokyo. The screen map flashed red with numerous street closings, funneling both the Inagawa-kai Ferrari and the Yamaguchi-gumi motorcycle toward Ginza. It would be a nightmare getting through there, but it was also the perfect place to catch him.

Sasaki Kohei tapped in queries and commands. The screen flashed the results. "Ginza, Yon-chome Crossing. That's where we'll catch him." It was the busiest intersection in the world. Tomorrow, those people would have a story to tell.

Kasumigaseki, Tokyo. Minutes passed and their location converged upon the motorcycle. Tokyo streets streaked past at 100 km/h. Kohei howled, exultant, and pounded the roof with his palm.

At least their quarry had good taste in women. Makiko was just beginning to make a name for herself in the "floating world" but she had the looks and charm to be star. In a crowd of ten thousand women, she would be a swan among chickens.

The unsecured body bag rolled and thumped with the massive accelerations. Kohei heard her crying inside it.

"Just think, sweetheart," Kohei said over his shoulder. "If the Inagawa-kai gets what we want, they'll pay me enough to buy you outright. Call this your initiation."

The only response was a muffled whimper.

Ginza, Tokyo. "We're on Chuo-dori," Shintaro said. He gritted his teeth with concentration.

Kohei gripped the dashboard with anticipation. The courier was rocketing down Harumi-dori to intersect with their path.

The Ferrari zipped between cars. The sidewalks were choked with humanity's chaff. The gods of Ginza smiled upon emperors and commoners alike with light from a thousand neon signs and plasma screens, showering them like shards from a rainbow.

Yon-chome Crossing lay just to the north, coming fast.

The traffic light turned red and thousands of pedestrians began to cross the intersection from six directions, including diagonally. The motorcycle was less than a hundred meters away, flying toward them.

Shintaro laid on the horn. Pedestrians scattered and dove out of the way. A cacophony of screaming terror filled the air.

From the west, the motorcycle roared into the intersection with the sound of ten thousand angry hornets.

Shintaro punched the gas, aiming for the motorcycle.

The courier swerved but too late. The motorcycle T-boned the driver's door with a crash of steel and glass. Something warm, wet, and pulpy sprayed the side of Kohei's face. The rider catapulted over the roof and plowed, heels up, into a grimy mound of freshly cleared snow.

The impact addled Kohei's head. The smell of blood and other fluids filled his nose. He tried to wipe his eyes.

With startling alacrity, the rider rolled backwards to his feet and ran, staggering, back toward the twisted conglomeration of car and motorcycle.

Kohei struggled with his seat belts, fumbling for the scabbard of his katana, tucked alongside his seat.

The motorcycle's front fork, designed to connect the front wheel and axle to the frame, was instead sticking through the side of Shintaro's head.

Kohei grimaced, then thrust open his wrecked Ferrari's door and leaped out, dragging his katana with him.

The rider dragged another such scabbard from the rear of the motorcycle seat, where space for it had been built into the motorcycle's frame. He saw Kohei and turned to run.

"Hold it, asshole!" Sasaki Kohei roared.

The rider picked up speed, running toward the packed throng of a thousand pedestrians.

"I got your geisha bitch!"

The rider skidded to a halt. He turned.

Kohei snapped the seat forward, reached inside, and dragged the body bag onto the pavement. The sound of terrified weeping emanated from the body bag. Kohei drew his sword and raised it over her.

The rider unbuckled his pavement-scored helmet, tore it off, and tossed it aside. He brushed a layer of sweat off of his shaved head and fixed Kohei with a look of flinty hatred.

With a single, deft slash, Sasaki Kohei laid open the bodybag. A brightly colored kimono began to kick free like a butterfly from a chrysalis. Kohei grabbed hold of the bag and dumped the rest of the rumpled butterfly into view.

Kurosawa Makiko's hands were tied and her mouth was gagged. Her distinctive geisha hairstyle stuck out, frizzed into complete disarray, and her porcelain-white makeup was smeared. Her beautiful eyes glittered with terror and blood trickled from her nose.

"Bastard!" the rider snarled. He whipped his sword free, tossing the scabbard next to his helmet. The blade shimmered in the neon Ginza night.

Kurosawa Makiko

Makiko gasped for breath around the sodden cloth gag in her mouth, spitting out the blood running from her nose. Her vision swam from the horrific ride in the body bag and from the impact of being dumped onto the pavement. The street was cold, wet, and gritty under her hands as she struggled to right herself.

Kohei called across the intersection to Ryu. "Come and get her, loser!"

Kusanagi Ryu unzipped his stiff leather motorcycle jacket and stripped it off. In the winter cold, the sweat steamed from his crimson silk shirt, like an oni fresh from Hell. Then he ripped the shirt open and peeled it off. He stood bare chested. Powerful muscles rippled under his skin, as if the tiger on his flesh were alive. Neon light limned the rugged planes of his handsome face.

A flash of silver flickered through her vision. The gag parted and fell away from her face, and she spit out the awful wad of cloth in a trail of spittle.

"Ryu!" she wailed. "Help me! Please!"

Kohei sneered. "A millimeter deeper and her geisha days would have been over. Are you sure you want a fight?"

Ryu's hard jaw worked silently.

Kohei said, "Just give it to us. You and your slut can walk."

Makiko knew it was an empty promise. No true yakuza would take such an offer, even had it been sincere. She squirmed onto her hands and knees, wrists tied before her, and began to edge away from Kohei, hoping to remove herself from immediate slicing range.

"Makiko, are you all right?" Ryu called.

Kohei raised his katana into the middle-guard stance, two-handed, with its point extended toward Ryu's throat. Ryu stalked forward, blade swinging at his side.

Kurosawa Makiko was not a weapons expert, but even she could discern that Kohei's weapon was fashioned in the traditional style, with the silk-wrapped, ray-skin grip. The grip of Ryu's weapon looked like textured rubber, with a circular guard of plastic or ceramic.

"If you want it," Ryu said. "You're going to have to peel it off my body." He thumped the tiger paw on his chest.

Standing three paces away from Kohei, Ryu raised his weapon. Both men planted their feet like roots into the earth. The two combatants edged closer, until the tips of their blades almost touched.

The space between heartbeats slowed to years. Blades hung motionless with the gathering force of tremendous wills behind them. Thousands of eyes from the surrounding throng gleamed. Many of the onlookers cracked hesitant smiles as if this scene were some entertainment spectacle organized for the amusement of the visiting foreigners. Giant video screens played music videos and advertisements, flashing the logos of the multi-billion-yen corporations that owned most of Tokyo.

The combatants began to circle each other, edging forward, then edging back in a silent, subtle dance of distance and measurement: of feeling the other man's mettle. Kohei smirked, and Ryu showed a steadfast scowl.

It happened too fast for Makiko to tell who struck first. A quick scuffle of Italian shoes, the glimmer of blades, shards of neon light, then the simultaneous clash of steel. And the crackling flash of blue lightning.

Kohei dropped like a ragdoll, crashing hard onto the street and twitching spasmodically. His katana skittered away. His eyes blazed with confusion and hate, and his fingernails clawed at the pavement.

Ryu placed the point of his katana against Kohei's breast. Another snap of blue electric arc, and Kohei's body jerked into a painful arch. Ryu drove Kohei back against earth with a hard thrust that sent the sword point into Kohei's ribcage, through his heart, and spearing into the pavement.

Screams erupted from the onlookers, screams mixed with uncertain applause. The circle spread wider as people scrambled to push away from the scene of death.

Kusanagi Ryu smiled faintly, jerked his sword free, and rushed to kneel beside Makiko. A flick of the tip severed Makiko's bonds. "We have to go," he said.

She threw her arms around his neck, kissing him with all the ferocity she could muster and breathlessly pressing herself against him, clutching his shaven head into her neck.

And pressing the tip of her fingernail against the base of his skull for just a moment.

No larger than the proboscis of a mosquito, the needle went unnoticed in the flurry of feminine wiles.

Within seconds, the strength drained from his arms and his face went slack. He collapsed beside her. Injected at the root of the spine, the neurotoxin would paralyze the victim almost instantly. The new Sumiyoshi-kai oyabun, Ishii Naoki, had not been lying about its effectiveness.

Men were so predictable.

She dragged the inductive data-cuff from her voluminous sleeve, slapped it around Ryu's wrist, and keyed the download sequence.

He was already struggling to breathe.

She had to get the data downloaded within three minutes after the heart stopped, or the data would die along with his brain.

With this data and the right buyer, perhaps the U.S. government or the Soviets, she could set herself up in unimaginable luxury. No woman had ever been a yakuza boss before. She intended to be the first. In the interstices of the endless wars between the yakuza gangs, she would bide her time, preserve her own skin, and build her influence and strength until it was time to declare herself as a power in the Tokyo underworld.

The crowd murmured and collapsed in toward her.

"Somebody, call an ambulance!" she screamed. Then she threw herself over Ryu's struggling chest. "Hang on, my love! I'm here!" she wept for the benefit of the audience: she was an incredibly skilled performer, after all.

But the light in his eyes was already going out.

About the Author

Freelance writer, novelist, award-winning screenwriter, editor, poker player, poet, biker, and roustabout, Travis Heermann is a graduate of the Odyssey Writing Workshop and the author of the *Ronin Trilogy*, *The Wild Boys*, and *Rogues of the Black Fury*. He has also written short fiction pieces in anthologies and magazines such as Fiction River's *How to Save the World*, *Historical Lovecraft*, and Cemetery Dance's *Shivers VII*.

As a freelance writer, he has produced a metric ton of role-playing game work both in print and online, including the *Firefly Roleplaying Game*, *Legend of Five Rings*, d20 System, and the MMORPG, *EVE Online*. After three years of living in Japan, he is back stateside watching his hard-won skill at Japanese slowly erode. He enjoys cycling, martial arts, torturing young minds with otherworldly ideas, and zombies. He has three long-cherished dreams: to produce a screenplay, become a *New York Times* best-seller, and get a seat in the World Series of Poker.

東京極道

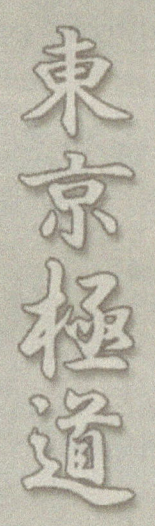

東京極道

Tokyo Yakuza
#20

Stoneheart

by Torah Cottrill

Japan won the Second World War; Now the yakuza are starting the Third!

Stoneheart

BY TORAH COTTRILL

February 7, 2020. Monzen-nakacho, Tokyo. Paper prayers thrashed against their strings like trapped birds, then broke free and tumbled through the morning air. The grove's slender trees shuddered in the thunder of construction equipment. A bulldozer clawed the ground into muddy chunks, rumbling to a stop with its blade against a stone well. The driver shut off the engine and climbed down from the cab.

"Hiroshi!" he shouted. He tilted his cap to wipe his sweaty forehead.

"What is it?" The return shout came from further down the slight hill.

"Come here!" The driver pushed his cap back down and lit a cigarette.

"Any excuse to take a break, eh?" Hiroshi, the foreman, climbed the hill and stood next to the driver, who offered him a cigarette.

"Look here," the driver said. He pointed at a small stone, half buried in tall grass. "It's a shrine."

"So?" said Hiroshi. He lit his own cigarette. "Boss says to level this section, we level it."

"Okay," the driver said. He climbed back into the bulldozer with the cigarette between his teeth. The smoke mingled with the stink of exhaust as the engine belched to life.

Kokoroishi woke in the dark, in middle of a field of dirt. Still half-asleep, she lay with her face pressed against the dead soil, reeking of solvents, trying to remember where she was. She'd fallen asleep to the silken sound of the wind in the trees and the shamisen plink of water dripping into the well. The young woman stood and turned in a slow circle. Where were the trees? Where was the well? Kokoroishi's eyes darted across the blank landscape as panic exploded in her chest. Where was she?

A tall rectangular shape blocked the bright haze of city lights. The sign was written in kanji and some other curly language she didn't recognize:

Discover Tomorrow!
Future Site of Olympic Village
Morishita Construction (a CBI-Hitachi family company)

She stared at the sign and back at the wide scar of dirt. Her home should be right there! Kokoroishi squeezed her eyes closed and clenched her fists, willing herself to see the grove of trees, the long grass, and the cool well: everything back again. This was only a dream.

She opened her eyes.

The ruined field stared back at her, clods of dirt like clotted blood in the moonlight.

Kokoroishi's long hair whipped around her in black ropes, thrashing the chilly air. What would happen to her without the well? Would she fade away now that it was gone? She studied her trembling hands, looked at the hem of her red kimono blowing in the wind, and her writhing hair. She felt solid enough.

Slowly, Kokoroishi gathered her hair in both hands and twisted it into a knot, securing it with the silver pins she kept tucked into her obi.[144] Someone had destroyed her home, but she was still here, so the well must be here somewhere, too: the well, the cool stones, and her shrine. If she could find the people who did this, maybe they could put it all back again! Wiping the dirt and tears from her face, Kokoroishi started walking toward the lights of the Tokyo night.

Nihombashi, Tokyo. After walking for hours, Kokoroishi was tired. Edo had changed since the last time she'd been here. Signs bright with with moving words stained the sidewalks with melted-candy colors. The streets were clogged with asymmetrical vehicles leaking music she could feel in her bones. People crowded the sidewalks and surged through intersections, like one great insect with a million legs, and Kokoroishi was pulled along, barely able to keep her feet in the crush.

Kokoroishi ducked into an alley, finding it only slightly less busy than the street and stopped to catch her breath. A knot of young people blocked the narrow sidewalk. The women wore layers of loose, filmy tunics over legging with bright patterns; the men had elaborately styled hair and dramatic makeup.

One of the young men noticed her. Unlike the others, his face was plain and he wore long hair pulled back into a rough ponytail.

---

[144] The ribbon-like sash used to hold a kimono closed.

His steel-framed glasses appeared to have only one lens.

"Hello," he said, stepping away from his companions. "You look lost. Do you need help?"

"Nobu, come on!" one of the girls shouted. "We're going to King of System[145] for karaoke."

"Go ahead," the young man called back. "I'll catch up." Looking back at Kokoroishi, he asked again, "Do you need anything?"

Kokoroishi studied his face. She was lost and she did need help.

"I'm thirsty," she said, deciding to trust him.

The young man smiled. "Then let's get a drink. I know a place right around the corner."

Kokoroishi followed him back into the crowded street and then down a few stairs to a tiny basement izakaya. They sat at the bar. Kokoroishi ran her fingers over the dark, polished wood. It felt old; a thousand, thousand memories brushed along the edges of her thoughts.

"Irasshaimase,"[146] the bartender said, startling her. "Your orders, please?"

"Beer," said Nobu. "And … ?"

"Water," Kokoroishi finished. "With cherry blossoms."

"We don't have cherry blossoms, sorry," the bartender apologized. His expression showed bemusement. "Would you like a slice of lemon?" Kokoroishi shook her head. The last time she'd been in Edo, the vehicles had been slower and the crowds less dense. People had recognized her and offered her rice and scented water. She didn't like this new Edo at all.

"Cherry blossoms?" Nobu said as the bartender turned away. "I've never heard anyone ask for that."

---

[145] A chain karaoke parlor with hostesses and rooms you hire by the hour.
[146] "Welcome!"

"It's the smell," Kokoroishi explained. "Especially when the water's cold."

Nobu smiled over the rim of his glass. "You must not live in Tokyo."

"No," Kokoroishi said. "I live in Edo. And I came to find someone. Maybe you can help me?"

"Who are you looking for?" Nobu asked.

"Morishita Construction," she told him.

"I've heard of them," the young man said. "They're a subsidiary of CBI-Hitachi, a competitor of my employer, Mabuchi Cyber. They have a lot of the Olympics building contracts. CBI-Hitachi and Morishita are really run by the Sumiyoshi-kai. You know that, right?"

Kokoroishi shook her head. "Does it matter?"

"They're a pretty powerful yakuza clan," Nobu explained. "Are you sure you want to find somebody with the Sumiyoshi?"

Kokoroishi took a long drink. The water tasted flat. "I'm sure."

"Well, if that's what you want." Nobu touched the frame of his Kyocera glasses. A white shimmer in the single lens hid his eye briefly. Kokoroishi leaned forward, fascinated, but before she could see the megane extensions that made the quick flicker of light, it disappeared. The young man borrowed a pen from the bartender and sketched a map on the back of a cardboard coaster. "You can find Morishita in Ueno," Nobu said. He circled one part of the map. "In the northeast part of the city."

Kokoroishi studied the coaster, then tucked it into her obi.

"Hey," Nobu said. He finished his beer and slid a ¥500 coin toward the bartender. "You want to come to King of System?"

Kokoroishi shook her head. "No. Thanks for your help, though."

The young man lingered, standing beside her. "Are you sure you're going to be all right? Are you on 'Line'?"[147]

---

[147] Japan's most popular social network and mobile dating service.

"I'm sure I'm fine, and I don't know what 'Line' is." Kokoroishi said.

"Well, good luck then," Nobu said. He gave her a final smile as he left.

Kokoroishi drank the last of her water.

February 8, 2020. Ginza, Tokyo. It was another long walk before she reached Ginza in the first pale light of day. Kokoroishi combed the streets, reading shop signs and fluttering banners. Finally, she saw a small, neatly lettered card taped to a window of a tobacco shop: Morishita Construction, second floor. She climbed the stairs with quick steps. Soon, she'd have her well back!

The dingy office was deserted.

"Hello?" Kokoroishi called. After several minutes, an old man in an ink-stained shirt appeared.

He stared at Kokoroishi, trying to focus his shortsighted vision. "Eh?" he said.

"Who's in charge here?" she asked.

"Eh?" the old man repeated. "No one's here now, come back later."

Anger flashed through Kokoroishi, bright and hot. Why was everything so hard in this miserable city? Kokoroishi took a step toward the old man and he finally met her eyes, his own widening behind thick glasses. "Who runs this company?" she demanded.

"Takegawa-san," he blurted.

"Where can I find him?" Kokoroishi asked. She'd never felt so hot before, in the cool shade of the well; it felt … it felt good. Kokoroishi smiled.

"Th-the Pink Room,"[148] the old man said, stammering. "He's usually there." He bowed several times to her departing back.

The Pink Room wasn't hard to find. The sign outside said it was a tea room, but when Kokoroishi came through the street door and saw the small photos of women on the wall, she knew what kind of place it was. She pushed through the inner curtain.

"Girls use the alley door," a woman said. She wore a severe kimono hissed at Kokoroishi. "Don't make me tell you again! Now hurry, customers are already here." She flicked her fingers toward a narrow hallway.

At the end of the corridor was a small kitchen area. A tall gaijin girl, wearing a green cocktail dress several sizes too small, was inexpertly making tea. At Kokoroishi's appearance, the girl's face lit with relief.

"Oh, thank god! Onesan Ozu Chieko said that the bosses were sending someone after Fatma ran off, but I was beginning to worry. You can make tea, can't you? Takegawa-san's already asked twice."

Kokoroishi took the teapot, rinsed out the girl's mess, and whisked matcha into clean water. "Here you are."

"Thank you!" the gaijin girl said, taking the teapot. "Wait here, I'll be right back."

Kokoroishi watched the girl struggle to open the sliding shoji door without spilling the tea. When did all of these foreigners come to Edo? After a few minutes, the girl reappeared, awkwardly shuffling through the door and sliding it closed.

"Whew!" the gaijin said with a huff. She stood. "I was born Mathilde, back in the USSR, but I go by Midori in Japan. What's your name?"

"Kokoroishi," she said.

---

[148] A Sumiyoshi-kai teahouse-themed hostess club in Ginza.

Matilde rummaged through a cabinet to emerge with another teapot. "Takegawa Yoshi wants more tea and a second hostess." She handed the teapot to Kokoroishi. "Kokoroishi means 'Stoneheart,' doesn't it?"

"Heart of the Stone," Kokoroishi corrected, whisking more tea.

"You'll need a working name. How about 'Amaya?' It means 'Night Rain.' I think it's pretty!"

Kokoroishi put the top on the steaming pot of tea. "I think I'll keep my name," she said. She walked toward the shoji screen.

"Wait." Mathilde stopped her with a hand on her arm. "You can't go in there looking like that! Where'd you get that kimono, your grandmother? Next time, bring a sexy dress. Let's see." The girl quickly untied Kokoroishi's obi, leaving her red kimono belted with only the narrow koshi himo sash. Mathilde studied the effect. "It'll have to do. All right, let's go! Sumiyoshi-kai gokudo like Takegawa Yoshi don't like to be kept waiting."

"I can't wait to meet him," Kokoroishi said. She followed the harried gaijin.

A man with torn clothes was sprawled on the floor just inside the tatami room. As Kokoroishi glanced down at him, he lifted a cigarette to his bloody lips. In the next room, four men played cards at a low wooden table, wreathed in clouds of smoke. A younger man with a ground-in sneer leaned against a wall nearby. His narrow eyes shifted to Kokoroishi as she passed, then returned to the card players.

"Takegawa-san, your luck is terrible today!" a man at the table cried, fanning out his cards.

Another man tossed the rest of his hand onto the table with a grunt. "Where's that idiot with the the big tits?" he muttered. "Midori! Tea!"

"Please, allow me," Kokoroishi said. She knelt beside Takegawa Yoshi and poured.

"Who are you?" Takegawa asked, his voice raspy. He tapped the ash from his cigarette onto the floor.

"My name is Kokoroishi," she answered, trying to keep her voice soft and pleasant.

"Is that so," Takegawa said. "And what's this?" he asked. He pulled the top of her kimono open to expose the tattoos at her neck and over her heart.

Kokoroishi felt another hot rush of anger at his touch, but she pushed it away. She needed this man to get her well back for her. She forced herself to smile and shrugged her kimono open a little more.

Takegawa snorted. "Tattoos? You think you're a lady yakuza?"

The other card players guffawed at Takegawa's joke as the winner dealt a new hand.

"Oh, no, Takegawa-san," she said. She dipped her head to hide her eyes. "I'm only a hostess."

"That's right!" Takegawa Yoshi said with a grunt. He picked up his playing cards. "Too much ambition in a woman is an ugly thing."

Kokoroishi watched the men smoke and slap cards on the table. She poured more tea into Takegawa's cup. "Takegawa-san," murmured. "Can I ask—"

"I've got you, Sozen!" Takegawa shouted. With a grin, he laid his hand on the table. "Cherry blossoms, just like the lady yakuza's tattoos."

The other men threw their own cards onto the table as Takegawa rose. "What's that, fifty thousand yen you owe me now?" With a flourish and wink in Midori's general direction, Takakura Sozen, the youngest card player, counted bills into Takegawa's outstretched hand. Takegawa thrust the fold of money into his pocket and turned to the door. Sozen ran his left hand through his Mohawk. Takegawa snapped his fingers. "Bunrakuken!" Takegawa yelled.

Katayama Bunrakuken, the tough leaning against the wall, straightened.

"Come on, cherry blossoms," Takegawa said to Kokoroishi, looking back at her over his shoulder. "I'm ready for something besides tea."

Kokoroishi stood, straightening her kimono, and hurried after him.

Outside, the tough held open the door of a shiny black car. Takegawa climbed in and gestured for Kokoroishi to sit next to him. Bunrakuken closed the door and slid into the front. There wasn't a steering wheel, Kokoroishi saw. Or a driver.

The car pulled smoothly into the late afternoon traffic. Takegawa laid a heavy hand on Kokoroishi's thigh. Kokoroishi made herself sit still, even though she wanted to fling his hand away. After all, this is what she'd come here for, a chance to ask this man to dig out her well and uncover her shrine.

"Takegawa-san," she began. She turned toward him.

"No!" he said, angry. Kokoroishi jumped. "I said three weeks. If they can't do it by then, the deal's off."

Takegawa Yoshi removed his hand from her leg and gestured to the tough in the front seat. Bunrakuken passed back a lit cigarette.

Takegawa pressed one hand to his ear and continued to talk. Kokoroishi sat in the growing cloud of smoke and tried to think of another way to find her well.

Kayabacho, Tokyo. The car stopped in front of a tall glass building, crawling with luminous advertisements. The door slid open as Takegawa strode toward it, one hard hand on Kokoroishi's elbow. She barely had time to notice Katayama Bunrakuken lean against the lobby wall, sneer firmly in place, before Takegawa hauled her into a glass-walled elevator. They rose so quickly Kokoroishi felt her stomach drop. Outside, the lights of a Tokyo evening spread out below, falling fast.

The door slid open on a Western-style living room full of heavy, soft furniture and chrome tables. Takegawa released Kokoroishi's elbow and walked across the room to a mirrored cabinet, lined with jewel-colored bottles. He poured himself a glass of amber liquor.

"Look out there," Takegawa said. He stood by a wall made entirely of glass. Kokoroishi approached cautiously and looked out across the city. Takegawa waved a hand in front of the window and the view tilted and zoomed, responding to the motion. Kokoroishi stepped back, startled. "I've got contracts all over the city, more every day. Now that old Sugawara's dead and Ishii Naoki is the new oyabun, the clan's got to pick a new wakagashira." He took a deep drink. "No reason it shouldn't be me instead of Sato Fukui."

"There!" Kokoroishi pointed at a field of bare dirt as it swung across the view. Takegawa's hand paused, twisted, and the field swung back to the center of the window.

"Takegawa-san, there was a well, there." She pointed. "And a stone. Could you find them again, in the dirt?" Her hand shook.

Takegawa laughed. "Why bother?" He put an arm around her waist and pulled her close. "In another six months, that's going to be apartments for the Olympic athletes. All the amenities. You like the Olympics, don't you, Cherry Blossoms?" He nudged her kimono open. "If you're nice, maybe you can watch the opening ceremonies with me. You'd like that, wouldn't you?"

Kokoroishi twisted away, her breath tightening in her chest. Why wouldn't this man listen? "No!" she said. "It's important. There was a shrine there, and a well. Could you find them again?"

Takegawa put his empty glass down with a thud. "Enough, stupid girl! No, I couldn't find any well, or one rock, even if I wanted to. Look." He pointed at the window. "Whatever used to be there is gone now. That's progress, Cherry Blossoms."

Kokoroishi stood, staring at the smear of dirt that was all that was left of her home. She felt Takegawa's hard hand yank her kimono from her shoulders and whirled to face him.

"Don't touch me!" She jabbed a finger at the window. "Look what you've done!" Kokoroishi pulled the silver pins from her hair, freeing the knot. Her hair lifted around her, twisting like silky black ropes in unseen currents. The anger like fire in her veins was nothing like the cool peace at the well, but it was all she had now.

Kokoroishi stared into Takegawa's white-rimmed eyes. His breath in her face was sour with whiskey and fear. Kokoroishi smiled as her hair lashed the air and wrapped around Takegawa's throat. "You enjoy destruction?" she asked. Takegawa's eyes bulged. He clawed at the tightening ropes of her hair. "Then you *are* lucky today," Kokoroishi said.

She drove the silver pins into his eyes.

Kokoroishi was wiping the hair pins on Takegawa's green shirt when she heard the elevator door open. The tough with the sneer, Katayama Bunrakuken, stepped into Takegawa's apartment and looked around. When he saw Kokoroishi standing over Takegawa's body, ropes of hair twining above her head, the sneer faded. He pressed a hand to his ear and spoke quietly. Looking back at

Kokoroishi, he removed a button from his pocket and extended it toward her.

She looked at the device, frowning. Her hair coiled around his wrist.

"You put it in your ear," he said, and gestured at his own.

Kokoroishi put the button in her ear. Immediately, she heard a woman's voice.

"My name is Matsuoka Noriko. I understand you've had a disagreement with Takegawa?"

"He took something precious from me," Kokoroishi said. "So I killed him."

"Bunrakuken did some research on you when he heard your name in the Pink Room. He told me about the Kokoroishi shrine. He looks like a thug, but the street samurai's really quite valuable. Takegawa, on the other hand, was not. Too much ambition in a man is an ugly thing, don't you agree? But now, lady kami, what will you do next?"

Kokoroishi paused. She hadn't thought about what would happen if she couldn't go back to the well.

Into the silence, Matsuoka Noriko said, "Allow me to make you an offer."

"Go on," Kokoroishi said. She watched Katayama Bunrakuken wrap Takegawa's body in a sheet of plastic. His sleeves were rolled up to reveal a rainbow of tattoos.

"I am the widow of our deceased oyabun, Sugawara Hirono. I took over the Sumiyoshi-kai temporarily after his death, until the senior clan members agreed to promote his wakagashira, the computer-loving otaku Ishii Naoki, to replace him," Noriko said. "I have other plans. Tell me, did you enjoy killing Takegawa?"

Kokoroishi smiled. "Oh, yes," she said. "It was even better than cherry blossoms."

"Perfect," Noriko said in her ear. "I could use someone with your talents."

Bunrakuken straightened and reached into his pocket again. This time, what rested in the palm he extended was a small lapel pin engraved with the Sumiyoshi-kai clan emblem. Kokoroishi considered it. Without her well, she couldn't be the Heart of the Stone. But now that she'd found this lovely, hot anger, she could be something else.

Kokoroishi took the Sumiyoshi-kai lapel pin and fastened it into her hair.

About the Author

Torah Cottrill is an evil mutant editor from Seattle. Her stories have appeared in *Stupefying Stories, Luna Station Quarterly, By Faerie Light,* and *The Awakened,* among other publications.

Weed in the Garden

by Stephen D. Rogers

Japan won the Second World War;
Now the yakuza are starting the Third!

Tokyo Yakuza #21

Weed in the Garden

By Stephen D. Rogers

February 9, 2020. Roppongi, Tokyo. Takakura Sozen of the Sumiyoshi-kai slapped the prisoner again, hitting him hard enough that the chair would have tipped over if not held in place by the chimpira, Eguchi Bunta.

Blood spilled and the sound of the blow echoed. He felt the sting in his hand.

Sozen relished the thrill of raw violence, here in this nothing basement, hidden from the goings on above.

He drew in a sharp breath. He'd never experienced anything quite like this, and now that he had, he couldn't imagine *not* doing it again and again and again.

How could he ever go back? He couldn't. He wouldn't.

Again the street samurai slapped his victim, channeling into the strike every injury he'd ever suffered as the second born in a family that only honored the first.

In the corner, in the darker shadows, Sumiyoshi-kai professional killer, and former rat, Okoshi Takeshi raised a hand.

Sozen stepped back, panting from the exertion, the animal physicality of beating a man down and reducing him to something less than he'd been.

Sozen's chest heaved, his heart singing. It seemed inconceivable that only eighteen hours ago, he'd been the type of person who enjoyed a quiet picnic lunch with family.

February 8, 2020. Yoyogi, Tokyo. Takakura Sozen took a bite of his apple before thanking his sister-in-law for the invitation to lunch. "You know, this is actually quite nice. I never would have come and spread a blanket in the park here unless you had suggested it."

"Every day should be magical. If you can't find it in your ordinary world, you just have to create it."

"Well, what you've managed is nothing short of miraculous." Over his brother's left shoulder, Sozen watched a girl band play for the sheer enjoyment of it, entertaining passers-by for no better reason than music was theirs to share. "I need a little magic."

His brother, Takakura Gin, lifted the bag of weed that Takakura Sozen had brought. "Is that what this is all about?"

"It's a gift. Help you relax."

Gin frowned, tossing the bag back to Sozen. "No thanks. Mom says you're always working."

"I'm staying busy."

"She didn't say what kind of work you were doing."

Sozen shrugged, stuffing the bag back into his pocket. "A little of this, a little of that, making ends meet in the middle. You've got it easy, dear brother, running the club. You always know where the money is coming from."

"Not so easy, no. Not these days," said Gin.

Sozen turned to his twelve-year-old niece. "And what about you, little lady? Where's your money come from? Your dad giving you an allowance?"

"She earns the money she gets every week," said Gin.

"Is that right?" replied Sozen.

His niece nodded. "I feed the dog and take out the trash. There's never any end to it."

The girl's mother rolled her eyes. "I keep waiting for the day you decide to stop eating and getting your clothes dirty."

"Ha-ha-" The two syllables, slang for "mom," stretched out to the count of four.

Midori leaned forward to say, "We used to have a dog when I was growing up in Soviet Union. We called him Zero."

Sozen sniffed in surprise. "You were a child?" Wearing little more than a teal wig and a bikini, his new girlfriend from the Pink Room didn't seem the type to ever have been innocent.

"Of course I was a child. Isn't that how we all start out, as itsy-bitsy babies?"

"You're a sunset, Midori. A sunset doesn't start as a candle. It's a sunset. It's always a sunset."

Sozen's sister-in-law turned to her husband. "Your brother's a poet."

"He's something, all right," said Gin.

Sozen laughed off his brother's disdain. "The sunset's the poem."

His sister-in-law smiled. "I always preferred the sunrise. There's so much more promise."

Midori straightened the tiny hat that had started to slip off her head again. "I can't remember the last time I saw the sun rise."

Sozen winked. "Maybe I can arrange to keep you up until then."

His brother cleared his throat. "You should visit mom more often."

That was his brother all over: family first, last, and everything in-between. Gin hadn't so much as looked at Midori, born Mathilde, this entire time. She was the outsider, the threat, not to mention a gaijin from the world's last holdout against the new order of global fascism.

That said, Sozen himself probably wouldn't have been here if not for his sister-in-law. She'd been the one who issued the invitation. Sozen was family, yes, but not family in any way that mattered: at least, not to his elder brother, Gin.

"I see Mom when I can. And then when I do, all she wants to talk about is my older brother," said Sozen.

"She understands my life. I'm married. I have a daughter. I have a job," said Gin.

Sozen put a spin on his words to hint at his own disdain. "I can't imagine Mom would want me to be more of the same."

"With that Mohawk, you'll never be more of the same."

"Listen to that, everybody. I think my brother just paid me a compliment."

"No. I didn't."

Midori placed a hand on his thigh. "I love your hair. It makes me think of ducks in a row."

Sozen's sister-in-law laughed. "Another poet. I'm eating a picnic lunch, surrounded by poets. And to think my daughter said this was a dumb idea."

"Haha." The word was condensed this time rather than lengthened. "I asked you not to repeat that."

Sozen nudged his niece. "So this is dumb, huh? What would you rather be doing?"

"No, it's just, you know. I just didn't think you'd be interested in a boring picnic."

"How could this be boring? You're here."

His niece huffed.

"Midori, what was I saying on the way here? My brother might a stiff, but his daughter; the little lady's got it going on."

She nodded. "That's what he said. The whole time. I'm telling you, Sozen talked about nothing else."

"I'm just a kid." A red-faced little kid, but obviously pleased.

"Your uncle spoke so highly of you, I thought maybe I picked the wrong man to date."

Sozen took another bite of the apple. "But then you remembered my hair."

"Ducks in a row."

Gin wiped crumbs off his pants. "This is fascinating, but I need to be getting back to work. That's what life is like when you have responsibilities."

"Remind me to stay away from them."

"I don't think you need that reminder." He kissed his wife as he climbed to his feet. "Thanks for lunch."

Sozen tossed his apple into the air and caught it backhand. "Except for the company, dear brother, is that right?"

"It was good to see you again, Sozen."

"Let me walk with you a little." Gin added to Midori as he stood, "Don't you be teaching my daughter all about life in the Soviet Union."

"Be quick or I can't make any promises," Midori answered in Russian-accented Japanese.

"I guess I'm counting on you, little lady. Revere the Emperor."

The girl took a quick glance at Midori. "I will, dad. You don't have to call the Kempeitai."

Sozen stood and stepped over his niece. "Brother!"

Gin kept walking, like man on a mission, striding away as if no one was calling him.

Sozen rushed to catch up. "I wanted to talk to you about something."

"I'm not sure if I'm interested in anything you have to say."

"You'll be interested in this. It's an opportunity."

His brother didn't slow down, didn't turn to look Sozen in the face. "No thanks."

"Hear me out. There's a local businessman looking to help businesses in the neighborhood. When one does well, everyone does well. It's like the Olympics."

"What do you know about the Olympics? That they're being held in Tokyo?"

"You can mock me all you want, dear brother, but you can't buy the additional security the club is going to need without an influx of cash."

"And this friend of yours is going to provide that? In exchange for what?"

"Did you not just hear those girls playing music? They weren't entertaining people because they wanted something in return. They played because they could. What does the sunset get in return for its poetry? Or, if your wife prefers, the sunrise?"

"Those girls were playing for free because nobody in their right mind would pay them to play," said Gin. "And besides, they were only playing music. They weren't giving out money."

"Music is what they had." Sozen wished his brother would slow down. "Money is what my friend has."

"Your friend, is he? What kind of rich man is this that he has you as a friend?"

Takakura Sozen swallowed his first response but couldn't stop himself from asking, "Why do you have to be this way?"

"Our father always wanted you to make something of yourself, but he always knew you wouldn't."

"So now you could read his mind?"

"No. I talked with him, and he talked with me. That's what fathers and sons do, but you wouldn't know that because you were always off with your trash."

"Dad gave you everything," said Sozen.

"He gave me nothing. I earned everything I have."

"Half that club in Roppongi should be mine."

"What, to repay all the money and time you didn't sink into it? I worked around the clock on that club when you couldn't be found anywhere. You don't deserve a thing."

Takakura Sozen bit his tongue before he made his brother even angrier. Unfortunately, he couldn't settle for a negotiated silence. He had to close the deal.

"Okay, maybe I didn't put anything into the club. I realize that now, and I want to make amends. This is my chance to help out."

"I don't need your help."

"Not my help. My friend's help. He's the one with the money to invest."

"Invest? That means he wants a piece of the club." Gin hissed through his teeth. "You said he wanted to help the neighborhood."

"He does. But that doesn't mean he's going to give it away. Where would the sense be in that? If he can't afford to stay in business, he can't afford to help other businesses. Like yours."

"Mine. Exactly. Whether you like it or not, Sozen, the club's mine, and if I'm not giving my brother any say in how it's run, I'm certainly not giving any to some stranger."

Sozen tried another angle. "Hosting the Olympics is going to send Tokyo through the stratosphere. You need a partner who knows how to navigate the system or you're going to get left behind."

"A partner now? I thought he just wanted to help."

Gin hadn't ended the conversation; that was a good sign. "He only wants to make sure his money is well spent. He's just being a responsible citizen."

"I'm sure. This friend of yours have a name?"

"Doesn't everybody?" Takakura Sozen pressed on, hurrying further and further from Midori, from the picnic, from his lunch. "Believe me, brother. You don't want to miss this opportunity. Once in a lifetime you get a chance like this."

His brother finally stopped. He finally faced him. He finally gave his full attention. "And what's in it for you?"

"Family. Family helps family."

"You've never made an effort before."

"I've changed."

"Yeah, the Mohawk and the cyberware. It's you. You're a cyber-chimpira." Gin shook his head. "You don't know how many times I've said to myself, 'all my waste-of-space brother needs is a punk haircut and some electronics under his skin. He gets that, he might actually be worth something.'"

"You always disrespect me just because I'm not like you," said Sozen.

"That's right, you're not, and you never will be."

"I wouldn't want to be."

"Listen, Sozen-kun, I've given you my answer. No. There it is again, just in case you didn't hear me." He turned away. "This conversation is over."

✦　✧　✦

February 9, 2020. Roppongi, Tokyo. Takakura Sozen stepped forward, twisting at the hip, putting everything into the heel strike.

His brother's nose exploded blood and snot. The chair rocked back, caught at the last second by Eguchi Bunta, and then Gin's head dropped forward, his body limp.

Bunta felt for a pulse. "He's dead," said Bunta.

Having been transformed from a rat back into a man by his secret mistress Suki, the kitsune wakagashira of the Inagawa-kai, Okoshi Takeshi stepped out of the darkness. Takeshi was now Suki's spy within the Sumiyoshi-kai.

"Speak to his wife," Takeshi said. "Make her the same offer. Do a better job of selling the benefits of having me as a partner."

Sozen nodded. "I did try to convince him," he said.

Takakura Sozen had just beaten and killed his brother.

His dead brother, slumped against the bindings that held him in the chair, for the first time allowed Sozen to have the final word.

His brother.

Takakura Sozen calmed his deep breaths. After what just happened here, he should feel different: changed, horrified. Something other than satisfied. Anything other than satisfied. "My brother …"

Okoshi placed a hand on Sozen's shoulder. "Whatever he may have been to you, the Sumiyoshi-kai are your family now. Talk to his wife. Make her understand."

About the Author

Stephen D. Rogers is the author of *Shot to Death* and over 800 shorter pieces, half crime/mystery and half SF/F/H/Other. "Magpie" appears in the anthology *The Lost* (based on the RPG of the same name by Galileo Games). "Four and Twenty" appears in the anthology *Once Upon an Apocalypse* (Chaosium). And contracted to appear in Third Flatiron's *Abbreviated Epics* is a piece of Wuxia fiction, "Qinggong Ji."

Tokyo Yakuza
#22

Everyone's Talking About Ryuk-kun

by Vishal Wilde

Japan won the Second World War;
Now the yakuza are starting the Third!

Everyone's Talking About Ryuk-kun

BY VISHAL WILDE

February 10, 2020. Shinjuku, Tokyo. "Everyone's talking about Ryuk-kun, Kitano-san, and what this means for the clan."

Naruse Riko spoke while she lay naked on black silk sheets and smoked a cigarette. She was a mature woman who had aged gracefully and, with that body, those eyes and that voice of hers, she held countless men by the balls.

"Hardly surprising. It was quite a scene, as you must recall," I answered.

"Quite."

I buttoned up my shirt, reached over to the cupboard, and lit a cigarette for myself. I didn't usually smoke, but I was a social smoker in high school so whenever someone else was smoking, it tempted me to join in. Not that I always gave in to temptation, but smoking a cigarette with Riko held a certain allure that I consistently succumbed to.

"Is that all?" I asked.

"You know it's not …" Her eyes sharpened and she laughed playfully. "If it were, you wouldn't have just lit that cigarette." *Damn, she got me there.*

"Right."

"I know what you're trying to do," she said. My heart skipped a beat, but my face betrayed nothing. Why was I not surprised? It was only a matter of time before Riko caught on. It was funny that my heart reacted the way it did.

"And what am I trying to do?"

"No need to play dumb. We both know that you want to take Kitano-san down."

"For such an intelligent lady, you make wild inferences, Riko. My loyalty lies with Oyabun Kitano-sama and the Yamaguchi-gumi." Lies were necessary. Don't worry though, I don't always lie. Riko smirked and gently ran her fingers through the ripples of silk.

"You know what your problem is?"

"I didn't pay for a counselling session and I'm getting one: that's my problem."

"You paid for conversation and I'm giving it to you," she snapped. "Your problem is that you don't trust people." A silence descended upon the bed chamber. I wondered, *who did trust anyone?* That was irrelevant; as far as I was concerned. Trust is a luxury that was far too expensive for my taste.

"Well, you know, Riko, trust is difficult to develop in these times and in this world. Anyway, enough of your amateur psychoanalysis." Amateur is definitely what it is … See, I told the truth then, didn't I?

"Very well." She stood up and walked toward me; her flawless, naked body strode through the moonlight that lit the room. Finishing her cigarette with one last puff, she then proceeded to take mine from my hand. Riko walked away and lay back on the bed with the remaining half of my cigarette. Any other geisha, and I might have slapped her down, but this was Riko. And I tried not to hit girls.

She could even have had me killed; she held *that* kind of power in Kabukichō. Though the kumicho of the Yamaguchi-gumi back in Kobe and Oyabun Kitano-san in Tokyo offered the geishas protection, it was not a relationship of dependency; the geishas were fully aware of the financial importance of Kabukichō to the clan. If any harm befell their leaders, there would be an instant revolt against the Yamaguchi-gumi and a severance of crucial revenue in those problematic times: that was a strategic chokepoint if I had ever seen one.

That power made Naruse Riko a warrior-woman in my eyes; she had politicians, bureaucrats, businessmen, and yakuza alike all by the balls and, like all good warriors, she had a strong sense of integrity. Her integrity lay in this; she would talk to her clients and provide certain amounts of information with varying degrees of accuracy, but she would never give away enough to reveal the source of that information: no names, *only information*. Of course, I knew from first-hand experience that some of it was false and some of it was true … at times, it got difficult to find the truth in a basket of lies, but I liked to think I'd gotten pretty good at it.

She walked a fine line and she played a dangerous game but she walked it gracefully and played it well. Naruse Riko, the deadly warrior-woman.

"It's not just you, y'know?" she continued. "Sure, there's plenty of people that do little things here and there but there aren't many that play high stakes."

I put on my jacket and proceeded to walk toward the door. I had to act as if I had no idea what she was talking about, but I paused briefly at the door as she began to utter her last words to me on that night.

"You're an insider trying to bring him down from the inside. Well, there's an outsider, trying to bring him down from the inside. Just thought you might find that interesting." An infiltrator? Now that *was* interesting. Nonetheless, I didn't know his capabilities and I wasn't a staunch believer in the idea that "the enemy of my enemy is my friend," not necessarily at least. Plus, Riko could have been talking nonsense. I decided to give it some thought and figure it out. The door scanned my iris and slid open.

"Good night, Riko."

February 11, 2020. After that meeting where Kitano-san gave Ryuk an ultimatum and the kid met his end, I went to a relatively unknown bar in the back alleys of Kabukichō. They let a bunch of amateurs and frequenters sing up on stage but every now and again they had someone half-decent. I was half-listening to the lyrics a lady was singing but I was also in my own thoughts. Half-pondering, half-wondering: whatever you'd like to call it: it's a state where we're impressionable and, in many ways, at our most vulnerable. Nonetheless, I catch myself slipping into it fairly often.

Ryuk-kun, interesting character, wasn't he? Perhaps he really was a coward after all. Tears streamed down his face as he was about to take his life. Maybe he wondered why he was crying? Perhaps he wondered why he was so afraid of dying? The thought of death is fraught with fear; that's why I never give it much thought. And maybe that was because I've never felt the sands of time catching up to me.

January 10, 2020. The night I took Ryuk-kun to a shaman, we had come to this same karaoke bar. A particular song was playing, which was a favourite of the folks here. As I recalled the lyrics, the voice resonated throughout my mind; it activated the dormant recesses of my memory and transformed that same memory of those fateful, calculated nights into a vivid reality.

"Tired of walking, tired of moving," she sang.

We had both had a few drinks and were just chatting away. The subject of divinity and the spiritual realm happened to pass into the conversation.

"So when you wear that mask," she sang.

"You know, I really do believe in something higher than all of this. When I was a kid, my parents used to take us to an astrologer," Ryuk-kun began. "I found that a lot of the things he read about my future from the stars were just too true. Sure he got some stuff wrong, but so much more of it was right that it can't possibly be bullshit, y'know?"

Ryuk-kun sighed and looked down at the table while the waitress served him another Sapporo beer. He was a bit surprised when she came to pour it, having forgotten that he'd made the order through a touch screen just a few moments ago. Yes, Ryuk-kun was in that vulnerable state we find ourselves in as our minds wander.

He waited until she had gone, out of earshot, before he continued speaking again. "It's a strange thing to say in this era, but I feel like I can trust you enough to say that I believe very strongly in God." He smiled and looked up at me, but the look in his eyes betrayed fragility. I couldn't believe it. Here was Ryuk-kun, a gangster-slayer, opening up to me!

"In fact," said Ryuk. "I think God works through us. I think that he talks through the mystical people like astrologers. In fact, in my heart, I know that the very reason I told you this was because it is all part of God's plan. Who knows why I had the sudden urge to mention it? I haven't told any of our yakuza brothers."

Idiot, I thought. That "urge" he was talking about came from the beer. The kid couldn't handle his drink. My mind went wild and almost rabid, conjuring ways to exploit this.

"I admire you, Ryuk. In fact, I'm Catholic too. I believe in the same things that you do: that is, everything happens for a reason." I smiled and drank some more. "What we differ in are our views on astrologers. My view is that although astrologers certainly do speak some truth, they omit important details and they tend to embellish the rosy aspects of that divine forecast. There are other mystics who are far more honest, though they can be slightly cryptic."

"Tell me more." Ryuk-kun was fascinated. "Mysticism captivates me. If you could introduce me to people like them, that'd be swell."

I laughed and gulped down the rest of my beer. The thoughts were too wild right at that time to make full use of that immediate opportunity. I had to give it some time. Constant refinement was the call of duty.

"Isn't it clear?" the singer continued. "That this city has no love."

"Some other time," I said. "We should talk about this again when we're both sober. You'll get more out of it that way."

February 14, 2020. Yamagashi was a well-built cyborg who owed me. I didn't even need to tell him why it had to be done.

"Just tell me what to do," he said. The power of giri.[149]

---

[149] A sense of duty owed to another. The need to do one's duty often conflicts with ninjo, feelings of compassion for those who suffer as a result.

He was a war veteran, ex-Special Forces, and a loyal killing machine, but in addition to losing his arm in conflict, the military doctors felt he'd lost his mind. Post-traumatic stress disorder "of a considerable magnitude" was what they diagnosed him with, and those were sufficient grounds for his discharge.

They were, however, kind enough to replace that lost arm of his with a prosthetic, robotic arm that linked directly to his brain. Yamagashi's cybernetics, combined with his almost complete lack of ninjo,[150] made him even more capable as a killing machine. The cybernetic arm, more than the brain damage, was a constant and visible reminder of his war wounds.

I accompanied him to Shinjuku's official data storage facilities. As dignitaries, athletes, and tourists from foreign countries were anticipated to flood into Tokyo for the Olympics, the Emperor had ordered the administrative head of Shinjuku to clean up the streets and remove the sleaze of Kabukichō. Of course, this was just for appearances' sake.

Everyone knew that the yakuza and the administration each got slices of the Kabukichō red light district's profits. The government just had to be *seen* to be doing something, even if all that meant was a few more good-for-nothing parasite cops like Detective Kato on the streets of Kabukichō. Of course, the expenditure on the games made it difficult to invest more into Kabukichō, so the Emperor simply told the official head of the district to "redistribute his resources."

Kitano-san told me that some of his men had observed that, on Fridays, the official data storage facilities' security guards were diminished in number, probably as part of this effort to redistribute funds and make the streets appear well enforced. The problem for

---

[150] Empathy or compassion for others, often in conflict with the objectives set by one's superiors.

them was that information was power and official data was one of the most valuable commodities in the market for power.

Kitano-san had been planning to raid the offices soon and he kept ruminating over the plans with us, but when I analysed the floor plan and the number of guards, it was clear that the operation would be easy. So why was he so hesitant?

Well, on the off chance that we were uncovered, the repercussions would be huge, what with the sudden official backlashes against yakuza and all. Kitano-san was, therefore, understandably hesitant.

Such is the nature of power; if one is not willing to risk everything, one will gain nothing. Leave the modest, risk-averse gains to the armchair generals. My battle cry consists of a call to arms whilst I charge full speed ahead.

Yamagashi didn't give a fuck about all that. He would help me out whenever I needed it and he was loyal. He didn't talk like Riko did, so there was no worry about stuff slipping out. He considered me his only friend, and I considered him one of my most useful tools. Though big and strong, Yamagashi was stealthy, being a former Special Forces operative during his time in the Imperial Army, and this made him the perfect partner for this operation.

The perimeter was lightly guarded on that Friday night, just as Kitano-san's agents had predicted. Too bad he wouldn't be reaping the rewards of his own operation. The best part was that he had told this plan to so many of his inner circle, and there're a lot of people in that fuckin' circle, that he would never suspect me of treachery. Even if he did, he couldn't suspect me any more than anyone else with whom he'd shared this information.

Yamagashi and I hid behind the bushes. Though I was the boss, field operations were Yamagashi's specialty, and I listened intently to his instructions.

"Attach the silencer on your handgun and start clearing the West perimeter in exactly five minutes. After studying the facilities' specifications, I realized that I can temporarily distort the surveillance equipment's signal processing mechanisms so that it simply looks like a malfunction, rather than hacking. Then they can't call for back up. Once I'm done, meet me in the inner chamber. Don't worry about passwords and access keys, it'll all be wide open by the time I'm done with them." A warrior with hacking capabilities; Yamagashi put geeks and gladiators alike to shame.

"How will I know when you're done?" I asked.

"You'll know." He smiled a stonefaced smile. After pressing some buttons on that robotic arm of his, it generated a gentle, rhythmic, pulsating signal. "In five minutes, the perimeter guards will be responding to my incursion. Pick off the ones that aren't facing you. Don't face anyone directly."

"No need to tell me twice," I said.

Indirect combat, that's my specialty. Hidden warfare.

"Five minutes." He repeated. He leapt out of the bush and climbed effortlessly up the barbed wire, probably cutting some flesh in the process but not giving a damn. Hell was about to break loose just a hundred yards away from me and I was waiting for the fifth minute.

The first minute passed. I heard nothing; the cyborg was probably stealthily slitting a few throats. The second minute passed, still nothing. *Probably still picking them off stealthily*, I thought. Then, once my timer hit 3:24, I heard automatic machine gun fire.

That sounded more like Yamagashi.

I heard screams, shots, and calls for backup, but not the dreaded sirens which would have jeopardised the operation.

At exactly five minutes, I leapt through the night and climbed the same barbed wire fence. I wasn't particularly adept at this kind of thing, so I was cut across the forearms a couple of times, just minor flesh wounds. I saw two guards, who seemed to be quivering in fear, and listened as they spoke. They were the only two who remained by the west end of the compound while the killing-machine slaughtered their comrades on the east.

"The signals are jammed and we can't call for backup!" one of them shouted.

"Who the hell is this guy?" his partner asked. They were both gripping their rifles tight whilst trembling from that unique rush you could probably only ever feel if you think your life might end sooner rather than later.

"I can hear them screaming …" His conscience kicked into play. "We need to go around and help them."

Lurking in the shadows and hearing this, I waited until they started moving and snuck up behind them. As they began to turn a corner, I took the first one, who lingered behind the second, and held a sword to his throat. He gasped and called for his friend, who was only a few paces in front of us. While my left hand held the blade to guard's throat, my handgun was aimed directly at the back of his friend's head.

"Don't move," I said. "I'm a sharpshooter and I've got a clear head shot. Obey my instructions or both you and your friend will face certain death." His friend's legs quivered and I could smell liquid shit from the punk I was holding close. Ugh, no control. Then again, it was a natural fight or flight response. "Drop your weapons," I said. Both men obliged. "I want you to take me into the inner chamber, take me to where the data is stored."

I quickly turned the silenced handgun back to the self-defecating imbecile's temple and let a bullet loose through his brain.

No way was I going to give his filthy blood the honour of staining my blade.

The remaining guard heard the body fall and he immediately knew what had happened. "Now you know I'm not fucking around. Keep your hands on your head." He obeyed. I closed in to let him feel the gun's barrel on his back and the blade on his throat. I thrust the barrel into his back and he started walking. All the while, we heard Yamagashi exchanging gunfire with the guard's comrades at the other end of the compound.

Sure, I was disobeying Yamagashi's orders here, but only because there was still the chance that he might have failed, and I couldn't make success contingent purely on his part. No, I would make my way into the inner chamber with or without Yamagashi's help. That said, I was sure that I'd meet him there.

The facility was a labyrinth and it would have been impossible to navigate without the guard.

I find it funny how people tend to discard loyalty when their life is threatened.

We kept going through several iris scans and, eventually, we reached the inner chamber.

The chamber was filled with at least a hundred desktops that acted as the visual interfaces to access the data, even though we'd come a long way since the era of shitty, huge hard drives.

There were five geeks who seemed to have been petrified even before I had walked into the room. Some of the surveillance equipment must still have been on; Yamagashi was excellent at what he did but he certainly wasn't perfect.

The scrawny little kids silently stared at me. I let them know that I wasn't fooling around and slit the guard's throat. No need to take him hostage any more; his value had expired. He fell to his knees and I pointed my gun at the geeks.

"Now listen up. You're going to help me or I guarantee that you'll meet your maker, understood? Don't fuck around or double-cross me; I have a friend coming and he'll make sure that I find out if you do." Two of them were in tears and snivelling while the other three were paralysed in fear. "Got it?" I yelled. They all shrunk into their seats and nodded vehemently in agreement.

Yamagashi entered the room.

"Bah! You're here before me; you didn't listen!"

"I listened and I had faith in you, but you know me by now. I have to make sure that the mission is a success and there's always the chance that your death might have been a possible setback."

"Well, I'm not dead and we're both here now. You'd have been a shit soldier: not following orders properly," he said.

No matter Yamagashi, I was never born to follow, I thought.

"Anyway, let's handle these geeks." He ordered one of them to boot up a visual interface for our use.

From the corner of his eye, he spotted two of them communicating through subtle gestures. What the hell were they thinking? He walked over and slammed his robotic arm across one of the cyberpunk's face, knocking the geek's glasses right off and spilling blood everywhere.

They all winced at that blow.

Disciplining prisoners of war prior to an interrogation was a specific art, but at the moment there wasn't enough time to paint the right picture, since I was only looking to add another stroke to my masterpiece.

"Don't fuck around. I'll know." He pointed back to the corpse of the guard by my feet. "Don't you little bitches get it? Can't you see what happens when you fuck around with the wrong guys? Give us what we ask for and nobody gets hurt." He turned to me, waiting for me to give them orders.

"First. I want you to erase all the remaining surveillance data. I know you have it. Get on with it." It was going to be a quick job, but a long night.

February 15, 2020. Aoyama-itchome, Tokyo. Rumours circulating in high places suggested that a certain Shizuka-san, from a Hananoka Wine Shop, made a particularly fine wine that was infused with memories of exquisite intensity and beauty.

Sure, there was a chance that it was bullshit but … if it worked, then who knew? Memories: powerful things, depending on the psyche of the subject. That night, all I kept thinking about is Angel and it had, rather paradoxically, sapped me of the motivation required to avenge her properly. Maybe it was because I couldn't clearly remember the time we spent together. The memories just weren't as vivid as they used to be.

I never drank to get drunk, but who could blame me if I got drunk on the memory of her?

Entering the wine shop, I saw Shizuka-san, a lady who clearly aged well, like the wines she sold.

The fibre-optic threads entwined throughout her hair gradually turned from green to blue upon seeing me. The look in her eyes exuded indomitable confidence and class.

"How can I help you?" Her voice was soothing and calm, as if she had been expecting me and this had all been pre-ordained. She asked the question but she already knew what I had come for.

"I'll have one of your memories in a bottle, if there is such a thing."

"Sure. It'll cost you though."

The opportunity to relive the past: I couldn't decide whether it was a blessing or a curse. Anyway, it was worth a try.

The Outliar

by Ash Crestfelt

Japan won the Second World War; Now the yakuza are starting the Third!

The Outliar

BY ASH CRESTFELT

February 14, 2020. Ogawamachi, Tokyo. Uchida Ryoto walks the loveless streets of downtown Tokyo. The nightlife buzzes. He passes a sign that reads "2020 Olympics" with four colored circles neatly clasping each other, entwined, but disconnected. He raises his head and blows a streak of white fire into the sky, a reprieve from the shrouding shadows of his hood. *It should be a knot*, he tells himself at the sight of the circles. *A giant knot that can't be undone.*

Clicking his tongue, he burrows his hands into the pockets of his hoodie, faces the cracked ground, and marches past three grand flagpoles stationed in a cascading line. First is Japan, just behind are Germany and Italy, and at the very end are the United States and the Soviet Union (China and Korea no longer have flags): this is the new world order.

Ryoto smiles grimly as he steps past the American flag. *Were they ever a leading nation?* he asks himself. He doesn't move his eyes from their fixed point on the pavement. He remembers the order of the flags well; after all, walking these streets is a habitual practice of his.

"Those greedy Germans should disappear like the Americans," he mutters under his breath. He shakes his head and spits: a crime to cleanliness in the eyes of the Kempeitai Thought Police, indeed, but a member of the Inagawa-kai like him couldn't care less. *Politics is just a load of bullshit*, he tells himself.

Uchida Ryoto turns a corner and enters an alleyway, the gate to the red light district that conveniently borders one of many nightlife quarters of the city. A look to the left gives him a glimpse of some men in suits. *Yakuza. Looks like that ban on us backfired. The politicians must've loved our money too much. Too bad it isn't shared too well among us dirty workers.*

"Hmm … we're dead. But commercial," Ryoto says, barely holding a chuckle. He relishes the times when his thoughts amuse him. He looks at the sky once again and smiles. "Sometimes I wish I were paid by the second like those Yamaguchi-gumi chimpira. But of course thirty-year-olds won't ever make good gigolos."

To hell with it all. Just got to live, that's it. He glances at his watch. It's eight-fifteen in the evening. *Thirty minutes to go.* Ryoto passes an abandoned building. The sound of thunder booms out of it with lighting illuminating its semi-shattered windows. Shouts, cries, and pleas fill the air, creating a whirlpool of incoherent, empty sound. Ryoto calmly strolls past the building, but at a distance. He knows what's going on in there.

Gang war. Must be a bunch of mangled and tangled bodies in there. Ten? Twenty? No, probably about thirty or forty by now. Damn, the Yamaguchi-gumi really knows how to use its dogs, making them fight each other so they can "qualify" to keep living. Sick bastards. No wonder society's fucked up. He clenches his teeth. *When were we never fucked up in our minds? Once you're yakuza, you can't go back. That's how it goes. It can't be helped. But someone's got to do the dirty work and pay the bills with blood money, and it sure as hell isn't the YG.*

Ryoto stops in his tracks. *The fruit of the laborers' work,* he thinks. He stays in place, eyes forward. His gaze locks on a thoroughly tattooed man, trudging towards an abandoned shed with a thick rope in his hand. Ryoto grimaces but watches intently. *The gang-life pressure must've gotten to him. Looks like he wants out, or rather up, with that rope. Better hope it doesn't snap.* Still eyeing the man, Ryoto begins to walk away. He examines his watch again. *Nineteen minutes to go.*

Ryoto enters a building with a falling sign on the exterior that reads, "Kami Delivery Service." He knows that another grueling job and measly paycheck is just up the unstable stairs and down the dark corridor. It's the room on the right, the one with messy *IK* letters scrawled across the exterior of the door.

Too cheap to afford some paper? Talk about a fitting image. Things really have gone downhill for the Inagawa-kai since the deaths of Oyabun Noboru Akira and Ryoto's old drinking buddy, Shio. Ryoto shoves down the rusted and uncooperative door handle, then flings it open: quite an entrance for a part-timer with the Inagawa-kai, indeed.

Inside the office, Ryoto looks around for his yakuza brother. "Took ya long enough," says Kaz. The Inagawa-kai gokudo emerges from the shadows of the sparsely furnished room, smoking a cigarette.

"I still got about two minutes or so," Ryoto replies, joking.

"Sure thing, whatever ya say."

"I thought you were the boss around here."

"Not for this job, I ain't," Kaz mutters, nonchalantly. He shoves one hand into his pocket, placing the other on the butt of his cigarette. He takes a long drag as Uchida Ryoto eyes him carefully.

"What do you mean?" asks Ryoto after a pause. Kaz leans against a table.

"I got a job for ya. And it's a mighty fine one, too. This one's got big money on it."

"Well, what do you have in store for me?"

"Kill Kitano Takumi," Kaz orders, grinning. Ryoto's eyes widen with surprise.

"The oyabun of the Yamaguchi-gumi? Why? And how?"

"The mission's simple. All ya got to do is get in there, get close, and screw them over when they aren't looking at ya. Got it?"

"You better be joking."

"The other day, a little birdie said there's a purpose to the gang war. Something about natural selection to find the worthiest sets in the Yamaguchi-gumi."

"I'm not stupid. There are plenty of factions within the YG. I know at least that much."

"Right, then let me ask ya something: why do ya think they need the bloodshed?" asks Kaz. Ryoto frowns.

"To find the best guys for their odd jobs?"

"Maybe. But I just got word that it's to help them Germans."

"What's the source?"

"Our little tip-off was sent by a delivery boy dressed up as a butler." Kaz pauses for a smoke. "I think the cosplayer was sent by some panty-twisted politician that didn't agree much with the shit that's going down up in the Diet."

"So he's hiring us."

"Ya know, I don't care who hires us Inagawa guys. If the pay's good and guaranteed, then we might as well be sold. So, deal?"

"What do the Nazis have to do with the YG?" Ryoto asks. He stares at the ground.

Kaz sighs, blowing out a breath of smoke.

"I wonder that myself. I think the Germans want the Yamaguchi guys to start killing off other Japs: important underworld or even political figures, for a while. Then maybe, one day, the Third Reich will be the leading nation and all that crap again. It's a hunch, but it's all I got from the info."

"Sounds like messy business. Sure we can't just take the money and split?"

"Do ya want a couple of bullets in your head? One of our guys tried that the other day. He's pushing up daisies now. Besides, why would ya want to do that if there was plenty more yen to come?"

"Aren't we a little tight on people for this op?"

"Like I said, I came up with a plan that doesn't demand much of us. And you're our front man."

"You mean dead man."

"No worries. We got a newbie, Izumi Goseki, some chimpira who idolized Shio before his death. He faked a defection to the Yamaguchi-gumi and will be your partner out on the field."

"Good to know." Ryoto's reluctance shows in the way he grumbles and he rolls his eyes. *Some reassurance that is.*

"So, ya in?" asks Kaz. A long silence fills the air. Ryoto looks out the sole window in the room. Moonlight pours through, but only enough to make a rectangle of light amidst the darkness. He closes his eyes. He hears nothing; not a soul moves about. He opens his eyes. Kaz stands before him, this time attentively observing his behavior. They lock gazes, but Ryoto quickly looks away.

"What's the plan?" he asks, breaking the deafening silence. A smile plays on Kaz's lips.

"Glad to have ya onboard, partner."

"Sure thing, captain," says Ryoto. "Now what's the plan?"

"Right, right, so here's the plan," says Kaz. "We got a guy from the Yamaguchi-gumi who's been incommunicado, in solitary in Sugamo Prison, for the last two years or so. We managed a get a pretty good fake ID for him and he looks a lot like you. So you're going to take his ID and his place in the YG."

"What if I'll be found out?" asks Ryoto. It's a calculated question.

"Ya won't. All the guys that knew him well are long gone. It's basically just his name that's out there now, and you're going to take that name. Once you're inside, I want you to get all chummy with the guys there, especially clan boss Takumi. Seriously pretend to be like them. Then, on the night when they break ground on the stadium for the 2020 Tokyo Olympics, there'll be a little celebration to mark the new truce between the Yamaguchi-gumi and the Sumiyoshi-kai. When they're all being happy out there, ya give us the cue and we'll storm the place, take out Takumi and any targets of opportunity. But ya got to do it right, otherwise we're all damned to hell. Wakarimasu-ka?"[151]

"Roger that."

"Great," Kaz says. He tosses Ryoto a leather jacket. Ryoto grabs it, surprised.

"What the hell's this for?"

"You're going to need it. Check the pocket, his ID's in there. Hatori Junichi's your new name. Judging from how ya look now, I guess you're ready to start. There's a car waiting for ya downstairs. So get going."

---

[151] "Understood?"

"Aye aye, captain," Uchida Ryoto mutters. He tosses his hoodie aside and puts on the leather jacket. He fiddles with the collar, and then heads for the door. Kaz watches him leave in silence.

"Good luck, soldier," he says quietly. Kaz closes door abruptly.

February 15, 2020. Kasuga, Tokyo. The next day, just a couple stops down the Mita line from Sugamo Prison, Ryoto sits in the waiting car sent by Yamaguchi-gumi Oyabun Kitano Takumi. *Leather never felt so cold*, Ryoto thinks. He leans against the inside of the car door. Boredom is the essence of the moment. Though leather is a fashionable item for feigning intimidation, it's hardly practical for a man like Ryoto.

What the hell am I doing? Looking like some ex-con wannabe gangster. At least now I'd be able to pass off as someone who makes money. Some disguise this is. He glances out the window. The nighttime city lights flicker on and off: blurry, distant, and Christmas-like, but cold. He yawns. *This is going to be a long trip*, he reminds himself. He begins to doze off. *Better get some rest. Hell awaits.*

Higashi-Shinjuku, Tokyo. Ryoto feels a shudder. He wakes up, a little startled, and looks around. The car has come to a halt.

"Good evening, sleeping beauty. Rise and shine, because you've got some work ahead of you!" says a cheerful voice from the driver's seat. Ryoto blinks several times as his eyes adjust. He can hardly make out his surroundings, let alone the figure before him. After scrutinizing this person for several seconds, he finally gives up.

"The hell are you again?" he blurts out, still groggy.

"Well aren't you a feisty one? I'm your new partner," says the driver, casually.

"So you're some newbie, huh? Good for you. Now I'm off," says Ryoto.

"Hey, the name's Goseki: Izumi Goseki. Used to be with the Inagawa-kai but I switched to the winning team. You sure you don't need any help?"

Formerly Inagawa-kai? Strange. "I'm fine. Just stay out of it."

"Sure thing, partner. Take care," says Izumi.

"Shut up," says Ryoto. *Fucking traitor. With Oyabun Noboru Akira dead, it seems everyone in the Inagawa-kai's jumping ship.* The car drives off. He stares at yet another disheveled building. *Must be a trend.*

Uchida Ryoto burrows his hands into the pockets of his leather jacket and enters the building. A group of Yamaguchi-gumi men in suits await him on the ground floor. A large man with a smart suit and gray hair steps forward, from the center of the gathering.

"Well, well, look who decided to join the party," the man says. He scrutinizes Ryoto. *That must be Kitano Takumi,* Ryoto tells himself, self-consciously tilting his head away.

"What, you not gonna say 'hi' to us, man?" bellows a voice from the crowd.

"Relax. This guy just got out of prison. You should be apologizing to him that we weren't able to welcome him properly," Oyabun Kitano barks. He turns back to Ryoto, "You sure have changed. Makes me wonder if you've still got those shooting skills from back then," he says. "With the gang war going on, you'll need them." Kitano pulls out a gun.

Ryoto reaches into his pocket for his switchblade, just in case. Kitano laughs. "Whoa there, hotshot. I'm not going to hurt you or anything. We're just going to do some friendly shooting, like old times. I mean, I got to make sure it's still you and not some other guy. After all, you did contact me out of the blue. I didn't know you were still alive or even remembered us; you were only with us a short while, after all. So, what do you say about catching up a little?" he suggests, acting casual.

Ryoto gives a reluctant nod. "Sure," he says.

"That settles it, then. Boys, set up some cans outside," Takumi orders.

A man in a suit hurries into the room. "Sir!" yells the man.

"What is it?" Kitano asks, irritated.

"We just got info that some Inagawa-kai guys are askin' for a fight," says the man. He glances nervously at Ryoto, clearly nervous. Ryoto frowns. *The hell? Kaz said nothing about this.*

"What? Those little chimpira … I thought the Seven Star Mob more or less wiped them out for us."

"No, sir. Apparently some nutcase called Miike and his girl Suki took over after Oyabun Noboru Akira got whacked and Wakagashira Minami Akio got driven out of town by the Koreans. They're attacking our guys outside The Bijou in Kabukichō . It's a shootout."

"Why are they picking a fight with us? Those little flies should know better than to want to get squashed," says Kitano Takumi. He sighs, "I want everyone at The Bijou in twenty minutes. Go put those Inagawa chimpira in their place. Junichi, do your shooting practice there," he says, eyeing Ryoto carefully.

Uchida Ryoto barely keeps his composure. Thoughts race through his mind, questions but not enough answers. He scratches his head as he heads for a van holding the other Yamaguchi-gumi men.

What's going on? We're not supposed to be going loud or anything. So why are the Inagawa-kai making a move already? What the fuck is Kaz thinking?

"Come on! I said move it, people!" booms the Yamaguchi-gumi oyabun. *Shit. They'll blow my cover, but I have to play it off. This is a test, after all.* Ryoto gets in the van. *Here goes nothing.*

Shinjuku, Tokyo. The lower floors of an older building adjacent to The Bijou. Bullets fly on all sides. The smell of gunpowder fills the air. Any moment now, the ceiling could give in, because this is a building that has been damaged by years of wear, tear, and earthquakes.

Ryoto ducks behind a tiled pillar, bullets exploding near his ear. He clings to the flimsy 9mm Makarov pistol Kitano Takumi gave him. The last time he was in a gunfight was five years ago. *Better hope my aim's still good,* he prays. He closes his eyes for just a moment to steel himself. Then he sticks his head out from the side of the pillar. *Three guys on the left and two on the right, all armed with high capacity pistols. They've got good aim, but they're not spot on. Reload time also isn't quick. Alright. Three … two … one …*

Ryoto snaps off the pillar and fires three shots, each hitting either the arm or shoulder of his three Inagawa-kai brothers on the left. He takes aim for the two on the right, but a bullet comes flying towards him, barely missing his neck. He scurries back into cover and glances in the direction of fire. There, crouching behind a wall, is Izumi Goseki. Ryoto's eyes widen. *What? What's this guy doing here?* He watches a little longer as the Yamaguchi-gumi take advantage of the fact that there are only two assailants left.

"Bail out!" orders Izumi. Ryoto frowns. *So … he's working for the Inagawa-kai after all … and the double-agent's calling the shots on this op.*

The Inagawa-kai members jump into a car that screeches as they make their escape. Bullets shower them from all directions.

Ryoto glares at the retreating car. *Why start a gunfight if you're not going to stick with it till the end?* He spits, then tosses the empty Makarov aside. *Something's rotten in the city of Tokyo tonight.*

It's late evening. Ryoto ducks into a Kabukichō alleyway, pulls out a cellphone, and contacts Kaz. He makes sure no one else is around as he waits for Kaz to answer.

"What's up?" Kaz answers.

"Why did you attack the Yamaguchi-gumi if you knew I was with them?" Ryoto demands.

"What are ya blabbering about? I didn't plan anything like that."

"Really? Then why were our guys in a shootout with the Yamaguchi-gumi?"

"Oh, that. A bunch of guys went astray and just caused trouble. Don't worry, they aren't around any more."

"They better not be. They're lucky to have escaped."

"What are ya talking about?"

"The guys that escaped. You expelled them from the clan, right?"

"Um … no one escaped. They all died," says Kaz. Ryoto's eyes widen with surprise.

"What are *you* talking about? I saw them: the other double-agent, Izumi, and a bunch of Inagawa-kai guys retreating."

"Izumi was here the whole night. He didn't go anywhere."

"Wha … the … hell …" says Ryoto. His breathing goes light. *Something's not right.*

"Ryoto?" Kaz asks. Ryoto hangs up. He sprints back to the scene of the shootout, the old building next to The Bijou. The lights of the city flash on and off, shooting Ryoto with spontaneous rays of light. He runs through it all and arrives at the base. He enters cautiously and searches for the dead bodies. They can't be found. He scours the grounds for evidence. No blood spatters, just empty shells and bullet holes. He stops dead in his tracks.

The bodies are gone.

February 16, 2020. A day later, Ryoto finds himself back in Kabukichō. The infamous red-light district is exactly as he imagined: *street after street filled with babes and big guys in suits.*

Turning a corner, he stands before a geisha ryotei.[152] He pulls out a piece of paper from the pocket of his leather jacket. He reads it, then looks up at the sign above. They match.

Well, Kaz got something right for once. But of course, it has to do with girls.

"Ugh. I hate this sort of thing," he says out loud. "Leading chicks on and getting info isn't my forte."

"Really? Then what brings you here?" inquires a voice. Ryoto turns, startled. He didn't expect anyone to be standing outside, nor did he expect anyone to hear him. It's a woman. He scrutinizes her for a bit, but comes to realize who she is.

"Riko …" he begins. He recognizes the famous geisha, known for her wealth of knowledge on gang leaders and members: at least, those who've slept with her.

"So you're my client for the evening. Uchida-san, was it? Pleasure to meet you," she says. A sly smile plays on her lips.

"Sure," he responds, his voice grim.

"Well, shall we get going? The night's still young, after all," Riko says gamely.

---

[152] A luxurious restaurant with traditional décor frequented by powerful men and their geisha companions.

"Let's just get this done with."

＋　　◇　　＋

February 16, 2020. The shower in the love hotel runs. Uchida Ryoto sits in the garishly decorated room, smoking an expensive cigar as he impatiently waits for Riko. He taps his foot. The clock ticks, ticks, and ticks away, burning the late night into early morning. He can't wait; he needs to know, and soon. *She can hear me if I talk from out here, right?* He wonders. Then he shakes his head. *I'll ask her. I can't afford to waste any more time.*

"Riko," Ryoto begins.

"Yes?" Riko calls out from the shower, her voice sensual.

"Tell me something: do you know about a guy called Izumi?"

"There are a lot of Izumis out there," she responds. He hears a squeak as the shower shuts off. "It's a common enough family name."

"I'm talking about someone who may have recently joined the Yamaguchi-gumi, an Izumi Goseki," Ryoto presses.

"That's interesting. And why would you suppose I know this sort of information?" Riko asks, toying with him. She calmly steps out of the bathroom with a towel wrapped around her.

"You've got dirt on everyone, so spit it out."

"I suppose I do. Well, I think you'd be surprised to know that there's no such person in the Yamaguchi-gumi at present, at least not here in Kabukichō. But there is a story floating around about how Chiba Shinobu killed an Izumi who tried to defect from the Inagawa-kai. Apparently, this Izumi chimpira was upset when the current Inagawa oyabun betrayed some guy named Shio, so this Izumi decided to switch clans. Big mistake. The Yamaguchi-gumi doesn't abide traitors." Ryoto stops tapping his foot. *This can't be good.*

"And?" demands Ryoto. Riko walks towards him. She puts her hand on his face and leans close.

"Oh, has that piqued your interest? Then perhaps you'd like all the details? Of course, I'll charge extra for them." She whispers in a business-like tone but adds a seductive wink.

"Charge it. So what's Chiba like?" Ryoto asks, unfazed.

"You're no fun." Riko pulls away from him and walks towards the dresser. "Chiba used to be an actor who performed kabuki at the local theatre before the old joint was replaced by a big pachinko parlor. He's a very outgoing person to most, but grim to those he works with."

"Is he a part timer?"

"No, a full timer, though a bit too close for comfort with some Sumiyoshi-kai types."

"What set is he part of in the YG?"

"None. He's part of the executive staff that runs the entire syndicate."

"No way …"

"More so, he's Takumi's right hand man, his wakagashira," she concludes, glancing at Ryoto. His blood runs cold. *Just as I thought. I've been set up.*

February 19, 2020. Shinjuku-sanchome, Tokyo. A few days pass. It's the eve of the planned celebration of the Yamaguchi-Sumiyoshi truce, CBI-Hitachi's breaking ground on the Spacecraft, and the Inagawa-kai's thwarted surprise attack on the Yamaguchi-gumi. Snow falls outside. Ryoto dons a hoodie to fight the cold. Every moment he doesn't act, he knows something will go wrong. His phone rings. It's from Kaz. He answers the call.

"What?" Ryoto shouts.

"Ryoto? We've got trouble. The real Hatori Junichi escaped from prison! I don't know where he went, but some of our guys are out to find him. But we're going to need your help, because we don't know if he'll get to the YG before tomorrow." Kaz spews his words out in a panic.

"Shit, you've got to be kidding me. How did he get out of Sugamo Prison in the first place?"

"I don't know. It's like someone let him out from the inside. Plus, he's in disguise. They found his prison clothes on the floor of his cell. There's no way he'd be running ass-naked out in this weather."

"Someone let him out? Who? Who did it?!" Ryoto asks desperately.

"Man, I don't know. But we're fucking screwed if the Yamaguchi-gumi finds out! Talk to ya later, I got to help the boys out."

"Wait," says Ryoto.

"What is it?" asks Kaz.

"Tomorrow, we're getting together at a warehouse to set the Yamaguchi-gumi agenda, before the meet up with the Sumiyoshi-kai, at the Spacecraft construction site, to celebrate this new truce. I guess it turns out the YG didn't kill Sumiyoshi-kai Oyabun Sugawara after all. And now, Kitano's planning some kind of time-limited truce with them, so the combined forces of the YG and SK can deal with the Koreans."

"What the hell do you expect me to do with that information? We have bigger problems to deal with ..."

"Just strike then. You need to take Kitano down at the warehouse before the Yamaguchi-gumi meets up with the Sumiyoshi-kai at the Spacecraft; there would be way too much security at the Olympics construction site. Remember, attack the YG warehouse. Trust me.

I'm counting on you," Ryoto says. He hangs up before Kaz can say anything else and shoves his cellphone into his pocket.

Now, what to do about the escaped prisoner. He feels his heart beat faster and faster with each passing moment. *Wait, calm down and think,* he tells himself. *Where would an escaped Yamaguchi-gumi guy be headed at a time like this?* Ryoto looks up in realization. *Of course, the Kabukichō red light district!*

✦   ◇   ✦

Shinjuku, Tokyo. With the increasingly heavy snowfall, unseasonable this late in the year, the Kabukichō streets never looked so empty. Ryoto waits in an alleyway near the east exit of Shinjuku-eki, leaning against the wall of the subway station.

Must be quite a storm coming. This is what I get for betting my money on this place. He shoves his hands into his hoodie pockets and pulls out Junichi's ID card. Amidst the smaller than usual crowd of pleasure-seeking humanity, a certain man in a suit walks by.

Ryoto glances at the card, then at the man's face. *Bingo, it's him.*

He pushes himself off the wall and begins to tail the real Hatori Junichi through the winding streets and back alleys of Kabukichō. Junichi senses Ryoto and turns to face him, but Ryoto lands a fist into Junichi's abdomen. He gasps for air and falls over, looking up at Ryoto.

"You ..." he barely manages to cough out.

"Pleasure seeing you, Junichi. Sorry, but I'm going to have to ask you to leave now."

"You Inagawa fuckers think you pull strings with the Kempeitai and get me transferred to solitary so you steal my identity? Well, guess what? I set plans in motion to screw you and your guys over from the start! So even if I die, you're going to die soon too. Bastard!" Junichi spits out.

He knows too much. How did he even know about our contacts in the Thought Police, or our identity theft plan? Damn it. I've got to do something about him. Ryoto reaches into his pocket and pulls out his knife. Junichi gets up, backing away.

"We can do this the easy way or the hard way. You choose," says Ryoto with menace. He advances towards Junichi, switchblade drawn.

"You want to kill me? Go ahead and try! My partner is still going to reveal you and then ambush your buddies!" Panic shows in Junichi's voice.

Ryoto grins. He lunges at Junichi with the knife. Junichi screams.

February 20, 2020. Shinjuku-sanchome, Tokyo. At a warehouse on the outskirts of Shinjuku, the Yamaguchi-gumi holds a meeting. The yakuza discuss how best to work with the Sumiyoshi-kai to take down the Koreans and profit off the Olympics by plying the athletes, and commissioners, with call girls. Things seem to be looking up for Tokyo's two largest clans.

Ryoto enters the building, arriving a bit late. The men at the door step aside when they recognize him. It's quiet on the inside, too quiet. *It's like someone died in here*, thinks Ryoto. Kitano Takumi stands at the head of a long table with "Izumi Goseki" at his side, smiling. Ryoto spits. *Bastard, so this is the game he was playing all along.*

"Well, Junichi, looks like you made it after all," Kitano says. Ryoto sighs.

"You can drop the act and just get on with it," Ryoto says, He shoves his hands into his pockets.

"Good one, Ryoto. Perhaps you were always this witty with your fellow flies."

"Not really. Wit doesn't put bread on the table."

"Oh, doesn't it? Perhaps you're suited to be a comedian, then," says the oyabun of the Yamaguchi-gumi.

"Not at all. Wit might not do the trick, but guns sure as hell do," Ryoto says and whips out his personal .45 H&K subcompact. Takumi's eyes go wide by the sudden development, and just as he makes a move, Ryoto's Inagawa-kai backup bursts through the doors, armed with guns and blades. Within seconds, the room erupts into a mosh pit of smoke, men, and blood. Ryoto ducks behind a table for cover and fires shots at all the targets he can.

Shit, I'm almost out. Where's my knife? Ryoto fires his last few bullets and fumbles for his switchblade, but before he can draw it, he feels something cold and wet against his skin. He looks down. A knife protrudes from his side, trickling blood from the open wound. Ryoto goes silent with shock.

Yamaguchi-gumi Wakagashira Chiba Ken, who had been masquerading as "Izumi Goseki," has stabbed him.

Outside, Ryoto limps as fast as he can. Off in the distance, fireworks go off above the Spacecraft, decorating that part of the night sky with an array of colors. CBI-Hitachi's subsidiary Morishita Construction has broken ground. The mob cheers.

Uchida Ryoto looks to the sky above his head. It's an empty black canvas punctuated by falling white snowflakes. His heart feels heavy; it becomes more and more difficult to breathe. He gasps for air. The knot inside him tightens, but in an instant, it snaps. Ryoto falls to the ground.

"All according to plan," says Kitano Takumi. He approaches the body from behind, grinning.

"I'll bet it was. Caused chaos tonight, didn't you?" asks a pale man. He has a big nose and a strong foreign accent, and wears a pinstripe suit. "Thanks for your hard work, right? Isn't that what y'all say over here?" he asks. He hands Kitano a briefcase. Kitano eyes it carefully, then takes it.

"Sure. You're not actually from Germany, are you?"

"Not at all. I'm American, but that'll be our little secret. Blow the whistle on us, and you'll end up like this poor fuck," he says gesturing at Ryoto's body. He walks off into the distance. Oyabun Kitano smiles. Wakagashira Chiba approaches.

"What's up with that guy?" he asks.

"Looks like our 'German' employers are actually American," says Kitano, amused.

"Guess the isolationists are also in on stirring up trouble in our great nation, eh? But doesn't everyone think it's the Germans making us do the dirty work?" asks Chiba.

"I might consider moving. Italy sounds nice," Kitano Takumi says. Other thoughts preoccupy him.

"Why? The Inagawa-kai are fucked, especially if this last idiot was the best they could do, the Sumiyoshi-kai are coming to the table, and the Seven Star Mob won't last long against our combined strength." Chiba says. Kitano Takumi's demeanor concerns him.

"Because sometimes late at night, when I sip my whiskey, I get tired of this life. Wars are brewing," says Kitano, "and not just between us yakuza. Why else would the Americans pretend to be Germans and stir up direct conflict between us and the Inagawa-kai?"

About the Author

Ash Crestfelt (born Ashwini Singh) made her writing debut on Off the Wall Plays in 2013 with the one-act play, *Someone to Remember*. In 2014, she proceeded to speak at the American Community School of Abu Dhabi's first ever TEDxYouth event. Shortly after this, she commenced working on various multimedia projects, most of which are yet to be released. When she's not terribly busy, Ash enjoys watching anime, surfing the net, and photographing our amazing world.

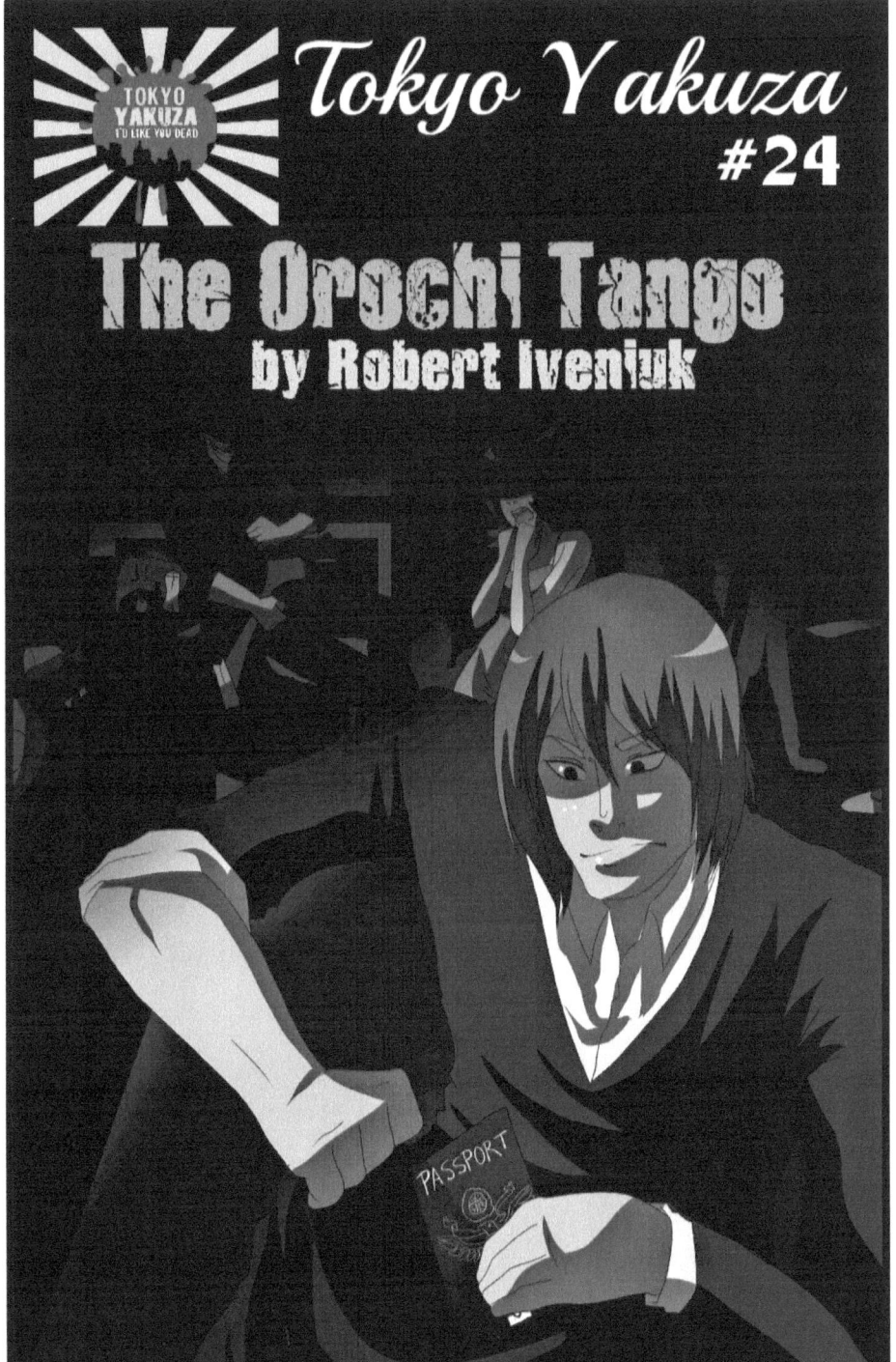

The Orochi Tango

BY ROBERT WILLIAM IVENIUK

February 21, 2020. Ryogoku, Tokyo. The rain stopped once he reached the abandoned factory. Puddles reflected moonlight as the last drops hit the ground, sending ripples across their still waters. Shun Kondo parked his scooter on the side. Removing his helmet, he set it on the seat of the worn-out old thing and started walking. It was alone in the middle of an old lot. Dirty brickwork spread across its boxy, rectangular shape. Rusted iron chimneys loomed overhead, and figures moved behind dirty windows.

On the horizon were the Tokyo lights, faint and distant as the stars above. Shun gazed out at them as he flipped his hood up and pocketed his hands. He thought of his family. Were his parents arguing over dishes while Tomoki read math books in the den? He pictured them, switching back and forth between Japanese and Korean as they bickered, and he smiled at the notion.

Metal ground together as double doors slid apart just up ahead. Unseen gears spread them open. Shun squinted as light spilled outward and filled the lot. Someone stepped into view.

"Kondo!" said the familiar, gravelly voice of his handler. They carried a particularly arrogant tone that night. His arms opened wide. "I was wondering where you were! Shopping for candy?"

Shun squinted, trying not to look into the glare. "I got lost. So sorry I'm late Kaz—uh, aniki. And sorry about what happened to Ryoto yesterday."[153]

Kaz took another step. The Inagawa-kai gokudo became more visible. That night, he wore a grey suit and a salmon-coloured dress shirt. His grinning, craggy face was hideous, and his hair was dyed a darker shade of auburn.

"Fuck Ryoto; he failed his mission," said Kaz. "If you're going to apologize for anything, it better be the lack of respect you're showing me," he added. "You're making me look bad in front of my boys!"

"S—So sorry, aniki!" Shun immediately put his arms to his sides and bowed. He saw himself in a puddle just below him. Spiky hair covered his forehead, surrounding his slim jaw and wide eyes.

A laugh from his handler. "I'm just busting your balls, kid. Here."

Shun looked up in time to see something flying towards him. With clumsy grab, he caught it. He gasped at the sight. In his hands was a red-on-silver tanto, fitted neatly into a slick, organic sheath.

Kaz smiled as his pupil examined it. "You might need it tonight."

"It's real?" Shun asked. Wary, he inspected the weapon.

"Monofilament edge. You could cut through a man like paper with that baby. Now, come on."

They entered the factory together. Shun's jaw slacked.

Scattered everywhere were screens of various sizes, airing security camera footage from all over Tokyo. Shun caught glimpses of empty alleyways, late-night scrambles through malls, and the

---

[153] Yakuza brother, a gruff and thuggish way of saying brother.

insides of restaurants. One large screen in particular showed long, cylindrical shapes being carefully loaded into the back of a silver truck. Inagawa-kai men were everywhere, patrolling around with their hands on an array of weapons or fiddling with wires and foldable control panels, fitted into the smaller monitors.

Shun wondered what he got himself into. Life was hard for a half-Japanese like him. His dock-worker father, an expat from Busan, and cleaning-lady mother barely made enough to make ends meet. It was not enough, though, especially not with inflation affecting prices while their wages remained much the same.

When job agencies and hand-delivering resumes failed, Shun got desperate. He trained himself to tail people and learned how to fleece wallets and jewellery without being noticed. He got good at it: good enough to be noticed by Kaz during a Ueno job. It was then that he was offered steady work for dirtier jobs: passport thefts; credit card fraud; even modelling for doctored photos. It put food on the table and kept debt collectors at bay.

Nobody knew about his ethnicity. He wondered if that helped somehow. Three months under the Inagawa-kai was difficult, but rewarding. Staring at everything around him, however, filled Shun with an overwhelming sense of dread.

Kaz punched Shun's arm. "What're you daydreaming for?"

Shun snapped awake. "Sorry! So, uh –"

Kaz pointed to the truck on the big screen as it was closing up. "We're driving that into Tokyo. I've got the address fitted into the GPS."

"What's in it? I mean, those boxes."

"*Very* precious cargo, kid. You'll understand when we're there."

"Okay. Er, lots of men out tonight."

"It's going to be that kind of night. We'll be close behind, keeping you good and safe."

"Our cargo must be pretty important."

"The Olympics are around the corner, kid. Things are hectic. Government's crackin' down on a lot of honest business, and *everybody's* locking horns." He wound his arm back, taking on a lazy posture. "With that old bastard Kitano Takumi mowing down Ryoto and some of our other Inagawa-kai brothers, we need this to mission to succeed more than ever."

"But, what are we mov–"

"Tsuki ga … de-ta, de-ta … Tsuki ga … de-ta …"

Everything slowed down. Whispers circulated. Each man on site looked round for the noise. Shun's blood chilled when he heard it. It was soft and sweet, a girl's voice to be sure, but with a sinister edge to it.

A woman in a long red dress glided out of a shadowed corner, entering the light. A pair of geta[154] shuffled as she moved. Her outfit stopped just before her ankles and long, wide sleeves covered her arms. Golden, serpentine patterns were embroidered into the neckline and shoulders. In her hands, she spun a simple umbrella with ivory frills. White hair fell over a thin, pale face. Amethyst earrings twinkled. Pink eyes blinked at them, curious.

"I wonder, I wonder, am I in the right place?" she asked. She turned on the heel. "By any chance are you all Inagawa-kai?"

"What's it to you, woman?" one of Kaz's men barked. "How did you know we were here?"

"Snakes always know where mice hang out." One of her long-fingered hands slid into a wide sleeve.

---

[154] Wooden sandals.

"No mice here," another man said. He stepped forward and looked her up and down. Lechery flickered in his eyes. "But you're one hell of a snake."

A giggle. "I like you," she said. Shun heard something *click* near her.

"Aniki," Shun started. His fingers danced across his tanto. "Something's —"

Across the woman's face came a terrible and predatory smile. "I wonder how you'll taste."

There was a ticking noise that stopped as the woman snapped her arm outward. A silver ball flew across the room. As it neared the man who flirted with her, it flashed. The front half of it glowed bright red and erupted into flame. The man thrashed around, trying to put out the flames that immolated him. Shun shielded his eyes and tried to block out the man's horrified screams.

Curses rang out as the yakuza raised their guns, opening fire on her. Just as quickly as their weapons went hot, however, she ducked down and lifted the umbrella. Lead bounced off of its frilly surface as though it were made of iron.

Above her, the windows shattered. Two men flew outward: one was a svelte bleached-blonde in a grey suit and tie; the other sported an anaconda-skin jacket, with dyed red hair and a wolfish grin. The blonde snapped his arms outward. Small shapes flew out of his hands and curved around the room.

Shun yelped as one of the gunmen fell, bleeding from the neck. He ducked as something flew overhead, arced, and went through another yakuza. From where he lay, he saw what was sailing around the room: knives. Flat, triangular blades with blinking lights in their bottoms whipped around like locusts and sent Kaz's men scattering.

As the newcomers landed next to the woman, the red-haired man gave a triumphant yell and shot his arms forward. Two long, whip-like appendages sprang out of his sleeves. An Inagawa man was impaled by them and lifted into the air as the assassin yanked back, sending him flying. Another howl and the crimson killer sprang forward, brawling with Kaz's men.

Shun was aghast, wide-eyed and paralyzed with fear. Blood splattered. Bones broke. The smell of burnt flesh assailed him. He became so engrossed in watching the carnage that he hardly noticed as Kaz pulled him off the ground and dragged him to the other side of the room.

"It's the Orochi!"[155] Kaz screamed. He produced a key-card from his coat and they headed for a bare wall in the far corner. "Kondo, we need to leave *now!*"

Shun's heart stopped. The Orochi: a Sumiyoshi-kai hit squad, rarely seen, and hardly survived. Whispers spread across the underworld of their power and danger. He was seeing them in action that night. A terrible fear clutched him.

A light blinked and the wall opened. Iron walls stretched into a snaking corridor. More men spilled out, weapons raised.

Kaz and Shun ran past them, veering left. Something shattered behind them and they kept running. Shun looked back as he heard men shouting orders, pointing at something down one bend of the hall.

The largest man Shun had ever seen suddenly barreled out of the passageway. His massive hulking body, which stretched against the confines of its black suit, slammed into them. The man's wide head nearly reached the ceiling.

---

[155] The Sumiyoshi-kai's most powerful squad of professional killers. Sent to liberate the dead oyabun Sugawara's illegitimate daughter from the Inagawa-kai so Sugawara's widow could gain win over certain potential supporters.

Kaz and Shun, hurting, got back to their feet as the man turned his attention to the other yakuza in the room. Ham-like fists knocked men back. Face red, his beady eyes flared as he let out a warbling battle-cry.

Another light flashed and Kaz led Shun into another part of the factory, filled with scrambling men. Iron walkways flanked an open truck-yard.

Shun recognized the silver truck from the screen. Kaz flashed a set of keys and the truck's lights blinked on. As Shun ran, a crimson spray hit the ground beside him.

Fighting its way across the walkways around them was some manner of bronze automaton. Man-shaped and half-dressed, its layered body moved with lightning speed. In each hand was a paired vibro-katana that shivered as it cleaved men in half. Shun caught sight of a sharp and slick face, featureless save for a single visor, and the kanji for "wind" painted on its back.

Another sound. On the opposing walkway was another figure, brutally murdering her way through a gang of six. She was a far different sight, a girl no older than Shun with a high forehead and thin hair. Clogs tapped against metal as she ran, clad in a pleated skirt, black blazer, and pink sweater. Two flat, circular drones flew around her. Machine gun-fire blazed from their shells, cutting down whoever came near.

She stopped and saw them. Ducking down, she brought a phone to her ear. Shun didn't know what she said, but didn't want to stick around to find out. He saw the truck's doors open and ran for them.

Jumping into the passenger side, he saw Kaz slide the key into the ignition and hit the gas pedal. They sped off before Shun had a chance to buckle up or even close the door. His body jerked back. Grabbing the dashboard, he reached over and yanked the door shut.

It was then that he noticed the screen in the middle of the dash. Kaz jerked the truck back and forth and ran his fingers along the glass. Information came up. Shun saw EEG readings, pulse monitors, and infrared scans of warm bodies in canisters flying past.

Shun paled. "We've got people back there?!"

"Girls, man!" Kaz scoffed. He saw the expression Shun shot him and shook his head. "I wanted it to be a surprise!"

"*We're trafficking prostitutes*?" Shun shouted.

"They're not prostitutes! Well, not *yet.*"

"Kaz—aniki, did you seriously just *kidnap* a bunch of people?!"

"God, when you put it like *that* –"

"Is –? Aniki? Why are the Orochi after us?"

"I'll tell you later!" Kaz yelled.

"Tell me now! Who's back there?!"

"I can't say! We need to –"

A burst. The truck jerked. Cursing, Kaz spun the wheel and fought against gravity. They began to veer. Metal screamed against asphalt. All at once, they stopped.

Kicking open the door, Kaz jumped out, fuming. Shun unbuckled and joined him. His heart stopped. One of the wheels had been torn apart. The rip in the rubber indicated that a bullet as big as a melon did the damage.

"Plan B." Kaz reached into his pockets. From out of his left pocket came a slim black handgun; out of the right came a little silver device, like an egg. He flicked open the top and revealed a red button.

Shun shuddered. *A detonator. How serious was he?*

They ran to the side of the truck. Just ahead, the factory was burning down. Smoke billowed out of shattered windows and fires rose out of one side.

The Orochi were lined up, backlit from the blaze and watching them. The blonde and red-head stood beside the colossal man. The girl, suddenly quite sheepish, hid behind the automaton. Next to them was the albino woman. She was eating a lump of charred flesh; grease and meat chunks stuck to her cheek. Near her was a robed man in a face mask and a wide-brimmed sandogasa.[156] Smoke trailed out of his left side and Shun recognized the smell of cordite.

An eighth figure drew near. Long-limbed and tall, a woman stepped in-between the colossus and the robot. Hair tied back in a ponytail, loose strands fell around her chiseled features. She wore a black suit with a white dress shirt and her high-heels clacked against the pavement. She gripped a large, silver revolver, and a pair of thick sunglasses covered her eyes.

The woman stopped and regarded them. Shun felt his blood freeze.

"So you're Hitomi, eh?" Kaz scoffed, levelling the detonator in his other hand. "The Orochi's *bitch supreme*?"

"You have someone we want," she said. Her voice was cool, professional. "Stand in our way and you die. Hand her over, and we'll just cripple you."

Kaz laughed. "The hell is that? Who taught you how to negotiate?"

"You made a big mistake." Hitomi tapped the revolver against her thigh, getting impatient. "This is us being fair."

"You made a mistake in abandoning her, if she mattered so much to you, damn it!" He held the detonator up. His gun-hand shook. "None of you move, okay? You move, and I blow the truck up and kill them all!"

Shun put his hands in the air. "Aniki, we should —"

---

[156] A samurai's travelling hat.

Kaz wasn't listening. Fury filled his eyes. "You hear me? You want to spend the evening scraping her off the pavement?!"

The Orochi weren't reacting to his threats. They stared at him in silence, as though expecting him to press the button. Desperately, Shun grabbed his handler by the arm and shook. "Kaz, listen, just let her –"

"*They killed my men!*" His handler shook him off with a roar. "*Fifty-four* of my best men, dead over some *halfie bitch* their oyabun made before he got his head blown off!"

Shun stopped. He quivered and stared at Kaz.

"What the hell is she to you?" Kaz shouted at them. "Her mother was some Dubai *whore*. That old fart, Sugawara, had already named Ishii Naoki his successor when he bit it! *She's nobody!* We're making her useful!"

Hitomi said nothing and released the revolver's safety. Her comrades shifted their feet and clenched their fists, preparing to strike.

"Damn it, Kondo, back me up!" Kaz said. He brought his gun up. "Looks like we're going down fighting. Take that tanto out! *Kondo!*"

Shun's breathing grew heavy. Anger filled him as Kaz spat his orders. The callousness and self-righteousness of the man began to bite at the youth, agitate him. His fingers clutched tight around the tanto. Gradually, he took the sheath off.

Then he turned to Kaz and drove the blade deep into his back.

Kaz stuttered. Body twitching, his fingers opened and his tools dropped to the ground. He grit his teeth and his eyes went wide. The Orochi watched in silence. Shun's hands shook. Breathing heavy, mind blank, he tightened his grip on the handle.

With a tug, Shun loosed the tanto. Blood spurted from Kaz's wound, staining his hoodie and shoes. Kaz fell without a sound, slumping forward like a marionette with its strings cut. His face hit the pavement with a sickening thud. A crimson pool spread. The tanto slipped out of Shun's hands. He stared at the Orochi, suddenly very afraid of himself.

Hitomi tucked her revolver into her suit jacket. "That was unexpected."

"Let ..." Shun heaved. Words wouldn't come. Every thought collided with another. He wanted to run. He wanted to fight. He wanted to cry. The blood on his hands felt heavy. Shun looked at the assassins, the monsters, and fumbled with his tongue. "I. Can I. Please."

He kept stammering. The seven-foot Orochi and the red-head broke away and headed for the back of the truck. Shun felt as if he were made of wood. He turned to watch them. With a jerk, the red-head shot both tendrils forward and they hit the door. With a tug, it came loose.

"Your heart's racing," Hitomi said. As her colleagues worked, she tilted her head. There was a clicking sound that came as she did. "I can see it. Neurons are firing everywhere. You're not made for this, are you?"

"I just ..." Shun turned to her. "My family. Please, my family. Mom, Dad, Tomoki."

The colossus turned to the others. "Which one is she?" he asked. His voice came out in a low baritone.

"Second row, third one down, left side," Hitomi said. She sighed and made a motion with her chin. "Go. Stay out of this world. For your family's sake."

"Thank you," he said. Shun quaked and started walking away, his body stiff.

"Don't be so soft with him." The automaton hummed like an electric tiger. "You should take a finger, or an ear, so he remembers us."

"Look at him," said Hitomi. Behind her, the large Orochi dragged one of the containers out of the truck. "He'll never forget this night," she said.

And so he walked. Shun only looked back once more as the container's lid was thrown off. A slender, tanned girl with bowl-cut hair was lifted gingerly out of it. He told himself not to watch any more. Still stunned, still smelling of Kaz's blood, he dragged himself back to his scooter.

The downtown Tokyo lights seemed farther away than before.

About the Author

Robert William Iveniuk is an author from Toronto, Canada. His short fiction has been featured in *Schlock Magazine*, *The Alchemy Press*, and Crossed Genres Publications' *Long Hidden* anthology. He has two years' worth of articles on the lifestyle and entertainment website, BlogTO, and presently contributes articles to *Archenemy Magazine*.

JAPAN WON THE SECOND WORLD WAR. NOW THE YAKUZA ARE STARTING THE THIRD!

TOKYO YAKUZA
I'D LIKE YOU DEAD

東京極道

The Morning Rats

BY MELISSA NIEBUHR

TOKYO YAKUZA BONUS ISSUE 1

The Morning Rats

BY MELISSA NIEBUHR

February 22, 2020. Ikebukuro, Tokyo. The rats came streaming through the cracks, running across her bare legs. Tachibana Suzume lay still and allowed the rats to go about their morning commute. The van was due in ten minutes and she wasn't about to give her position away.

She wished that her cover had allowed her to wear pants, but unfortunately, the getaway plan required the elaborate geisha kimono. The white face paint was also an annoyance. It didn't feel much worse on her skin than her normal makeup, but it was slick on the stock of the sniper rifle.

She could hear the clients stirring in the tea house below her attic vantage point. If their routine held, the geishas and kisaeng[157] would be bowing out their overnight guests just about the time that the van entered the kill zone. She expected a rather spectacular crash when she took out the driver. Considering the contents of the van, a fireball was not out of the question.

---

[157] Korean geishas.

ZomB got the users bombed out of their minds. It was a quick-acting, long-lasting, intense high. It rotted minds just as quickly.

ZomB was also an exceedingly volatile chemical compound. It was expensive to make, expensive to buy, and produced by Bosseu Tu-bong of the Seven Star Mob, one of the fuckers extorting free autobody work out of her dead brother's maimed best friend, Tanaka Shinobu.

Suzume couldn't get close to Tu-bong, not yet, but she was going to give him one hell of a headache. The shipment in the van was worth more than one billion yen.

The driver was a bonus. Yeoum had hired Shinobu to steal Eugi's Ferarri and done nothing to help the night that Suzume's brother, Tachibana Michi, was eviscerated and burned alive. It was too bad that he'd be dead before the van burned.

She could hear the geishas below begin the ritual of seeing out their guests. Excited by the noise and activity below, the sedate, two-lane highway of early morning rat commuters suddenly became a six-lane expressway, boiling up from the tea house. Hushed and delicate conversations were replaced by blood-curdling screams.

"Rats! Rats!"

"Follow them! Kill them!"

"Get them, Han Tae Hee!"

Oh, shit, thought Suzume. *If they follow the damn rats, I'll be busted. Shit! Fuck me, motherfucker.*

Enthusiastic shouting and chaotic footsteps rang out as the guests all rushed to prove their manhood and become the saviors of the squealing geishas. Just as the pursuit gained coherence and headed for the attic, the van she had been watching for pulled around the corner.

Sixty seconds to the kill zone.

Would the guests follow the rats to attic before she could get the shot off? Suzume had nowhere to go, but at the least, she was going to take Yeoum with her.

Suzume steadied the stock against the shoulder of her white and blue kimono. Yeoum was driving down the alley, slow and steady, like any other delivery van.

Thirty seconds to the kill zone.

Fresh screams erupted below. More frantic than before, these screams came from the front of the tea house, opposite her sniper's nest. A terrible crash shook the building, momentarily jerking her scope off the van. *What the fuck?* she thought. Distantly, she heard the men's footsteps retreating down the stairs toward this fresh outrage.

The van entered the kill zone; the driver was in her sights. Suzume took the shot.

The .308 sniper round put a small hole in both the windshield and Yeoum's forehead. The back of his head did not fare as well; his brain tissue left the back of his head at supersonic speed. He was bowing before Amida Buddha so abruptly the Buddha's head spun.

The van leapt forward as the dead weight of Yeoum's foot pressed the accelerator. The van swerved toward the concrete wall of the factory on the opposite side of the alley.

Suzume dropped the rifle down a shaft between the inner and outer walls of the tea house and raced for the stairwell. She heard the crump of the van impacting the concrete wall as she reached the top floor of the tea house. She put on a burst of speed. The white clouds on her blue kimono flashed as she got to the top of the stairs, leading down to the ground floor.

The ZomB didn't react well to the sudden deceleration. As she'd hoped, it exploded, igniting the tank of the van. The dual concussion lifted Suzume off her feet and blew her down the steep stairs like a leaf in the breeze. Luckily for her, she landed on a rather plump guest. Luckily for him, he'd glanced up in the direction of the explosions in time to try and catch her. The two ended up in an undignified heap at the bottom of the stairs.

"Oh, so sorry. Please excuse my clumsiness. Are you all right, lord?" asked Suzume. She put on a breathless, subservient voice. She didn't even have to fake it. The blast had really knocked the wind out of her.

"I am honored to save so beautiful a lady from injury. You are quite all right?" The guest grunted. She'd winded him and he was trying to fake a normal voice.

"You saved me, lord. I am so grateful. Please, help me up." Suzume deftly rolled to her feet, taking the disoriented guest with her. She bowed deeply. "You are so powerful, lord. I was so fortunate you were here."

He sketched a wobbly bow in her general direction in return and plopped back to the floor, landing on his butt.

"I must go and see to Mama-san, lord. Oh, please forgive me, but I fear for her." Suzume bowed again and rushed toward the front door.

Geishas and guests were rushing everywhere: in and out, out and in. The assault to the front of the tea house and the explosions behind had created the perfect scene for Suzume's escape.

"What happened behind us?" asked a geisha.

"I don't know!" Suzume said. "What happened in our garden?" She rushed past the girl into the front yard.

Black tire tracks ran up to, then away from the ruined front gate. Everyone was in a state of shock and took no notice of Suzume as she sidled through the crowd and out the skewed gate.

Suzume adjusted her kimono and discretely checked her hair as she walked away from the building.

"What happened at the tea house?" asked a passerby.

"It was terrible. The beautiful gate is ruined," Suzume said. "I couldn't bear to stay and see such desecration." Giving a shallow bow, Suzume continued on.

Four blocks away, Suzume slipped behind the wheel of her ancient Lexus. She put the key in the ignition, started the powerful motor, and rested her head against the steering wheel for comfort.

"Take me home, Lexi-sama," Suzume said to the kami of her Lexus.

✦   ◇   ✦

Kit Yamaguchi watched the geishas and clients chase the rats out with disinterest. She hated rats of the two legged kind. The four legged variety were beneath her notice. She was calmly sipping her tea when a crash from the *front* of the teahouse startled her. She expected an explosion from the back. *What was this?*

The crash stopped the rat hunt in its tracks. They paused, and then went running toward the wreck. Kit reached for her kugo[158] case. Something had gone balls up on this. She would have to deal with it. Just as she flipped the latches open, a shockwave and blast of sound struck the building from the rear. The tea house shook hard enough for her to lose her grip on the instrument. As Kit regained her footing and flipped open the case, she saw Suzume run past, her kimono streaming about her.

The blast drew the geishas and men back into the teahouse.

Kit closed her eyes, focusing her mind.

---

[158] A traditional Japanese stringed instrument.

Her telepathic command stopped the first arrivals, geishas worried about the house. Kit wiped their memories of the blast and sent them back out to the crash site. The next three to enter were Tu-bong's men.

Kit grabbed their minds. She held them still as she shot them between the eyes.

Kit continued to use her mind to redirect the innocent and slaughter Tu-bong's men as they entered the room where she reclined, at ease, with her beloved MP7 submachine gun.

When the last of the men lay dead at her feet, Kit Yamaguchi reached out to her backup team to come gather and dispose of the bodies. She then seized the minds of the people crowding in the forecourt and froze them. The geishas and remaining clients stood still; time paused for them.

Kit exited the teahouse headed to the alley to survey Suzume's handiwork. As she walked, she erased people's memories of her. Kit bowed slightly as her Yamaguchi-gumi clean-up crew passed her. The crew members knew that they could release each person from Kit's hold with just a small touch, as if to get their attention.

Being a kami, able to control mortals with her mind, made this type of work simple and enjoyable for her. Though they remained enemies, Kit Yamaguchi had nothing but admiration for Suzume. To achieve success with only beauty and determination must have been far more stressful. It was too bad that after killing the Koreans who hired Shinobu and continued to torment him, Suzume would inevitably come after Eugi and the Yamaguchi-gumi for killing her brother.

Suzume hit the garage door opener and pulled into Shinobu's auto repair shop before the door was even all the way up. She parked the SC430 behind a lift and let out a sigh. Her eyes felt gritty. The kimono smelled like rat, she could feel sweat trails in the caked-on white makeup, and she had to pee.

Suzume absent-mindedly patted the fender as she headed out of the garage toward her room. She wanted to scrub off the makeup and change clothes before heading for the public baths. As she left the garage, she smacked the wall mounted door controller and paused to listen as the garage door started to shudder and shriek its way closed.

Suzume's pet, Ryuu, burst into the garage, wagging his tail so hard that his whole butt wiggled.

"Who's a good doggie? Oh, you so good doggie!" cooed Suzume. She stopped to scratch the big pit bull's ears. Ryuu responded by jumping up and licking most of the white off of her face. "Yuck, Ryuu, that had to taste nasty! Let me change and we'll go walkies? Who wants to go walkies?" Ryuu fell in behind Suzume, his back end still dancing.

"Who's a good Lexi? You're a good Lexi!" A male voice, carrying a sneer in the tone, came from the ether in the vicinity of a Kawasaki Ninja, leaned against the wall.

"Shut up, Saki. I had a hard night." A female voice came from the Lexus.

Suzume couldn't hear a thing. She wasn't a medium like Shinobu. She wasn't even remotely sensitive. Suzume had no idea that the kami hated how she treated the vehicles, to which they were bound, no differently than she treated her pit bull, Ryuu.

"Want to talk about it, Saki? Or is the little Lexi-sama too tired?"

"I got parked in the Hanamachi district overnight, away from the good tea houses. A drunken businessman pissed on my tire, I had to make a deal with the house kami, and I rammed a gate. It was not tiring at all, Saki."

"A drunk pissed on your tire?"

"Out of all that, you want to know about the drunk?"

Suzume crossed the garage, trailed by a still enthusiastic Ryuu. She headed in to bathroom, shutting the door on the dog. Ryuu whined, then ambled over to the Lexus, sniffing her right front tire.

"See, even Ryuu wants to know about the drunk who pissed on your tire."

"And now I've been pissed on by a drunk *and* a dog. Thanks a lot, Ryuu."

Saki laughed so hard that the Kawasaki Ninja shook against the wall. "At least you know the dog!"

"Saki, I am so going to run you over one day."

"Do it and I'll take out your oil pan!"

Coming back into the garage, Suzume whistled for Ryuu. She fastened his lead, fumbling with the simple catch. Her face was grey without the elaborate makeup. With a grunt of effort, she flung a tote over her shoulder, then flicked off the garage lights. "See you soon, guys. This is going to be the best hot shower ever." She blew kisses at the vehicles as she locked the door.

"So, is that a new dent?"

"Yes, Saki, it is. I rammed a gate, remember? That was after the deal with the kami and the drunken business man."

"So how drunk was he?"

"Drunk enough to piss on a tire! Why are you so fascinated by a man pissing? Are you missing something, Saki?"

"Ha! You wish! Why did you have to make a deal with the kami?"

"Changing the subject. Subtle, Saki, but I'll go along. I made a deal with the kami because I didn't like Suzume's plan. I wanted eyes on the inside. She'd have stabbed a guest if one had tried to get frisky and I couldn't risk that. Shinobu would send me to jigoku[159] if I let her die."

"But Suzume was visiting the Mama-san to talk about her mother. Why would a guest bother her?"

"Because she's prickly. One guest says one thing wrong and boom! Dead guy."

"Suzume's not that mad. What was really bothering you?"

"It's a tea house, all rice paper walls and tatami's. The rifle wasn't silenced. The sniper's nest was over the kitchen. Her mother's kimonos are twenty years out of date and she sucks at makeup. Pick one."

"You left out that she's clumsy walking in geta."

Shun didn't reply.

"You're right. It was a sketchy set up."

"Thank you."

"So, the dent?"

"Rats."

"You were dented by rats? How big were these rats? Human-size big? Like that rat that orders the turtles around?"

"I come home tired, dented, pissed on, and you just have to give me grief, don't you, Saki?"

"Lexi, if I behave, will you just tell me?"

"If by 'behave' you mean you'll shut the fuck up and stop screwing with me, then yes, I will tell you what went down. Deal?"

"Deal."

"Getting in was easy since Suzume's mother was once employed by the Mama-san. She was going to be safe all night, drinking tea, giggling, and telling stories about the old days while the Mama-san made her up. It was the sniper's nest I didn't like. So I promised the house kami that we'd never do this sort of thing out of her house

---

159 Buddhist hell.

again. Easy promise, but the kami had to be talked around. Took hours. Turned out it was a good thing that I made the deal, but not for the reasons I was worried about. Suzume was right. The kitchen noises masked the sound of the shot. The cooks do make a god awful racket to encourage the guests to leave."

"What went wrong?"

"The house has rats: not a few rats, a shit load of rats. Hundreds of the nasty little motherfuckers. They even ran across Suzume's legs while she waited for the van. She was tough. She just laid there while rats, fucking nasty, dirty rats, ran over her."

"That's hardcore. But what do the rats have to do with you ramming the gate?"

"They didn't clean up the gods damned supper. The rats found the leftovers. The geishas found the rats. The rats ran away to the attic. The guests were chasing the rats to impress the geishas."

"So there was a parade of would-be *heroes* chasing the rats straight toward Suzume?"

"And the van was entering the kill zone. She was going to take the shot, no matter what."

"Fuck."

"Yes, fuck. The house kami came to me when the geishas found the rats, but I couldn't do shit about the rats. So I distracted the *heroes* the only way I knew how."

"You rammed the gate."

"I rammed the gate."

"Did anyone see you?"

"No one in the tea house, but there was a drunk guy."

"The drunk guy who pissed on your tire?"

"Back to pissing. You really are missing something, aren't you, Saki?"

"Well, I'm missing a new dent."

"Fuck you."

"You wish."

The lock clicked as Suzume entered with a still-wiggly Ryuu. "Home sweet, rat free home!" Suzume kicked her zori[160] off at the door. She unlatched Ryuu's leash and wobbled toward her room. "Good night, Lexi and Saki!"

Suzume whistled for Ryuu as she crawled into bed. Ryuu jumped on top of the covers and settled in against her. Suzume hugged the red and white dog as he gently licked her face. As she drifted off, Suzume wondered about the accident at the tea house. The gods themselves must approve of her mission. How else to explain a drunk hitting that particular gate at that exact time?

About the Author

Melissa Niebuhr has two hobbies; reading, writing and fast cars. Okay make that three! Melissa has three hobbies! She became a librarian to be as close as possible to one of her hobbies. When not working on programming at her library, or buying books, she loves driving her car. Anywhere, it doesn't matter.

Melissa's show car is a 1970 Chevelle SS 454 with 559 dyno tested horses living under the hood. Her daily driver is a 2008 Infiniti G37 with a paltry 330 hp. Melissa shares her home with her husband, Roger, and their two rescue dogs. Scout is a boxer/black mouth cur mix and Coco is a Catahoula Leopard Dog. Melissa's friends have been pestering her to write for years, and this is the result.

---

[160] Flat, Japanese sandals made of rice straw.

Glossary

14K Triad: The Chinese criminal clan in Tokyo. Their gang colors are red.

Akechi Mitsuhide (1528-1582): A general who rebelled against daimyo Oda Nobunaga, leading to Oda's death.

Aniki: Yakuza brother, a gruff and thuggish way of saying brother.

Appa: "Daddy" (in Korean).

Arigato gozaimashita: "Thank you so much!"

Bakuto: Gamblers. A traditional profession of the yakuza and the specialty of the Inagawa-kai, Tokyo's oldest clan.

Bento: Wooden lacquered lunchbox.

Bijou, The: The Yamaguchi-gumi's premiere hostess club in Shinjuku, Tokyo's Kabukicho red light district.

Bliss, The: A mental state of distraction caused by being placed under the spell of a kami.

Boseu: Korean for "boss"—used to refer to the clan underboss of the Seven Star Mob. The clan boss is called "chairman" or "uijang."

Chang na: 짱나 - Korean, Short for 짜증 나. Idiomatic expression used to express feelings of annoyance or frustration when something does not going as planned.

Chems: Illegal drugs and pheromones.

Chikushō : "Oh hell!"

Chimpira: A street punk. Literally, "prick."

Chon: チョン - Japanese vernacular nickname for Koreans, with strongly offensive overtones.

Daigo Fukuryo Maru: 第五福龍丸 - Lucky Dragon 5. An oceangoing fishing vessel.

Daikoku-ten: The god of great darkness and five cereals. One of the Seven Lucky Gods of the household.

Dai-Nippon Teikoku Rikugun: Army of the Greater Japanese Empire.

Dō han: Dates outside the house of pleasure.

Edo: Edo is old Tokyo—the capital of the Tokugawa shogunate. Tokyo was destroyed by Allied firebombing during World War II but was rebuilt. The new Tokyo is sometimes called "nouveau Edo" or "Neo-Tokyo."

Fuhyo: Pawn, in Shogi or Japanese chess.

Gaijin: A casual, somewhat offensive, term for a foreigner.

Ggondae: 꼰대 - Korean, clueless old man, normally an authority figure, who takes advantage of his power and resists any changes.

Giri: A sense of duty owed to another. The need to do one's duty often conflicts with ninjo, feelings of compassion for those who suffer as a result.

Gokudo: A yakuza gangster, or made man. Literally, a follower of the "extreme path" or "ultimate way."

Haha: "Mommy."

Hai: "Yes."

Hakama: Baggy pants for kendo fencing.

Hebi: Snakes, designer drugs that come in the form of pills.

Hi no tama: Colorful floating balls of soul-fire.

Hitoppori: Getting tattooed for two hours a day.

Horimono: Full body tattoo, aka. full body suit.

Hoshi no tama: A kitsune's fox ball, or shapeshifting amulet.

I Ching: The *Book of Changes*, an old Chinese book of fortunetelling.

Ill-boonin: Korean description of a Japanese person.

Inagawa-kai: The third largest criminal clan in Japan and the original yakuza family of Tokyo. Their gang colors are black.

Inari: Nine-tailed fox god of the kitsune.

Insanity: A dance club in Ueno-hirokoji frequented by college kids where the Inagawa-kai deals in ecstasy.

Irasshaimase: "Welcome!"

Irezumi: Yakuza tattoo done by hand with traditional tools.

Izakaya: Pubs serving beer and skewers of grilled meat, inner organs and green onions.

Jimmy Fong's Authentic Chinese Emporium: A place where rich Tokyoites could buy war trophies scavenged from conquered China.

Jingasa: Soldier's cap.

Jjokbari: 쪽발이 - Korean, racial slur used to describe Japanese Imperialists living in colonized enclaves on the Peninsula.

Kabuki: Traditional Japanese performing art.

Kabukichō : Tokyo's most infamous red light district. A place in Shinjuku where a kabuki theatre was planned but never built. Full of hostess clubs, soaplands and love hotels.

Kaiju: A movie monster, like the radioactive creature born from the sea when Japan tested the first atomic bomb in history on Pearl Harbor during World War II, knocking the United States out of the fight.

Kakashi: Scarecrow, often set up in rice paddies.

Kami: A Shinto nature spirit.

Kanji: Traditional Chinese characters adopted into the Japanese language for written communication.

Kannon: Goddess of Mercy, "Guan-yin" in Chinese.

Katana: Samurai longsword.

Kawaii: Cute.

Keisatsu-cho: National Police Agency. Japan's version of the FBI.

Keisatsu Dai-gakkō : The National Police Academy of Japan.

Kempeitai Thought Police: A secret police operating independently from routine law enforcement as the Emperor's eyes and ears. The Thought Police serves as judge, jury and executioner where lack of patriotism is concerned.

Kendo: The Way of the Sword. Fencing.

Ketsumeisha: Someone who has taken a blood oath, used here to connote a "blood brother" relationship.

Kimchi yaro: キムチ野郎—literally, "kimchi bastards" in Japanese.

King of System: A chain karaoke parlor with hostesses and rooms you hire by the hour.

Kobun: Son. A subordinate yakuza.

Kodokushi: 孤独死 - "lonely death" refers to the phenomenon of people dying alone and remaining undiscovered for long periods of time. Additionally, used as slang to describe those who are lonely, appear lonely, or as a derogative term.

Kohada: Gizzard shad, a kind of sardine eaten as sushi.

Koi: Carp, often found in pools in Zen gardens.

Konbanwa: "Good evening!"

Koya: 荒野 - desert wilderness or wasteland.

Krugerrands: Gold coins minted in South Africa and used continuously in world trade since 1967.

Kumicho: Clan godfather or "Chairman." The "capo di tutti capi," "boss of all bosses," or "oyabun of all oyabun." Each clan has a kumicho who stands at the top of the pyramid and controls one oyabun for each city in Japan where the clan operates.

Kunoichi: Female ninjas.

Kuso: "Shit."

Kwanjangnim: 관장님 - Korean, grand-master of a martial or combative art.

Kyabakura: Hostess club. A place where women pour drinks, light cigarettes, and make small talk with lonely men.

Line: Japan's most popular social network and mobile dating service.

Maiko: Geisha-in-training.

Maria Theresa thalers: Silver coins minted in Germany and used continuously in world trade since 1741.

Masu: A square wooden box, often used to hold sake cups and catch the overflow from culturally mandated, overly enthusiastic outpourings of sake.

Megane: Smartglasses.

Mempo: Samurai mask and helm.

Menko: A simple card game played by placing a card on a surface and trying to flip the other's player's card by throwing one of one's own cards at it. The menko cards are beautifully illustrated with samurai, ninja, soldiers, baseball players or anime characters.

Moshi moshi: "Hello?" (when answering a phone).

Mu: 巫 - Korean, the supernatural energy harnessed by sessŭ mu shaman through ritual practice, tattoo channeling (both simple ink and bioaugmentative), and martial discipline.

Namu Amida Butsu: "I take refuge in the Buddha of Immeasurable Life and Light."

Namazu: The earthquake-causing catfish of Shinto myth.

Ninjo: Empathy or compassion for others, often in conflict with the objectives set by one's superiors.

Noren: Traditional fabric divider.

Nosae: 노새 - Korean, mule. Beast of burden.

Obi: The ribbon-like sash used to hold a kimono closed.

Ofuro: Wooden soaking tub.

Ofuro No Osama: 風呂の王様 - King of Baths. Chain of semi-legitimate Japanese style bath houses found in and around Tokyo and elsewhere. The Inagawa-kai is paid protection money to ensure Thought Police compliance and also maintains a limited trade in prostitution, drugs and body modifications through these establishments.

Oji: Uncle.

Otaku: Obsessive fans.

Onesan: Older sister, the woman who runs a geisha house or hostess club.

Oni: Demon.

Onigiri: Rice balls.

Oreiboko: The final year of five year apprenticeship where all money made goes to the master.

Origami: The art of folding paper to resemble animals and other things.

Oshou: King, in Shogi or Japanese chess.

Oyabun: Father. Yakuza clan boss.

Poju: 포주 - Korean, pimp.

Pon hiki: Pimp.

Pusnaegi: Punk, in Korean.

Reichsmark: The official currency of the Third Reich, introduced in Germany in 1924. The exchange rate for RM in the world of Tokyo Yakuza is $\mathcal{RM}$ 1:$4 or ¥400.

Rodo: 主 - Lord, master or head of the house. Chief, person in charge. Used to denote management of Inagawa-kai owned property.

Sake: Traditional Japanese rice wine.

Sakura: Cherry blossoms.

Sashimi: Slices of raw fish.

Seiiki: "Sanctuary"—an unassuming sushi-ya in Shibuya, Tokyo.

Seiza: Literally "proper sitting," it means kneeling on the floor in a traditional posture.

Senpai: Senior. Elder classmate.

Seonsaengnim: "Master" or "teacher," a respectful term of address in Korean.

Seven Star Mob: The Korean criminal clan in Tokyo. Their gang colors are blue.

Shamisen: A three-stringed Japanese musical instrument.

Shinagawa: A part of Tokyo that literally means "River of Products."

Shinjuku-eki: "Shinjuku station."

Shink: Short for "shinkansen" or "bullet train."

Shinyuu: "Best friend."

Shitagi: Samurai undershirt.

Shogi: The Generals' game or Japanese chess.

Sinzo: 신도 - Korean, "way of the gods." Korean ritualistic shamanism which may incorporate martial art, augmentative technologies, and sessŭ mu religion/mythology. Forbidden by the current Imperial Japanese governor.

Spacecraft, the: The nickname for the new 2020 Tokyo Olympics stadium in Shinjuku.

Soju: Literally "burned liquor," a grain alcohol originally from Korea.

Solntsevskaya Bratva: The Russian Mafiya in Tokyo, run by Andrei.

Sou desu ne: "I see."

Sugamo Prison: Colloquial for the New Sugamo Detention Facility, an infamous yakuza prison in Tokyo.

Sumiyoshi-kai: The second largest criminal clan in Japan. Their gang colors are purple.

Tabi: Split-toe traditional Japanese socks.

Tanuki: A Japanese raccoon-dog spirit, which like the kitsune (fox spirit) has the powers of shape shifting (itself and others) and possession (mind control).

Tokkuri: 徳利 - Ceramic sake flask or service container used for delivering warmed rice wine.

Torii: A red wooden Shinto gate. Oftentimes, a path to another dimension.

Ttong: 똥 - Korean, dung or shit.

Udon: Noodle soup served in a hot ceramic bowl.

Ueno Gakuen University: A private university near Ueno park specializing in music. Formerly an all-girls school.

Uijang: "Chairman" in Korean. The clan boss of the Seven Star Mob.

Umeboshi: Pickled Japanese salt plums.

Uncle Sam's: A wartime propaganda American-themed Sumiyoshi-kai pub in Ginza.

Velours, The: A high-class hostess club in Ginza run by the Yamaguchi-gumi.

Wakagashira: Clan underboss.

Wakagashira-hosa: Deputy underboss.

Wakarimashita: "I understand."

Wakizashi: A samurai short sword, often used in the off-hand for blocking in the dual sword style with the katana held in the main hand for attacking.

Waseda University: The second best university in Tokyo, after Todai or Tokyo University.

Whiskey Chandler, The: An authentic Scottish whiskey bar in Ogawamachi - at the top of the hill and hang a left.

Yako: A kitsune devil.

Yamabishi: The diamond-shaped clan emblem of the Yamaguchi-gumi.

Yamaguchi-gumi: The biggest criminal clan in Japan. Their gang colors are green.

Yamaguchi-gumi, Sixth: Each kumicho reforms his own clan from the ashes of its predecessor. The fifth Yamaguchi-gumi was operated by a relatively wise kumicho who managed to die peacefully, of natural causes, at age 96.

Yakuza: Japanese organized crime/mobsters. Literally, 8-9-3, adding up to 20, the losing hand of cards in a certain illegal gambling game that can be played with hanafuda, flower cards.

Yakuza Graveyard, the: The yakuza are known for hosting lavish funerals for their dead leaders, but few realize that their souls all end up here.

Yen: The exchange rate for JPY in the world of Tokyo Yakuza is ¥100:$1 or $RM0.25$.

Zainichi: Japan-born but of Korean ancestry.

Zen: Extinction of the affect.

Zori: Flat, Japanese sandals made of rice straw.

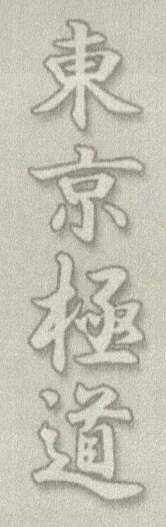

東京極道

Cast of Characters

Appearing below are the characters of Tokyo Yakuza, including the board game as well as this anthology. The characters grouped by clan affiliation and ordered by rank. After each character's name is a parenthetical listing every issue number in which they appear, i.e. (#23) or (#B1) for bonus issue #1, or (BG) for board game. This section should help you follow the fates of your favorite characters or use them in the Tokyo Yakuza roleplaying game (RPG).

Yamaguchi-gumi

Yamaguchi-gumi Leaders

Yamaguchi-gumi Clan Boss (Oyabun) Kitano Takumi (BG, #1, #2, #3, #8, #10, #17, #19, #23): The undisputed leader of the most powerful clan in all of Japan.

Yamaguchi-gumi Clan Underboss (Wakagashira) Chiba Ken (BG, #9, #10, #14, #19, #23): Secretly working with Eugi and Moji to earn the support of the Sumiyoshi-kai by winning a no-bid contract for the Sumiyoshi-kai controlled corporation CBI-Hitachi to build the 2020 Tokyo Olympics stadium, Chiba plans to overthrow oyabun Kitano with the Sumiyoshi-kai's support and seize control of Japan's largest clan for himself. A former professional actor, he killed Izumi Goseki and assumed his identity after Izumi tried to defect from the Inagawa-kai.

Yamaguchi-gumi Fighters

Yamaguchi-gumi Professionals

Kamei Daichi (BG, #7, #10, #15): This Professional with a dragon tattoo carries a submachine gun and learned to kill at an early age. Now in his late fifties, his skills have only gotten better with time. Ordered Jared Santos' murder. Afterwards, Kamei was shot and killed by Moji during a gunfight with Paul on January 30, 2020.

Matsuhono Eugi (#1, #2, #3, #9, #10, #14, #15, #B1): Yamaguchi-gumi wakagashira-hosa, this pimp in a white suit operates the Bijou hostess club in the Kabukichō red light district of Shinjuku.

Tobi (#7, #8): A stealthy pickpocket and sniper who inhabits the foreigner bar in Roppongi. He assassinates Sumiyoshi-kai clan boss Sugawara in Shinjuku on January 22, 2020, the day after Sugawara's actions at CBI-Hitachi headquarters, and is killed the same day by the Tokyo Stock Exchange AI.

Yamaguchi-gumi Made Men (Gokudo)

Fog, The (#10, #22): A tax collector who loves the late geisha, Angel, and who seeks to avenge his dearly beloved's murder at the hands of oyabun Kitano. A brilliant strategist who uses swords and guns in "this era of cyber-kinetics, artificial intelligence, digital dog-shit and all that crap ..."; most importantly though, amongst these "traditional means", is the psychological guerilla onslaught he wages upon his opponents. His name remains unknown.

Moji Sumio (BG, #1, #7, #9, #15): The Yamaguchi mobster with a cruel smile and wraparound sunglasses packs a Desert Eagle .50 caliber heavy pistol and a mean attitude to boot. Moji was a bosozoku biker punk as a teen. He worked for Eugi and Chiba. Received Angel's head from Jared Santos. Shot and critically injured by Paul at The Bijou on January 30, he recovered but was killed by Hikaru after betraying him in a warehouse on February 16, 2020.

Ryuk (#10, #22): A senior warrior who fled from battle in the streets of Kabukichō and was executed by oyabun Kitano for his cowardice. The Fog "set him up" without his knowing; Ryuk, though once a senior warrior, was merely a tool used by The Fog.

Yamaguchi-gumi Street Samurai

Asahara Hikaru (#1, #2, #3, #8, #9, #15): A Yamaguchi-gumi soldier and pimp with a catfish tattoo shot by Eugi at the Seiiki sushi-ya during a night of drunken revelry. A waitress, Yoshiko, saved his life and received his tattooed skin (which he replaced with cybernetic dermal plating) in repayment for her kindness. Hikaru operates The Velours, a high-end hostess club in Ginza. By mid-February, he becomes the only man in Tokyo to know the depth of the conspiracies within the Yamaguchi-gumi and the Sumiyoshi-kai.

Kusanagi Ryu (BG, #19): This half-Japanese, half-American older brother with a bushido tattoo on his left arm carries a katana and wakazashi, just like the samurai of old. He is slow to anger but quick to victory. A data courier, he was killed by his crush, the geisha Makiko, on the streets of Ginza on February 5, 2020.

Yamaguchi-gumi Martial Artists

Doi Tyrone (BG, #7): Favoring use of a judo hip toss to drop an opponent to the ground, this half-Nigerian, half-Japanese thug likes to finish them with brutal ground-and-pound straight to the jugular. Messed up by his step-dad as a kid, Tyrone is a big tough thug who hangs out in a foreigner bar in Roppongi where he pimps out Filipinas.

Takami Godan (BG, #1, #2, #15): A tanuki, mischievous raccoon-dog spirit with an oversized nut sack, who works the streets of Kabukichō as a tout, luring passers-by into the overpriced, mobbed up Bijou hostess club where his girlfriend, Kit Yamaguchi, works as a hostess. Godan has the supernatural ability to disappear without a trace, and he practices an esoteric form of kenpo karate.

Yamaguchi-gumi Punks (Chimpira)

Akiyama Jiro (BG, #1, #15, #16): A thick-necked bruiser and low-ranking yakuza and, before Soto, Yayoi Himetsu's most recent client, of whose payment she skimmed a little extra off the top. Carries a pair of brass knuckles, a birthday present given to him by his senpai who later died while fleeing rival gangsters; his senpai drove his motorcycle the wrong way against traffic and off the Rainbow Bridge into Tokyo Bay. Akiyama is more careful now. Killed by Kusama Mariko on January 31, 2020.

Hatori Junichi (#23): Locked up in solitary in Sugamo Prison, Chiba helps bust him out but he is stabbed and killed by Uchida Ryoto, who had assumed his identity.

Jared Santos, aka. Jiro Satani (#7): A wanna-be gangster from America who gets more than he bargained for.

Yamaguchi-gumi Workers

Yamaguchi-gumi Geisha

Naruse Riko (BG, #10, #22, #23): The daughter of a deposed yakuza boss, Riko has risen through the ranks by taking on a yakuza identity, differentiating herself from the typical Gion Kyoto geisha. She plays the shamisen.

Angel (#10, #22): A deceased geisha who was the lover of The Fog. She was raped and murdered by oyabun Kitano. She never told The Fog her real name and her past remains shrouded in mystery.

Yamaguchi-gumi Hostesses

Akarui (#15): Former hostess at The Bijou, quit when she married Paul, died of cancer.

Asuka Higashino (#5, #8, #9): Art student who has the only existing proof that the Tokyo Stock Exchange AI, not the Yamaguchi-gumi, ordered the hit on Sumiyoshi-kai oyabun Sugawara. She is reward with a hostess job at The Velours after giving the information to Hikaru and sleeping with him. Her ex-boyfriend and classmate is Inagawa-kai chimpira Hiroto Itou.

Hanako (#1, #2, #14, #16): A new hostess at the Bijou hostess club and a former waitress from the Seiiki sushi-ya who was recruited by the pimp Eugi. Yoshiko borrowed her waitress outfit, the dress and wearable cat ears she had left behind. With Eugi's permission, she remains Kichiro's girlfriend even after he leaves the Yamaguchi-gumi to join the Sumiyoshi-kai. Killed by Kusama Mariko on January 31, 2020.

Kusama Mariko (#16): A cybernetically enhanced hostess with few qualms about killing her way to the top.

Kinugasa Tamika (BG, #9): A former promo model for fast cars and videogames, Tamika joined The Velours as a hostess and married Yamaguchi-gumi wakagashira Chiba Ken. Look but don't touch! She is a chain-smoker. Tamika loves to collect fine weapons of all kinds.

Kit Yamaguchi (BG, #1, #2, #10, #15, #B1): A mysterious kitsune fox spirit who works in the Bijou and hangs out in parks. She plays mind games with males and always hides an MP7 submachine gun and a katana nearby, just in case. She also helped urged Ryuk's death, and she wiped out the survivors of a vigilante attack on the Seven Star Mob.

Yayoi Himetsu (#1, #15): She wears plastic cat ears and works in the Bijou for Eugi Matsuhono.

Zafa (#15): The onesan of The Bijou, she joined about the same time as Paul's dead wife, Akarui. Now she manages the girls whom Eugi recruits and is guarded by kunoichi.

Yamaguchi-gumi Schoolgirls

Deguchi Suko (BG): The daughter of a mid-ranking yakuza, popular kogal Suko alternates between an austere fashion sense and a sporty gyaru valley girl look. She acts like a queen and expects all others to play along.

Yamaguchi-gumi Maids

Aiko (#2, #3, #16): An empty-headed waitress at Seiiki who doesn't mind wearing see-through clothing. She works hard to give off the appearance that she lives to make horrible men like Eugi happy. Killed by Kusama Mariko on January 31, 2020.

Matsumoto Tokie (BG): A natural bunny girl kami. Tokie was born this way. Her best bud, Hikaru, thinks customers are soooo dumb. Still, they pay. Tokie, on the other hand, is super enthused about everything. She loves playing video games or just watching boys play games. DD bra size. Big ears.

Yoshiko (#2): Born in Okinawa, a half-kami waitress at the Seiiki sushi-ya in Shibuya. She saved the life of Hikaru, a Yamaguchi-gumi street samurai, and she has an affectionate relationship with the tanunki, Godan Takami, whom she nicknamed Kakashi, meaning "scarecrow."

Yamaguchi-gumi Foreigners

Vera Rogozin (BG): When she showed up at Narita airport, her charming gokudo "friend" took her passport for safekeeping. The blonde Russian with a ponytail is often pictured in yakuza photo shoots wearing a suit with a short tie, and holding a champagne bottle or a dildo. Vera still makes more in a day than you make in a month.

Sumiyoshi-kai

Sumiyoshi-kai Leaders

Sumiyoshi-kai Clan Boss (Oyabun) Matsuoka Noriko (#20): Widow of the deceased oyabun Sugawara Hirono, she wants to kill Ishii Naoki with the help of Kokoroishi and Bunrakuken and take over the Sumiyoshi-kai.

Sugawara Hirono (BG, #3, #6, #8, #20, #24): Was working with Eugi to get contracts for the construction of the Olympic Stadium and for various other services involved with setting up for the Olympics. He was killed by a Yamaguchi-gumi sniper and replaced by the Tokyo Stock Exchange AI who used his clan underboss, Ishii Naoki, as a puppet.

Tokyo Stock Exchange AI (#8): An artificial intelligence with the power to manipulate the Tokyo Stock Exchange. Created by Sugawara Hirono, the AI committed patricide by means of a Yamaguchi-gumi sniper, Tobi, and ignited a war between the clans. Now the Tokyo Stock Exchange runs the Sumiyoshi-kai from the shadows, controlling Ishii Naoki, who is in awe of its computing power. The TSE AI also killed Tobi and his mother. Through the Sumiyoshi-kai, the AI owns a majority stake in CBI-Hitachi corporation, which makes cybernetic clones and won the right to build the Spacecraft, the Olympic stadium.

Sumiyoshi-kai Clan Underboss (Wakagashira)

Ishii Naoki (BG, #3, #14, #19, #24): Marco's master until Marco decided to join the Seven Star Mob with the girl he rescued. Naoki, a computer loving otaku, is enthralled by the majesty of the Tokyo Stock Exchange AI and worships it as a god. Ishii was promoted to oyabun after Sugawara was killed, but he takes orders from the TSE AI in private and acts as his wakagashira.

Sato Fukui (#6, #20): Sumiyoshi-kai professional hitman, wakagashira-hosa, and technology-fearing "pro-human terrorist." Sato led a team to take out CBI-Hitachi's Maihama-based cybernetic cloning facility. Promoted to wakagashira after oyabun Sugawara's death, Sato remains blissfully ignorant, for the time being, of the depth of "oyabun" Ishii's subservience to the TSE AI.

Sumiyoshi-kai Fighters

Sumiyoshi-kai Professionals

Hitomi (#24): Leader of the Orochi hit squad.

Kokoroishi (#20): An Edo-period kami tied to a shrine and a well in Monzen-nakacho which was bulldozed to make room for the Olympic Village. She killed Takegawa and works for the former oyabun Sugawara's widow, Matsuoka Noriko.

Okoshi Takeshi (BG, #12, #21): Packing a shotgun, this Professional doesn't mess around and isn't afraid of close quarters. The clan only calls in "the Animal" Okoshi when things get hot. Suki turned him into a rat for a few months when he lost his shirt betting against her. After becoming wakagashira of the Inagawa-kai, Suki returned Takeshi to his human form on the condition that he serve as her eyes and ears in the Sumiyoshi-kai. He gets Sozen to kill his brother over a family owned club in Roppongi.

Sumiyoshi-kai Made Men (Gokudo)

Takegawa Yoshi (BG, #6, #20): Sato's second in command and a long-time member of the Sumiyoshi-kai, from back when it was not a kai but a rengo, Takegawa keeps a Beretta 92FS light pistol always close at hand, just in case. Sometimes, simply giving his target a glimpse of the gun is enough to achieve the desired effect. Killed by Kokoroishi in his apartment on February 8, 2020.

Sumiyoshi-kai Street Samurai

Nakashima Kichiro (#14): Disgraced and tasked by the Yamaguchi-gumi with one final mission, Kichiro delivers Yamaguchi-gumi wakagashira Chiba's message offering a truce to Sumiyoshi-kai "oyabun" Ishii, following oyabun Sugawara's death, joining the two clans together in a pact to destroy the Korean Seven Star Mob. He is Hanako's boyfriend and still lives with her in Shinjuku. When Hanako is killed, Kichiro vows to avenge her death.

Takakura Sozen (BG, #20, #21): Along with his ninja-to sword, this urban warrior with a Mohawk wields an Okinawa sai and has pockets full of sharp throwing stars for starting off fights with a momentary advantage. Sozen also has six Eurasian girlfriends. Lost a bundle of cash to Takegawa while playing hanafuda in the Pink Room in Ginza. He killed his brother over the family club in Roppongi.

Sumiyoshi-kai Martial Artists

Katayama Bunrakuken (BG, #14, #20): Loves anime and kickboxing. A Muay Thai expert with an undefeated streak 32 fights long in Bangkok, Bunrakuken loves to grab dudes by the back of the head with his left hand and punch them repeatedly in the face with his right.

Sumiyoshi-kai Punks (Chimpira)

Eguchi Bunta (BG, #14, #15, #21): Never far from his baseball bat, Eguchi-san is a huge fan of the sport. When disciplining deadbeat clients, he takes it relatively easy on them. Not so, enemy gangsters, whom he cripples by striking them in knees first. Beat up Kichiro upon first meeting him. He held down Sozen's brother for him to kill.

Sumiyoshi-kai Workers

Sumiyoshi-kai Geisha

Kurosawa Makiko (BG, #19): A traditional geisha with a large headdress and restrained yet flirtatious look, if you are good perhaps she might lift her kimono to show a bare leg. Makiko always arrived by rickshaw pulled by college kids in need of extra money. She stole Ryu's data after betraying him.

Sumiyoshi-kai Hostesses

Ozu Chieko (BG, #20): A typical big haired hostess with flashy "elegant" look, Chieko has fake boobs and dyed her hair red. She wears a crown because she is a princess. Everyone loves her the best. Ozu is the onesan of the Pink Room in Ginza.

Sumiyoshi-kai Schoolgirls

Miyamoto Sakuro (BG): Something of a bokukko tomboy, Sakuro once kicked the crap out of a girl for calling her a futanari. She only dates hipsters and wealthy old men. Sometimes on the same dinner date.

Sumiyoshi-kai Maids

Kobayashi Wattan (BG): Wattan was born a normal girl but started turning into a cat girl just before puberty. Now 20 years old, Wattan works in a maid cafe, serving colorful cocktails in test tubes in test tube racks to patrons from around the world. She loves Germans and hates it when her Sumiyoshi-kai boss blackens her eyes.

Sumiyoshi-kai Foreigners

Fatma Uhuru (BG, #20): Fatma will trick you out of your hard earned money and not give a shit what that means to you and yours. It's your own damn fault anyway for being a perv. A Kenyan in a hip-hugging, tight dress with handcuffs and whip, Fatma is ready to dominate you. No man stands a chance with her. Fatma used to work at the Pink Room but, one day, she ran off.

Mathilde, aka. Midori (#20, #21): A big breasted, compliant gaijin, born in the USSR, who works at the Pink Room in Ginza. She is dating Takakura Sozen.

Inagawa-kai

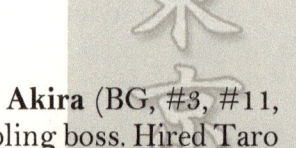

Inagawa-kai Leaders

Inagawa-kai Clan Boss (Oyabun) Noboru Akira (BG, #3, #11, #12, #17): Tokyo's most renowned gambling boss. Hired Taro to find Oda Nobunaga's bones in order to make a clone. Known as the father of the bakuto (gamblers). Killed by Marco on January 16, 2020.

Miike Yuki (BG, #13): With a briefcase that opens up to reveal a bolt-action, high-powered, unsilenced sniper rifle, the Inagawa syndicate killer has only one shot. And that's always just what he needs. Miike worked with Shio, a popular drunk, until he betrayed him so Miike, the clan's top hitman, could be elected the new oyabun of the Inagawa-kai. A serial killer who leaves behind "a promoted pawn" at the scene of the crime, Miike is known to the media as the Shogi killer.

Inagawa-kai Clan Underboss (Wakagashira) Minami Akio (BG, #11): Takes over as interim oyabun after Noboru Akira is killed, until a new oyabun can be elected by the surviving senior clan members. Minami enjoys a close working relationship with the Kempeitai Thought Police. He ends up being manipulated by Jihoo and Shon of the Seven Star Mob. Hounded by a large majority of the Inagawa-kai for his obvious betrayal, he ends up being run out of town.

Suki (#12, #13, #21): 'Susanoo's' devilishly sexy kitsune companion who turned Sumiyoshi-kai yakuza Okoshi Takeshi into a rat, and later murdered two Inagawa-kai thugs who crossed her. Suki offered Miike, the Shogi Killer, a path to the position of oyabun. As a reward, Miike named Suki his wakagashira. Suki then transformed Takeshi back into his human form to use him as her spy inside the Sumiyoshi-kai.

Inagawa-kai Fighters

Inagawa-kai Professionals

Shio (#13): A popular drunk and a fixture at The Whiskey Chandler in Ogawamachi. A favorite to replace the slain oyabun, he was betrayed by Miike while playing a prank on the chimpira, Izumi.

Inagawa-kai Made Men (Gokudo)

Kaz (#23, #24): He orchestrates a failed plot to assassinate Yamaguchi-gumi oyabun Kitano by having Uchida Ryoto take on the identity of imprisoned Yamaguchi-gumi yakuza Junichi Hatori. Killed by Shun Kondo for being a prick to women.

Sasaki Kohei (BG, #13, #19): A scrawny kid in his youth, Sasaki was always running his mouth off anyway and getting his ass into some serious trouble. Nowadays, his Taurus Raging Bull revolver and his katana help him get out of it. Kohei wrecked his Ferrari and died in a swordfight in Ginza on February 5, 2020.

Inagawa-kai Street Samurai

Ito Shintaro (BG, #13, #16, #18, #19): "No-nonsense" Ito starts problems with his nunchuks and ends them with his combat knife. A killer through and through, Ito smokes a pack of Golden Bat cigarettes every time he does a dude in. He helped Taro and company dig up Oda's milk tooth. Ito died in a car wreck in Ginza on February 5, 2020.

Inagawa-kai Martial Artists

Isamu (#12): An enforcer and friend of Gorou killed by Suki the devil fox spirit.

Sachi (#5): Inagawa-kai Ecstasy dealer who lures teenagers to the dance club, Insanity.

Uchida Ryoto (BG, #13, #23, #24): Studied mixed martial arts under his father from a young age. Uchida-san styles himself after Bruce Lee, employing the star's door-busting side kick to great effect at the start of fights and when least expected during a flurry of blows. Upset by Shio's death, he is chosen to infiltrate the Yamaguchi-gumi, masquerading as old YG chimpira Hatori Junichi, to assassinate Kitano and is killed by Chiba in a warehouse shootout on February 20, 2020, the day ground is broken on Spacecraft and the Yamaguchi-gumi celebrates its truce with the Sumiyoshi-kai.

Inagawa-kai Punks (Chimpira)

Gorou (#12): A coder and friend of Isamu killed by Suki the kitsune gambler.

Hiroto Itou (#5): College kid, Inagawa-kai chimpira, and lapsed Catholic.

Izumi Goseki (BG, #13, #14, #23): Izumi uses a long, heavy stick about an inch thick. He often jokes that it is an extension of his chimpira and has nicknamed it "Little Brother." He went out with Shio on a mission because his half-Chinese half-sister wanted to scare him straight, and he ended up witnessing Shio's death at the hands of Miike and Suki, who went on to lead the Inagawa-kai. Goseki was killed by Yamaguchi-gumi wakagashira Chiba during his attempt to defect from the Inagawa-kai to the Yamaguchi-gumi.

Shun Kondo (#24): A good natured kid caught up in a much larger, more perverse, and deadlier, game than he ever imagined.

Inagawa-kai Workers

Inagawa-kai Geisha

Mizoguchi Sui (BG): A lightly tattooed maiko with ornate fan, Sui is famous for wearing rare shidare kanzashi, composed by long chains of silk flowers. Despite a mark on her left ear from being hit with a crystal ashtray, Sui is still highly sought after among politicians.

Inagawa-kai Hostesses

Teshigahara Sayo (BG): Sayo has had a tough life, but it wasn't always that way. At first, she was addicted to kawaii street fashion and alternated between dekora, fairy, mori, visual kei and sweet lolita styles. Then she went and got her face cut up. Now she's the punk lolita hostess.

Naka (#13): A rotund woman with nasty breath and bad attitude, reduced to working in the cheapest of the cheap hostess clubs after her philandering husband Shio was blown apart by grenades and submachinegun fire.

Inagawa-kai Schoolgirls

Asahara Shino (BG): A dandere nerd who needs glasses but doesn't know it yet, Shino likes to hang out with her friend, Hi. She is scared of her step-dad. Her favorite color is pink. Shino likes The Three Kingdoms story from China.

Izumi Akane (#13, #14): Half-Chinese, half-Japanese high school girl who is trying to look out for her asshole half-brother, Goseki. She despises the Inagawa-kai, indeed all yakuza, but that doesn't stop them from controlling her anyway.

Inagawa-kai Maids

Yamashita Amaya (BG): Formerly a maid at Maidreamin', Amaya has traded in her standard cutesy French maid outfit for a Gothic lolita style. She likes black and blue roses and hanging out in Catholic churches, just staring blankly into the stained glass and giving the cold shoulder to whoever paid the yakuza to be with her that night.

Reiko-ni (#11): A bathhouse android.

Inagawa-kai Foreigners

Millie Natad (BG): Millie is sooo nice. She might look goth, but this Filipina in a miniskirt and open shirt is happy to play dice and cards with you all night into the early morning. Then go home with you afterwards. Really. Only problem is half her pay goes to her tattooed Inagawa-kai masters. Mille can cook great fried rice.

14K Triad

14K Triad Leaders

14K Triad Clan Boss (Dragon Head) Andy Leung (BG):

14K Triad Clan Underboss (Incense Master)Jimmy Fong (BG): Pretends to be a civilian who runs a small antiques and curio shop in Azabu-juban; secretly conducts initiation rituals for the 14K Triad. He knows where Paul's daughter is (working for the triad in the dance club, Insanity) but feeds Paul false hope to use him against the 14K's enemies.

14K Triad Fighters

14K Triad Professionals

Xia Tian (BG): Bringing a standard-issue, military-grade assault rifle to bear on a domestic situation, Xia Tian is the cruelest mofo in the entire HK 14K. Ho-ho-ho biatches, I got an assault rifle.

14K Triad Made Man (Gokudo)

Gao Hei (BG): Gao Hei is not one for fooling around. Every pocket holds a grenade. Not to mention, he has 27 kids and doesn't give a f**k if they live or die …

14K Triad Street Samurai

Chen Jie-shi (BG, #5): A fanatically racist Han Chinese supremacist, Chen is bad news for anyone of the wrong type who meets him alone in a dark alley. He bears a single Chinese broadsword with tassel and has trained extensively from a young age in the famous Shaolin Temple.

14K Triad Martial Artists

Xu Hongfeng (BG): Xu practices 48 styles of kung fu daily. You never know what to expect out of this dude, but he has been seen to punch a rival in the face while kicking in his knee in the same moment. Xu used to be a traveling warrior monk until a certain gambling debt.

14K Triad Punks (Chimpira)

Wu Laifu (BG): In a land of sashimi knives, Wu lugs around a jungle-chopping machete. Having made Roppongi his favorite haunt, Wu dares anyone from a different gang to try to take it from the 14K. His favorite food in Pikachu Burger on Roppongi Hills.

14K Triad Workers

14K Triad Geisha (Da Mei Nu)

Wang Wan Ning (BG): Wang Wan Ning is the first Chinese geisha to achieve widespread popularity in Roppongi. She likes to hang out with taikomochi, male geisha who play the drums. Originally from Heilongjiang "Black Dragon River" province in north China.

14K Triad Hostess (Xiao Mei Nu)

Li Shu Zhen (BG): Li is the country lolita in a club with a very pretty but somewhat frightening gothic lolita hostess. They are besties. Also, Li loves fresh tuna sashimi and cats! And diamond earrings! And LV!

14K Triad Schoolgirls (Shao Nu)

Xie Cai Ping (BG): While she can play kawaii when she has to, Cai Ping prefers to be kuudere, an almost emotionless, cool girl with dark eyeshadow and hair dyed purple. Cai Ping has one goal in mind: money. All else comes second. And love third.

Sodaina Migotona (#15): She was supposed to be matriculating at Chiben Gakuen but was snatched off the streets by the 14K Triad and forced to work in the dance club, Insanity, which the Chinese took from the Inagawa-kai. Jimmy Fong was lying to her dad, Paul, all along, sending him on vengeance-fuelled missions against his enemies in the Sumiyoshi-kai and Yamaguchi-gumi.

14K Triad Maids

Tsuji Ema (BG): Everybody is stupid. Last week she was a Victorian steampunk cosplay girl, this week the half-Chinese, half-Japanese Ema is showing her loyalty to the 14K by wearing a short qipao and decking herself out panda clips. Why can't everyone be as smart as Ema? Well, too bad - they'll have to be losers forEVs.

14K Triad Foreigners (Lao Wai)

Ping Ping (BG): Born in the willow fringed lake city of Hangzhou, in south China, Ping Ping prefers to dress in miniskirt or short qipao. She smokes after sex and always carries cigarettes and a lighter. Ping Ping's grandfather was a friend of Chairman Mao and diplomat Zhou Enlai. She believes in ping pong diplomacy and fancy sports cars.

Seven Star Mob

Seven Star Mob Leaders

Seven Star Mob Clan Boss (Uijang)Shon Kyowon (BG, #11): Master of the shakedown, smuggling boss, ruler of the liquor trade in Tokyo. Dominates Inagawa-kai wakagashira Minami after assassinating Inagawa-kai oyabun Noboru.

Seven Star Mob Clan Underboss (Boseu) Kim Tu-bong (BG, #B1): Mastermind behind the designer drug ZomB. One of the vigilante Suzume's targets.

Seven Star Mob Fighters

Seven Star Mob Professionals

Kim Jae-sang (BG): Strapped with tube rocket launcher he carries on-board the Tokyo Metro subway system in a mutha-f**king knapsack, this Korean bad boy is more than happy to show you the business end of his boomstick.

Seven Star Mob Made Men (Gokudo)

Park Yeoum (BG, #B1): Nicknamed "Sicko," he ain't a Saturday and Sunday banger; this is what he is 24/7. The Korean Mobster is never far from his trusty .357 magnum snub-nose revolver. Hired Shinobu to steal Eugi's car, touching off the events that led to the deaths of Shinobu's best friend Michi. Killed by Suzume on February 21, 2020.

Seven Star Mob Street Samurai

Kim "Mago" Jihoo (#11): A spiritual cyborg with a frog tongue balled up in his robotic right arm, Jihoo was the operative who helped Uijang Shon bend Inagawa-kai wakagashira Minami Akio to his will.

Marco (#3): A warrior monk whose father was an American soldier and whose mother was Japanese. He worked for the Sumiyoshi-kai as the equal of any street samurai until he rescued a Korean girl and turned inevitably to the protection of the Seven Star Mob.

Roh Hong-jip (BG): Roh walks the streets in the early morning, totally sober, afraid of no man. In addition to the ssangsoodo, a 2-handed Korean saber with a 5-foot long blade, strapped to his back, Roh is also known to use a traditional triple bladed bamboo spear to skewer his foes from a distance. Stay away.

Seven Star Mob Martial Artists

Pak "Haegol" Sun Ho (BG, #11): This black belt has achieved the taekwondo dream of a one-hit knockout by head kick at the start of a fight: 53 separate times. You could say he's something of a living myth. Yet, the women he has been with, and the guys he's destroyed, know Haegol is real enough.

Haegol is also a champion at lane defense multiplayer games, where he goes by an online moniker meaning "Skull."

Seven Star Mob Punks (Pusnaegi)

Hidekazu Shiomi (#11): First mate of the Fukuryu Maru, a smuggler.

Kwon Hyung-tae (BG): A big fan of Korean soap operas and manga, Kwon protects himself with a big length of chain he wraps around his fists and unwinds to strangle his enemies. He is also happy to kick a man while he's down and enjoys rupturing eardrums to disorient them.

Tanaka Shinobu (#4, #B1): Took on a freelance job to steal Eugi's Porsche but crashed and burned and lost his legs. Now he is in debt to the Seven Star Mob for his hospital fees.

Seven Star Mob Workers

Seven Star Mob Geisha (Kisaeng)

Han Tae Hee (BG, #B1): A blind geisha who tells fortunes and reputed to prophesy the deaths of one's enemies, she wears a skull headdress and carries a paper umbrella. Tae Hee has a twin sister who lives in Seoul and is happily married with seven children. On holidays, Tae Hee often goes to visit her and her family, since she has none of her own.

Seven Star Mob Hostesses

Gong Bo Young (BG): A yanki who got pregnant and dropped out of high school, she would take her baby to class reunions. Bo Young is into rockabilly fashion and has two bosozoku boyfriends right now, neither of whom is the baby daddy. She is good at saving money. Her bosses don't know she is looking for a way out.

Seven Star Mob Schoolgirls (Sonyeo)

Song Hyo Jin (BG): She wants to bite off your sex organs. A true psycho yamanba, Hyo Jin takes the yandere love of brutality to the next level. From a childhood spent throwing cats off high rise apartment building rooftops, comes the schoolgirl who can't stop laughing and beating your bloodied face with that bottle of Dom Perignon.

Seven Star Mob Maids

Kim Hyuna (BG): Also known as "Alice," Hyuna is lost in the Wonderland of Tokyo, dressing up as a playing card girl, most often the queen of hearts. She works out of a dingy maid cafe in the heart of Akihabara. Hyuna has a collection of British theme costumes and doesn't want to grow up.

Seven Star Mob Foreigners

Mee Sun Lee (BG): A diva in the sack and mother of three, this Korean in a hanbok pours soju for customers from an ornately decorated bottle into glasses with ice cubes. Sun Lee is happy and at home in Tokyo. She only sometimes feels a twinge of guilt that she hasn't visited her parents in Seoul for almost a decade now. Plastic surgery keeps her young forever.

東京極道

Non-clan Affiliated Characters

("Civilians")

Aristocrats

Kujo Michihiko (#9): An imperial prince who agrees to help Yamaguchi-gumi wakagashira Chiba win a no-bid construction contract for the CBI-Hitachi corporation. Kujo often hangs out at The Velours with his old friend Hikaru.

Bar Patrons

Jaques (#5): A foreign English teacher killed by the 14K Triad in their takeover of an Inagawa-kai dance club.

Corporate Executives

Hiro, Chairman (#6): Chairman of the board of directors of CBI-Hitachi and the force behind the decision to create cybernetic clones to augment Japan's workforce.

Shigeru Akagi (#6): A director and major shareholder of CBI-Hitachi, killed by the Sumiyoshi-kai in a raid on January 21, 2020.

Drifters

"Susanoo" (#12, #13): More of a title and a role to play that Suki forces upon helpless street trash. One was the pauper emperor of back alley menko gambling who was killed when Suki the kitsune gambler had to recycle his implants. Suki found a replacement "Susanoo" the next day, a homeless old man, and has been creating "Susanoo's" like this for a long time.

Yamagashi (#22): A cyborg war veteran (former Special Forces operative) and loyal killing machine. Yamagashi lost his organic arm in combat but its replacement—a bionic one—more than compensates. It is unclear as to why he obeys The Fog unquestioningly—perhaps it has something to do with his past?

Imperial Army

Soto Tasami (#1): A veteran who served on the mainland, in the Imperial provinces of China and Korea.

Kami

Okawa (#4, #18): A mischievous oni who possessed a pink teddy bear.

Monks and Priests

Takenaka Kenji (#13, #14, #18): Shinto monk in crimson robes, loves whiskey. He used his magic on Oda's milk tooth.

Kawaguchi (#14): Shinto head monk in a small shrine in the heart of Kabukicho.

Russian Mafiya

Andrei (#17): runs the Solntsevskaya Bratva, the Russian Mafiya in Tokyo.

Salarymen

Nobu (#20): Mabuchi Cyber salaryman who likes karaoke and competes with CBI-Hitachi.

Small Business Owners

Ryuu, Oji (#2, #3): Uncle of Yoshiko, and owner of the Seiiki sushi-ya in Shibuya.

Shizuka (#22): Owner of the Hananoka Wine Shop, which deals in memories.

Students

Tomoki (#24): Shun's innocent younger brother.

Tattoo Artists and Street Docs

Horiyoshi VII (#2): Tokyo's most famous irezumi artist, willing to take on Yoshiko as an apprentice.

Tokyo Metropolitan Police Department

Kato, Detective (#3, #8, #14, #22): A corrupt vice squad detective who often hangs out with the Yamaguchi-gumi and likes to rock an open purple silk shirt when off-duty. He tipped off Eugi to planned police crackdown. A smoker who despises clueless gaijin, Kato hangs out in the Philippines foreigner bar in Roppongi anyway. Kato was seriously injured by the Sumiyoshi-kai at Kichiro's request.

Ueda (#14): An amateur boxer before joining the police and working the Kabukicho beat. A friend of Detective Kato. The "hero cop" was killed by the Sumiyoshi-kai at Kichiro's request.

Wage Slaves

Hiroshi (#20): A foreman for Morishita Construction (a CBI-Hitachi family company) working on the Olympic Village in Monzen-nakacho.

Kaede (#2): A cook at the Seiiki sushi-ya. And a friend of Ryuu and Yoshiko.

Tachibana Michi (#4): He was Shinobu's best friend until the Yamaguchi-gumi killed him in January, 2020 out of retribution for Shinobu stealing Eugi's Porsche.

Unknowns

Jise Hirabayashi (#16): One of Mariko's former idols.

White Witch (#16): Another of Mariko's former idols.

Vigilantes and Freelancers

Hoshi (#17, #18): A yako kitsune married to Taro.

Oda Nobunaga (#17, #18): A clone made using DNA from the historical figure's bones.

Paul Bitaendo (#15): A family man on a mission to rescue his daughter from mobsters.

Tachibana Suzume (#4, #B1, #B1): Michi's sister, was always off-limits to Shinobu. Wipes out Shinobu's debt to the Seven Star Mob by wiping out Bosseu Kim Tu-bong.

Kobayashi Taro (#17, #18): A freelance thief and explorer hired by the Inagawa-kai to find Oda Nobunaga's bones. Married to Hoshi, the kitsune.

www.ingramcontent.com/pod-product-compliance
Lightning Source LLC
Chambersburg PA
CBHW030849030726
47495CB00005B/1438